T0361688

PRAISE FOR ANNE BEREST'S *THE POSTCARD*

A *NEW YORK TIMES* EDITORS' CHOICE

Best Book of the Year
Library Journal • NPR • *Hudson* • *TIME*

Most Anticipated Book of the Year
Globe and Mail • *Toronto Star* • *Bustle* • *Book Riot* • *Vogue*

"Stunning." Leslie Camhi, *The New Yorker*

"A can't-miss novel." *Chicago Review of Books*

"Compelling." *The Washington Examiner*

"A testament to the power of imagination and an investigation of empathy." *Vogue*

"A beautiful, affecting portrait of mother and daughter searching for their family history." Nichole LeFebvre, *On the Seawall*

"Riveting, poignant and unflinching . . . This brilliant novel, at times harrowing in its telling, is surely one of the finest of the year." Janet Somerville, *The Toronto Star*

"A work of rare grace and importance." Rachel Seiffert, *The Guardian*

"I loved this book so much. I cannot stop thinking about it . . . It's a book that will haunt you and make you think about family legacy, traditions, and so much more." Elisa Shoenberger, *Book Riot*

"[A] powerful literary work . . . that contains a single grand-scale act of self-discovery and many moments of historical illumination." Julie Orringer, *The New York Times Book Review*

★ "Phenomenal . . . powerful . . . brilliant." *Publishers Weekly* ★

★ "A moving reflection on loss, memory, and the past, in equal measures heartwarming and heartrending. Highly recommended." *Library Journal* ★

★ "Electrifying . . . A commanding family memoir." *Foreword* ★

★ "Exceptional." *Shelf Awareness* ★

★ "Unique . . . moving." *BookPage* ★

"Full of suspense and emotion."
Leïla Slimani, author of *The Perfect Nanny*

"One of the most beautiful novels I have ever read, and certainly the most beautiful I've read in recent years."
Valérie Perrin, author of *Fresh Water for Flowers*

"Moving . . . engrossing . . . Let's hope that a book like this, which encompasses both the monstrosities of the past and the dangers of the present, will guard us from complacency."
Heller McAlpin, *The Wall Street Journal*

"Masterfully blends elements of drama, mystery and philosophy. It's propulsive yet deep—an intimate, exacting contemplation of loss that somehow ends in love." Kate Tuttle, *People*

"A powerful exploration of family trauma."
Lauren Elkin, *The Washington Post*

"Intimate, profound, essential." *ELLE*

GABRIËLE

Anne Berest and Claire Berest

GABRIËLE

*Translated from the French
by Tina Kover*

Europa
editions

Europa Editions
27 Union Square West, Suite 302
New York NY 10003
www.europaeditions.com
info@europaeditions.com

Copyright © Editions Stock, 2017
First publication 2025 by Europa Editions

Translation by Tina Kover
Original title: *Gabriële*
Translation copyright © 2025 by Europa Editions

Library of Congress Cataloging in Publication Data is available
ISBN 979-8-88966-089-7

Berest, Anne and Berest, Claire
Gabriële

Cover design by Ginevra Rapisardi

Cover photo by Anne Spratt/unsplash

Prepress by Grafica Punto Print – Rome

Printed in Italy

C O N T E N T S*

* All chapter titles are taken from works of art by Francis Picabia

For Frida and Léonore,
who were born while this book was being written

"Gabriële is a King, Gabriële is a Queen.
She adores bewitchment. Even caught in
a spider web, she remains bright as day."
—JEAN ARP

"Gabriële Buffet enjoys danger . . .
She is ever rich in spirit; her spirit
is a wellspring at the side of the road. She will
do what she has always done: draw into her depths
those who can only live on the surface."
—FRANCIS PICABIA

"I've just this moment received a letter from Gaby P__ . . . "
—MARCEL DUCHAMP

"And so, from earliest youth, Gabriële
knew the incomparable pleasure of fighting the
establishment—and winning."
—MARIA LLUÏSA BORRÀS

Our mother's name is Lélia Picabia. A beautiful name concealing a great deal of pain. Growing up, we didn't know the origins of her name. Our mother never talked to us about her father, or her grandparents.

In 1985, Lélia's grandmother (our great-grandmother), Gabriële Buffet-Picabia, died of natural causes at age 104. We didn't go to her funeral, for the simple reason that we didn't know she existed. It wasn't until we were adults that we became aware of the silence surrounding her. We had a sense that this woman, unknown and unremembered, had been an extraordinary individual. Unknown to us. Unremembered in the history of art. Why this double disappearance?

And so we set about reconstituting the life of Gabriële Buffet, visionary art theorist, wife of Francis Picabia, mistress of Marcel Duchamp, close friend of Guillaume Apollinaire.

We wrote this book four-handed, as a kind of duet, hoping for beauty in the strangeness of it. We looked at it as an experiment, our words intertwining and overlapping until only a single voice existed. We wanted to recapture the old joy of writing, to write the way we used to have fun together—with the intensity of children at play. And sisters always turn back into children when they're together.

We played, yes, but we didn't make anything up. There was no need. Gabriële's life was like a novel. In writing this book we relied on works of history, archival documents, and interviews. Still, we aren't historians, and we don't claim to be. We hope art experts will understand that, despite our careful research, our subjectiveness as writers played into our interpretation of our great-grandmother's feelings. The events in this story really did happen to its main characters, though we've told them in our own way. And we've chosen the present tense, the *living* tense, to recount the life of Gabriële Buffet.

Anne and Claire Berest

1
ENCIRCLEMENT

She doesn't particularly catch the eye at first. There's no flamboyance in her average stature, her demure figure, her long chestnut hair pulled into a low chignon, her outfit—dark and alluring, but never revealing. There's nothing sweet about Gabriële Buffet's face. No whimsy in it. Her chin, especially, is too large. Her forehead, too. Her eyes are narrowed in perpetual thought, like two coal-black slits beneath strongly marked brows that obscure the color of her irises. This woman, neither beautiful nor ugly, is something *else*. If you're curious enough to study her unremarkable face at more length, you see that the corners of her pale mouth curve upward like the wings of a bird in flight, that her cheekbones stand out prominently. The overall impression is terribly determined. Her gaze invites you to look into it. To follow it.

In 1908, Gabriële is 27 years old. She's in Berlin to complete the musical studies she began in Paris. She's an independent young woman. No husband, no children, no attachments. Her life is good, carefree, more like a young man's. She earns money playing in orchestras. She's not accountable to anyone.

Gabriële has just spent the summer in a Swiss chalet with her new friends from Berlin. There, she had a startling encounter: "At the time, in the area around Geneva, there were a lot of holiday cottages rented by Russians. And I met Lenin, because he was staying next door to me. I saw him coming out of the house once, but that's as far as it went—though I did notice that he was very handsome."

Family legend has it that Gabriële had a fling with Lenin. There's no documented proof of this, and we're skeptical. But what's interesting is that the story exists: the idea, perpetuated through the decades, that Gabriële was only attracted to revolutionaries, whether political or artistic.

After her holiday in the mountains of Switzerland, Gabriële returns to France to visit her mother and her brother Jean. Like many servicemen of the time, her father retired to Versailles, that quiet, well-heeled town with its own electric (formerly horse-drawn) tram system.

Gabriële doesn't much like spending time in Versailles. What's pleasant at first quickly becomes boring: the family rituals, the unchanging routines, the same stories told again and again. Gabriële isn't a "family" person, and she never will be, even with her own children. Especially with her own children.

It's a beautiful day in September 1908, the summer drawing to a close. Gabriële's mother sets the table beneath the arbor in the garden, happy to have her two grown children home. She wears a rose-pink dress; the sun shining through the trees casts a dappled light on the tablecloth. It's a scene straight out of a Renoir painting.

Madame Buffet's heart is heavy. This will be their last family lunch of the summer. Gabriële is going back to Berlin, while Jean, a painter, has settled in Moret-sur-Loing. Soon she'll be alone in the too-large house.

Jean chose the small town in Seine-et-Marne because it was painted many times by the Impressionist Alfred Sisley, whose work he admires deeply. Sisley painted Moret-sur-Loing's church, its bridge, its poplar trees and its rue des Tanneries—and so Jean does more or less the same thing, fifteen years later. Fifteen years too late? To Gabriële, herself an up-and-coming member of the musical avant-garde, he's no artistic visionary; he might even be called a has-been. Jean belongs to a generation of young neo-Impressionists, "a new follower of a movement that is already old." Certainly, he's talented—very talented, in fact—but Gabriële is unmoved by the prettiness of his subjects, or the sensitivity of his compositions, or his ability to imbue his snowscapes with real chromatic power. To her, while the Impressionists may have scandalized the public in her parents' day, they're now as dull as a set of classroom exercises.

But let's go back to that September afternoon in the garden with Gabriële and her mother. The wisteria has flowered late. Mother and daughter speak only to keep the silences from stretching out too long. They get along perfectly well but don't have much to say to one another. Jean isn't there yet, and they're waiting for him to have lunch. He promised not to be late.

After a while, Gabriële and her mother begin the meal—*he'll turn up as soon as we start*, they tell each other—and eventually move on to dessert, gradually resigning themselves to the thought that he isn't coming, each concealing her worry by going about her own business. The afternoon passes. Gabriële packs her bags for her return to Germany. She's eager to get back to Berlin; the summer vacation has been like one long sleepless night, and she feels as if she's suffocating. She paces her bedroom. The bureau smells of furniture polish, its drawers holding modest dresses in shades of blue and gray. Pretty and insipid, like reseda.

The bells of Versailles Cathedral ring for evensong. There's still no sign of her brother. Gabriële listens to the chimes, the heavy bronze bodies of the bells resonating deeply, solemnly. Suddenly, an unexpected noise: the loud crunching of gravel. She runs to the bedroom window. A car has just pulled into the courtyard. The sight is as incongruous as it is extravagant in these early years of the twentieth century; people react the way we might if we saw a helicopter landing on the front lawn. It doesn't take Gabriële long to figure out what's going on.

For several weeks now, her brother Jean's talked of nothing

but the "wonderful fellow" he met "*sur le motif*" in Moret-sur-Loing—that is, out in nature, engaging directly with the subject of their art, as the masters do. They were both painting, setting up their easels in the same places, and they ended up becoming friends. Gabriële has heard the man spoken of in Germany; he's the fashionable painter of the moment, a young Impressionist with a Spanish name whom everyone finds extraordinary: Francis Picabia.

For reasons she doesn't understand, Gabriële gets irritated whenever her brother mentions his new friend around her. And the more Jean sings the young painter's praises, the more unbearable she finds Francis. "I'd heard a great deal about Picabia before I ever met him," she will say years later, "and I despised that sort of bourgeois type, you know, with the rich grandfather . . . "

Watching "this small, slim man with quite a graceful figure" emerge from his car, Gabriële is annoyed. When her mother calls her downstairs to greet the young men, she steels herself for the ordeal of dinner. She straightens the collar of her dress like an actor adjusting his costume in the wings backstage. She glances around the room, feeling lost for a moment, wondering what exactly she's looking for, but no answer is forthcoming.

At last she goes down to dinner. Everyone else is already at the table, waiting for her. She finds herself seated across from the painter, who has smoldering dark eyes, an olive complexion, thick eyebrows, a small peach-fuzz mustache, and the relaxed air of those whose wit and intellect, combined with substantial wealth, allow them to be at ease in any situation and with every sort of company.

This young man represents everything Gabriële loathes. He's flirtatious, though he's trying to pretend otherwise. She looks him over surreptitiously. His clothes strike her as faintly ridiculous: impeccable black silk socks, baggy brown velvet trousers with hems worn threadbare by hours spent painting outdoors, and narrow black leather shoes, new and shiny. The overall impression is both luxurious and nonchalant—and deliberate, down to the smallest detail. He also wears a typical collarless painter's shirt, white and loose-fitting, its sleeves with their buttonless cuffs rolled up to the elbow. He smells strongly of linseed oil, resin, eau de Cologne, and gasoline. A pungent combination. Her stomach flips.

Very quickly, the air between Gabriële and Francis becomes charged. Between the antique rose-pink porcelain soup tureen and the clock with its gold-plated pendulum and bronze elephant, Gabriële suddenly feels very warm. To hide her discomfiture, she picks up her spoon and starts on her soup before anyone else.

Madame Buffet, embarrassed at her daughter's faux pas, hurriedly seizes her own spoon. With obvious pride, the men regale the table with the story of the auto breakdown that made them late. The swarthy young painter apologizes for depriving the ladies of their dear Jean's company—taking advantage of the opportunity to meet his sister's gaze. The truth is, she's the reason Francis Picabia has come to Versailles. Ever since Jean told him about his sister, Francis has been obsessed with meeting her, this girl who composes music and lives alone in Berlin. He finds the idea of her incredibly exciting. Becoming friends with Jean, driving him back to the Buffet home in his auto—all of it was done for the express purpose of being invited to dine with the family. And now, finally in Gabriële's presence, he's trying to establish some kind of complicity, a secret understanding. He wants to know what makes her tick, this free-spirited girl. But Gabriële keeps him at arm's length. She has no desire to play his game, or even to be nice to him. Her answers to his questions are brief, non-committal. "They asked me what the exhibitions in Berlin were like; I boldly confessed at once my utter ignorance and incompetence with regard to painting, the boredom and the great efforts it cost me to visit exhibitions and museums . . . "

Gabriële's not merely playing dumb; she's lying. She convinces Francis Picabia that she's never heard about the exhibition of his work—even implies that she's never heard of him at all. "I knew of Picabia by reputation," she will admit years later, "and I knew he was a prominent figure in the art world. But he'd fallen in love with me at first sight, and I was very nasty to him. I told him I hadn't seen his exhibition in Germany."

Gabriële's apparent indifference stings the painter's pride. Francis is used to people being intrigued by him. He's a star, a phenomenon whose work is sought after in fashionable galleries. Taken aback, he protests, committing one gaffe after another: *What? No, impossible! How can she not have heard about his exhibit in Berlin? It was a dazzling success!* He boasts and brags, puffing himself up like a blowfish, mentions a book that's been published about him—already, at not even thirty years old, he's the subject of scholarly study! The book's (pompous) title is *Picabia, le peintre et l'aquafortiste*, and it was written by one Édouard André—a great connoisseur, Francis assures Madame Buffet and her daughter, promising to send them a signed copy the very next day.

Francis is boorish, Gabriële thinks. Even vulgar. She's spent time with globally renowned musicians—true masters—humbler than this flash-in-the-pan little Impressionist. And Francis, for his part, is all too aware of how he's coming across. He can't think of a way to get out of the hole he's dug for himself—to act modest now would be even worse. He spills a glass of wine all over the tablecloth, babbling apologies. Jean, who doesn't understand why his normally affable sister is treating his new friend with such disdain, tries to pick up the pieces of the conversation. She used to love paintings, he reminds Gabriële, back when her music teacher encouraged her to visit art galleries. That was then, she says coldly. She doesn't care for museums anymore, much less galleries.

The discussion, and the meal, are over. The men have to return to Paris that same evening. Gabriële lets it be known that she has things to do in the city, and Francis proposes that she drive back with them. The three young people set off, but they've hardly made it any distance at all when Picabia's car breaks down again. In these early years of the twentieth century, "successive and incomprehensible" incidents of engine trouble are part of the adventure of traveling by car, and a trip without a breakdown is the exception rather than the rule.

By some miracle, there's a garage only a few hundred meters from where they've broken down. They have to push the car. Picabia watches, astonished, as Gabriële calmly rolls up her sleeves. "Resigned," as she'll recall later, and likely at the end of her patience with this pretentious driver who can't even manage his own car, she reaches the garage covered in engine grease and sits down to rest on a pile of old tires. And it's there, on that uncomfortable makeshift perch in an obscure garage somewhere between Paris and Versailles, that fate takes a turn. Francis Picabia, who, abashed by Gabriële's lack of interest in him, has been all but silent since dessert, approaches her pile of tires and blurts, with mingled exasperation, sincerity, and anger:

"Painting bores me even more than it does you, you know!"

"Oh? Then what *does* interest you?"

"Everything—everything but what I'm doing!"

"Then why are you doing it?"

"If I weren't bound by contracts and exhibitions, I wouldn't. I'd never pick up a brush again."

"Really? You'd quit painting?"

"Well . . . at least the way I do now. I just know there's a different style of painting out there—a style with a life all its own . . . something more than just objective representation . . . "

That makes Gabriële's ears perk up. Finally. He's speaking her language now. She's intimately familiar with these concepts in music—but she's never considered that they might be applicable to painting, as well.

"Then . . . what *will* you paint?"

Gone is the dismissive, sarcastic expression Francis has been confronted with all evening. Gabriële waits avidly, certain his answer will be something truly surprising. But the young painter doesn't know how to answer this question—so abrupt, so unexpected, and yet incontestably the most important question anyone has ever asked him: *What will you paint now?* Here in this garage, this old wooden building full of stacked barrels and spokeless wheels and disassembled carts, as the mechanic, interrupted in the middle of his family dinner, shows Jean how to fix an engine by the flickering light of a naked bulb hanging from the ceiling, Francis Picabia does exactly what you're supposed to do when you don't know how to answer a question: he asks one of his own ("Which I answered using musical logic," she will recall years later.)

"Well, if you're so smart, you tell me: What should I paint?"

"What you paint should be purely a creation of the mind conceptualizing it."

The words send a shiver down Francis Picabia's spine. He pushes Gabriële further.

"That's all well and good, but how can a person *create* when there are so many things there to be copied?"

"Just don't copy; that's all."

Like a flash of light, Francis glimpses, *senses*, the sublime chaos that these words could call into existence. The possibilities are enough to make him dizzy. Gabriële's words are the key, an echo of the thoughts he's been wrestling with for months, the visions that slip out of reach the moment he stands in front of his easel. Visions of paintings that are chaotic, unchained, free—but that he's never been able to sum up in words until that instant. "And suddenly, at that moment, a deep understanding emerged between us. A general sense of agreement, not just about art, but society, too."

After an hour of conversation, they're able to resume their journey. "After a few failed attempts to start the engine, it came to life with a deafening roar, and we got into the car, beneath these sort of grayish driving blankets, and we left." Gabriële and Francis are silent during the drive, both of them stunned, thunderstruck. They watch the road, the night rushing past, illuminated by the car's headlights. This magic of speed and electricity strikes them both as the perfect metaphor for the ideas seething inside them, a thousand thoughts and arguments and examples sparking and jostling and whirling. They have so much to talk about.

In Paris, Gabriële and Francis manage to rid themselves of Jean, to be alone together and continue their conversation. It's almost two in the morning when they park the car in front of 15 rue Hégésippe-Moreau, near the Montmartre cemetery. Here stands the Villa des Arts, built during the reign of Louis XV to provide working space for painters. Despite the lateness of the hour, Francis is set on showing Gabriële his studio.

Normally, he brings young women here to seduce them. There's something erotic, something heady about the place, with the hustle and bustle of the studios, models coming and going, art dealers' representatives browsing. When Francis invites a girl to see his paintings, it's for one reason: to get her into bed. But tonight, the thought never even enters his mind. What he wants is to show Gabriële a canvas that will prove to her that everything she's been talking about has already germinated in his mind.

On this warm September night, the candlelit studio windows of the Villa des Arts turn the place into a vision straight out of the Enlightenment. The perfect setting for a first romantic encounter. But romance is the furthest thing from their minds. Focused on their conversation, they're oblivious to the beauty around them; there are important things to be done. Francis promises to show Gabriële a painting "that no one could possibly take as a mere representation or transposition of natural forms as we usually perceive them—I mean, as distinct from their surroundings—through ordinary visual and pictorial interpretation . . . " He stops, there in the cul-de-sac, and turns to look at her.

"You understand what I'm trying to say, don't you?"

Of course Gabriële understands. Indeed, she's the only person in the world who does, the only one who *could*. Francis Picabia knows this. He takes the young woman's face in his hands—not to kiss her, but to reassure himself that she's real. At last, after a lifetime of being endlessly frustrated by "the inability of those around him to comprehend a way of thinking that they generally dismissed as madness," he's found an equal, someone to listen and understand.

In his studio, Francis lights candles and a few oil lamps and begins to flip through the multitude of canvases propped against the walls. There's a chill in the room, and the sharp, almost nauseating smell of turpentine makes Gabriële a bit dizzy. She doesn't know where to sit, or put her suitcase, or even look. Her unease is the kind you feel when you first get close to someone with whom you suspect you'll not only make love, but possibly share whole days and nights and years. She gazes at the canvases, and the books, and the clothes tossed carelessly around the room—an entire life revealing itself all at once, childhood photographs and jars of paintbrushes lining the rim of the white ceramic sink, piled letters and keepsakes and postcards thumbtacked to the walls, mismatched crockery, a few coins spilling from a leather wallet, newspaper clippings. But also (and Gabriële should have taken note of these, and been wary) a discarded pair of high-heeled shoes, a powder compact, and a tube of Guerlain Forget-Me-Not lipstick—the sort of paraphernalia generally associated with loose women and actresses.

As Francis rummages unsuccessfully for the canvas he's seeking amid the room's appalling clutter, Gabriële glimpses the dozens of landscapes he's recently painted in Moret-sur-Loing alongside her brother Jean. He asks her for her frank opinion of them. "Be brutally honest," he entreats.

"The truth is, all this Impressionism rubbish makes me sick to my stomach," she admits.

"Yes! Me, too!" Francis shouts, like a crazy person.

Snatching up the landscapes, he throws them one by one into a pile in the center of the room, ranting:

"They're no better than a batch of rolls! Though at least the baker has the satisfaction of feeding people. I get no reward from this—nothing but money!"

Suddenly, he leans down and grabs another canvas, this one a mass of indefinable shapes in garish, violent colors. It's the one he's been looking for. *This* painting is no copy of reality; it has nothing to do with "ordinary visual and pictorial interpretation."

"There! You see, I wasn't lying," Francis says triumphantly. But Gabriële frowns.

"It's . . . interesting. Yes. But it's not enough."

Instead of taking offense, Francis sees the vast range of possibilities opened up by the remark. This woman is right—he must go further, strike harder. Everything falls into place in his mind. Encouraged by Gabriële, who nods in emphatic agreement, he launches into an impassioned soliloquy, the words pouring forth in a torrent:

"I want to paint shapes and colors that are freed from their usual sensory associations. A kind of painting situated in the realm of pure invention, one that recreates the world of shapes according to its own desires, its own imagination. From the dawn of time to the modern age, the artist has successfully reproduced what any man of ordinary intelligence would be able to recognize immediately: the original model of a given thing. But I—I want to do something else altogether."

"Seeing that I was virtually spellbound," Gabriële will later recall, "Picabia continued to develop his arguments, pushing them to the very heights of intellectualism, with an incredible richness of images and words."

And this is only the first night, of all the nights that will follow.

Gabriële will never speak of love. Never will she say, *I loved him, and he loved me*. What happens between them is a meeting of the minds that gives rise to a wave of thought and creation; it's the beginning of a never-ending conversation, in the etymological sense of the term; a journey down the same river in the same shared land.

Like a streak of electric-blue paint, the day begins to break in the sky beyond the studio's large windows. Both Francis and Gabriële are starting to tire. They don't speak. They know that, soon, their lips will meet. They know it will happen because they won't be able to resist, but right now they have other things on their minds.

"The night is heavier than the day," Francis says.

"How do you know?"

And Francis tells Gabriële how, when he was a little boy, his father gave him a scale. A wonderful thing, a Roberval 10 kg, with large copper pans and round, gleaming weights. He began to weigh everything within reach: his toys, the kitchen forks, his grandfather's eau de Cologne, sugar, hair, books, even flies. One day it occurred to him to put his scale on a windowsill, in the sunshine. He put a screen in front of one of the copper pans, so that one would be in sunlight and the other in shadow, because "he wanted to see if light weighed more than shade."

The needle pointed toward the dark side. Francis drew his own conclusions.

The sun has risen fully now. The first night is over. They haven't made love, only talked for hours—but with just as much pleasure. Francis suggests that Gabriële lie down on the bed in his studio while he goes out for a short walk, so she can have a bit of privacy and rest. She agrees. Francis steps out into the fresh early-morning air and heads in the direction of Montmartre, which looks like a country village at this hour, with its smoking chimneys, its houses huddled along the rise of the hillside, its uneven cobbled streets.

Dazed by what he has just experienced, stunned by the reality of meeting Gabriële, Francis drinks a cup of black coffee at J. Arvis's, which has just put up a new advert for Munich Beer, and then buys a 20-centime liter of milk at La Goutte de Lait. The rue de Clignancourt is stirring to life, the Bazar National beginning to bustle with activity. He catches sight of Pablo Picasso and Max Jacob some distance away, returning to the Bateau-Lavoir after a night of carousing. The two "Picas"— Picasso and Picabia, both Spaniards—are less than fond of one another, so Francis crosses to the other side of the street, not wanting to spoil his euphoric mood.

Around him, Paris continues to awaken: street vendors and newsboys, laborers on their way to work, gamboling children. He buys croissants at the Boulangerie de la Galette and a beautiful apple from a village woman with her fruit-and-vegetable cart. A feast for Gabriële. He's completely besotted with her. She's his lifeblood, already. He never wants to be parted from her again.

There are men who worship at the altar of youth, others who are helpless in the face of beauty, and yet others who fall in love with feminine kindness and generosity. In September 1908, Francis Picabia loses his heart to a woman's mind. He's just met the most intelligent woman he's ever known, one whose intelligence is "instinctive" as opposed to "the kind one meets everywhere, in sophisticated gatherings, at concerts and in theater boxes and conference rooms."

There can be no question of letting Gabriële board that train to Berlin.

* * *

"Gabriële Buffet was twenty-seven years old when she met Francis Picabia. That's the same age our grandfather, Vicente Picabia, their youngest son, was when he died by suicide."

"You're right. I'd never noticed."

2

YOUNG GIRL IN PARADISE

It is not surprising that Picabia was captivated by the young woman's personality. She was extremely cultivated and notably independent in her opinions; in her way of thinking and behaving, she really was very advanced for her time and her social position."

To understand why, we need to start over at an earlier point in time. Ten years to be exact. To the moment Gabriële decided to become a composer.

Gabriële Buffet is seventeen years old.

She wants to change the world of music. She's determined not to marry. Music will be her sole lifelong companion.

Gaby is a modern girl.

It's 1898. For a woman to be accepted into music school, she must be the absolute best, so dazzlingly talented that her superiority can't possibly be called into question, even by the most misogynistic member of a judging panel. Gabriële knows this, and still she chooses to enter *le concours*—that is, to compete for acceptance to Paris's Conservatoire National de Musique.

The most prestigious music school in France has accepted only a very few women in its history. The first was in 1851, when the father of a young violinist requested that his daughter be permitted to audition. The reply to this iconoclastic patriarch was clear: women were not allowed in the institution's hallowed halls on the rue Bergère.

But the father refused to take no for an answer. Week after week, month after month he persisted and pleaded, sending letters that piled up on the director's desk, requesting face-to-face meetings that were invariably refused, haunting the corner of the rue de Trévise like a ghost to shout at every professor who emerged from the building: "My daughter plays like a man!"

Finally, exhausted, the Conservatoire's director, Daniel-François-Esprit Auber, agreed to let the young violinist play Pierre Rode's Fourth Concerto, hoping the token gesture would rid them of her father's harassment once and for all.

On the day of the audition, young Camille Urso, aged nineteen, showed up with violin in hand, serious and solemn-faced in a long white gown that accentuated her voluptuous curves, the sight of her as jarring to the *messieurs* on the jury as a trumpet-blast in the middle of a string quartet.

The men's uneasy smiles, sniggers, and condescending murmurs lasted precisely until the opening notes of the first movement rose, quivering, into the air—and then every whisper died, ears perking up, souls pierced to the quick. A stunned silence reigned after she lowered her bow, and then there were a few timid smatterings of applause before Rossini, composer of *The Barber of Seville*, rose to his feet, clapping, and the king's former principal violinist Delphin Alard followed suit, then the composer Michele Enrico Carafa, until the whole jury was on its feet. The impossible had happened. Camille Urso's musical power had conquered hearts and shattered precedent. She was admitted to the Conservatoire National de Musique by unanimous decision, ahead of every one of the seventy male candidates.

Since that day, women have been permitted to participate in the competition to become *cons'*—the nickname for first-year students—but in truth, it isn't much of a victory. Female students are still few and far between: a battle or two won, but not the war. Forty years after Camille Urso, places at the Conservatoire remain elusive, and Gabriële knows it.

A further obstacle is posed by the fact that she wants to study not piano, but composition. Though it's true that the Conservatoire occasionally admits a small number of women to study voice or musical theory, and an even smaller number to study a particular instrument, the composition course—the most prestigious of all—remains virtually inaccessible. People will accept a female singer; they'll tolerate her being a pianist or violinist. But a composer? That's a step too far. Composition requires abilities that God would never bestow on a woman, not least the capacity for abstract thought.

Gabriële, though, is undaunted. With a brave heart, a brave *spirit*, anything is possible. She bucks up her courage by recalling the few female composers who have managed to make their music heard: Louise Farrenc, born in 1804, composer of piano music, chamber music, and three symphonies; Augusta Holmès, goddaughter of Alfred de Vigny and composer of operas and dramatic symphonies (and the object of Camille Saint-Saëns's passionate infatuation); and Loïsa Puget, born in 1810, whose success was such that her work was performed at the Opéra-Comique. These artists are all but forgotten now, their names unmentioned by their contemporaries and omitted from histories and dictionaries of music. No matter. Galvanized by their pioneering talent, full of rage, Gabriële applies for entrance to the composition course.

But rage, in the late nineteenth century, isn't yet enough.

The jury rejects her.

Now Gabriële finds herself stuck. Without a conservatory placement, her parents soon start pressuring her to consign her piano to the parlor and find a husband to share her bed. The thought horrifies her. Gabriële doesn't share the aspirations of most young girls. At age seventeen, she dreams of the endless whiteness of solitary mountain rambles, of going to Bayreuth and meeting Cosima Wagner, of one day composing a daring new opera freed from the weight of musical tradition. Anachronistic dreams, ambitions unacceptable in that era.

She'll just have to change her dreams.

Or her era.

Gabriële knows she must come up with a new plan, and fast. Desperate to avoid marriage, her only hope is to find a music school that will accept her. But where? There's no point in approaching any of the institutions that have opened their doors in the past half-century; none of them are welcoming to women. The highly renowned École Niedermeyer, a school of religious and classical music, doesn't even allow them to audition, and the Institution Royale de Musique Religieuse, founded in 1817 by Alexandre Choron, isn't much better, its female students relegated to the lowest ranks.

Then, miraculously, Gabriële hears about a new school, very recently founded by Charles Bordes, Vincent d'Indy, and Alexandre Guilmant: the Schola Cantorum. Rumor has it that this establishment is open to avant-garde thinking—and, apparently, to women. There are naysayers, of course, claiming that the Schola Cantorum accepts female students because it can't afford to turn down the fees they represent. Well, so what? All roads lead to Rome. The competitive auditions take place in November. With Sisyphean persistence, Gabriële registers. It's her final chance before the matrimonial noose is placed around her neck.

To prepare, Gabriële sits in on the classes taught by the composer Gabriel Fauré and is quickly impressed by his unorthodox methods. With his "olive complexion, snowy white hair and beard, and dark, dreaming eyes," this Eastern-looking man always arrives in the classroom slightly late, murmuring apologies, then shuffles through his sheet music and sits down at the piano. He begins by lighting a cigarette from the butt of his previous one and then, this ritual complete, he asks his students not about their homework, but about what they did the night before. Professor Fauré invariably wants to know all the town gossip; he adores nothing more than imbibing the froth of Parisian nightlife second-hand. "That was how his 'classes' always started," one of his former students will remember. "Fauré did correct our homework sometimes, and critique our compositions, but mostly he *talked* with us. He made his lessons seem like a conversation; he imparted his wisdom to us with casual ease and passion but without dogma. He left all the criticism and lecturing to his teaching assistant. We were truly able to commune with him. He gave us total freedom, never forced any specific ideas or concepts on us."

Gabriële, who has read Montaigne's *Essays*, knows that this deceptively informal, relaxed style of learning is far from a waste of time. Fauré is instilling his ways of thinking in his pupils' young minds, teaching them that things must be considered from every angle, that true foolishness takes root in the rigid and overly serious mind, and that depth can sometimes be found in apparent lightness. One day he tells them about the time when, after a performance of his "Nocturne No. 6 in D flat op. 63," a "highbrow" lady asked him:

"Tell me, which magnificent landscape were you viewing when you were touched with such divine inspiration?"

And Fauré answered: "I was in the Simplon Tunnel!"

The class bursts into laughter. But while the professor is entertaining his students, it's true that he's jarring them at the same time, forcing them to reflect. Twenty years ago, he says, he traveled to Zurich with Camille Saint-Saëns to meet Franz Liszt, then aged seventy-two.

Fauré's voice throbs with emotion as he tells his students how, as a bold young man, he'd handed one of his ballads to the master, saying, "I'm afraid it's too long."

"Too long? Young man, there's no such thing. We write as we think."

Liszt's answer, so simple on the surface, was earth-shattering. In it lay the first flickers of the philosophy behind Cubist painting, summed up decades later by Pablo Picasso's statement, "I don't paint what I see; I paint what I think."—uttered, by the way, at around the same time Francis Picabia is repeatedly asserting, "I paint what's in my head." Now, at the tail end of the nineteenth century, music is thirty years ahead of painting, and it's into this caustic bath that Gabriële now plunges herself.

Fauré, her teacher, is an avant-garde composer in a musical culture that considers modernity to have stopped with Wagner. His song cycle *La Bonne Chanson*, composed from 1892 to 1894, caused shockwaves. Too unstructured! "Fauré has gone completely mad!" spat Saint-Saëns, furious. Marcel Proust, though, admired it. "Did you know that young musicians almost universally dislike *La Bonne Chanson*?" he wrote to his friend Pierre Lavallée in a June 1894 letter. "Apparently it's pointlessly complicated. [. . .] Bréville and Debussy (who they say is a much greater genius than Fauré) both think so. But I don't care; I adore it."

When she's finished auditing Gabriel Fauré's classes, Gabriële retreats to Étival in the Jura to prepare, alone, for her audition for the Schola Cantorum, which is scheduled for the autumn. She's no more a Parisienne than she is a Versaillaise. She doesn't belong anywhere. But, since childhood, she has claimed the Jura as home. She loves this tiny, mountainous region, drawing inspiration from its strength, its endurance, its tranquil beauty. There she roams the mountain paths for hours, humming the counterpoint out loud with only cows to hear her, feeling the music physically enter her body, the joy and pain infusing each adolescent muscle. Certain melodic sequences rouse incomprehensible emotions in her as she practices the audition piece, her very skin reacting to *appoggiatura* and changes in harmony, the strange notes moving her deeply. Her connection to music is a primal, bodily thing. Men, on the other hand, don't interest her at all.

On August 31, 1898, summer ends with the slash of a razor—the one used by Colonel Hubert-Joseph Henry to cut his own throat the day after his confession to having forged evidence in the Dreyfus Affair. Gabriële is back in Paris. The capital is already a hive of activity following the torpor of the summer months. Construction of the first underground train line, the *métropolitain de Paris*, has begun; when finished it will connect the Porte Maillot to the Porte de Vincennes. Once again Gabriële adds her own colors to the city's vast palette of workwear: the gray and coal-black worn by the denizens of the Latin Quarter, the blue of the plumbers and zincworkers, the white of the masons and builders, the thick corduroy trousers favored by carpenters. Gabriële, too, wears a costume for her exam at the Schola Cantorum: that of the corseted young student, complete with new (and uncomfortable) spool-heeled boots. She already misses the simplicity of her mountain life, but she's willing to wear any corset, as long as she passes her exam.

Which she does. With flying colors.

The jury's verdict is that the young woman indisputably possesses the qualities needed to become a good composer. Still, she's summoned to a meeting with the school's director, who wants to assess her stamina. In scheduling this interview, Vincent d'Indy is taking every precaution; if Gabriële were to drop out of her course partway through, he would be criticized for having wasted a place in the composition program on a mere girl.

D'Indy is approaching his fiftieth birthday, which makes him old enough to be Gabriële's father. He has a receding hairline and a curling mustache and is always impeccably dressed. Arms folded, tone calm and serious, he explains the curriculum.

"The first condition for completing a Schola course successfully is to love art, and to have a sophisticated and well-rounded intellect. I require a five-year commitment from my . . . militant students, if you will . . . that is, the ones truly destined for a career as a composer. One mustn't lose sight of the fact that art is long, and it takes a long time to learn it. And make no mistake—art cannot be learned in books."

The term "militant student," which Gabriële has never

heard before, appeals to her immediately—as does the prospect of hard work, which, far from discouraging her, stirs her blood. Her whole life is waiting for her here, at this school. A straight line to her future, to her fate. And the Schola's director, for his part, sees this young woman with perfect clarity. He can sense her hunger. If he doesn't accept Mademoiselle Buffet into his school's renowned composition course, he knows he'll be condemning her to a life of unhappiness.

By the end of the interview, Vincent d'Indy needs no more convincing. He accepts the young woman, who will be the only one in that year's class, and he does it despite the risk it entails. A great risk, in fact—for accepting a woman into the prestigious composition program could harm the reputation of his school, already the subject of much scandalized disapproval among Paris's do-gooders, not to mention the Schola's enemies at the Conservatoire National.

To understand fully the magnitude of d'Indy's decision, we have to remember what it means to be a young woman like Gabriële in 1898. She isn't allowed to wear trousers unless she's astride a horse or a bicycle. She isn't allowed to work without a husband's permission. She isn't allowed to practice certain professions, to teach Latin, Greek, or philosophy. She isn't allowed to apply for a passport on her own, or vote, or run for political office, or make decisions about her own body, or manage her own earnings. But—and this is truly an earth-shattering *but*—Gabriële is authorized, in the autumn of 1898, to study composition at the Schola Cantorum.

The start of a revolution.

There is a photograph of Gabriële, taken two years after her admission to the Schola. It's 1900, the year she turns nineteen. She looks directly, confidently, at the camera. By now she's one of the school's stars, those composition students who never really mingle with the others, who swan around in a constant state of apparent inspiration and importance, dreaming of the glittering destinies that await. She is the anomaly among all the male faces with their Belle Epoque mustaches. The error. And proud of it. Her teacher, Vincent d'Indy, stands next to her: "He wore his hair parted in the middle and smoothed back on either side, though he let it grow a bit longer than was typical. He favored low, starched collars, always with a tightly knotted black tie—there was none of the unkempt look of the *artiste* about him."

On the other hand, there's nothing stylish about Gabriële, at least in the sense that she doesn't follow the current trend for *robes bicyclettes*, which reveal young women's ankles, or show off her figure by wearing one of the new straight-front corsets, which slim the hips and arch the lower back. Silk and lace do not interest her.

Gabriële doesn't seek out the company of her fellow (male) students. Nor does she go straight to the concert hall at the end of a day's work. The Schola's schedule is very strict: students must start work at dawn, studying instruments and music theory as well as composition history, harmonic rules, arranging, and orchestration. It's a crushing workload, but Gabriële, like every pupil at the Schola, is buoyed by the exhilaration of being part of a new institution that is poised to become a school of musical thought. Here, all will be reinvented—the way in which music is taught, played, and written.

In less than ten years, the Schola Cantorum has surpassed its competitors to become the Conservatoire National's only rival. Accordingly, it has recently moved into more spacious premises in order to accommodate more students—specifically, the former English Benedictine monastery at 269 rue Saint-Jacques.

On Saturday, October 27, 1900, arriving at the Schola's new location, Gabriële feels as if she's breathing in more air than her lungs can hold. It's unseasonably hot in Paris, the blistering temperatures only heightening the sense of fevered stimulation among the school's young artists. This evening they're giving a free concert for the laborers who renovated the buildings on the new site. The Schola's directors have also invited the local residents, their new neighbors, who have endured weeks of noise during the construction work. The students have sacrificed hours of sleep to rehearse the new Vincent d'Indy symphony they'll be performing—learning along the way that music is a gift in every sense of the word, and that people must be generous with their talent.

It's almost time for the concert. The Schola's final-year musicians are deep in one last practice session. Suddenly, a kind of panic sweeps through the school: there are shouts in the corridors and classrooms, a call to arms: every student must stop what they're doing and go in search of chairs and stools! Curious spectators are already crowding the lobby; no one's ever seen so many people here at once! It's a sign. Something is *happening*. Gabriële's skin prickles with goosebumps. "The auditorium only held 450, and there must have been at least a thousand people out there!" Vincent d'Indy will exclaim afterward. "A handful of adversaries, annoyed at the sight of our success. Masses of people stood through the entire concert, for there wasn't another chair to be found in the whole place—others listened from outside on the balconies, et cetera. An enormous success—an astonishing turnout. The young are with us!"

The Schola Cantorum soon becomes *the* home of the Parisian musical avant-garde. It's difficult to imagine, today, how people felt about music then. For both musicians and the listening public, there was no music except what was played in concert halls. Music wasn't a thing you could *own*. There were no recordings, no albums. And when a composer was no longer fashionable, he was quickly and quite naturally forgotten. Numerous works, even whole repertoires, disappeared in this way.

But now, at the end of the nineteenth century, a few musicians are undertaking to rediscover these forgotten works, republishing and then playing them. Vincent d'Indy is among these few. He transforms the Schola Cantorum concert hall into a vibrant theater of musical rebirth, staging revivals of forgotten pieces alongside the newest, most cutting-edge creations, mingling past and future.

D'Indy's deepest interest is reserved for the most pivotal, original music, for pioneers such as the Italian composer Monteverdi, who is now considered the inventor of opera but who, in 1900, was virtually unknown to both musicians and the public. Thanks to his research, d'Indy is able to have his students recreate several of Monteverdi's operas—and these create such a sensation that people start coming from all over Europe to attend concerts at the Schola. The establishment on the rue Saint-Jacques soon has the ear of musicologists like the German Hermann Kretzschmar, who sends a student to Paris to take detailed notes on a performance of *L'Orfeo*.

Vincent d'Indy is the kind of beloved educator who "opens windows to other artistic worlds." He urges his students to read poetry, to lose themselves in museums and art galleries. Thanks to d'Indy's teachings, Gabriële will dazzle Francis Picabia with her knowledge of painting; despite feigning ignorance, she can describe in detail the paintings of Goya and Velasquez at the Prado in Madrid.

The students rediscover Christoph Gluck and Jean-Philippe Rameau, whose music has been forgotten since the Revolution. Vincent d'Indy arranges for them to hear performances of all Bach's cantatas—incredibly, unknown up to this point!

Inevitably, d'Indy's success makes him a target for attack by jealous adversaries. He's accused of using his students to operate a cheap music hall, a criticism he refutes in strong terms: "The concerts we give are in no way intended to earn a profit, but solely to provide our students, who are composers, instrumentalists, and singers, with a musical education by enabling them to hear and perform works they cannot hear or perform anywhere else." The rue Saint-Jacques becomes a battlefield, one on which Gabriële cuts her teeth and experiences with pleasure the first skirmishes in what will become a lifelong crusade for her: championing the avant-garde.

Claude Debussy is a regular attendee of the Schola's concerts—despite the fact that this innovative composer, aged forty, detests academies in general and the Conservatoire National in particular. He's been a favorite among music students since his "Prelude to the Afternoon of a Faun," a free interpretation of Stéphane Mallarmé's poem, was released to extraordinary success in 1894; at its premiere, the audience was so amazed at the sound of such utterly new music that the orchestra was obliged to play the whole thing over again then and there. His work, which seeks to infuse sound with fresh colors, combining compositional freedom with a new way of marrying instruments, marks the beginnings of modern music.

When Debussy appears on the Schola's grounds, he's quickly surrounded by an eager mob of young people. His profile is immediately recognizable; his forehead bulges almost grotesquely, like a Beluga whale's. His manner of speaking appeals to Gabriële, as does his biting sense of humor, always ready to rail at the musical establishment. This son of ceramics and pottery dealers, born into a social sphere that in no way fitted him for a career as a composer, calls it as he sees it. More than anything he loves to stir up young minds, to provoke the students that swarm around him by badmouthing their teachers—though gently. He encourages them to be suspicious of rules and institutions, endlessly repeating the aphorism that will mark a whole generation of young artists: "*Les règles ne créent pas une oeuvre d'art*"—Rules do not create art.

He delights in making fun of a famous critic to the students who gather clamoring to hear about his success, imitating the man's voice and mannerisms: "You have talent, and I don't. This can't go on much longer!" He skips lightly over the criticism, arrogant and sardonic at once about his own gifts:

"I'm pretty quick at composing, but I'm very slow at actually deciding to do it."

When asked about his musical preferences—and particularly his dislikes, a far spicier subject—Debussy loves to make his young listeners laugh. "Much more worthwhile to watch a sunrise than listen to the *Pastoral Symphony*."

Then, abruptly, his mood darkens, a shadow crossing his face. Gazing intently at the assembly of up-and-coming faces, young souls swelling with ambition, he issues a warning:

"Since time immemorial, there have been certain people who perceive beauty as a kind of secret insult."

When Gabriële meets Francis Picabia, she sees in him a strong likeness to Claude Debussy. The defiant character, the provocative nature of his writing, the insolent genius, the free-flowing way of expressing himself—and the insatiable hunger for worldly pleasure and the company of women. Both men claim that their creative activities are simply recreational, a way of amusing themselves—that is, detached from any notion of work or effort—but in both cases, behind this seeming ease lies perfection of technique and an extremely deep and rigorous understanding of composition, whether of a painting or a sonata.

In 1901, Gabriële is enchanted by Debussy's *Nocturnes,* composed of three movements entitled "Clouds," "Festivals," and "Sirens" and inspired by a series of paintings by Whistler. Instead of an explanatory introduction, Debussy writes a prose poem for his listeners: "*Clouds*: the unchanging aspect of the sky, with the slow and melancholy march of clouds ending in gray death, softly tinged with white. *Festivals*: the movement, the dancing rhythm of the atmosphere, flashing suddenly with light." Debussy is seeking to reinvent music completely, seeing it not merely as something to be written down on paper, but "for the ears." Above all, we are *physical bodies*.

The questions raised by the new piece are dizzying for the young woman, life-altering: *what is the purpose of musical notes? Can we play them with other instruments? Or even with things other than instruments? Is every sound musical?* All questions that modern painting will ask itself in the years to come. What is the purpose of color? Can we change it—disrupt the color spectrum? Can we paint with substances other than paint? Can all things be represented in a painting?

A force grows within Gabriële during her time at the Schola: the idea that we must draw inspiration from all the emotions unleashed by art, the storms of painting, the floods of poetry, to find a new musical language.

It's in this state of intellectual euphoria, something near enlightenment, that Gabriële pursues her studies. She writes to her brother Jean: "I've begun to realize that any unfinished project—any work left on the shelf—is wasted time, and that progress will only ever come on the heels of an act of will, one we see through all the way to the end of an idea, unspooling the thread until the bobbin is empty." Her precocious and extraordinary sense of determination grows ever stronger in this place that educates even as it defies convention.

The years at the Schola pass quickly, and Gabriële spends every day of her education filled with the intoxicating sensation of being part of a radical movement. For the rest of her life, she'll keep chasing that feeling, as if this youthful experience were a drug she can't live without. When a reporter asks her, long after her time at the Schola, about her mindset while composing, she'll reply, laughing:

"The Cubist spirit!"

In 1906, two years before meeting Francis Picabia, Gabriële is awarded her diploma. She spends the summer with her family in Étival, in her beloved mountains, luxuriating in the silence of the great outdoors and composing. Her parents are as impatient as ever: when will she bring home a young man?

The idea repels her.

Gabriële is almost twenty-five, and the idea of having to make love with a man is utterly alien to her. She can scale a mountain peak with gusto, but a man's body? No, that's another story. She remains oddly uninterested.

But there are whispers of a suitor. So Gabriële flees to Paris, on the pretext that she has to participate, as a former student, in organizing the entrance exams for new applicants to the Schola. She celebrates her birthday alone in the capital. A few days later, on November 25, the city drapes itself in yellow and green, the colors of Saint Catherine. On that day, *Catherinettes*, unmarried young women aged twenty-five, don extravagant hats in yellow and green and parade through the streets to "do Saint Catherine's hair," a tradition begun by female workers in fashion houses. Displays of headgear, sweets, and pastries in shades of sun and leaf fill the shop windows. Florists sell little sprays of orange blossoms, and street flower-sellers even offer ironic little bunches of dandelions, which young women pin into their hair. Sometimes the girls are jokingly called *midinettes*, since the fashion workers who started the Saint Catherine tradition came mainly from the *midi*, or south, of France.

The Catherinettes traipse through the streets in groups, rebellious and gay, greeted by both teasing and cheers as they pass. Male students from the Latin Quarter, sons of the bourgeoisie, gather to heckle the working-class girls and end up drinking with them, invited to the regulation evening dance—the "last-chance dance"—where it's not uncommon for the police to be called to calm the hullabaloo.

Gabriële picks her way unhappily through the boisterous crowds. It isn't just her family; it's the whole *world* that's determined to marry her off! The masses of lonely hearts parading past look like nothing but a bunch of bodies seeking their master. She wants to travel the world—to live for music—to create—to write. How can her dreams of composing come true if she's busy changing diapers?

Once again, Mademoiselle Buffet turns to her professor, who has also become her protector. Her admiration for him is boundless—except for their fundamental differences of opinion regarding the Dreyfus Affair.

Vincent d'Indy can see only one way for her to escape the typical young woman's fate: to go away, far from her family. Berlin is a cosmopolitan city, young, musical, and jolly. The poet Jules Laforgue, who lived there in the 1880s when he was employed as a French reader to the Empress Augusta, called Berlin "the musical Mecca." Gabriële needs her parents' permission to go. Vincent d'Indy writes them a letter, assuring them of their daughter's bright future and promising to see to it that her time in Germany is perfectly comfortable. He also writes letters of recommendation that will enable Gabriële to take masterclasses from Ferruccio Busoni in Berlin, and finds a family willing to host the young woman in exchange for French lessons.

With the matter all settled, Gabriële takes a final walk through the buildings of the Schola Cantorum. In the dim hall where students congregate before lessons, she greets the austere Monsieur Raynaud, who manages the schedule with an iron fist, one eye always on his watch, calling out when it's time for each class to begin. It's this gray-haired gentleman who's always provided Gabriële with her student card, stamped each month with a round seal reading "Schola Cantorum."

One last time, she passes the door of the office where Vincent d'Indy holds court, "a vast, beautifully proportioned room with lovely Louis XV woodwork painted gray, at its center a wonderful pink marble mantelpiece with an immense mirror hung above it." One last time, she listens to the two grand pianos being played. She lingers, gazing at the easel where the portrait of some obscure ancestor has been replaced by a blackboard, the sight of which strikes terror into the hearts of hundreds of students on exam days, all afraid to confuse semiquavers with demisemiquavers, syncopation with contretemps, key changes with changes in time signature.

The sun is setting, and it's time for Gabriële to leave this place she has come to know by heart over the years, to confront the unknown once again. She passes beneath the rectangular portico and out into the rue Saint-Jacques, whose cramped pavements frequently threaten to tip you off your feet and into the path of a horse-drawn omnibus. Walking away, she can sense behind her, receding into the distance, the Schola's chestnut tree, grown so massive that it dominates the courtyard, a few branches even reaching beyond the campus wall.

Back home, Gabriële resolutely hands her mother Vincent d'Indy's letter:

Chère Madame,

It seems to me that this plan can have no drawbacks, for, if we accept the fact that she doesn't desire to continue in her current situation, and that marriage (as is the general rule) would take her away from her music, what better arrangement could there be for a young woman than to have, at least until she does marry, a steady occupation that she enjoys and that will provide her with work? Do not refuse her this; your daughter's gifts are far too real to be neglected . . .

The professor is an undeniable master of *captatio benevolentiae*, the ancient art of appealing to another's goodwill. Yet Gabriële's parents are categorically opposed to her departure, "considering with a certain anxiety [her] determined and independent nature, whose profound ambitions they [are] incapable of understanding." At a loss as to how to harness the lion—the lion*ess*—that is their daughter, they simply refuse to give her a *sou*. No money, no train ticket.

So Gabriële will do without their approval. Without their money. Without their love, if she has to. She quickly finds work teaching piano to the children of bourgeois families, takes German lessons, and, secretly, plans her grand adventure.

3
COMPOSITION

G abriële is still a young woman when she completes her studies at the Schola Cantorum. She arrives in Berlin in 1906 with two *open sesames*: 50 marks (the equivalent of a month's middle-class salary) and Vincent d'Indy's letters of recommendation.

She might be alone in an unfamiliar city, but Gabriële isn't afraid. On the contrary! Here it is, the life she's been waiting for. A new start. Freedom. Everything about this place appeals to her. She loves it all. Berlin is an extraordinarily modern city for a young Frenchwoman. The wonders of electricity, the luxury cars with their powerful engines, the trams whose rails crisscross the city amongst its profusion of parks and flowerbeds, the electric trains, the little chocolate-and-cream omnibuses— all of it makes her feel as if she's part of an era in the process of creating itself. "The power of imagination in such a vast city is startling, overwhelming," the playwright Jean Giraudoux observes when he visits Berlin this same year.

Berlin glitters like the eyes of a man possessed. New districts pop up like mushrooms, sturdy edifices rising in an endless display of industry. "Paris is a pigsty in comparison," writes the artist and traveler Charles Huard, "London a cesspit, New York a wallow." Berlin has a more organic quality than Paris, its trees seemingly more resistant to the installation of gaslights and the presence of steam engines.

Gabriële loves the exoticism to be found in even the city's small details. Everything is different: the cookie tins, the greetings, the signs printed in Gothic type, the sickly-sweet taste of cakes slathered in buttercream, the uniforms of the mounted police, and the order and silence that reign in the vast department stores, where the concern for cleanliness is such that gentlemen are required to deposit their cigars in tiny copper boxes before entering, to be retrieved upon exit.

During these early days, she immerses herself in the liveliest neighborhoods with abandon. The most popular area is the one around Unter den Linden, the Champs-Elysées of Berlin, lined with chestnut and linden trees. This is where the luxury hotels are found: the Bristol, the Savoy, the Metropole, the Royal. Here too are the elegant offices of the German steamship lines, their windows replete with maps showing the dotted lines of sea voyages all over the globe—Gabriële lingers in front of these longer than other pedestrians. This part of the city is popular with tourists, and every language can be heard, Russian and American most of all. Sitting at a table on the terrace of the Café Kranzler, Gabriële orders a hot chocolate with whipped cream and a *Baumkuchen*, a thick, round cake shaped like a tree trunk. In the shops, she surveys the local cuisine with a certain trepidation: boiled potatoes, myriad varieties of cabbage, black radishes, carrots, Harzer cheese. There are sandwiches, some open-faced and thickly buttered, others of black bread and smoked fish; there are poppy-seed tarts and sweet-and-sour beer soup with macaroni, all washed down with *Rote Ente*, "red duck," the national beverage, a mixture of red and sparkling white wines.

Berlin is a city designed for the young, especially if you're a musician. Gabriële, obliged to pay for her own room and board, starts looking for work as soon as she arrives in town. She easily finds a place in a chamber ensemble, specifically the house orchestra at a bar-restaurant. Music is everywhere in Berlin, part of everyone's daily life, regardless of social class. "Whether at the opera, at a concert by the Philharmonic Orchestra, or in a smoky *brasserie* where people come on certain days to hear a military band play, the most admirable musical performances can be heard everywhere at minimal cost," enthuses a French travel guide of the period. Gabriële begins to carve out a niche for herself among the city's musicians and to familiarize herself with the *Berliner Dialekt*, influenced by both Dutch and English, in which g's are pronounced like y's.

Gabriële becomes acquainted, too, with the flip side of day. She who was always so sensible in Paris, so solitary and aloof, develops a taste for the aimless hours of the night. She learns to drink, opening herself up to the pleasure of intoxication, to lighthearted flirtation, and to the crowded emptiness of urban nightlife. She has no more need of a chaperon; in Paris it was Vincent d'Indy who looked after the girls on evenings out at concerts. In Berlin, she's on her own at last.

She rapidly earns enough money to become independent. It's wonderful to be paid to play music, to give joy to others, to entertain them, no matter who they are—bourgeois husbands in no hurry to return home, families celebrating a special occasion, down-and-outs with no place to go, romantic students who only feel at home outdoors—all those denizens of cabaret culture who she'll meet again, years later, in the work of Bertolt Brecht.

At around 7:00 in the evening, as soon as night has fallen, darker and denser than the Parisian night, the city's countless bistros awaken (most of them tavern-style places with medieval décor, very German), every one of them with its own little chamber ensemble in the back of the dining room. The patrons smoke pipes or cigarettes, drink beer, and play cards and *Skat* and, if the bistro has a back room, *Kegelspiel*, all while eating *Appetithappen*, "little canapés," which, despite the name, aren't actually small at all.

It takes Gabriële only a few days to grasp the rules and hierarchies of seating in the brasserie where she works. The best tables are reserved for the best customers, those who come every day to drink up their last marks. These old regulars are always the first to arrive and the last to leave, which they do just before closing time—the *Polizeistunde*, or "police hour."

If a regular doesn't show up, it invariably means he's shuffled off this mortal coil. His ceramic pipe is then covered in black crepe and set at his empty place at the table, his fellow patrons drinking silently to his memory. There is no more laughter that night. But the assembly's joie de vivre always returns the next evening, as they engage in a lively debate over who will inherit the vacant seat.

In the Berlin night, Gabriële becomes delicate and feminine. Robust and solid, with sturdy legs made muscular by long mountain hikes, she was never one to turn heads in Paris. In Germany, though, she trails in her wake the intoxicating perfume of France. In the midst of so many impressive male figures, she feels daintier than she did in Paris, for in Berlin all the proportions are magnified: the bodies are larger and so are the streets, and even the plates with their extravagant quantities of food.

For the first time, Gabriële enjoys the sense of being looked at. *Gazed* at. Desired. Even so, she doesn't take a lover. She makes no attempt to "date," as the Americans are calling it these days, and turns down every invitation. Male-female relations are very different in Germany from what she was used to in Paris; men and women don't engage in banter, their conversations are less ambiguous, less mischievous. Gabriële's dresses, simple and modest though they are, still draw attention; it's considered chic to wear French- or English-style clothing. This awareness of being noticed, approved of, does more than give her confidence; it teaches her things about herself she didn't know. It's a new, intimate experience, a dialogue between the girl she still is and the woman she's in the process of becoming.

This hard-won independence, this unprecedented feeling of being pleasing to the eye—it all makes her happy in a way that's hard to define. How can it *not* change you, to be in a country where everything is so different and unusual? That's the advantage of being a stranger in a strange city: you can reinvent yourself.

In Berlin, Gabriële softens, becomes less rigid, more

spontaneous. She's more surprised than anyone when she catches sight of her reflection in a mirror—why does her face look so odd?

It's because she's smiling.

One evening, she comes home to the news that her father has died. Stooping to pick up the letters that have been slid underneath her door, she finds an envelope edged in black. It's a shock, completely unexpected. Gabriële doesn't cry. Instead, she locks herself in her room and sleeps for days, unable to get out of bed. The weeks that follow are marked by crushing fatigue, as if she's covered in a damp wool blanket.

It's not long after this that the small group of French, Swiss, and Germans who make up Gabriële's circle of friends decides to go to the art opening, or vernissage, of a fashionable new painter who's the talk of Paris but has a Spanish name: Francis Picabia. It's 1906. The future lovers haven't met yet, and this is the first time Gabriële has heard of Francis. He's known for painting Impressionist landscapes worthy of the great masters, modeling himself on Cézanne and Sisley.

Arriving in Berlin covered in glory, this 27-year-old's name is on every tongue in the expat community. Rumors fly. People say:

He came to Berlin in his *own* automobile.

He's a brilliant, spoiled child.

His first solo exhibition was a dazzling success, his fame growing in leaps and bounds both in France and abroad ever since.

They say that he's known as a "fast liver" and a rowdy presence in many a Paris bar, fond of alcohol and fistfights; that he once wrought havoc at Maxim's, overturning tables with his bare hands.

That he spends money like water, ready to do anything for a few hours' fun or to get a girl into bed.

That the old Impressionists are jealous of him, including

Pissarro, who is said to have written disparagingly about him in his letters.

That he's throwing a huge party for his vernissage at the famous Kasper Kunstsalon, and that it's the social event of the season, not to be missed.

"Are you coming, Gabriële?" her friends ask.

"No. No. I can't stand Impressionism and all that 'modern antique' rubbish."

Gabriële and Francis missed meeting by a hair's breadth in 1906 Berlin. Our whims and opinions, no matter how minor or fleeting, can change the course of the future forever. If they *had* met at that precise time in their lives, they would undoubtedly have hated each other, and neither of us would exist.

Vincent d'Indy's letters of recommendation enable Gabriële to join a class taught by Ferruccio Busoni. The composer, considered the greatest pianist since Franz Liszt, is also a teacher whose skill as an educator is as highly sought-after as his musical talent. As Marc Le Bot, one of Picabia's future biographers, will put it, "Busoni's students gained immensely from him, but without being forced to relinquish any of their individuality. Busoni never tried to alter anyone's brilliance." The maestro's pupils all share a hunger for new creative experiences. They're fiercely curious, open to iconoclastic theories. And they come from all over Europe.

Ferruccio Busoni is an art theorist whose musical research will result in his 1907 manifesto *Sketch of a New Aesthetic of Music*, published in Trieste, the tenets of which he will instill firmly in his students' minds. His philosophies may not be as radical as those of his contemporary Arnold Schönberg, the apostle of so-called "atonal" music, but they're subversive enough for his theoretical opus to cause a scandal in the musical world. Busoni "[is] the musician that most interest[s] Gabriële in those stirring times in Berlin, perhaps because he reject[s] French Impressionism and its imitative music."

Musical instruments, Busoni explains to his pupils, are limited by their own range and timbre, and, as artists, composers must free themselves from these limitations. He entreats them to explore abstract sonorities, to aspire to unlimited tonal freedom, broaching possibilities never before imagined, including electroacoustic and microtonal music. He galvanizes their minds and kindles their creative spirits, ending every class with the words:

"All those born to create must first accept the great responsibility of unlearning everything they think they know."

Busoni enthuses about new musical possibilities, but he will not explore them himself. However, under his influence, one of his pupils, a young man of twenty-three who joins his masterclass in 1907, will invent electronic music. With his wild hair and stormy expression, Edgard Varèse gives off an air of intensity, even danger. He arrives in Berlin with a bad reputation; he was expelled from the Conservatoire National, they say, for having refused to take his fugue test. A few days before that, he'd said baldly to none other than Camille Saint-Saëns:

"I have no desire to become an old fuddy-duddy like you."

And so Edgard Varèse leaves the Conservatoire under a cloud, accompanied by a young classmate studying dramatic arts, Suzanne, whom he impulsively marries. The couple lives for a while in a small apartment on the rue Descartes, visited by friends including Charles Dullin and Louis Jouvet, and Varèse enrolls in the Schola Cantorum. Without an income to live on, he joins the large number of student musicians living hand to mouth. At a Schola concert one evening, he's literally caught with his hand in the till. But Vincent d'Indy doesn't expel him; in fact, he even finds him a job in the library. It's unthinkable to let him get away, this extraordinary young talent who wrote his first opera at the age of thirteen. D'Indy is impressed, too, by Varèse's confidence when he takes the stage in front of the other students, by his blazing eyes and the way he faces down his fellow musicians. The director arranges for a scholarship so that his protégé can attend Busoni's masterclasses in Berlin, and Varèse and Suzanne settle at 61 Nassauische Strasse, poor as church mice and unable to speak a word of German. To keep them from starving, Edgard finds work as a copyist.

His fellow student Gabriële Buffet catches Edgard Varèse's attention from the first. They have a great deal in common: they're both French and around the same age, and they both attended the Schola Cantorum in Paris. Most importantly, they're both estranged from their parents. Just as Gabriële fled France to escape being married off, Edgard Varèse left behind the engineering career planned for him by his father.

At first, Gabriële's a bit uncomfortable around this young man so bent on becoming her friend. He looks at her so intensely that it disturbs her; he gives her the impression—as she'll admit later—of being almost unhinged, a quality she finds both unsettling and interesting. He's handsome, too; *that* part doesn't hurt anything, even for the obstinately single Gabriële. Romain Rolland, who meets Edgard two years later, will describe him as "tall, with wonderful black hair and light eyes, an intelligent, energetic face, like a young Italian Beethoven painted by Giorgione."

Edgard is drawn to Gabriële. He follows her through the streets after class, seeks her out among the cosmopolitan masses of Berlin's student musicians, lingers in the brasseries where she plays, invites her to Philharmonic Orchestra concerts. After a few weeks, the young woman gives in and accepts his friendship: she sees in him the sounding board she needs, and she's overwhelmed by the new worlds Busoni's teachings have opened up to her still-developing intellect. Years later, Varèse will echo the sentiment: "Busoni had the gift for stimulating my mind to explore bottomless depths of prophetic imagination." He and Gabriële emerge from class with cheeks flushed and heads bursting, needing each other to go over the maestro's words again and again. Berlin has ceased to exist; it's as if the city has vanished from their mental landscape, wholly replaced by the idea of creating a new kind of music. Following in the footsteps of the professor, they construct musical utopias and invent outlandish new instruments, seeking to create different notes the way a painter would try to invent nonexistent colors. "We wanted to free ourselves," Gabriële writes later, "to break away from every traditional technique, all the old syntax and grammar, to explore what we called pure music."

Gabriële and Edgard walk for hours in the Tiergarten Park, with its many brasseries and orchestras. Watching them stroll together along the pathways bordered with triumphant statues, one might think they're lovers, but nothing could be further from the truth. They're two revolutionaries in the process of questioning every artistic principle they know. They discuss section XIX of Aristotle's *Problems*. Edgard explains to Gabriële the scientist Hermann von Helmholtz's discoveries involving the perception of sound and color and introduces her to the writings of Leonardo da Vinci, while Gabriële translates journal articles for him about Max Planck's work on the development of quantum theory. She also translates *Entwurf einer neuen Ästhetik der Tonkunst*, the book their teacher has just had published in Trieste. Dissecting Busoni's manifesto together, they work to create a new universe, and thanks to him they envision "liberating music from the tempered system, from the limitations imposed by the instruments in use and by the many years of bad habits we wrongly call 'tradition.'"

Instead of talking about "music," they speak of "organized sounds." Instead of calling themselves musicians, they say they work with "rhythms," "frequencies," and "intensities." Their great ambition is to find new instruments with which they can produce other sonorities, sounds beyond the seven notes possible on the piano. "This gave rise to a stream of discoveries,"

Gabriële will recall, "and so Varèse then composed his own music, which led to pop art and current music, unshackled from the old techniques, from all the grammar and syntax musicians once had to obey."

Edgard is younger than Gabriële, just twenty-three to her twenty-five. He sees in her a reference point, a beacon in the rushing torrent of his creative energy. Varèse still has trouble managing his own brilliance. He fumbles around, starts a new piece, burns it, starts several more, doesn't finish any of them. His musical gestation is painful, so much so that he finds he needs the comfort of his classmate's company. Edgard is the type of artist who needs the support and attention of others to create. One day, he asks all his musician friends, including Gabriële, to help him complete a two-line theme he's just composed. Unable to get any further, as Gabriële will remember, "an idea came to him that could surely be classed among the first attempts at aleatory music: he asked each one of us to improvise on that theme." A sort of pre-Dadaist experiment in the creative process. "The result was surprising. But everything we did during those years in Berlin . . . all of it was lost."

One day at the end of class, Busoni informs his students that the famous Eugène Ysaÿe is passing through Berlin. This Belgian who towers above his audiences at two meters tall and looks like a mountain woodcutter crammed into a three-piece suit, is the greatest violinist in Europe, perhaps the world. Ysaÿe is a living legend, ticking every box on the list, including a childhood similar to Mozart's, complete with a violent, authoritarian father who trotted him out to play at balls from the age of four and confined him in the cellar to develop his talents. Temperamental and defiant, the boy was expelled at age eleven from Liège's Conservatoire Royal de Musique. The staff's parting words to his father? "Better to make him a dung-collector than a violinist."

Like all good legends, Ysaÿe's includes an element of chance. One day, the very famous composer and violinist Henri Vieuxtemps, who was passing through Liège, heard the sound of a violin drifting from an open window: someone was playing his very own Fifth Concerto to perfection. Never had he heard it executed so well. Vieuxtemps knocked on the door of the house from which the music was emanating, and a man opened it. The maestro eyed him.

"Who's playing the violin here?" he demanded.

"It's my son Eugène, sir."

"Can he play for me now?"

Eugène was fourteen. Henri Vieuxtemps arranged for him to be accepted back into the Conservatoire de Musique. No more defiance, no more dung-collector. The teachers, floored by his talent, now had him play for the other students to show them how pieces should be interpreted. When he won his first prize in 1873, the conservatory's director jotted in his notes: "He plays the violin the way birds sing."

That was the beginning of the "phenomenon." Henri Vieuxtemps took his protégé all over Europe, and he was acclaimed everywhere he went. He had a tempered-steel constitution and lived like a Cossack. In Paris, he drank absinthe with pretty girls and played with the virtuoso pianist Anton Rubinstein, then met César Franck and became friends with Gabriel Fauré, Claude Debussy—and Vincent d'Indy. All these composers would dedicate works to him, and Ernest Chausson would write a sonata for his wedding. To earn a steady living, young Eugène accepted the position of *Konzertmeister* at the Konzerthaus in Berlin, a convivial meeting place where men gathered for a beer after leaving their offices. Here, the house orchestra played Strauss waltzes and operettas by Offenbach, Schubert, Schumann, and Wagner, music that struggled to rise above the incessant hubbub of the customers' shouts and laughter—except when Ysaÿe played. Then, the room would fall silent. Everyone listened, and wept.

At the Konzerthaus, Ysaÿe met Clara Schumann, the late Robert Schumann's muse and a legendary virtuoso pianist in her own right, who encouraged the young prodigy to embark on a career as a soloist. Abandoning the path of easy success and a comfortable income and following the advice of Camille Saint-Saëns, Eugène returned to Paris, where there was a desperate need for artists capable of understanding and performing the new music being created. Even the great Rodin invited him to give recitals at his studio.

It's this bearlike celebrity, whose massive physical presence belies the infinite delicacy of his playing, who has just returned to Berlin from a triumphant tour of Russia. Ferruccio Busoni has asked Ysaÿe to meet with his students when he passes through the city, to give them a sort of informal masterclass. Gabriële, Varèse, and the others are deeply impressed by the Belgian, who tells them:

"Virtuosity without music is nothing. Every note, every sound must live, sing, express pain or joy. Be a painter, even in those 'brushstrokes' that are merely a rapid series of notes."

He encourages the students to ask questions but, afraid of sounding stupid, no one dares to raise a hand. Gabriële, humbled, is silent. Edgard Varèse, however, stands and asks Ysaÿe if he'd be willing to listen to one of his compositions. Edgard's classmates are stupefied, but Ysaÿe willingly accepts, on the condition that the performance takes place as soon as possible; the violinist has to go back on tour and can only squeeze Varèse in the next morning. As soon as class is over, the students ask Varèse what he's planning to play for the virtuoso, but Edgard admits that it was a bluff. He doesn't have anything ready. He'll have to spend the whole night composing. Gabriële suggests that he play for Ysaÿe a piece he's already begun, a musical poem entitled *Bourgogne*, which she calls, "A remarkable experiment."

Edgard asks Gabriële to help him finish the piece that

night. Without a moment's hesitation, the young conspirators climb aboard a passing *berline*—one of the large, heavy black vehicles that serve as the city's tram cars—in the direction of 61 Nassauische Strasse. The atmosphere there is strained. Suzanne, Varèse's wife, has never been thrilled about her husband's friendship with Gabriële; she finds this young woman, of marriageable age but not married or even engaged, slightly suspect. But how can she be made to understand that Gabriële doesn't care about Edgard as a man, only as an artist? Suzanne is more than welcome to be saddled with a husband. Gabriële's only claim is on Edgard's creative spirit.

The truth is that, for some time now, Gabriële's been realizing how much her status as a single woman is impinging on her freedom. People *wonder* about her. Women are suspicious of her and shy away from her friendship. Men sometimes become combative. Society's perception of her as an old maid is beginning to wear on her.

Edgard and Gabriële spend the whole night working on *Bourgogne*. It's a night Gabriële will never forget, far more significant in her eyes than any lovers' interlude. For the first time, she experiences a pleasure she'll seek to recreate for the rest of her life: the pleasure of being the midwife, the one who urges and assists, the one who finds just the right words to restart the stalled creative machine. Whenever Edgard works himself into a temper, huffing and grumbling, Gabriële calms him, encourages him, throws out ideas, lifts his spirits when he doubts his own ability, praises him when he picks up his pen again. They alternate between arguing and moments of kinship, the friction often generating good ideas. Edgard proves himself capable of being nasty at times, snapping at Gabriële that her observations are useless, and she threatens to leave. He'll do anything to keep her from abandoning him, though, for he feels lost without her. "We worked all night trying to put flesh on the bones of his theme, but all we did was spoil it. It was incredible on its own, absolutely new in terms of sonority and as a musical idea. He just couldn't take it any further. He was blocked.

"In the end, we had nothing to show Ysaÿe."

Gabriële and Edgard don't speak for several days. Then, finally, the holidays arrive. Varèse manages to get beyond his creative block and finish composing his symphonic poem *Bourgogne*, the score for which he intends to shop around in France. Gabriële, for her part, decides to spend a couple of weeks in Versailles with her family, planning to do some composing herself. She was so busy helping her friend "give birth" that she hasn't done any of her own work.

She doesn't know it yet, but the weeks she's about to spend in France will put an end to her musical career.

4

FRANCIS PICABIA BY FRANCIS PICABIA

G abriële's musical career ended when she met Francis Picabia." Reading that sentence, it feels sudden and violent, like an accident. Yet the reality of the situation was more ambiguous, perhaps. Gabriële was a free being, free enough—why not?—to exercise that freedom by sacrificing it. As counterintuitive as it might appear, it seems that her subjugation was voluntary. She was *created* to form and to champion ideas. Ideas, through men. Ideas *more* than men, in truth.

Let's return to 1908. Gabriële has been introduced to Francis Picabia at her mother's home in Versailles. Let's take a closer look at that summer. What's been happening during the weeks preceding that first meeting? Edgard has gone to Paris, manuscript in hand, with the firm intention of presenting it to anyone who will listen. But what about Gabriële? What is she writing?

Gabriële will never speak about her own musical compositions. It's strange, when you think about it. She defines herself as a musician; it's her essence, but it stops there. She will remember "realizing" that she had a special gift for music; it's an objective way of describing herself. Yet nothing remains. We don't have a single piece written by her, no sheet music, not even the title of a musical poem. But it's certain that Gabriële Buffet composed music during her ten years of study. So why this silence?

There are several possibilities. It's perfectly feasible that Gabriële suffered from some kind of musical writer's block. We might even wonder if, subconsciously, she was actually writing about herself when she recalled, on the subject of her years in Berlin, "Edgard Varèse used to start things and never finish them. He wasn't yet able to concretize his ideas, to make them a reality." This first possibility would explain why she embraced, without apparent frustration, a career as a maieutic, that is, a sort of muse for the creative processes of others. A bit like a midwife who, unable to give birth herself, dedicates her life to helping other women through labor.

The second possibility is that she was as uncompromising with herself as she was toward others. Did she apply that needle-sharp perspective, that cold judgment, to her own work, too? She knew she was talented, but not a "genius." Why add more mediocre music to the existing cacophony?

In addition to these two possibilities, we must consider the personality of Francis Picabia. The painter had such a deep need for her, for her mind and her eye and her constant availability, that he may not have encouraged her in her own creative endeavors. Being his companion was a project in itself, a daily occupation. Picabia, vampire-like, destroyed any other artistic energy around him. It's not that we think he actively prevented her from working—no one prevented Gabriële from doing anything—but he must not have contradicted her when she expressed doubts about her own musical ability.

But what if she was wrong? Could she have been, like Edgard Varèse, a great composer in a totally new style?

We'll never know.

She burned all her sheet music.

We think the manuscript of her valedictory composition for the Schola Cantorum has survived, but despite our research we've been unable to find it. Perhaps it lies sleeping somewhere beneath a blanket of unfeeling dust, fading to illegibility as the years creep slowly by.

Gabriële and Francis have met. They've spent a sleepless night together. It hasn't occurred to them to kiss.

Francis has gone out to find Gabriële some breakfast. But in his absence, she's preparing to flee. The rising sun has dispelled the last vestiges of alcohol, and sentimentality. Her train for Germany leaves in a few hours. It's time for her to leave this studio tucked away behind Montmartre Cemetery.

Hurriedly, she finds a piece of paper and a pencil stub, scribbles a farewell note, hesitates. Just then, Francis returns. Gabriële, caught mid-escape, her cloak already buttoned to the chin, freezes at the sight of him. He's bright-eyed and fresh as a daisy. Despite a night without sleep, he looks rejuvenated, refreshed even, by their hours of feverish discussion—vampire-like as ever. She reads the surprise in his expression: *You're leaving? Just like that?* It's ridiculous. He only met her yesterday, but today he believes his fate depends on this petite woman with average looks.

Gabriële feels her blood run cold. She knows there's no over-ruling the look on his face. The die is cast. She should have left when she could; the night was far too intense, their exchanges too passionate. She isn't going anywhere.

Picabia's off again: "You have to understand—painting has become meaningless for me!" he cries. "Just a way of earning a night's drinking money so I can forget I've got to spend my days painting. I hate it, all of it. If you go back to Berlin today, I'll never paint again, and it'll be your fault. I *need* you. My own thoughts tell me where I am, but not where I'm going. You can't leave—you're the only one who can help me."

Gabriële, who yields to nothing and no one, makes the decision to stay. It takes a bare split-second. Immediately, a chill sweeps through her. She may be free, but society isn't. Propriety must be maintained. This is 1908, and she can't just move in with some strange man. She goes to her brother's flat: can he put her up for a few days, just long enough to wrap up some matters that are keeping her from heading back to Berlin? Jean agrees without hesitation, swallowing the lies hook, line, and sinker, delighted that his sister is showing some interest in him for once.

But the days pass, and Francis doesn't appear. After begging her on his knees to stay in France, the bird has taken off. Flown the coop. Gabriële is stunned. When she asks Jean, casually, if he's heard anything from that odd friend of his, her brother replies that no, actually, he hasn't seen him in a while. Gabriële is furious. No way in hell is she going to stoop to making the rounds of Paris's dive bars like some nagging shrew, searching for a man who means nothing to her. Jean, too, is trying to reach Picabia; they've talked about going to Brittany for a few days, just the two of them, to walk the Painters' Way. But Francis is unfindable. Jean even goes by his studio, thinking he's shut himself up there to paint. Empty.

Gabriële is incandescent with rage. Classes have started back up in Berlin, the orchestra she plays with must already be looking for her replacement, and here she is stuck in Paris, waiting for some arrogant Spaniard. Furious, her pride stung, she packs her bag. She'll catch the train that ridiculous boy was so determined for her not to take. Next stop: station.

But abruptly, a horn blares in the street outside. Brother and sister rush to the window.

There's a raving lunatic sitting behind the wheel of a flashy automobile in front of the building, waving his hat like a victory flag. Who is this conquering hero? None other than Francis Picabia, showing up—as always—at the very last moment. In his other hand, he's brandishing a bottle of champagne, and the back seat of the car is stuffed with all the other accoutrements necessary for a car journey: fur coats, blankets, and driving gloves for everyone. He's bought a new car for the occasion, too. It's magnificent; he's head over heels in love with it.

The young men try to persuade Gabriële to come with them. The trip will be a riot; Brittany's the most beautiful place in the world at this time of year. She's torn. If she gets into this car, her life path will veer toward the unknown. If she doesn't get into the car, her career as a musician awaits. Ideally, she should be able to make her choice knowing where her destiny most likely lies. But she has only an instant to roll the dice. Almost mechanically, her hands reach out to put on her coat and hat and pick up her bag. It's so hard to resist someone who desperately wants you. It's unthinkable to resist Francis Picabia.

They set out for Brittany in a mood of exhilaration that only intensifies as they drive west. They've left with no map, no plan, no guide to help figure out where they're going, but who cares? Squeezed between the two young men, compass in hand like a navigator, Gabriële laughs, abandoning her usual reserve. Jean's presence only makes the air between her and Francis crackle more hotly. She closes her eyes, and suddenly an image surges into her mind's eye of the train she was supposed to catch, the train for Berlin that's already left without her, taking away a part of herself, an idea of herself, of the musician she may never be, now.

Gabriële realizes that Francis is watching her. Gradually, surreptitiously, they begin to exchange looks smoldering with possibility, their arms brushing. When he helps her out of the car, the young painter's hands grasp her waist a bit more firmly than necessary.

The landscape around them is breathtakingly beautiful. They stop occasionally to ask for directions, the local Breton dialect as harsh as the slapping of waves against the rocky shore. Early September marks a major religious event in the region, the Grand Pardon de Notre-Dame du Folgoët, and Jean and the lovers encounter crowds of pilgrims on their way to the celebration. They've come from all over Brittany on foot and on horseback, by wagon and carriage, to join the procession. Their car is quickly surrounded by a mob of children intrigued by the gleaming machine, who rattle hundreds of tiny bells with all their strength. The pilgrims advise them to delay their journey to Lorient and take a side trip to Folgoët, even though it's significantly out of their way; the distance doesn't matter, after all, and they might even get to touch some sacred relics, which have the power to grant wishes. They'll be able to buy religious medals and rosary beads in Folgoët that will protect their families. Francis is enchanted by the idea; it reminds him of Seville, where he has cousins. They won't have any trouble finding a barn to sleep in on the way to Finistère; the local farmers happily accommodate religious travelers during this period, and a modest offering might even get you a comfortable bed to sleep in.

It's tradition for pilgrims to present the country-dwellers who lodge them with a white chicken, and so the trio is advised to stop at any farm where these snowy birds are pecking in the yard, as it means the residents will take them in. The Breton women are so beautiful in their tall white lace coifs and black frocks, which contrast strikingly with the multicolored banners they carry. The traditional clothing suits them, accentuating their round, doll-like faces and large blue eyes. Francis, Gabriële, and Jean come across dogcarts, lacemakers, and a devotional singer who intones grim Biblical stories for the price of a few coins. There are cotton-bonnet-makers, ragpickers married to sailors or wheelwrights, swaddled babies in pushcarts, and women balancing heavy baskets of shellfish on their heads. Compared to these throngs of people in traditional costumes and working attire, our three citified young artists in their luxury automobile look like extraterrestrials from the future.

But the fun times don't last long. The happy bubble of their trio bursts when Jean finally realizes that Francis is romancing his sister. The Spaniard has gotten a bit too daring, holding Gabriële's gaze for a moment too long, the air between the two of them humming with silent complicity. The whole trip to Brittany, Jean realizes, was thought up and planned by Francis for the express purpose of seducing his sister. He, Jean, is just a pretext, a part of the cover story. Do they take him for an idiot? "Jean Buffet found himself playing the role of outraged brother," Maria Lluïsa Borràs will write in her biography of Francis Picabia, as if his anger is feigned, or perhaps hiding some ambivalence. Does he feel as if he's lost a friend? Jealous that his sister has taken on greater importance in a relationship he invested so much energy in establishing? Or is it that, knowing Francis's reputation as a playboy, he sincerely wants to keep his sister's heart from being broken? In any case, their lighthearted jaunt quickly turns sour. Jean orders Gabriële back to Versailles and threatens to blacken Francis's reputation.

Picabia, desperate to avoid a confrontation, abandons Jean in the middle of Brittany without a moment's hesitation. He simply leaves him there amid the thronging pilgrims, the pardon ceremony, the lace coifs, the Breton bagpipes, the choirboys. He does it without a moment's remorse, without looking back, thinking only of saving his own skin. He flees. And kidnaps Gabriële in the process, heading for Cassis in his latest toy, his shiny new roadster. This young woman who has so far refused him, Francis knows, will end up giving in. The car is like a particle accelerator; romantic liaisons are forged in the heat of danger. "The mad speed of our getaway," he will write in his 1924 autobiographical novel *Caravansérail*, "bound me to this woman more closely than years of togetherness could have done. We were united by the force of everything the two of us had risked."

It's a full two days' journey to the south of France by car. Francis does it in twenty hours flat. A madman. Gabriële may act cool and level-headed, but she finds the whole thing incredibly exhilarating. Picabia is hers. She's abandoned her brother without a backward glance, her blood running hot from the thrum of the engine and the thrill of Francis's nearness. She's never spent so much time pressed up against a male body this way, feeling the cavalier heartbeat of a bad boy on the run.

What to say? Where to begin? Picabia, despite the considerable noise of the car engine, talks nonstop, solely about himself, telling stories of his life, explaining who he is and where he's come from. Gabriële has to know everything about him, understand it all. He has to make up for all the years that passed before she met him. He recounts every important thing that's happened in his life. Tells her the whole story of his childhood. He unburdens himself completely to her, wanting her to grasp his essence in full, determined that she, and she alone, will be the one person on earth who truly knows and understands him.

He starts at the beginning: his birth, which took place on January 22, 1879. His grandfather and his father were born in Cuba, but not Francis. He was born in Paris. This will give him a sense of being left out, excluded from a sort of hereditary club; he's merely, boringly French, a feeling made worse by the fact that his father never speaks Spanish to him. Already he's been branded as marking a break in the male genealogical chain. The Picabias are actually Spaniards, exiled to Cuba in the seventeenth century. Why this banishment to the other side of the globe? It's said that an ancestor, Pedro Martinez de la Torre, was friends with the king of Spain. Unruly and sardonic, one day his teasing went too far, and he fell into disgrace. Punished by his former friend the king, he went into exile in Latin America. *Hasta luego, Pedro. Go tell your jokes to tropical birds in the Caribbean.* So goes the family legend, but in the end it doesn't really matter whether the story is true or not; what counts is that the Picabia family has its very own founding hero, complete with the hallmark characteristics of irreverence, glibness, daring, and humor.

This rebellious great-grandfather landed on his feet, gaining a fortune in Cuba by investing in sugarcane. He had a son, Juan Martinez Picabia, whose nickname was "the Indian"— we haven't been able to discover why. Maybe because of his unique physical appearance, his broad, smooth-skinned face. Maybe he wore his hair long. We don't know. The Indian had six children with his first wife, and after her death he married Josefa Delmonico, who was seventeen years his junior. She was a beauty, an Italian-Swiss woman born in Berlin and raised in the Ticino region of Switzerland whom he met in New York and married in Havana. They, too, would have six children. Prolific, that Indian. He was also an entrepreneur, and in 1855, when Spain needed a bigwig to launch the railroad, he was summoned from Cuba pronto, agreeing to gamble his intellectual and financial resources on the Spanish train venture on one condition: that he would be allowed to choose the route. The line he built connected Madrid to his family's home province, A Coruña, and a statue of him would be erected near the station. One of these days, we'll have to go and see if it's still there.

Francis likes to define himself as a Cuban; it gives him an air of mystery and exoticism, to be from the other side of the world. He's never actually set foot in Cuba, of course, but he shows off for Gabriële, bragging that the tropical blood flowing in his veins has always set him wonderfully apart:

"What can I say, we're Cuban . . . the people there paint their houses pink and blue and pale green . . . it's a shame I don't live there, but I deal with my ideas the way they deal with their homes. I paint dark thoughts blue. Nice, eh?"

In Madrid, Josefa, the Indian, and their children lived at number 60 on the Calle Mayor. Sadly, the building has since been torn down, replaced by a hideous supermarket complex and parking lot begrimed with damp patches.

Pancho, Francis Picabia's father, is the fourth of the couple's six children. He's a strange, fanciful fellow, very different from other men of his time. He stands 1.8 meters tall, extremely tall for the nineteenth century and unusual even within his own family; even his son will be shorter than him. He's thin, and dresses like a dandy. Part sophisticate and part diplomat, he officially works for the Cuban embassy in Paris but prefers to stay at home, smoke three packs of cigarettes a day, and avoid exerting himself too much. "His favorite occupation consisted in swatting flies with a whisk and feeding them to the ants." Quite an interesting character to have for a father.

Francis's mother, for her part, is the epitome of all things French. She comes from a family every bit as wealthy as her husband's. They live at 82 rue des Petits-Champs.

Francis describes the French side of his family to Gabriële in amusing detail. He imitates the shrill voice of his maternal grandmother, whom he detests:

"Marie, how many eggs did you put in the omelet yesterday?"

"Twelve, Ma'am."

"Are you sure? Bring me the shells."

Francis hates this sort of bourgeois stinginess; imagine going through the garbage to make sure the maid hasn't wasted too many eggs! Money, he says, is made to be drunk, spent, eaten, and otherwise burnt on the altar of pleasure.

Young Francis's mother's name is Marie-Cécile Davanne. He will remember her as a woman just as mild-mannered and dreamy as her husband. Francis's parents' marriage is a love-match, their individual eccentricities fitting together perfectly. Francis will be their only child, adored and cosseted by his mother. People advise Marie-Cécile to keep her distance, to avoid coddling the little heir too much, or he'll end up spoiled and unmanageable. Marie-Cécile's health is fragile; she suffers from a complaint of the lungs. As she grows weaker, she's urged to keep even further away from her son, who becomes temperamental, demanding gifts and attention. The more overindulged the little boy is, the sadder he becomes, pushing back against these adults who "deprived him of the contact he longed for with his mother."

One day his father presents him with a truly extravagant plaything—a shiny little buggy drawn by two ponies—seemingly for no reason. Francis is seven years old. The family is spending a few days at their country house in Saint-Cloud. He gazes out his bedroom window at the enormous toy his father has had brought onto the lawn. The child-size buggy is like something straight out of a little boy's dream. Slowly, he turns from the window and looks at the two large Swiss women in white aprons who are looking after him. He's just realized the reason the buggy has appeared out of nowhere in the garden. "My mother is dead," he says simply.

Indeed, Marie-Cécile Picabia died on September 21, 1886, of pulmonary tuberculosis. Francis will never say anything else about it. We can imagine the child stunned by the news, silent and stiff-bodied with grief, going outside to run a hand along the gleaming body of his new buggy. *So,* thinks the bewildered little boy, *according to adult logic, this machine can replace a mother.* Fair enough. Picabia will collect cars all his life—he'll own one hundred and forty-two in all. And he'll collect women, too, though it's hard to be quite as exact about the number.

"I've been alone ever since," he tells Gabriële.

His relationship with his father will continue to deteriorate. As Gabriële will write, "He was a secretive child, weighed down by boredom and loneliness. He didn't start to thrive until the day his father took him to a beach in Normandy. There he discovered the ocean and freedom, learned to run and to swim."

Of his mother, Francis retains nothing but a portrait, an oval painting of a lovely, delicate-featured young woman. Marie-Cécile's son will keep that portrait, his only memento of her, all his life. The boy takes refuge in art so that he can touch his mother's face. He searches for her in every female portrait he produces, in every mouth he kisses.

"The lack of women enervates me and, for anyone who has acquired the habit, the absence of a woman in his bed may even prevent him from sleeping," he tells Gabriële.

We have to give Francis this: he told it like it was, if you knew how to listen. And so Gabriële considers herself warned. Maybe she doesn't even need the warning. Maybe she understands, instinctively, that Francis is one of those men whose faithfulness will be other than physical.

With Marie-Cécile gone, little Francis is raised by his father, his uncle, and his grandfather. He'll refer to the Picabias as "a family of four without a woman"—this from a man who will claim some four hundred notches on his bedpost. He will develop an obsession with doubles: "After his father gave him a magnificent horse-drawn buggy after his mother's death, he always worried about losing his toys and often had two of a particular one." The theme of doubles will recur throughout his life and characterize his work.

We've mentioned that, after Marie-Cécile's death, Francis plunged himself into art. Let us add, too, that he was absolutely brilliant at it.

His uncle Maurice, a curator at the Sainte-Geneviève Library in Paris, is also an art lover. In his living room hang paintings by the so-called lesser masters: Ferdinand Roybet, Félix Ziem.

"I made copies of them and hung them in place of the originals," Francis recalls. "And then I sold the real paintings to buy stamps for my collection. I was twelve or thirteen years old. The adults never suspected a thing."

The following year, young Francis announces his intent to study at the École Nationale Supérieure des Arts Décoratifs. His father balks at first. He's dubious, even suspicious. To see whether his son actually has talent, he implements a ruse.

"I was fifteen," Francis will recall. "My father submitted one of my paintings to the jury of the Salon des Artistes Français. He did it under a false name and date of birth to see how it would be received. Not only was I accepted, I got a special mention. So my father agreed to let me continue down that path."

The experts have judged Francis's work on its merit alone. His father has no further excuse to withhold his approval, and, armed with the endorsement from the Salon des Artistes, he enrolls at the École du Louvre and then the Arts Déco. There, he meets the painters Georges Braque and Marie Laurencin. He also works regularly in the private academy run by Fernand Cormon, where he learns the techniques of classical painting: landscapes, portraits, historical scenes.

Francis is nineteen when he discovers the Impressionist painter Alfred Sisley. It's as if he's been struck by lightning. Immediately he applies his remarkable gifts to following in his idol's footsteps. In 1899, when he's twenty, his work is exhibited at the Salon de la Société des Artistes Français—and he's singled out by critics as an exciting young Impressionist.

"We award a special mention to the luminous canvas by Monsieur Francis Piscalia [sic] entitled *A Street in Martigues*." Suddenly, the press is extremely interested in this "unique artist" who possesses "a great talent for silhouettes and distant perspectives," despite the fact that he's just an overgrown schoolboy. Picabia's Impressionist canvases are exactly the sort of thing that pleases the "establishment," which adores precocious young prodigies. His paintings start to sell—and well. Exceptionally well. And the money Francis earns quickly burns a hole in his pocket. He squanders it on trifles, on modish clothes, in fashionable restaurants and nightspots. He gains a reputation for always being surrounded by a gang of unlikely friends, whom he always invites back home with him in the wee hours for, if he doesn't have a female companion for the night, he can't sleep without the noise of a party swirling around him.

In 1900, his Davanne grandmother—the eggshell-counting harpy—dies and leaves Francis a handsome legacy. The first thing he does is buy his first roadster, the second, move out of the family apartment. Financially independent, he's eager to be on his own, accountable to no one. He allows himself the luxury of renting a large studio in the Villa des Arts, the very place where his illustrious predecessors Gauguin and Cézanne painted before him. Delusions of grandeur.

He goes through phases of near frenzy in which he paints compulsively, locking himself into his studio for whole days and nights together. He travels the countryside, going from village to village, exhilarated by the painter's life he's chosen. He goes away to live alone on a farm in Pierre-Perthuis in the *département* of Yonne—weeks of drinking, solitude, and work. "What happy times those were," he'll recall later. "I had such belief in myself, and in the people I considered friends. Life seemed ideal." His friend of that period, Manzana Pissaro (third son of the painter Camille Pissaro and an anarchist sympathizer), is so astonished by the number of paintings Francis churns out that he writes, in a letter to his famous father, "Picabia is here. He's already done nine canvases." But these frantically productive periods alternate with moods of deep melancholy, during which he doesn't paint, only drinks, avoiding the studio and losing himself in the Paris nightlife, becoming cynical, sometimes morbid, and even violent.

In 1903, he exhibits eight Impressionist canvases at the Salon des Indépendants—and becomes the darling of the event. His work, critics gush, is "of peerless ardor."

His first solo exhibition takes place in 1905. The critics fall over themselves to praise him; buyers line up to acquire his work, and the press prints miles of type. "An exhibition that has been the subject of much prior discussion will open tomorrow, Friday, at the Galerie Haussmann at 67 boulevard Haussmann: that of Picabia's landscapes. This assembly of fifty of his canvases will undoubtedly be of great interest and brilliance." The papers, from *Le Figaro* to *L'Écho de Paris* to *Le Gaulois*, are unanimously laudatory, singing his praises and predicting a future to rival those of Renoir, Corot, Manet, and Pissaro. They compare him, too, to his idol Sisley. He's hailed as a young genius. Everyone wants to have him over for dinner (and many want him to stay for breakfast, too). Francis abandons himself to it all with pleasure.

In 1906, he holds a solo exhibition in his own studio (unheard of!), mainly to flaunt his defiance of the painter and poet Marie de la Hire's remark that "one shouldn't hold an exhibition of their own work until after the age of 40, if they're famous." It's a bit easier to understand, now, why Francis was so upset when Gabriële pretended not to have heard of him.

At last, the couple reaches Cassis. Francis hasn't stopped

talking the whole way. He's dumped his entire childhood right in Gabriële's lap.

* * *

"Whenever I try to picture Picabia as a child, I find him unsettling. Too precocious, too sad, too solitary. With Gabriële it's even worse, because I think she was too strong as a little girl. It's like she was enclosed in a suit of armor. We're bringing them back to life in this book, so I feel like they belong to me, like they're my children. Like I need to take responsibility for them, understand them. I feel like I need to love them. Do you love them?"

"I don't know. I've never thought about it like that. But since we started writing this book, I *have* asked myself, would they have loved me? I don't know, but I'm making sure the answer is yes. Sometimes I act in a certain way because I think it's what they would have wanted me to do. I feel like the dead are watching me. And I think, generally, I've lived my whole life that way, ever since I was small."

5

Man and Woman by the Sea

assis, September 1909. The small fishing village is all
but deserted this time of year. The light is magnificent.
All of a sudden, Paris no longer exists for the young
couple, who feel as if they've come to the very ends of the
earth, like characters in a romantic novel. They check into a
hotel Francis knows, the Cendrillon, and he asks for a room for
himself and his wife. Gabriële's heart starts to pound. For an
instant, she hesitates. Not because of the lie—she couldn't care
less about that—but because this will be the first night she's
ever spent in a man's bed, and that man doesn't seem to have
realized that she's a virgin. She comes across as so confident, so
unheeding of convention, that Francis perceives her as a feminine double of himself, in every sense. He's a ladies' man. Sex is
a given. She feels a brief surge of panic—which keeps her from
noticing the frown on the desk clerk's face. He doesn't believe
for one second that these two are married, and with good reason; this isn't the first time Francis has shown up here with a
"wife." But he doesn't say anything.

Imagine the emotion, the awkwardness of these two intellectual beings about to go to bed together, naked, for the first
time. It's not easy to move from an interaction of the mind to
one of the flesh, and the transition is not a smooth one.

Francis is surprised. He wasn't expecting this independent
woman of twenty-seven, especially one who's been living alone
in a foreign country, to still be so *innocent*. And Gabriële,
who was being chaperoned by her older brother on the trip to
Brittany as recently as yesterday, wasn't prepared to become a
woman so abruptly. Their night of love is not a success. Francis

and Gabriële were designed to talk together, to exchange, theorize, create—but not to make love. Their understanding isn't
physical, but metaphysical. Together, they "produce material."

Slightly dazed from their disappointing night, our young
couple walks silently on Cassis's wide, pebbled beach. Changed.
Discomfited. But irrevocably linked.

Francis picks up a flat, smooth stone and flings it into the
sea with uncharacteristic violence, angry that everything seems
to be going wrong. The euphoria of their initial departure and
the pleasure of their long drive have all dissolved into a kind of
malaise, like a pernicious ooze. Gabriële asks him if he wants to
go back to Paris. He dithers. There's something he hasn't told
her. A secret is gnawing at him.

He's already living with a woman. And she must be half-
dead with either anxiety or rage right now, because he didn't
tell her he was going away. He simply said he was buying a new
car, nothing else—"I'm going out to buy a car," the way you'd
say "I'm going out to buy cigarettes"—and then he didn't come
back.

Now he doesn't know what to do, he explains, in the tone
of someone politely asking another person for a solution. *Is he
serious?* wonders Gabriële, normally the picture of sangfroid.

What do we know about this woman who was living with
Francis Picabia at the time? Virtually nothing. We have no
photo of her, no painted portrait, not even a letter. She was
older than him by six or seven years, according to our research.

We don't know how they met, or what Ermine Orliac did
in life. But we do know that she was the official mistress of
someone prominent, perhaps Eugène Letellier, a businessman who founded a newspaper called *Le Journal* (that is, *The
Newspaper*—laziness or genius?) and who may have been the
mayor of Trouville. In any event, Francis and Ermine had to
keep their relationship a secret from the moment they met.
They rapidly fled to Switzerland, to the Hotel Mont-Blanc in

Morges, supposedly at the same time Nietzsche was staying there, but Francis might have made that part up. They went without a sou to live on, and legend has it that, to pay for their hotel room, the young man painted landscapes on the shores of Lake Geneva and sold them to tourists.

Now Francis tells the stunned Gabriële the story of his odyssey from those Swiss shores to the pebbled beach at Cassis. He's lived with Ermine Orliac for almost ten years now. She might as well be his wife. It's like a cold shower. Gabriële, who at twenty-seven has never succumbed to the slightest romantic whim, now finds herself—on the morning after losing her virginity—in a novel situation, to say the least. The problem is that this impossible, irresistible young man now swears to high heaven that he stopped loving Ermine some time ago. She believed in him when he was only twenty years old, yes, but the same things that kindle a relationship can sometimes be the reason it ends, and now he can't bear any of the qualities that originally attracted him to her: her insistence on their continuing to be part of society life, on his remaining the fashionable darling of Paris. He stays with her out of cowardice, because he's afraid of being alone, and also because he feels sorry for her, this childless woman who was being supported by a powerful man but gave it all up to be with him. Now, though, meeting Gabriële has given him the strength to leave his longtime mistress.

And then he asks her to stay at the hotel in Cassis and wait for him. Casually, as if it's a given. She can't believe her ears. He wants to drive back to Paris to tell Ermine everything, leaving her here. Just like that. Faced with her guarded silence, Francis falters. He starts to beg. She has to stay here and wait for him. It'll only be for three or four days, just long enough to drive there and back. Then, he promises, he'll be free—*they'll* be free! Free to love one another in peace and, even more importantly, to continue their discussions.

Alone in Cassis over the next few days, waiting for Francis to return, Gabriële asks herself a thousand questions. Foremost among them? *What am I doing here?*

Her friends in Germany must be worried about her. Edgard Varèse probably has a million things to tell her. Her orchestra must be trying to contact her; they're surely furious that she's just disappeared without notice. And all this, for what? To end up alone at the other end of France, unemployed and aimless, waiting for a man capable of anything (especially the worst) who's just taken her virginity as if it were nothing. Her first night of "passion." It's absolute insanity that she's allowed herself to be abandoned like this by a man who's toted her around the country like a piece of luggage. Left alone on a rocky beach in mid-September. And Jean, who must have told their parents the whole story by now—how right he was to warn her. He knew. He knew all about Ermine. That's why Francis fled so fast; he was afraid Jean would tell Gabriële everything. Jean got so angry because he was trying to protect his sister without betraying his friend. And she was nothing but condescending to him. Didn't even try to understand why he'd reacted so intensely. Looking back at her own behavior fills her with shame.

Gabriële Buffet, admired and even feared by her male musician peers, mysterious and cool, elusive and detached, has somehow been turned into a disheveled, two-bit Ariadne deserted on the beach by her Theseus. She's known Picabia for all of a week, and he's already trotted out his tearful pleading-and-vowing act twice. It's all moving too fast. She feels like a player in some bad bedroom farce. It's ridiculous. Grotesque.

There are moments in life when everything around you is screaming out the absurdity of your situation, and yet some irrational, irresistible force holds you in place, appalled, watching the consequences of your own choices play out.

It's this force that's drawing Gabriële to Francis, that's keeping her in Cassis. As she'll say later, "I don't know why we met. I'd always kept myself isolated, apart from everything." It's an interestingly restrained way of referring to the improbable alliance that bound them from the first.

And Francis does come back.
He keeps his promise.
Gabriële never doubted that he would.
The next few days are strange and exciting. They send Jean a postcard. Written on it, with no further comment, is this Nietzsche quote: "The friend whose hopes one cannot satisfy, one would rather have as an enemy." It's an odd missive, perhaps meant to spare Gabriële from admitting, "I was unfair to you. I know you just wanted to protect me."

They laugh about the difference between the reality of what they're doing and the way they look to the rest of the world. People treat them like an established couple even though they've only spent a few days together since meeting. People are always fascinated by young lovers. They ask questions, and not always discreet ones. One American, to whom the hotel manager has explained that Monsieur Picabia is a famous French painter, even snaps a photo of them. A paparazzo ahead of his time.

After that, everything happens at the kind of surreal speed common to dreams. Time ceases to exist, events blurring and squashing together rather than occurring in a normal calendar sequence. The couple remains in the south of France for a few weeks, returns to Paris, moves Gabriële's things into Francis's studio, introduces one another to their families, plans a wedding. Yes, all of that in mere months.

Gabriële is stripped of her *self*, as if she's suddenly living in someone else's body, allowing herself to accept and act out events without really understanding the stage directions. She has no desire to marry, later writing, "It was really for him that I got married, because his grandfather had very old-fashioned ideas about marriage and that sort of thing . . . "

The marriage certificate tells us that Gabriële and Francis wed in Versailles on January 27, 1909—five days after Francis's thirtieth birthday. The groom's profession is listed as "artist painter," the bride as "no profession." Gabriële is recorded as living with her mother, Francis with his father. A perfectly respectable young couple as far as the authorities are concerned. Gabriële's brother Jean serves as her witness along with their uncle Maurice Buffet, retired colonel of the cavalry and Officer of the Legion of Honor. Francis's witnesses are his grandfather Alphonse, the photographer, and Uncle Maurice, the curator at the Sainte-Geneviève Library.

Gabriële looks around at the Picabias, at all these men to whom she's just bound herself. Father, grandfather, uncle, son— all of them live at the same address, 82 rue des Petits-Champs, a magnificent building located near the Place Vendôme. All those overgrown boys living together, with no women and no real profession, all with their own strong personalities and personal obsessions. What a tableau. As quirky and annoying as a Wes Anderson film.

Signing her name in the civil register, Gabriële thinks to herself that she might as well be using the pen to draw a line under her time in Berlin. She's made her choice. She's numb, but strangely sure of herself. Francis has bought a new car for the occasion. He pulls round to pick her up, giddy as a schoolboy. They're leaving on their honeymoon immediately.

Another car, she thinks.

* * *

Francis Picabia will own an "abnormally large" number of cars in his lifetime. Somewhere between 110 and 150, depending on the source. The gallerist Gérard Rambert tells us what the act of buying a car represented in the early twentieth century:

"Things were different back then. You didn't just buy cars 'ready-made.' Picabia had his automobiles custom-made. A customer began by contacting a *constructeur*, or automaker, which would build the chassis and the engine—it'll come as no surprise that Picabia's favorite constructeur was the luxury company Delage. After that, the customer would go to a *carrossier*, or car-body builder, for production of the interior and exterior of the vehicle. Then everything was designed, put together, and painted. Sometimes customers' requirements were extravagant; for example, they'd ask the carrossier to make the inside of the car look like an eighteenth-century boudoir.

"Most carrossiers were located between Puteaux and Levallois-Perret, north and west of the center of Paris. They were multistage complexes hundreds of square kilometers in area, with dozens and dozens of carrossiers working by hand, using a technique called hammerforming. One can easily imagine Picabia spending whole days at the garages, watching those craftsmen work. I think he was far more passionate about that than he ever was about the history of painting! His attraction to the carrosseries is understandable when you think about the fact that, beyond the mere symbolism of car-building—that is, beyond the idea that a car is an extension of the self, beyond the statement 'this is who I am,' once you've gotten past all that, his love for carrosserie was a love of FORMS.

"Carrosserie, at that time, was a veritable work of sculpture. It was about reflecting on the proportions of fenders, hoods, trunks, roofs. These cars were works of art. Unique pieces, single copies. Works of art that also had the virtue of being useful.

"If you asked an expert to estimate the value of an automobile collection like Picabia's, you'd be talking about a FORTUNE. It was a collection worthy of an English lord, or a maharajah. Which means that Francis Picabia, who was wealthy, yes, but certainly no maharajah, literally went broke buying cars, the way other people gamble their fortunes away at casinos. Well, as you say, he did both.

"Picabia loved gambling because it brought immediate satisfaction. Casinos compress time. You play, you lose or you win. It's a face-to-face confrontation with chance.

"Picabia owned yachts, too. Who on earth owns yachts?!
"The Danish royals own yachts.
"The Norwegian, British, and Spanish royals own yachts.
"Artists do not own yachts.
"But Picabia did."

The wedding, the marriage contract, a house, a family—Gabriële finds it all terrifying. Francis tries to reassure her: "If it's too tedious being married, we'll just get unmarried, that's all." The only children they need to worry about are the paintings they'll create together. The rest is just housekeeping.

Now it's almost time for the couple to embark on the traditional honeymoon, the prospect of which they both find horribly dull. Neither of them cares about playing tourist or making plans for their marital home. What home? The studio they're living in now isn't a sweet little two-story cottage fit for the perfect couple, though everyone's acting like it is. Francis's father wants them to honeymoon in Spain, so that Gabriële can be introduced to the family there. As is only proper. They can't leave quite yet, however, because there's another wedding on the horizon: in a few weeks' time, Francis's father will be able to remarry at last—something he couldn't do as long as his own son remained single. In the early twentieth century, custom dictated that a widowed parent had to wait for any children of marriageable age to do so before taking a second husband or wife themselves. Again, it was the only proper way to do things. And so Picabia *père*'s wedding is set for March 23, 1909.

The day after the ceremony, Francis decides to set off for Saint-Tropez with his luggage, his easel, and his wife. In that order. Closer and more convenient than Seville—and, most importantly, quieter. He's had enough of interminable family dinners and formal introductions. They can wait. For now, he wants his Gabriële all to himself. She's his, and his alone. The conversations he has with her in Saint-Tropez galvanize and inspire him more than ever. He paints a dozen canvases in only a few days. He wants to keep this little wife of his inside his mind; she must always be with him, watching him paint, giving her opinion on each brushstroke, ever-present, like a mother-muse coddling with her gaze her child prodigy's every gesture. Gabriële is a womb.

The young couple packs their bags. Just before leaving Paris, Francis terminates his contract with his gallerist, Danthon. Just like that, in the blink of an eye, without a second thought. He will never paint another Impressionist canvas. That life is over.

"What is he thinking? Has he gone mad?" Danthon wonders despairingly.

"It's all because of that wife of his," someone says.

That *someone* is Ermine Orliac. The mistress who had faithfully maintained Francis's social calendar and exhibition schedule for years has made her exit without a fuss. Embarrassed by her abandonment, she isn't about to demean herself further by being inconsolable. And Ermine, who has no spite in her, advises the gallerist to do the same. But Danthon is taking an enormous financial hit. Picabia's canvases sold like hotcakes. Danthon is furious. More than furious. Humiliated. Francis is clearly out of his mind, blinded by love. And why the sudden radicalism? No more high living, no more luxury cars and eau de Cologne, no more aphrodisiacal parties and easy money pouring in like fine champagne. He's turned his back on all of that, ever since that *Gabriële* got her hooks into the young genius. Now he wants to "save painting," to "show that it can be something more than an exercise in virtuosity for commercial ends, achieved by the endless reuse of pleasant clichés."

Danthon has lost his goose that laid the golden paintings, now flown away to a love-nest in the south of France. Picabia may have painted nearly three hundred Impressionist paintings for him in six years, but now, as far as the art dealer is concerned, he can go to hell. Danthon plans his revenge with icy calm.

It's midwinter, and the village of Saint-Tropez is cold and unwelcoming. Francis, though, is keyed up, overheated. He spends whole days painting, not changing his clothes and hardly eating, and Gabriële agrees to pose for him. Posing for a "great painter" isn't something she particularly wants to do, but it's the "must" of the time, the dream of every young girl, the feather in the cap of every society sophisticate, and a thing for which wealthy heiresses are willing to pay handsomely. Gabriële doesn't like being looked at or photographed, though, much less painted. The job of model isn't one she's ever coveted. *Be quiet and look pretty.* She isn't even pretty, for God's sake! No, what Gabriële likes is being *listened to.* And she rapidly makes it clear to Picabia that she isn't just going to settle into the role of "painter's wife." If Francis wanted a beautiful Fernande Olivier type to rival Picasso's mistress, he's married the wrong girl.

The few portraits of Gabriële painted by Francis during this period are full of movement, as if he can't quite capture her, can't pin her down. Picabia is feverishly productive in Saint-Tropez, obsessed with his canvases and his work. As Borràs will later write, "Francis [explored] the Divisionist technique and [made] much use of purples and violets, half-Nabi and half-Fauve, so that those days in Saint-Tropez may be regarded as a new impulse that would take him to horizons that as yet he could not even imagine."

From time to time, Francis pauses in his painting to play billiards in a Saint-Tropez watering-hole he knows well, where he's hailed by the regulars as an old friend. The clack of the colorful balls helps him to empty his mind and ponder his next canvas. He can spend whole days like this, the hours blurring together. And so Gabriële, always at his side, has the saddest, most depressing, worst honeymoon ever. The young bride who gritted her teeth and went along with social convention is well and truly trapped. "I felt very much alone, and I began to regret the decision I'd made," the newly minted Gabriële Picabia will recall.

Neither does it help matters that she's made another discovery about Francis's romantic past. The Picabia family has dramas within dramas, like Russian dolls, and one of these dolls is Louise, the young second wife of Francis's father Pancho. Around 1898 or 1899, Gabriële has learned, an intense episode took place. Louise was then twenty years old, a *petit rat* at the Paris Opera's school of dance, and Francis was about the same age. They met on a train, both chaperoned by their respective parents, Louise traveling with her mother and Francis with his father. A perfect mirror configuration. The young people began to talk, and Francis fell instantly in love with the lithe beauty. Unfortunately, so did Pancho. Both father and son began to woo Louise, and in the end Pancho carried the day. For Francis, this incident—his sweetheart becoming his stepmother—was a seminal one. Not only did it mark his first experience with a love triangle, it instilled in him a strange penchant for being in romantic competition with another man, his subconscious turning the paternal betrayal into something bizarrely erotic. To his dying day, Francis Picabia would seek out three-sided intellectual and sexual arrangements. And all his life, he would have a weakness for dancers.

Now Gabriële understands Pancho's hurry to marry Francis off; it was simply so he could marry in his turn. And Francis's rush to leave town immediately after his father's wedding makes sense, too.

As the hours, the days and nights of her honeymoon pass, Gabriële imagines the life she'd be living in Berlin right now if she hadn't made the choice to marry. Realizing the amplitude not of the waste, but of everything she's taken on. It's a bitter pill to swallow. Francis takes up all her attention, all her energy. He drains her strength until she has almost none left for herself.

For music. She thinks of the day in Versailles, not so long ago, when she played him a little air on the piano.

"Oh yes, that's wonderful! Play something for me, just for me. Make up a tune that's for Francis Picabia and no one else."

When she'd played the tune, and turned around to see what he thought, Francis was gone. He'd gone off to paint. Gabriële wasn't even angry. His painting was far better than her compositions. It was everything.

But all these trials must be endured for the love of art. Gabriële knows that. The hours of solitude, the hours of doubt. Not to indulge her husband, but to ignite an artistic revolution—an idea far more thrilling than any "successful" honeymoon.

She knows she's in the process of setting a match to gunpowder. Something very important is taking place. The two large portraits her husband has painted of her are the starting point. A (deserved) "homage to the woman who inspired many of the changes then affecting the artist."

Patience.

Meanwhile, in Paris, the gallerist Danthon is plotting his revenge. On March 8, 1909, he auctions off at Drouot ninety-nine Impressionist canvases by Francis Picabia—every one in his possession. It's a firm, even harsh move signaling that, as far as he's concerned, Picabia's artistic career is over, his work now worthless. It's like a liquidation sale, common and vulgar. *Clearance! Everything must go!* But Francis, far from being upset by the news, is delighted. Now returned from their honeymoon, he and Gabriële bid good riddance to his artistic past with a night of drunken rejoicing.

And as it turns out, Francis Picabia hasn't had his final word on the subject. Several days after the infamous Drouot auction house liquidation, from March 17 to 31, he holds an exhibition of his "new" canvases, born in the feverish days in Saint-Tropez, at the Galerie Georges Petit. On the opening night of the exhibition, gazing at the paintings lining the walls, the curious and the fashionable filing past, concealing their sneers and sniggers beneath a thin veneer of enthusiasm, Gabriële sees all the colors of her honeymoon. In this new act of creation, in the choices of shade and movement, lies the exaltation of their physical love, their shared conversations—and that's worth all the hours of solitude spent waiting for an aggravating husband, she thinks. These canvases are far dearer to her heart than the syrupy-sweet photos young couples take and keep all their lives just so they can look back and say, "Remember?"

Old canvases have been discarded, new ones displayed. Francis's father has remarried. It's the end of a cycle. Francis feels like a new man. He can finally take his wife to Seville. To his roots. They set off for Spain. In a new car, of course.

A Spaniard returning to his homeland (even if he's never lived there) is more than a cause for celebration, it's an EVENT. The sun dancing with the moon. Feasting and revelry. And when the returnee is a prodigal son into the bargain, that's when the blackest lace comes out, the best dresses, the fine wedding china. Now it's a proper *luna de miel*. The young newlyweds are hosted in Seville by Francis's Abreu and Picabia cousins. Gabriële's never been to Spain, and after Berlin, the South is a shock. The baking heat, the clinging scents of almond, olive, and fig trees. Women in lace shawls, their shining chignons black as pitch, seemingly in charge of this bustling ark teeming with children, donkeys, and bulls. For Francis and Gabriële have arrived right in the middle of the *Feria de Abril*, the annual Seville Fair, an intense week-long extravaganza of singing and dancing in the streets, of feasting and drinking, windows glowing bright until dawn. No one goes home, and no one sleeps in their own bed—ever. There are parades of children and adults in costume. Processions of horses. *La corrida*, bullfighting. The crowd, possessed, in the grip of delirium tremens, sways in rhythm from morning to night to the polychromatic, alienating sounds of the folk music of the region, the Sevillanas.

Gabriële's never seen anything like it.

Never heard anything like it.

She gazes in fascination at the thousands of red carnations tossed onto the sandy ground of the bullfighting arena, as if in representation of the blood about to be spilled. She, who has always been so firmly ensconced within her own areas of intellectual curiosity, feels as if she's been shoved naked into a geyser of beauty and brimstone. That's the sensation in her chest—the blossoming of her blood. And the mantillas come down and the garnet-red wine thick as a demure dress sets souls alight and the women spin their bracelets and the old ladies twirl their rosary beads with heavily beringed fingers and the girls conquer every male heart in the vicinity, the men brought to their knees by so much strength and grace.

After the absurdity of a wedding authored by others, after the coldness and solitude of Saint-Tropez, after all the misgivings about the stranger to whom she finds herself so intimately tied, Gabriële finally yields. Gives herself up. She doesn't want to be anywhere other than beside this man who is the first at the table to get up and dance, perfectly imitating the poses of the fierce *toreros*. This man who gazes at her as no one else does, dousing her in the sulfurous perfume of pigments and passion and who, after drinking several bottles to the dregs, pulls her to him and calls her, gently, as from a great distance, *mi oscuro corazón*.

To be another person's heart, dark or not, is something Gabriële had never imagined.

It's in Spain that their marriage becomes real, that capricious fate knits together at last these two beings *si imparfaits et si affreux*.[1]

---

[1] *si imparfaits et si affreux*: "So imperfect and so dreadful," from the poem "On ne badine pas avec l'amour" by Alfred de Musset (1810–1857)

In Seville, Francis pauses his painting at last. He still draws constantly, of course, but that's like breathing for him. He sketches Spanish women in mantillas like in Vélasquez's paintings. He sketches, too, his wife's eyes, narrowed in thought as always. Those unsettling coal-black slits. He draws sustenance from Seville, filling himself up with images of bodies in constant motion, images that will inspire not one, but two, series of paintings—his *Dances* and *Processions*—back in Paris.

Gabriële is happy, powerfully happy, gripped by what anyone *not* in love might call sentimentality, even mawkishness. The feverish discussions with Francis have stopped for now; there's too much noise around them, the urgency is elsewhere, in the rustling and brushing of passing bodies. After Seville, his cousin Pepe invites them to stay in his hacienda in the Sierra Morena mountains, a place luminous as a lighthouse amid the peaks, described by Gabriële as "a white spot, relentlessly white, on the top of a hill covered to mid-slope by the dark mass of cork-oaks." It takes an entire day to get there, climbing a steep trail on muleback. To make Gabriële laugh, Francis snaps at his mule: "Come on, Danthon! Move forward! Don't be so stubborn!"

Halfway up the slope, the little group is startled and intrigued by a delicate clinking sound. They dismount from their mules, glad of the excuse to rest aching backs. They listen carefully, the music becomes clearer, and they follow the distant melody like children lured by the Pied Piper's flute. At the edge of a brook, they discover a young girl dancing and playing castanets, watched quietly by her only audience—her herd of black pigs. The moment is duly captured by Francis, and the dreamlike vision will always be a vivid memory for him and Gabriële.

"I note these details of our time in Spain (the memory of which is precious to me alone) because, once we'd returned to Paris, they served for years to inspire the themes of compositions by Picabia that were nonetheless entirely abstract. There was a series of processions, one of which was exhibited in Germany. Another, dated 1912, is among the masterpieces of modern painting."

After their stay in the mountains, where the night is as black as the women's shawls and dotted with stars far brighter and more untouchable than those in the sky over Paris, the couple travels by train to Barcelona. On the way, they stop in Madrid just long enough for a visit to the Prado Museum, a quick tonic bath in Spanish painting.

In Barcelona, they're greeted by Uncle Perico, Aunt Francisca de Asis, and their three children, Perico, Manolo, and Muñeca, who are bursting with excitement to meet their French cousins. Once again, Gabriële sinks effortlessly into the rhythms of Spanish life, late dinners outside beneath the trees, long afternoon siestas. She and Francis stroll Las Ramblas for days, never growing tired of it, wandering the cobblestoned streets of the Barrio Gotico and, like many a young couple blissfully, distractedly in love, getting lost in the labyrinthine pathways of the Park Güell, still under construction.

But Barcelona is also a city of demons. Picabia is well acquainted with the districts where one can live it up without restraint, and he brings Gabriële and his cousin Manolo along. There's plenty of the usual singing and dancing here, but with an added component to relieve people of their inhibitions: drugs. Francis swallows the pills they slip him without looking at them twice. He asks Manolo to lead them to the narrow-streeted maze of El Raval, the seedy district near the port also known as the Barrio Chino, the Chinese quarter, packed with brothels, dance clubs, and opium dens. Here Francis indulges in a new experience, reclining for the first time in a haze of poisonous smoke that's as soothing as a warm bath, the perfect panacea for his tormented soul and the fierce Barcelona heat. One evening, he pulls a prank on Manolo, giving him a dose of pills that make the young man lose all sense of dimension and distance. Cubist pills! His dazed and disoriented cousin, thinking he's going through a door, falls out of a window right in front of Picabia, breaking both his legs.

Gabriële, who lacks neither nerve nor curiosity, has nothing against these psychedelic experiments, but she quickly decides that they're a waste of time, and dangerous into the bargain. The idea of losing herself in an opium haze doesn't tempt her. She, unlike Francis, has no need of escape. She can drink for hours, anchored to the table and hanging on every word uttered by an enthusiastic conversation partner—but without Francis's melancholic, foul-tempered drunkenness. Gabriële's drunkenness is subtler, more introspective, and it doesn't differentiate between night and day. It has an almost musical quality, as she allows herself to be lulled by the sounds of her own brain.

How did she feel back then, watching her new husband abandon himself to debauchery? To these plunges into the abyss, where she can't follow? Maybe she was entertained, sometimes—he surely remained charming even when high as a kite. Maybe she was scared, too, but with that double-edged fear composed of equal parts horror and excitement, the kind that runs down your spine like a hard little pearl, causing pain and pleasure at the same time.

And then one morning, a strange suspicion begins to awaken in her. A faint queasiness, an intangible, unexpected presence. She knows without understanding. What? That. The thing even the most naïve women have intuitively perceived since time immemorial, a common animality. In all the noise and movement, in the shadow of all those nights shared with Francis, whose body has become as familiar as a memory, she forgot about one small detail, one momentous possibility. It's time to go back to Paris.

Gabriële is pregnant.

"Any woman who has a child spends nine months ill and the rest of her life recovering!" retorts Francis Picabia, when congratulated on his impending fatherhood.

Gabriële feels much the same. She's not showing yet, so she can continue her day-to-day life as if nothing has changed, but she isn't exactly thrilled about what's to come. Right now, in 1909, the couple has no fixed residence. Their official address remains the Montmartre studio on the rue Hégésippe-Moreau, where their first night together sealed their fate as a pair, but they don't actually live there. Gabriële can't bear the place anymore, with its nauseating smell of paint and—ever since their time in Spain—opium. Francis loves to prepare the magical paste himself, the same way he likes to mix his own oil paints.

They divide their time between the home of Francis's uncle Maurice Davanne, the Buffet residence in Versailles, and the village of Crozant in the Massif Central. At a time when most young couples expecting their first child are nesting, the Picabas are in flight, more itinerant than ever. Like many women in denial of their pregnancies, Gabriële puts on little weight, refusing to allow herself to be *invaded*. She carries the living bloat with a certain grace, but also with the air of someone who's been made to pick up a heavy bundle and lug it all over the place before being allowed—*finally*—to set it down. Still, she's obliged to rest, reminded of reality by pains in her back and other inconveniences of the kind that women discuss with one another in whispers, as if these slightly shameful things are no business of men.

Gabriële chooses to rest at the Buffets' mountain home in Étival; the thought of taking Francis to her beloved childhood retreat is deeply appealing. Enthralled by the mysterious beauty of the Jura, Picabia captures it in paint. *The Church at Étival* and *Landscape at Étival in the Jura*. As Borràs would later wonder, "Were these the first tentative steps in the direction of a painting of form and colour, freed from any submission to nature?"

Gabriële loves trees, so that's what Francis paints.

Whatever Gabriële prefers.

* * *

Describing Gabriële pregnant feels . . . unnatural to me. Don't you think? When I write about her, I see her strange, beautiful eyes, her hair in a chignon, I see her with Francis in a cocktail bar or his studio. But I just can't picture her as a pregnant woman—or, actually, when I do write about her that way, I imagine her pregnant with Francis Picabia. I mean carrying Picabia in her belly and giving birth to him. It's like that was her mission, her calling, her destiny. It makes me think of the painting by Frida Kahlo that shows her husband, Diego Rivera, as an enormous, naked baby with a chubby-cheeked adult head, nestling in her arms like a burdensome newborn. Her baby. The baby that, thanks to a series of miscarriages, she would never have.

I think Gabriële would have liked to be another Frida Kahlo, keeping her stillborn fetuses in a jar of formaldehyde on a shelf.

Silent, objectified, eternal.

7

A Little Solitude in the Midst of Suns

It starts in dreams. Then images that arise even in broad daylight, unexpectedly. Like all women who are pregnant for the first time, Gabriële finds herself staring her own childhood full in the face. Expecting a child always makes us reflect on what kind of child we were ourselves, so that we can separate ourselves from that memory-child once and for all, to make room for the baby to come.

Gabriële has never really talked to Francis about her childhood. She's told him that she was a rebel compared to her very "provincial" family: "I was compelled to leave them behind. Not out of ill will; I never wanted to hurt them. It was just impossible for us to come to an understanding." But that's all.

We, too, know almost nothing about Gabriële Buffet's childhood.

Here is the little we've been able to find out.

She was born on November 21 in the palindromic year of 1881, at 9:00 P.M. Her birth certificate is filled out in the old-fashioned handwriting typical of late nineteenth-century bureaucrats, the loops and curlicues executed with a feather-pen dipped in black ink. Capital letters are unashamedly grandiloquent, family name initials lavishly adorned with curls and whorls. It's all very solemn and very pretty.

Solemn and pretty: there, in a nutshell, is what a whole generation about to be born will rebel against. Picasso, born the same year. Picabia, who's three. Guillaume Apollinaire, only a few months old. But also the younger ones: Marcel Duchamp, Arthur Cravan, Tristan Tzara, and many more. They're the children of the new century to come—and with them, a definitive farewell to conventional nineteenth-century "good taste."

The newborn girl is named Madeleine Françoise Marie Gabriële. The fourth name, relegated to the end of the list, is spelled in a strikingly different way, with an umlaut and a single *l* before the final *e*: Gabriële. It will become the preferred name of the little girl who carries it, finding its androgyny much better suited to her personality than Marie or Madeleine. Eventually she makes the decision to rechristen herself all on her own and demands that her parents call her Gabriële from then on—already she's acquired a taste for the strange and unusual. And all her life she'll vary the way she signs her self-chosen name: sometimes Gabriële, sometimes Gabrièle, sometimes Gabrielle. She refuses to consider herself bound by any laws, even those of spelling.

Her father, Alphé-Gabriel Buffet, is a soldier, a major in the 15th Regiment of Chasseurs à Cheval. Austere and solid, like most military men. His profile is firm and spare, his mustache immaculately trimmed. He always wears his uniform for photographs.

Alphé-Gabriel comes from an ancient Jura family, many of his forebears attorneys and judges trained at the Abbaye de Saint-Claude. He's older than his wife, old enough to be her father. This might have been an arranged marriage, or a loveless one, because there will be no more children after Jean and Gabriële. But of course, we have no real idea, and the dead aren't much for explanations.

Gabriële will refer to her father as "a very good soldier." But he resigns his commission in 1893, after a disagreement with his commanding officer. "Disagreement" is the word his daughter will use when she tells the story. A euphemism, surely, because the quarrel was serious enough to stop her father's career in its tracks. What happened, exactly? It's difficult to know. Alphé-Gabriel's commander, General Gaston de Galliffet, was an awful man, nicknamed the Town Executioner, for it was he who arbitrarily chose which prisoners would be shot on the spot, often simply because he didn't like their looks. Clemenceau's quip about the general was as cynical as it was brilliant: "Galliffet hasn't shot a prisoner in more than twenty years. How dull life is."

Gabriële's father retires to Versailles. A thwarted rise, a ruined career.

Even in retirement, a military man remains a military man. In 1905, Colonel Buffet is reprimanded for going to Sunday mass in uniform just after the government's official separation of church and state. More than a century later, this episode may seem surprising. But at the time, military officers were prohibited from mingling their duties in service of the state with their personal beliefs. An amusing anecdote from the life of Charles de Gaulle illustrates this dichotomy. One of the general's dinner parties happened to fall on a Friday, and his wife mentioned that she was planning to serve their guests fish. History records the following response:

"Fish to soldiers on a Friday? Yvonne, don't even think about it!"

Gabriële's father, then, is an upright and disciplined man, but one with strength of character and a liberal mind. His daughter may not have approved of his ideas or his choices, but it was from him that she inherited the courage to express her opinions.

Gabriële's mother, Laurence, is a retiring woman who has left little trace. She's been called gentle and kind. Gabriële will describe her, with a hint of acid in her tone, as "the literary-salon type, no matter where she was." The two women will never have much to say to one another.

Laurence is directly descended from the Jussieu family of botanists. The most famous of these maternal ancestors is Bernard de Jussieu, demonstrator of plants at the Jardin du Roi, now the Jardin des Plantes, France's best-known botanical garden. His rival, the Swedish botanist Linnaeus, said of him: "Aut Deus, Aut Dominus De Jussieu." ("No one but God or Jussieu can solve this problem.") So he must have been quite talented. In 1734, he planted the first cedar tree in France; legend has it that he transported the stolen seedling from England in a tricorn hat, holding the hat carefully beneath his arm during the homeward crossing, shielding it from wind and tide, ushering it to its eventual home in French soil. It was Condorcet, in his "Éloge de Jussieu," who described Bernard's unlikely theft of seedlings from France's neighbors across the Channel, and the anecdote made its way—not without pride—into family lore and then history. Even the painter Jean Arp couldn't resist mentioning Gabriële's famous ancestor when he sketched a word-portrait of her for his preface to her *Aires Abstraits*: "The great botanist Jussieu, that distinguished man, could never have imagined that his several-times-great-granddaughter would be, among the Dadaists, more than an *éminence grise*: a radiant eminence of every color of the rainbow."

The two most important figures in Gabriële's childhood are her grandmother and her aunt.

Her grandmother, because she's an essayist. Laure de Jussieu. An intellectual figure recognized by the establishment and honored for her work, she is particularly famed for texts including *Un Essai sur la Liberté, l'Egalité, et la Fraternité*, written in the wake of the Revolution of 1848, when she's just twenty-seven years old.

Her aunt, because she's a painter. The younger sister of Gabriële's mother, Alphonsine is the eccentric in the family. When she displays an early talent for painting, her family enrolls her in the studio run by the painter Charles Chaplin—yes, like the actor. A well-known figure during the Second Empire, Chaplin was the favorite painter of the Empress Eugénie, commissioned by her to execute grandiose pieces for the Opéra Garnier, the Palais de l'Élysée, and the Tuileries. A liberal and open-minded man, in 1866 Chaplin is one of the first painters to accept women into his studio, and it's there that Alphonsine pursues her artistic training, alongside a girl whose talents are equally precocious: Berthe Morisot. The two will become fast friends, and in fact their families live quite near one another in Passy.

To be free to paint all her life, Alphonsine must remain unmarried. She'll live for many years with her sister and brother-in-law, Colonel Buffet, thus becoming a key figure in Gabriële's childhood. She'll spend her last years alone, still brilliant but also half mad, living in a former chapel she's renovated herself. As a teenager, Gabriële will be afraid of ending up like her.

The Buffet family moves often, following the garrisons, the colonel's career forcing them to relocate constantly from one city to another. Fontainebleau, Vesoul, Bellevue, Marseille, La Rochelle, Versailles, and even a period in Algeria, where Gabriële will remember with awe the sight of pink flamingos in flight, an intense image that, along with other snippets of memory, imprints itself on her consciousness forever, establishing the foundations for her adult outlook.

The children learn not to get too attached to anything. Not people, not places, not things. All her life Gabriële will display an almost obsessive determination to get rid of things, to give away and sell everything she owns—a trait perfectly illustrated by the time when, as she feeds her children lunch in the kitchen, someone remarks on the value of the cups—ceramic pieces handcrafted and gifted to them by Pablo Picasso.

"Do you *realize*? For a simple children's meal!"

"You want them? Take them," Gabriële says, snatching up the cups—without even letting the children finish their snack!

No cherished possessions, no investments for the future, no money stashed away beneath a mattress. Material goods only weigh a person down. Gabriële has no taste for ownership.

From a childhood spent roving all over France, the brother and sister learn that the horizon is broad and that travel is always within reach for those who choose to undertake it. The Buffets crisscross the country, taking with them only what is essential, changing houses and friends with no room for hesitation and no time to develop a taste for home. These years will instill in Gabriële a lifelong taste for travel, an inextinguishable wanderlust. Distance and risk pose no obstacle—even for a young woman or, as she herself might have put it, *especially* for a young woman. The siblings don't start attending school until 1890. Before that, they're tutored at home by various German governesses with drab clothes and hair pulled tightly back, who teach the children their language, among other things—a skill that will serve Gabriële well during her time in Berlin.

In 1891, Gabriële enrolls in school in Marseille, where her father is in command of the military base. Just a short distance away, the poet Arthur Rimbaud dies in the Hôpital de la Conception aged 37, having been forced to cut short his African wanderings due to failing health. The very poet who, as a teenager, wrote in a letter to his teacher: "When the endless servitude of woman is broken, when she is able to live for herself and by her own means, man—heretofore abominable—having given her her freedom, then she, too, will be a poet! She, too, will discover the unknown!" Powerful words, and though the little girl can't have been aware of them at the time, they probably would have resonated deeply in her young soul. Discovery of the unknown will indeed be the destiny on which Gabriële sets her heart, and at a very early age.

There is one place that represents home and sanctuary to the Buffets, and that is Étival, a tiny village high in the Jura mountains with a name that smacks of summer—appropriately enough, as it's here that the family spends the warmest months of each year from 1884 onward. It's a place to be a child, a magical place. A place to put down roots, its trees changeless and reassuring. "Étival, that small village in the Jura that is my home," Gabriële will call it. The Buffets have an ancient house there, a solidly built old residence with a wide, steeply sloping roof, halfway between a farm and a manor, that has been in their family for so many generations that its origins are lost to time, giving the place a charming air of mystery.

Étival will be the setting for some of Gabriële's fondest memories:

"I was one of the first people to ski. Back then, no one thought the snow could be a source of fun and entertainment! I remember the children used to come out of the schoolhouse to watch me. They'd scream: 'There goes Gabriële over the snow without sinking!'" You can hear Gabriële Buffet laughing at this memory, with the high-pitched, innocent laughter of childhood, the adult woman lighting up and growing suddenly younger as she describes the mountainous landscape with its lakes gleaming like mirrors, its legions of pine and beech trees (which, like a good *jurassienne*, she calls *foyards*, pronouncing the local word with a long *a* and an *r* that rasps in the throat), its nights darker than the most impenetrable Pierre Soulages landscape.

Little Gabriële is comfortable in this late nineteenth-century rural life, taking a passionate interest in the production of Gruyère cheese under conditions she will later describe as "very interesting, very communist, and very free." She loves this sense of nature managed so as to suit the collective good—it just goes to show, really, that everything is political—even the production of cheese.

Standing at the front door of their Étival house, the Buffets see a vista of pastures, herds, fields. The home itself is a maze of rooms and corridors connected by ancient staircases, all of it dating back to the fifteenth century. The place has the gentle, old-fashioned charm typical of so many childhood homes, where behind every door lies adventure and enchantment, and whose smells of cooking and hay and roses stay with you forever, resurrecting through some Proustian trick of memory that magical time that never lasts, the time of life's first impressions. The mountain house is Gabriële's childhood, the Jura her homeland.

The seasons pass, one summer following another, and the Buffet children grow up, both of them setting their sights on an artistic future.

Jean wants to be a painter.

Alphé-Gabriel Buffet comes around to the idea that his son won't be embarking on a military career. In 1897, he allows him to enroll in the Beaux-Arts studio of Jean-Léon Gérôme, a classical painter and staunch member of the old guard vehemently opposed to modern painting. At the Exposition Universelle of 1900, as the President of the République is about to enter the gallery reserved for Impressionists, Gérôme will make a last-ditch effort to stop him, blocking the entrance with his body and crying: "Stop, Monsieur le Président! What's in here is a disgrace to French painting!" The man is in no way a visionary, according to Gabriële, who has decided to become a musician.

Colonel Buffet may be able to imagine his son transforming his painterly ambitions into a career, as long as he can show proof of both talent and perseverance, but there are limits to his indulgence where his daughter is concerned. She can dabble in music, certainly, but just until she makes a suitable marriage. That's her only means of becoming a respectable adult. A young female artist? Unacceptable.

But Gabriële will not budge.

All children are attracted to music, but Gabriële describes a true revelation. As she explains it, she grasps the world of sound even without prior musical education, "just as well as she feels hot and cold." From the age of five onward she's able to "see" notes and rhythms, which give her intense physical pleasure. This despite the fact that no one in her family seems to have any particular affinity with music. "I had these abilities,

I don't know why," she'll recall. Her musical comprehension is the manifestation of an absolute gift.

All her life, Gabriële will remember a melody sung by her nursemaid, the story of a soldier who kills his captain. The narrator of the song is the condemned soldier awaiting his execution. Even when she's a hundred years old, Gabriële will be able to sing the lyrics by heart: "*Demain avant le jour ce sera à mon tour . . .* " She'll say that this song was a revelation for her, that it touched her profoundly, introducing her to another language, the language of sound, of rhythm, of composition. "Touched" is the term she uses to recreate that seminal moment of her childhood.

It's then that she asks her parents for a piano. And gets one.

* * *

"There's something I don't understand."

"What?"

"Gabriële's family seems pretty 'open.' A grandmother who was a writer, an aunt who was a painter, a rebellious father . . . "

"Yeah, there must have been far worse families to be a part of, back then."

"And yet, Gabriële always swore up and down that her family was uptight and smothering. She said in one interview: 'I was the black sheep of my family, especially on my mother's side." In another interview, she said, 'I myself was born a revolutionary, into one of the strictest families that you could imagine, with values of the old nobility. I left—it was really madness.' I'm intrigued by the fact that she would make exaggerated, dramatic statements like that. Why did this little girl have so much anger at adults?"

"I don't know. Maybe because Laure de Jussieu, the grandmother who was a writer, stopped writing at age twenty-seven, as soon as she got married. Or because Alphonsine, a painter who never had children, was considered abnormal. Or because her mother Laurence was so meek and submissive. And then when Gabriële wanted to study music, her father reminded her that a young woman's destiny was marriage."

"I get that. But to say it was 'a mad situation' . . . it was really just what was normal for the time."

If we really want to understand the truth about young Gabriële, part of it may lie in that discrepancy. There's no real explanation for why this girl was, literally and from a very early age, a rebel.

In an unpublished text, she will even write: "I'd lived alone and without love until I met Francis."

Alone and without love. That's an extremely serious charge to level against her family, and perhaps an unfair one. Who knows. But Gabriële wasn't sentimental. There was no warmth in her memories of the past, and she would show little tenderness to her future child.

8

THE SHADOW IS MORE BEAUTIFUL THAN THE ACADEMY

Autumn 1909. Back in Paris after honeymooning in Spain, Francis and Gabriële relocate to the opposite bank of the Seine, moving into a small flat on the rue de Lille owned by a family friend. This is a long, narrow street that runs parallel to the river, extending from the rue des Saints-Pères all the way to Les Invalides. Gabriële quickly realizes that the move was a mistake. The young couple feels stifled in this tiny apartment in a middle-class neighborhood, the way you feel after putting on a new pair of leather shoes for the first day of school, after spending the whole summer walking barefoot on cool grass. The idea of looking like a "family" doesn't appeal to either of them even though, with Gabriële's pregnancy advancing, they have no choice but to play the role.

They miss Montmartre, with its cheerful dirtiness and its sense of community. Every day Francis has to travel all the way across Paris to reach the studio where he works. Some nights, he doesn't come home. But he isn't spending the night at his studio, or with another woman. Since Barcelona, he's become a regular at the opium den in Faubourg-Montmartre, where the hours pass like seconds. Gabriële finds herself alone, far away from her neighbors in the Villa des Arts, far away from her friends in Berlin, and—even though she never expected to miss her—far away from her mother. She could easily walk to the rue Saint-Jacques to see her former teacher Vincent d'Indy, or offer to teach at the Schola Cantorum, or pursue composition again. But she doesn't. She doesn't do any of that. When it comes to herself, this woman who moves mountains for other people isn't even strong enough to open a door.

Instead, Gabriële pursues the mission she's set for herself: to help her husband go through the mental processes that will enable him to change the way he paints. While Francis is out, she spends her time compiling journal articles, perusing books and catalogues, and studying the history of music and painting. She rereads her school texts, takes notes, conceptualizes. Searches everywhere for material related to painting. In Hegel's *Aesthetics*, which she reads in German, she finds a number of anchor points concerning the imitation of nature. Art, according to Hegel, must never imitate nature, no matter how perfect the imitation. As a rival of nature, like it and superior to it, art represents *ideas*, using nature's *forms* as symbols to express those ideas.

"Listen, Francis—listen to what Hegel says: 'Just as in music the single note is nothing by itself but produces its effect only in its relation to another . . . so here it is just the same with colour.' *That's* exactly what you must do, do you see?"

Gabriële also recalls hearing about a series of articles called *Clavecin pour les yeux*, or *Ocular Harpsichord, With the Art of Painting Sounds and All Sorts of Musical Pieces*. These were written by a fanciful Jesuit mathematician and physicist called Louis Bertrand Castel, a proponent of Newton's law of gravitation, who took great interest in the concept of harmonic proportions put forth by Jean-Philippe Rameau. In November 1725, Castel published in the *Mercure de France* his initial proposal for a harpsichord he had designed, one that would enable a player to transform sounds into colors "in such a way that a deaf person would be able to play and experience the beauty of a piece of music, and a blind person would likewise be able to experience the beauty of colors using his ears." The Jesuit claimed to have successfully produced his harpsichord using a prism "to make colors appear, with their combinations and every harmony corresponding precisely to those of the music."

Having searched every bookshop in Paris for a copy of the

Mercure de France, Gabriële returns home with magazine in hand and fire in her eyes, reading to Francis:

"Castel says here that there is 'another way of painting sounds, capturing them on canvas or in tapestry.' *Painting sounds!* Francis, that's it—you must paint sounds!"

Francis, appreciative of these arguments, is also aware that Paul Gauguin himself—who has recently died, making his influence on the up-and-coming generation of painters especially significant, explored the realm of music during his career: "Color," he wrote, "itself being enigmatic in the sensations it provokes in us, can only logically be used enigmatically, each time we use it not to create images, but to provoke the musical sensations that stem from the color itself, from its own nature, its interior force, mysterious and enigmatic." And: "Color is vibration, just as music is."

Picabia takes drugs and works night and day, a heavily pregnant Gabriële constantly observing, as if she's a parrot perched on his shoulder, one of those pet birds so intelligent it's almost frightening. She makes comments, he pushes back; he experiments, she asks questions. They live together in a bubble of their own, their conjoined intellects roaming innumerable new realms which they explore with the exhilarated excitement of children who have managed to infiltrate a forbidden place. In his novel *Caravansérail*, Picabia will write of "this woman [he considers] one of the most intelligent he's ever had the opportunity to know." Their minds overflow into one another, Gabriële's brain like a reservoir of material to be splashed over the canvas. The joy and intensity of the act of painting itself war inside Francis with his dissatisfaction at the results. He gathers himself, starts over, painting the way he breathes, cleansing himself of his old cultish devotion to Impressionist art. Gone is his desire to have his name on everyone's lips; the world he shares with Gabriële is a retreat, a cutting off of the superficial racket and clamor of his previous successes. They hardly go out. Driven by the mission of developing a new form of painting, neither of them pays much attention to that other gestation taking place. The baby. Yes, Gabriële's pregnant, but right now it's still just the two of them with nothing standing in their way.

But Francis Picabia has also taken up residence in that other country that is opium, with no scruples about how hard his wife is working on his behalf, formulating the ideas he needs to move forward.

When the couple reunites after a night or two apart, their discussions resume with more fervor than ever. As Gabriële will recall in *Aires Abstraites*, "Convinced of the arbitrariness and falsity of our poor creation, we were nevertheless compelled to press on with its development, with our work of finding a new arbitrary, one we had to create from whole cloth, with no tools other than our willingness to rely on chance and intuition." It's Gabriële who labors to develop her intuition, using it as the premise and the foundation for her own discursive musical reasoning. Chance, that unpredictable thing, is Francis's domain. He has a gift for it. In this particular case, chance goes by the name myopia—and it concerns optical phenomena.

During their stay in Spain, Gabriële realized that Francis was hiding something important from her. His vision is declining, and fast. He should be wearing glasses—though he doesn't, of course. This is out of vanity. Francis Picabia cares very much about how he looks. His clothes, cologne, travel accessories, his daily impeccable shave. Everything having to do with his body and the way he moves. The idea of wearing glasses is quite simply unthinkable. And now his young bride understands what will become key to the evolution of painting: it's no longer the details Francis is trying to see, but "the general organization of ensembles." His eyes failing him, the painter is now turning to broader forms, and with them a new, radically different style.

The creativity born of error, the physical failing overcome—these are the things that allow us to find what we weren't looking for, simply because we hadn't imagined that it could exist. The sparkling wines of the Champagne region came into being because some glass bottles were incorrectly stored. Chewing gum owes its existence to the latex used in making tires. Kellogg devised his famous corn flakes as a food to calm his patients' sexual urges. Francis Picabia's vanity—the preoccupation with elegance, the wish to be attractive that led him to forego glasses—accelerated the artistic revolution to which he devoted his life.

Gabriële, over weeks of long conversation, finally manages to put the question they're both pondering into these simple terms:

"We accept music, an arbitrary world of sound. Why not accept that form and color can be arbitrary, too?"

In other words, if modern composers can create "abstract" music, why can't painters do the same thing? This question will receive an answer. And that answer is called *Rubber*. The painting measures 47.7 cm wide by 61.5 cm high. It's a mixture of watercolor, gouache, and India ink on cardboard. It contains colored shapes and, at the center, overlapping circles outlined in black.

Francis Picabia paints *Rubber* in June 1909, shortly after his honeymoon in Spain. For the first time, a painter has painted something that doesn't represent ANYTHING. Before Picasso. Before Kandinsky.

With *Rubber*, the fruit of Gabriële's musician's mind, Francis Picabia paints one of the very first "abstract paintings"—if not, according to some historians, "the first abstract work in the history of art." Without knowing it, and certainly without ever *claiming* it, Gabriële has established herself as a "figure at the forefront of the artistic movement," exerting on Picabia "a profound liberating influence." As Borràs will write, "Never again, perhaps, was Gabrielle Buffet's influence on Picabia's work to be so decisive as in those days of 1909 and 1910."

The history of art, as written up to now, tends to claim that the first work of modern art was an untitled Kandinsky watercolor dated 1910. This painting does contain bright spots of color that seem to be whirling in every direction, and black lines that give an impression of threads or wires interlaced in the air. These lines and shapes take up the whole canvas in a manner that is fairly regular, rhythmic, giving a sense of harmony in what is really chaos. Some critics have questioned the dating of this work, denying Kandinsky the title of originator of abstract art. This watercolor supposedly dating to 1910, they believe, is in reality a sketch for an oil painting called *Composition VII*, completed in the autumn of 1913.

In the end, it doesn't matter whether it was Kandinsky or Picabia who produced the first abstract painting. The only way to be safe, to be sure of not being wrong, is to agree with Karl Ruhrberg that "abstraction sprang into being at almost the same moment in various places, without the individual artists being aware of it: with Delaunay and Kupka in Paris, Kandinsky in Munich, and Mikhail Larionov in Moscow."

On January 17, 1910, the Seine swells, rising dangerously hour by hour until it floods its banks. Paris's pipeline system gives way, the city's sewers overflowing and its metro tunnels filling with water.

Gabriële's water breaks on the same day. Less than twenty-four hours later, she gives birth to a tiny girl, a prettily crumpled package. The baby is given the first name Laure-Marie, after her great-grandmother. But this Laure of the new century is fragile, lacking the strength of her Jussieu ancestor. Laure-Marie Catalina Picabia is an intruder in her parents' relationship. It's only now that Francis and Gabriële realize, belatedly, that it will never again be just the two of them. Laure-Marie will bear the stigmata of this mourning, their mourning for their freedom, for the Picabias are not tender-hearted parents, even toward a newborn.

It seems that the gods of youth and insouciance, too, are angry. For each day the waters continue to rise, sharply and relentlessly. January 1910 marks the worst flood in the history of Paris, the worst on record since the seventeenth century. Paris is literally turned upside-down. In the warehouses of Bercy, barrels of wine float like snow-covered corks. At the Orléans automobile manufacturer's warehouse on the rue du Chevaleret, overturned cars drift on what looks like a steel skating-rink. People are rescued from their inundated homes by ladder to trudge single file along makeshift walkways, the way pedestrians in the Piazza San Marco have to do when Venice floods. And still the river continues to rise, turning even these walkways into useless bundles of planks carried away by the water. Old ladies are carried piggyback and hoisted into canoes, and anything that's seaworthy, or floats, or even just doesn't sink, is pressed into service, recycled into a fleet of life rafts. The elected representatives with their mustaches travel to the National Assembly in ramshackle boats, forcing a hollow laugh from the street clown on the Pont de l'Alma, who's in water up to his shoulders. Paris is awash, a city-turned-lake-turned-ocean, another Venice, frozen and chilled to the bone.

As the capital drowns, so does Gabriële. Maternity, the loss of her body and spirit—none of it sits well with her. She feels like a rabbit that's been disemboweled and then had its fur removed, leaving her skin raw. She doesn't know what's happened to her mind, but it seems as if someone—the child, undoubtedly—has taken it. Her brain—her great weapon of seduction, her erotic crowning glory—has been stomped on by a newborn's tiny feet. Memory gone, intellect gone. And the pain. Unspeakable. Something has shut down inside her with the arrival of this baby who never asked for any of this, certainly not to be born. And the Seine continues to overflow its banks. On January 21, at precisely 10:53 P.M., every clock and elevator in the city stops. The steam engine powering the factory of the Pneumatic Clock Company, sole provider of Paris's compressed air network, has been flooded. Gabriële staggers. Like the Colonne de Juillet in the Place de la Bastille, which is in danger of toppling.

In the span of ten days, Paris has sunk into the depths. Everywhere, people are confronted with the appalling sight of an inundated capital. The stations have closed; there are no more trains, no more passengers. The Gare d'Orsay is a giant empty swimming pool, the Esplanade des Invalides a rectangular lake. Silence reigns. Charon stalks the city at night, rowing soundlessly on his slow ferry.

In Paris and the suburbs, the damage is considerable. Rotting merchandise, small houses lifted right off their foundations, detached cobblestones floating in the water like books thrown out of upper-story windows by the hundreds, by the thousands, drifting aimlessly. The metal Pont de Sully, spanning the Seine and linking the Ile Saint-Louis to the rest of Paris, has managed to withstand the floodwaters without collapsing thanks to its iron construction, the river's rise halting a few centimeters below the keystones of its outermost arches, snagging waste, garbage, carcasses, and many thousands of tree branches, which clog like dirty hair in a bathtub drain.

The city's air smells foul, like rotten cabbage and vegetable peelings and swamp mud. All the filth of Paris overflows the sewers like sweat from a diseased body, forcing pedestrians to wade through unspeakable muck. The advertising posters emerging from the receding waters, singing the praises of Mercerou shoe polish, Fix jewelry, and Guerlain's Jicky perfume, seem as laughable and irrelevant as a cocktail dress on the evening the *Titanic* sank. The newspaper *Le Journal des Débats* remarks irritably that "from the excessive number of orange peels passing beneath the bridges, bright spots of color in the muddy, yellowish sludge, we've gotten a good idea of the role occupied by this fruit in the Parisian diet."

In the midst of this widespread disaster, Gabriële gazes at her fragile newborn, who chose the very worst moment to come into the world. An inauspicious debut for the first Picabia child. Outside, all is awash. There's no electricity, no running water. The radiators have stopped functioning. In the Jardin des Plantes, the animals are freezing to death. No Noah, no Ark. The snakes' house was the first to flood. The giraffe succumbs to pneumonia. Only the polar bears are able to adapt to the sudden watery invasion.

That little Laure-Marie doesn't perish, too, is nothing short of a miracle. A photo taken in January 1910 shows Francis Picabia standing near the flooded rue de Lille. He looks slightly ridiculous, still with his hat on amid the catastrophe, but he's lost none of his poise. We can imagine him having evacuated their apartment, some kind of canoe coming to rescue them, him and Gabriële climbing out a window with their baby, the newborn bundled up to within an inch of her life. Francis must have been thrilled by this chaos of nature. His smile in the photo isn't without a hint of satisfaction.

The flooding reaches its peak on January 28, 1910, with the waters having risen higher than at any point in history, up to 8.5 meters at the Pont de la Tournelle. But it's not until March 15 that experts can say with certainty that the Seine has settled back to its normal height. Gone back to bed, as they say. During this time, Gabriële longs to rise from her own bed, warm milk flowing from her swollen breasts in a seemingly inexhaustible supply.

Laure-Marie grows larger. A sweet baby, quiet and

unobtrusive. Occasionally, Francis pauses next to the cradle and looks at his daughter with concentration for several minutes together. Gabriële can almost hear him wondering: "What is that doing here, again?" And then he walks away.

Faced with the heart-rending sight of a father uninterested in his daughter, Gabriële's gaze shifts. Not to avoid the pain, but to settle on *Rubber*. Her eyes devour the canvas as if she can read their future in it. Painting, to prolong and contaminate life. Painting, more eternal than any baby. She draws strength from it. Summons her courage. Francis is . . . multitudinous. There are several of him inside that body. It's not posturing, not ego. It's something more dreadful. Gabriële can feel it.

Francis's opium-taking has increased significantly, as he flees new fatherhood and the responsibility of having a family. Opium has the wondrous ability to make you forget everything: your problems, your children, your money woes, your social relationships, your complexes. But Francis also forgets to work. He leaves. No ultimatums, no threats. Without even giving any thought to the significance of leaving. He simply takes his things and his car and goes off in search of *air and silence*. So he can paint. Of course. He needs to feel his body become one with his car, for hours and hours. He needs to look at boundless landscapes, with nothing standing between him and the horizon. And he needs that horizon to be his sole destination, endlessly receding, unattainable. He needs to get closer and closer to the sun, to go to meet it, to feel its morning embrace, its searing heat on his skin. He needs water, the infinite sea, the happiness of the early-morning swim, the fishermen just returning home. He needs to surround himself with men and women whose cares are not his own, to make friendships as deep as they are fleeting with villagers and country-dwellers. To be regarded as a visitor, a stranger, a demigod.

So he can paint. Of course.

No one wonders what Gabriële might need.

As a woman and a young mother, Gabriële is assumed to be satisfied with her life. But she's different from other women of her era. A stranger in her own society, just as she's a foreigner in her own country.

She remembers the lullabies of her childhood, the folk songs the nannies used to sing to soothe her and Jean and get them to sleep. She remembers, especially, the song about the rebel due to be executed before dawn for killing his commander. And yet she doesn't sing these songs to Laure-Marie. She simply can't force the sounds from her mouth. She, too, pauses occasionally next to the cradle for a long minute or two, lost in aimless thought, until she's jolted out of her reverie by the demands of the tiny pink body.

Francis has left. Again. She's stopped counting them now, his getaways, his escapes, his endless flights. His dodging of responsibility. Does it bother her? Yes, perhaps. On the other hand, she never wonders about other women. Francis's visceral, compulsive womanizing entertains Gabriële, the way you might enjoy watching ant build a tunnel under a magnifying glass. It's small and fascinating. Her husband's need for skin-to-skin contact, for casual sex, for the musky-sour smell of bodily fluids. She views it the way you develop an indulgence for other people's obsessions. She feels no resentment, no jealousy. Both are utterly alien to her nature.

After two weeks' absence, she receives this telegram from her husband: "Have discovered paradise on earth Stop Do come."

However hard Francis may try, he can't do without her. Gabriële. So he tyrannizes and orders, with a paucity of both words and *mea culpa*, in a hideously flippant message that still, somehow, retains an element of charm.

So she comes.

Gabriële arrives in Cassis loaded down with everything but

the kitchen sink; nanny, newborn, trunks, hats, dresses, provisions. It *is* heaven. Francis was right.

The telegram, so typically Picabia, has summoned her. She's come to him. And why not? Francis welcomes them with extravagant flourishes and embraces. A happy reunion. He lavishes affection on his wife and baby. He seems so delighted to see them. This is an entirely different man from the Francis in Paris, sun-kissed and salt-washed, the foul moods a distant memory. Gabriële is touched by his attentiveness. He had a local man help him set up a little crib to make everything ready for their arrival. That crib means that Laure-Marie exists, that Francis does remember, from time to time, that he has a child. In Cassis, Gabriële and Francis rediscover the happiness of their newlywed days at the studio in Montmartre, a life of odds and ends, of fruit and crusty bread for lunch. The warmth and pleasure of simply being together, dreaming. Francis has been prolific during his stay. He shows Gabriële the canvases, asks for her opinion. He's missed her so much.

Every morning, Gabriële goes swimming, very early, when there are still streaks of night in the blinding southern sunlight. She's the only one on the beach, the first of the household to get up. She takes her bathing costume along in a basket but leaves it on the sand and swims in the nude, even plunging her head beneath the water, her long, loose hair clinging to her neck and shoulders. It's 4:30 A.M., who would begrudge her this immodesty, this liberation?

Cassis. The scene of her abduction, the place of her ravishment. The beach where he asked her to wait for him. To wait while he broke up with his mistress, while he wrapped up his previous life. And the place to which he returned, where he asked her to be his. To stay with him. Forever.

Can a lucky choice lead to heaven?

The days pass, a holiday stolen from the rest of life. The

chaos restores Francis and Gabriële's equilibrium, as always. They never get along so well as when they're not living at home, not sleeping in their own bed, not where they're supposed to be. Theirs is a rogue love. A love between outlaws.

One morning, Gabriële finishes her swim and watches the sun rise. It promises to be a beautiful day, gentle and warm, just like yesterday. And yet she's just felt something jab at her heart, a kind of sting that she'll realize later is the pricking of intuition. A cramp from swimming, she thinks, or maybe hunger. Going back up the little path toward the house, she catches sight of the nanny rocking Laure-Marie in the garden. Inside, the air smells of freshly brewed coffee and the warm bread Gabriële has delivered each day along with the milk and the vegetables for lunch. Still, something is off.

"Is everything all right?" she asks the nanny.

"*Oui, Madame.* Monsieur just asked me to tell you that he was leaving."

"Leaving? Where?"

"I don't know, Madame. He also said to tell you that he's allergic to caterpillars. That's all."

Allergic to caterpillars?

Let it never be said that her husband lacks a sense of humor.

She's pregnant again. She hasn't told him. She didn't get the chance. She didn't want to.

* * *

"It's really sinking in for me that neither one of us really knows anything about Gabriële and Francis. We know nothing about their everyday lives. Or even the major events. I'm feeling it more and more deeply as we write this book. It's like a slap in the face, if you think about it."

"I feel it too. It's bizarre. The more we learn about them, the more shocked I am by how little we actually know."

"I can pinpoint almost the exact day I really became aware of being Picabia's great-granddaughter. It was at the private showing before the big exhibition of his work at the Musée d'Art Moderne. I must have been about twenty. Maman had unexpectedly invited us to go with her. Remember? We took the car into Paris that evening. Seeing those paintings made my head spin, like, *I can't believe it was our great-grandfather who painted all this madness! Where does it start and where does it end?!* I don't remember a whole lot about that night, but what I do, I remember like it was yesterday. The champagne was incredibly good, some old painter asked me to marry him, and I recall one painting in particular, which I looked at for longer than the others. It was the face of a Spanish woman, and the reflection on the glass made it look like my own face was superimposed on it, my eyes right on her eyes. But after that evening, I kind of closed the door on all of that. I lost interest in Picabia for a long time. *Picabia* meant my mother. Our mother. And that was fine."

"Yes—I know which painting you're talking about. You have exactly the same face shape, the same eyes, and that same way of smiling and smoking a cigarette at the same time. What I remember about that evening is being in line for the private showing, in front of the museum, in the middle of a crowd of invited guests, chic Parisians, the smart cocktail-party set. I was struck by the fact that we were dressed totally differently from them. We came from a very different world. And that difference made me feel a kind of shame: we weren't sophisticated. We weren't 'chic' like the Parisians. That really made a deep impression on me, and I've definitely tried to make up for that since then. On the other hand, I was very conscious of the fact that we were the painter's *family*. I became aware of Francis before you did. I must have been in middle or high school. Since Maman never talked to us about him, one day I secretly looked up the name *Picabia* in a *Petit Robert* dictionary. I felt like I was doing something forbidden. And there was a very broad chronology of Francis's life. Some dates and a few words about painting that I didn't really understand."

"It's strange to think back to that time. It makes me feel intensely nostalgic. Sad and happy at the same time. That's a *we* that no longer exists."

9

THE DOUBLE WORLD

Francis has fled the caterpillars to plunge, body and soul, back into the hubbub of Paris. Now that he's found his "path," or at least the way toward it, he's desperate to reconnect with the electric cultural atmosphere reigning in the city in this spring of 1910. Cassis served as a kind of rehab for him, his craving for opium diluted by the Mediterranean waters, and now he wants to take full advantage of the capital's boundless energy.

Gabriële travels back by train. These games of "Now you see me, now you don't" and hide-and-seek are getting a bit old for a woman pregnant for the second time in less than a year. She leaves her husband to his painting, his mood swings and made-up allergies. She takes her baggage straight to her mother's house in Versailles, where there's at least some order and support. Francis remains at his studio in Montmartre, going to his grandfather's house in Saint-Cloud whenever he wants clean laundry and a home-cooked meal. Still virtual newlyweds, the couple already finds themselves living apart.

Soon enough, though, Picabia comes looking for his wife, his car pulling up in the front garden of the house in Versailles just like the first time they met. He hasn't come to propose that they resume life as a family, however. No, he wants to go back to their old bohemian ways. And that's music to Gabriële's ears. It's hard to say no to a man who is never dull, who's always asking you to come out and play. And so, with a ringing peal of laughter, she climbs into the car and leaves behind her mother's house, her daughter, and all her domestic worries, which grow smaller and smaller as the auto speeds away, until they vanish completely. Just like that, the Picabias climb back aboard the glittering carousel of the Parisian artistic scene, accomplishing the feat—remarkable for a married couple—of becoming young lovebirds all over again, and once more consigning to the fire the too-new, too-tight garments of married life.

In no time at all, the Picabias resume their friendship with the group of painters who, when they aren't in Montmartre, are in Montparnasse. They live in a constant social whirl, frequenting the Café de la Rotonde and Le Dôme on the Left Bank, and on the Right Bank—Picabia's preference—the Élysée-Palace Hotel and the Café Weber. They're less conventional. More disreputable.

Francis wants to be both at the center of this wide social circle, and simultaneously always on the fringes. This results in a lot of movement and a certain schizophrenic quality to their lives. But Gabriële embraces all this activity with pleasure, one *salon de peinture* following another, their dance card perpetually full. Everything always at speed, everything in constant motion. And Francis's painting, which to this point has represented static things (a landscape, a seated man, a languishing woman, an object on a table), will now have to reflect that momentum and turbulence, too.

This new way of painting isn't to everyone's taste. As Gabriële mentions in her memoirs, "Francis began exhibiting again at the Salon d'Automne, and then at the Société Normande de Peinture Moderne. Every day, he received press cuttings and letters about his art, but now these contained abuse, insults, even threats. He found all the animosity hilarious, though, and it gave him the opportunity to make all sorts of scathing and witty retorts, which of course earned him a bunch of enemies."

A bunch of enemies, but also new friends. And not just any old friends. Francis becomes very close with Pierre Dumont, who coordinates exhibitions at the Salon de Rouen, where Picabia's work is also displayed. Together they plan to create a new event to be held in Paris. Francis and Gabriële also develop friendships with Hedelbert, the director of a contemporary art gallery on the rue Tronchet, and with the Villon brothers, Raymond and Jacques.

The Villons live in Puteaux, in a house at 7 rue Lemaître that they also share with the Czech painter Frantisek Kupka. They often host gatherings on Sundays, when the artistic minds of Paris gather to drink coffee and wallow in creative insurrection. Conversation topics range from occult phenomena to Henri Poincaré's work on dynamic systems theory. They exchange copies of Jean d'Udine's monograph on synesthesia and treatises on painting by Leonardo da Vinci, pausing in their talk to play boules or tetherball in the garden, which has been left to grow wild. These Sunday gatherings, which began as pleasant little afternoons of chess and conversation, become more and more radical, with the future of painting the main topic of discussion. At the heart of the debate in 1911? Cubism.

Even the word itself is new. It has its roots in a quip made by the painter Matisse at the sight of a canvas by Georges Braque, whose *Houses at l'Estaque* were shaped like cubes. The remark would become the name of an entire artistic movement represented by two groups: the "Braque-Picasso Cubists," working from 1908 onward, championed and exhibited by the gallerist Daniel-Henry Kahnweiler, and the Puteaux Group, the so-called "Salon Cubists," which counts among its members Albert Gleizes and Jean Metzinger, who work to theorize the movement. These two groups are aware of one another but keep to themselves. Picabia, for his part, tends to gravitate toward the Puteaux Group, though he's deeply wary of anything that smacks of a confraternity.

At the Salon des Indépendants in April, Francis exhibits a painting entitled *Spring* alongside the Puteaux Cubists—who were actually responsible for creating the event. Until now, the custom has been to hang paintings in alphabetical order by artist. The Cubists, though, have broken with tradition to hang all their work together in a single room, room 41. The decision results in a common vision, a unified impression. The public is shocked by the sight of these geometric shapes that are supposed to represent reality.

Gabriële's mind continues to evolve amid these painters with their great intellectual freedom and affluence. Her straining belly, on the other hand, is beginning to hinder her movements and her ability to travel around the city. As the end of her second pregnancy approaches, she starts to think—not unreasonably—that it's time to find a new shared base for her and Francis. She's found an apartment at 32 avenue Charles-Floquet, on the edge of the Champ de Mars. It's a roomy, quiet space on two floors, with its own studio, windows overlooking the leafy park, and enough rooms that they won't have to see one another too much, where they can coexist without smothering each other. It's Gabriële who has chosen this new anchoring place. Far from Montmartre. Elsewhere.

But it seems that whenever she tries to establish equilibrium, domesticity, Gabriële finds only chaos. She could have gone on this way, being the wife of Picabia, accepting the best of him—their shared vocabulary, their endless, boundless discussions—and sparing him the responsibilities of daily life. But two children are a lot of work, and it's out of the question for Francis not to take on his share of the burden.

During the move to the new apartment, Gabriële stumbles across some of her grandmother's writing, a small book bound in greenish-bronze leather. She opens the book on one of her knees—the other currently being occupied by her young daughter—and rereads this passage: "Everywhere, in ancient times, we find oppression existing alongside liberty. Slavery was no mere unfortunate, tragic accident; it is the foundation on which the power of nationalities rests." Suddenly, the ghost of Gabriële's grandmother seems to rise up and stand before her, to ask the uncomfortable question: "You think you've agreed, mindfully and deliberately, to be the tool of another. But isn't the truth that you've fallen into slavery?" And with that, Laure de Jussieu vanishes, leaving Gabriële in a state of torment. The answer isn't always clear. On some days, she's filled with the kind of satisfaction felt by those gray men who serve as shadow-advisors to heads of state. On other days, she feels like a woman. That is, less than a man.

Her son is born on February 28, 1911, in the middle of their umpteenth move and at the height of paternal disinterest. She names him Gabriel. Yes, Gabriële gives her own first name to her tiny boy. She's carried him, and continues to carry him. It's she who will keep him alive. He comes from her. That's what children are, small pieces of ourselves expelled to live outside our bodies. A strange self-mutilation.

Madame Buffet-Picabia is now a woman of thirty, a mother, a wife "extended" by two young children, with a household to run, yet still expected to provide a stable foundation for the development of a higher artistic understanding. All of this is dictated by the kind of conventional wisdom Gabriële never expected she'd have to advocate for one day. Paying the nurse, keeping up appearances, maintaining their social life, seeing to the practical side of things. Keeper of the household, of the temple, of the façade, of the agenda. Being the head of a family. It's all a big joke to Francis; he's so good at being a rogue. Even the idea of saving money is like a confinement, he explains to Gabriële. How *fun* it is to be thoughtless.

With the arrival of this second child, Francis has started using opium again. A predictable chain of events. "I can't stop myself from loving the atmosphere opium creates," he'll write in his unfinished novel *Caravansérail*, "and indulging in those delectable nights where all of life's sadness, all its worries remain behind the closed door." That's precisely what he does when he goes to the opium den—closes the door to all rational discussion. Pulls up stakes. And Gabriële finds herself relegated to handling life's worries. Is there any point in reminding him that *she* never wanted marriage or children at all? That *he* was the one who sold her on the whole thing? No. Because Francis always runs, getting into one of his cars and screeching off to repaint the night to match his mood. And yet, despite everything, Gabriële always keeps a foot wedged in the door, to keep from being hermetically sealed in, to keep the inside and the outside in communication. It's painful, but she does it.

* * *

"It's important to remember that opium wasn't illegal at the time," the gallerist Gérard Rambert reminds us. "The pharmacies even carried laudanum, a very common product that was, quite simply, an opium syrup. You'd rub a drop of it on a fussy newborn's lips with your finger, to get them to sleep. The effect was immediate. A doddering old person could enjoy a night of delightful dreams with just three or four drops. For a healthy adult, ten drops in the morning and ten drops before bed could keep you in a good mood all day.

"Opium is a dream-machine. It creates a kind of muffled atmosphere, instantly calming anxiety, depression, agitation, suicidal thoughts. It's not really surprising that Picabia was an opium-lover.

"Time stops existing, and so does hunger, thirst, even any sense of where you are. Nothing matters anymore. The drug silences a person's inner dialogue. You take it so you can have peace, to stop the voices in your head. The hours pass without your even being aware of it. You skip lunch, you skip dinner, you stop feeling any kind of anger or aggressiveness, and gradually you stop feeling any strong emotion at all until you've lost all will and desire. And finally you lose any sense of motivation. Opium is a powerful revealer of the pointlessness of everything.

"In Picabia's time, opium consumption was very much tolerated, just as the use of cocaine and morphine were. For example, with morphine, it wasn't rare to be at a dinner party and have a lady take a needle out of her personal kit and inject herself in the inner thigh, right in the middle of the meal. This would happen in wealthy and sophisticated homes, and the women would have these beautiful, engraved silver cases, with the syringe of morphine already prepared. They'd inject themselves through the fabric of their gowns, right there at the table. And no one thought anything of it. It was no more unusual than lighting a cigarette.

"In the early twentieth century, opium was made from a plant, *Papaver somniferum*, the opium poppy. A slit was made in the poppy's seed pod at dawn, so that the air could oxidize the product. A gel-like substance oozed from the pod, a white gum that oxidized in a few seconds and changed color to become caramel- or chocolate-colored. Once the resin had been collected, it had to be cleaned, because the harvested pods were piled on the ground, and dust, dirt, and small stones often ended up mixed with the gum. This means that pure opium could not be consumed in its harvested state, but had to be 'prepared.' Here's the recipe used by Jean Cocteau, who was smoking opium at about the same time as Francis Picabia.

"Cocteau insisted on preparing his own opium, and he was undoubtedly right to do so. He started with 100 or 150 grams of pure opium, which he put in a cooking pot, and then added a bottle of good wine. Diluting with Bordeaux—that was the Cocteau method. Then he'd let that simmer without boiling, to reduce it. The resulting syrup was strained through a wool or cotton cloth to filter out the impurities. After the first filtering, he started the whole process over again, for hours and hours. And it stank. A smell like animal urine, which got into everything. Eventually the syrup thickened into a substance the same consistency as paint out of a tube. Damp and soft, malleable but not liquid. Still with the same odor of cat piss. After the second filtration was finally done, what he ended up with was new opium, or 'young' opium, as it was called, which wasn't very nice to smoke—some English lords would have their servants smoke it, to recover what was called the dross, a hard, shiny material with a particularly high morphine content. This dross, mixed with 'young' opium, resulted in something called 'chandu.' You had to know exactly how to dose it, so the mixture would adhere to the pipe bowl. Inexperienced smokers would waste a lot of opium before they learned how to stick the little ball to the pipe bowl so it wouldn't fall off into the lamp when the pipe was turned over.

"All of that was a bit complicated to do by oneself, which explains why there were so many opium dens in Paris. The advantage there was that everything was simple. An old Chinese lady would prepare the opium for the customers, so all they had to do was lie down with their head on a hard little Chinese cushion. The old lady would hand them the prepared pipe, and ideally the smoker would just turn his head and inhale the vaporized ball, trapping the opium smoke between the top of the stomach and the sternum in a single long, deep breath."

Winter 1911. Francis Picabia can't get out of bed. He's lethargic this morning. Pale. Weak. Ill, he says. A cold. Gabriële knows his sickness is actually called *opium* but refrains from commenting, simply offers to take the paintings he owes Hedelbert over to the gallery herself. In the taxi on the way to the rue Tronchet, she curls herself into the smallest possible ball to fit in amid the paintings cramming the vehicle.

Approaching the gallery, Gabriële spots Hedelbert on the pavement, discussing something with a serious-looking young man. Their exchange seems heated, but with a kind of still, focused heat, nothing physical. As the taxi gets closer, Gabriële wonders how old the young man actually is; his expression is so intent that his features are slightly distorted. She studies his profile. It's sculpted, flawless, a high forehead curving down to striking brow bones, the gray eyes beneath them remote, unsettling. His mouth is an ambivalent line, the full, rather androgynous lower lip set in a frown that is firm but not disdainful, projecting an air of easy authority. The young man runs a hand unconsciously through his hair, undoing the effort he's clearly made, probably more than once, to slick back the light blond, naturally wavy strands.

She's crossed paths with him before, Gabriële realizes. And certainly not forgotten him. His lanky form is swamped by the cheap, possibly secondhand suit he's wearing, and he's tall, though probably not as tall as he seems. The pale smoothness of his neck is marred by the prominent Adam's apple common to overly thin men. She imagines him running his long fingers reflexively over that neck, the way you run a fingernail along the edge of some familiar object nearby. Yes, she's definitely seen this young man around here and there, at exhibitions and galleries. She even knows his name, because she knows his brothers—has been to their home more than once—and it's even possible that this man has been to her flat on avenue Charles-Floquet during one of their open houses, which last for hours and sometimes days.

Certain faces, like certain landscapes, arouse in us a kind of primal attraction, a disconcerting and instinctive desire for possession. Gabriële hasn't forgotten this young man, or the unexpectedly cutting remarks with which he peppers his highly intelligent conversation, or the solemn light in his gray eyes. His grace and his shyness, so quietly refreshing alongside all the shouts and laughter, have already stopped her in her tracks. It's like running into a wall because you aren't looking where you're going. Funny and awkward at the same time.

Gabriële steps out of the taxi, flustered, the driver hurrying to help her navigate the car's running board. The two men in front of the gallery break off their conversation. Gabriële watches the young man turn his spare, crescent-moon profile in her direction. He recognizes her, she's certain; he knows she's Picabia's wife. He dashes to the taxi and helps her out. Then, as Hedelbert goes to open the gallery doors, the young man gathers the paintings under his arms and, with incredible strength for such a thin body, picks them all up at once. They stand there on the pavement, the two of them, and the young man leans toward Gabriële and smiles dazzlingly, one of those smiles that makes you want to fall into it, to live in it forever. And with that, Marcel Duchamp introduces himself to Gabriële Buffet.

In the distance, deep in the gray eyes, the other bank.

To thank him, she invites him to dinner.

On the day of that encounter at the gallery on the rue Tronchet, Marcel Duchamp is twenty-four years old. He has two older brothers who are artists, the Villon brothers. The ones who host the dissident branch of Cubism at their house every Sunday. These are the famous meetings on the rue Lemaître, the "Puteaux Sundays." The two brothers, Jacques (whose real first name is Gaston) and Raymond, are Duchamps by birth, the older siblings of Marcel and a baby sister, Suzanne. It was Gaston, a painter, who chose the pseudonym; partly as a tribute to the poet François Villon and partly because he wanted to spare his true family name any potential disgrace. Raymond, a sculptor, goes by the name Duchamp-Villon. A happy medium. They come from a middle-class family in Normandy; their father is a notary, their mother plays the piano, and all the children are artistic. The older brothers moved to Paris in 1894, and young Marcel followed them in 1904 after earning his *baccalauréat*, determined to be exactly like them. Years later, he'll say, "When I was sixteen, I thought for six months that I wanted to be a notary like my father, but that was just because I loved my father. I *adored* my brothers."

When he first arrives in Paris, Marcel lives in Montmartre with Jacques/Gaston, where he becomes acquainted with both the impassioned community of penniless painters and the general atmosphere of the neighborhood centered around the Chat Noir cabaret. Marcel, too, wants to be a painter. He enrolls in the Académie Julian but plunges with equal enthusiasm into the district's bohemian scene and frequently skips class, preferring to fill his sketchbook with the vignettes of Parisian life unfolding on the city's terraces day and night. In 1905, he applies for entrance to the Beaux-Arts de Paris but is turned down. After a temporary return to Rouen and an obligatory period of army service, he moves back to the capital, to the rue Caulaincourt, alone and finally his own person, his brothers having relocated to Puteaux during his absence, to escape the depravities of Montmartre.

Marcel's character becomes more well-defined. He realizes that he prefers the company of humorists to that of painters, so he starts doing satirical sketches. In 1908, he moves to Neuilly and exhibits his work for the first time at the Salon d'Automne, sponsored by his brothers, who are members of the organizing committee. His work is ignored. He couldn't care less. Then, at the 1910 Salon des Indépendants, Marcel exhibits two female nude studies, and these don't go *completely* unnoticed—a March 19 article in the magazine *L'Intransigeant* mentions "some very bad nudes by Duchamp." Marcel finds this highly amusing, telling himself that, despite being negative, the review has at least brought him out of anonymity.

Marcel is a younger brother, a shy young man who dislikes both outrageous behavior and self-promotion. He enjoys being part of a group, but even then, he stays on the fringes, observing. He goes to parties but doesn't dance, attends the Puteaux Sundays but doesn't participate in the conversation. He keeps to the shadows, plays chess, and grows ever more appreciative of the peace and quiet to be found in Neuilly. And gradually, he stops seeking out the groups altogether. Already, his is a dissident soul. He has his share of liaisons but keeps them quiet. He's an attractive man, but he's no seducer.

In view of all these qualities, Gabriële senses that introducing Marcel Duchamp to Francis Picabia will make sparks fly. They share the same taste for shattered icons, for the art of irony and the irony of art, for jokes no matter the circumstance, and the idea that God is dead. Admittedly, it's also true that there's a ten-year age difference and that they have almost nothing else in common. One of them comes from a kind, loving, and respected provincial family; the other is the scion of a moneyed and dysfunctional aristocratic clan who holds his own inheritance in contempt. Young Duchamp is secretive, sensitive, and quietly modest, while Picabia is noisy, intemperate, and shameless, a flamboyant hotshot. But they are two magnets. And when Gabriële introduces Marcel to her husband, Francis will find himself face-to-face with a magnificent, sublime, un-hoped-for mirror image, a photo negative.

On the evening Gabriële has invited him to dinner to thank him for helping her carry her husband's paintings, Duchamp arrives promptly on time like the well brought-up boy he is, bouquet of flowers in hand. The maid who opens the door for him is startled by his punctuality; she isn't used to the Picabias' guests showing up when they're supposed to. The young woman asks Marcel to wait in the lounge, making excuses on behalf of Francis and Gabriële, who are still getting ready, as they've only just returned from the Jura, where they've left the children with Gabriële's mother—indeed, Marcel has to step over the half-unpacked suitcases still sitting in the foyer. He does so with grace and seats himself politely on the sofa, still holding his bouquet of flowers.

Eventually, Francis comes downstairs, hair damp, filling the lounge with the scent of his eau de Cologne. He's wearing an immaculate light suit, linen shirt, and bowtie, but no shoes or socks. Marcel's never seen anything quite like it. Francis pads barefoot across the rug as if everything is perfectly normal and pours the young man a glass of champagne, apologizing for making him wait. They've just come back from a trip, staying with his wife's family, his incredible wife—who should never under any circumstances be addressed as "Madame Picabia," he warns, because she hates that. Francis describes the family vacation to Étival as though he and Marcel have been friends forever, with ease and familiarity, as if they were just together last week.

"My wife had a painter aunt named Alphonsine, you see," he tells Marcel. "As a child, she used to see her aunt's paint-ings hanging on the walls of the family home, but eventually she started hating the sight of them—all those bad paintings lined up one after another like that. It was too much! So I'll tell you what we did before we left: my wife took down all of poor

Alphonsine's paintings and piled them in the garden, and I'll be damned if she didn't set them on fire. A great big joyful bonfire to celebrate the demise of academic painting. So, you see, my wife's a vandal. A bad girl. It's dangerous to spend too much time with her—she'll take the older generation's most beloved statues and smash them to pieces."

Francis steps closer to Marcel, who's listening, slightly over-whelmed, still clutching his bouquet of flowers, and refills his glass, which bubbles over, dripping onto the carpet.

"Have something in here," Francis says, thumping his own chest, "and you'll know whether you should paint! And if you want to be followed, learn to run faster than everyone else."

On this note, Gabriële appears, asking Francis not to scare off their guest. Not yet, anyway. Dinner is served. Marcel hands his bouquet to the mistress of the house who, instead of fetch-ing a vase, puts it into a drawer. During the meal, Gabriële gives Marcel Duchamp a taste of the questions she and Francis are asking themselves on the subject of painting.

"I had this idea, this feeling," she explains, "that since we'd created a new approach for music, why couldn't we create one for images?"

"The question of art today is what that new approach could be," Francis puts in. "In other words, we have to think about what we're going to put on canvas from now on."

Marcel listens attentively, first to one of his hosts, then the other. This is a new way of speaking for him, a new way of hosting a dinner guest, a new way of being a married couple. And their secret thoughts about painting resemble his own. Gabriële and Francis are so different from the couples he's met at his brothers' house. When the dessert course arrives, Francis proposes that they go for a drive in his car. They could go to Normandy, or even as far as Brittany, or—why not all the way to Cassis? If they leave right away, they'll arrive in time to watch the sunrise. Marcel is speechless. Gabriële glances at her watch and reminds Francis that, unfortunately, they're expected at a friend's place. He'd completely forgotten. He asks the maid to take the desserts back to the kitchen; they've got to leave right away. All three of them. Marcel is nonplussed. He doesn't want to intrude and offers to go home. But Francis won't hear of it. The evening's just getting started, he says, and Marcel is absolutely forbidden to leave them.

And they're off. Everyone readies themselves to go out. Gabriële retrieves the wilting bouquet from the drawer, so as not to turn up empty-handed, and they all head out. On the way, they have to stop when Francis's car is blocked by another in the road. Gabriële begs him to be patient and not to get out his pistol. She turns to Marcel and explains, rolling her eyes in exasperation:

"Picabia has a habit of shooting at the tires of the car in front of him if it doesn't let him pass quickly enough . . . "

Francis, Marcel, and Gabriële arrive at a large private home where all the guests, eyes glittering and heavy-lidded from drinking, kiss them sloppily on the cheeks. Not a single painter at the table, Marcel observes, just a group of happy, silly people who aren't taking themselves seriously at all. Francis plays with the asparagus tips left on a plate, throwing them at a couple of pretty young dancers preening in front of him. They simper back at him. Gabriële, at the other end of the table, is absorbed in a discussion with a doctor sporting a long beard, who seems utterly fascinated by what she's saying. Francis leans toward Marcel, pupils dilated, and murmurs, "What can I say, my wife has an erotic brain. It drives truly intelligent men crazy."

"Lucky for you, that type of man is rare," Marcel replies.

After that dinner, Francis takes a greater interest in the Puteaux Group, since it's an opportunity to see young Marcel every Sunday. Duchamp, for his part, emerges from his solitude to spend time with the Picabia couple. Gradually, the pleasure of being together becomes a necessity. Long evenings of conversation with Marcel replace nights spent at the opium den;

the former are, for the painter, every bit as intoxicating. He falls headfirst into the young man's bottomless intelligence.

Marcel Duchamp will speak of this period as the start of a revolution for an *us* comprised of only two people, himself and Francis. "The years between 1911 and 1914 were like an explosion for us. We were rather like two poles, if you like, each of us adding something, and making an idea explode because of those two poles. If we'd been alone—he by himself and I by myself—perhaps fewer things would have happened for each of us."

In November 1911, a few days after the Salon d'Automne ends, Pierre Dumont and Francis Picabia hold the Société Normande de Peinture's first Paris exhibition on the rue Tronchet. Marcel Duchamp shows a painting, *Sonata*, that represents the women in his family, depicted using a Cubist technique. Picabia exhibits three paintings, two of them entitled *Garden* and the third *Swans*. The event becomes the first formal exhibit for the Puteaux Group. Nevertheless, Duchamp and Picabia remain free electrons even inside the movement, experimenting with different techniques, questioning the knowledge gained, and refusing absolutely to be part of any theoretical or communal framework.

Gabriële had a feeling that the two men would get along, but she didn't expect them to become permanently inseparable. Very quickly the three of them forge a deep friendship, behaving like they've known one another forever. Whenever one of them appears at a party, the guests instinctively look around for the other two. Intellectual dialogue, that powerful river flowing between Francis and Gabriële, clogged in recent months by the debris of reality, begins to run freely again. With Marcel, they rediscover what naysayers claim no married couple can enjoy for long: the feeling of building something immortal together, solely through the strength of hearts toughened by the world's muck and misery. It's Duchamp who bursts the abscess that has formed in the Picabias' marriage since the births of their children, allowing them to love each other and to love Marcel, in chaos and in order, heads down, backs straight. The straitlaced Marcel accompanies the Picabias everywhere, on fantastical trips, drunken escapades, parallel worlds of drugs and visions, nights reborn and days filled with promise.

The weeks pass, and Marcel more or less moves into the avenue Charles-Floquet apartment. He plays with Laure-Marie and baby Gabriel, whom they call Pancho, bouncing them on his knees. He, Francis, and Gabriële create a group of their own, whose first rule is the absence of rules. Once again, thoughts flow freely. Marcel's presence is like a rebirth, a resurgence of vital energy in the quest to create another way of painting. Gabriële will write: "Behind a quasi-romantic façade of shyness, he had the most demanding mind in terms of dialectics, utterly passionate about philosophical speculation and absolute conclusions."

Along with philosophy, Marcel Duchamp has been interested in aeronautics ever since he witnessed the takeoff and landing of a plane at Toussus-le-Noble in the department of Seine-et-Oise. As it turns out, Francis knows a famous aviator, Henri Farman, who studied art in Paris; the two have been friends since their youth. Farman eventually abandoned the Beaux Arts to become a cyclist, driver, and finally a pilot. An adventurer and a pioneer in his field, he invented the term "aileron" and sets new aviation records every year.

One night Francis runs into Henri Farman by chance in a cabaret, the Âne Rouge, and the two men embrace warmly. Before they part ways in the wee hours, Francis asks his old friend for a favor: to organize a taste of flight for a young man he knows who would absolutely adore the experience. A sort of "baptismal flight." Farman agrees.

They arrange to meet at Chartres. On the appointed day, Francis, Marcel, and Gabriële set off in the car. At the last minute, Marcel's two older brothers ask to come along. The truth is that Jacques and Raymond are starting to be slightly irritated by Picabia's influence over their little brother. People used to talk about the three Duchamp brothers as "a litter of puppies who all do the same thing, say the same thing, react the same way." But ever since he met the Picabias, Marcel has split off from the pack. Afraid that this bad joke will end in an aerial disaster, the brothers are determined to keep an eye on the situation.

Gabriële will remember their arrival at the rendezvous point: the edge of an immense stretch of prairie, the home territory of the new flying machines. "We looked with astonishment at a totally new world of strange objects—rather like monstrous toys made of sticks and rope, equipped with antennas—that is, propellers, turning slowly." The men back down immediately at the possibility of danger, robbed of any desire for a baptismal flight by the sight of the plane, which they immediately nickname the "chicken coop." Francis is extremely annoyed. He's not in any great rush to board the plane, either, despite his fondness for new experiences. But he is angry with himself for having put his friend to all this trouble for nothing.

Then: "Have you got a flying suit for women?" asks Gabriële, who's been all but ignored.

The three Duchamp brothers turn and gawp at her, incredulous. It would be not just foolish, Raymond explains, but insane for "a mother [to] expose herself to danger." Francis, though, is delighted. His wife has shown once again that she's the *only* person he can always count on.

Gabriële, now dressed in a beige flying suit reminiscent of a construction worker's, her hair tied back in a scarf, climbs into the aviator's biplane. Without hesitation, without a hint of fear. Like a queen. She settles herself on a kind of half-stool, half-bicycle seat behind the pilot, in a small niche crowded with ropes and cables.

"Don't touch anything," Henri Farman warns her. "It's extremely dangerous."

The machine stirs to life, rumbles along the ground, and takes off. The noise, she will recall, is "infernal." It's like an earthquake, everything rattling and swaying. Farman turns occasionally to make sure his passenger is still alive. It's impossible to make oneself heard over the roar and clatter, so Gabriële indicates with hand signals that everything is okay. For the most part, she's absorbed by a sight few of her contemporaries will have shared: the earth in motion, just as the birds see it, a palette of yellows, greens, and blues. The flight lasts only a few minutes, but at thirty meters above the ground those minutes seem like an eternity, a sense of being outside time and space that only true shock can provoke, and then the plane begins its descent. The landing is bumpy, the return to earth a jolt. Her husband and the Duchamp brothers run to meet her, astounded, speechless. Gabriële thanks Henri graciously and climbs down from the infernal machine.

On this day of her baptismal flight, Marcel rebaptizes Gabriële herself. From now on, he will call her "Gaby." It came to him quite naturally while she was in the air. A nickname with nothing innocent about it. It's the same thing Raymond Duchamp calls his fiancée, Gabrielle Boeuf. Gaby—a lover's pet name for the Duchamp brothers. For those minutes in the air shifted something inside Marcel. He was terrified that there might be an accident, that Gaby might die before his eyes. Marcel has fallen in love with Gabriële.

Sometimes, it's simpler to love as a trio.

Two painters, one woman, three possibilities.

"I've always thought," Gabriële Buffet will say, "that the day spent with those aviation pioneers opened up wide new horizons for those who were pioneers in art. On our return to Paris, and for several days afterward, there were passionate discussions that culminated in the enthronement of the machine, that creation of men, in the highest echelons of art."

11

WATCH OUT FOR PAINTING

G *aby*. It's chic. It has panache. The pet name delights Francis, who soon starts using it himself. He loves, too, that the name is an expression of Marcel's desire for his wife. For it's become impossible to ignore the obvious: Marcel is hopelessly, irresistibly attracted to Gabriële. Still, it must remain an idea only. Marcel doesn't try anything, doesn't attempt to seduce her. He spends every possible moment by her side but considers her untouchable. Perhaps by design. The existence of a muse can serve as a galvanizing artistic force. The woman becomes the ideal, the unreachable, the *beyond*. For this deeply shy young man, loving an unattainable woman gives him an excuse to keep his distance from other women. Sometimes Marcel withdraws, escaping to Neuilly for a while to cleanse his mind of the overwhelming clamor at the avenue Charles-Floquet apartment, work in peace, and paint in silence, the better to plunge with renewed energy back into the Picabia pool. And, of course, into Lake Gabriële. This woman—for she is all woman, with her curving lines like those of some modern vestal virgin, her slanting eyes, fathomless and remote—is a heart-stopping being indeed. Yet Marcel finds himself experiencing tremendous equivocation: his desire for Gaby is every bit as great as his wish to preserve the couple he idealizes and adores. If only he could become one with this two-headed monster. Melt into them both.

Of course, none of this prevents him from accompanying Picabia on his nocturnal adventures, during which they invariably cross paths with ladies of the night. He's a man madly in love, which has nothing to do with sex.

For now.

Gaby, for her part, pretends not to see any of it. In all her writings, Gabriële Buffet, every bit as discreet and understated as Marcel Duchamp, deliberately omits herself from the equation. One must remain modest where posterity is concerned. But she is at the very heart of the trio, a direct and privileged eyewitness to the considerable and dramatic influence the two men have on one another. They share the sense, the deep knowing, that art cannot be reduced to a conception of life; no, art IS life.

Francis paints two canvases for the Salon de la Société Normande, *Horses* and *The Chicken Coop*. For the latter, he's immersed himself in images of the Miremont farm that inspired Edmond Rostand's epic verse play *Chantecler*. The Picabias attended the play's premiere at the Théâtre de la Porte-Saint-Martin in January 1910. A memorable evening, with Paris's most prominent critics and literati in the audience, and scalpers selling tickets for an arm and a leg. There were rumors that the young playwright had spent eight years writing the play. After the success of his *Cyrano de Bergerac*, everyone had waited with bated breath to see what he would do next.

The jeers had begun during the third act. The atmosphere in the room was charged.

"I'm going to buy a farm," Francis had announced, as they emerged from the theater.

"A farm?"

"Yes. I want to keep chickens, cats, donkeys. I want to be up to my eyeballs in straw."

"Donkeys aren't farm animals."

"I want a ruin! We'll rebuild it together!"

From the theater to wanting to live on a farm, Gabriële had thought, amused. But one thing was generally true about the way Picabia operated: if you pretended to go along with him, if you didn't directly oppose him, you'd always be surprised by the result.

Shortly after the flight with Henri Farman, Francis's rural fantasy cropped up again. He was determined to buy a country house. This hadn't been a surprise to Gabriële; she knew this was a way for him to build a sanctuary, a dream castle, a uto-pia—and the trio they'd formed with Marcel was a kind of ro-mantic utopia. Now, one morning late in 1911, after the Salon des Indépendants, the Salon d'Automne, and the Parisian exhibition of the Société Normande, with all the clamor and turbulence that came with them, he says to Gaby, "Someone told me about an abandoned Benedictine monastery. It's a few hours from Paris. Let's go see it! We could turn that into a farm, couldn't we?"

"When are you thinking?"

"We'll leave tomorrow! We can take the Peugeot."

"I'm seeing Heidi tomorrow."

"Perfect. We'll take her with us."

"Heidi" is Adelheid Roosevelt, whose husband André is a great-nephew of the American president. He's also an adven-turer: mountain climber, aviator, and filmmaker. He and Francis get along like a house on fire. Heidi is studying sculpture with Raymond Duchamp-Villon and was one of the first women in America to become a licensed architect. Gaby adores her.

So the two couples set out in the gleaming Peugeot to visit the Benedictine monastery/farm. In an era when travel is far less easy than it is today, when any trip requires a great deal of plan-ning, Francis Picabia is modern enough—and mad enough—to take off on the spur of the moment, and often. Every momen-tary whim becomes a quest. Going to look at the sea, searching for better light, buying a farm—all really for the pleasure of the rushing wind and the speed of the drive. "Momentary whim" is no exaggeration; it's not unheard of for Francis to get up from the table in the middle of dinner, bundle Gabriële and Marcel into the car, and take off for the night, finding immedi-ate relief in the vibration of the metal chassis in his bones, the way you satisfy an addiction. Driving is a release of adrenaline, engagement in a risky sport. The roads are inadequately paved; signs warning of danger are still a rarity; automobile engines—when you manage to start them at all—can stall out at any moment; and, of course, cars are not designed to protect passengers from the weather: a sudden storm can cause a flood of biblical proportions, not to mention the dust that infiltrates and coats the seats and their occupants. The deafening noise of the car's machinery, combined with the noxious odors of smoke and gasoline, can make for a truly hellish experience.

But today, everything runs like clockwork. The car behaves itself, the travelers are in a fantastic mood, and the farm is magnificent. Yet on the way back, Francis is glum. He's not going to buy the house, he says. Moreover, he's not going to buy anything. Ever again. He's finished. Hunched silently over the steering wheel, it's as if he's being assailed by some dark demon.

Gabriële understands. Now, at this exact moment, it dawns on her that her husband's moods are cyclical, the cycles succeeding one another sometimes slowly, sometimes rapidly. It's a kind of illness. Why does she realize this today, specifically? It's taken Gaby more than three years of marriage to fully comprehend the fact that Francis alternates periods of euphoria during which he spends money like water and works tirelessly, with periods of depression and despondency. In 1911, the term "manic-depressive insanity" wasn't yet widely used in the medical profession, having been employed for the first time only four years earlier. Two French psychiatrists had also worked simultaneously on the subject in the 1850s, one of them, Jean-Pierre Falret, describing the disease as "circular insanity" and the other, Jules Baillarger, dubbing it "dual-form insanity." Gabriële knows nothing of any of this, but she has observed that her husband experiences binary cycles. For a certain period, he'll immerse himself fully in the hustle and bustle of Paris, going multiple nights without sleep, painting canvas after canvas, rising to every challenge, taking on countless projects. An enchanted ogre with an insatiable appetite. Then, suddenly, he'll desire nothing but calm and silence, shunning the social whirl. At these times, too, he becomes a hypochondriac.

The drugs don't help. Marcel is fascinated by Francis's disappearances into the warren of Paris's opium dens. "He would slip off into worlds I knew nothing about," he'll recall. "In 1911 and 1912, he went to smoke opium almost every night." But ever since Duchamp has entered their lives, it seems to Gabriële that things have been different. Francis is more stable. And when he does disappear on some new escapade, some fool's errand, Marcel is still there, standing firm, holding down the fort. He has become her confidant, her dearest friend, someone she can rely on. The triangle must remain intact. "The young man from Normandy always managed to save the situation," Borràs will observe, "however tense or difficult it might appear." And when everything is calm again, it's Francis's turn to monopolize Marcel's attention. He likes their three-way relationship, but he also likes having Duchamp all to himself.

One morning, Francis and Marcel set off for Rouen to make arrangements for a Société Normande exhibit. On the way, their car is stopped by gendarmes. The two painters are unceremoniously handcuffed and taken to the police station. They have no idea what's going on. They're questioned for more than ten hours. Asked where they were going and why, where they'd been the previous month and the month before that, where they got the car. The same questions over and over again and in every imaginable tone. What's going on? Gabriële, notified the day after the arrest, arrives to verify their identities, and they're finally released, dazed by what's just occurred. Finally, a young gendarme enlightens them: they'd been mistaken for thieves who've been making newspaper headlines for three months, members of the Bonnot Gang. Marcel was thought to be Raymond Callemin, nicknamed "Raymond *la science*" because he was the intellectual of the gang. And the police had taken Francis Picabia for Jules Bonnot himself.

No need to draw him a picture. Francis has been obsessively interested in the whole affair since the beginning, and for good reason: the Bonnot Gang is committing history's first motorized bank raids. The robbery of the Société Générale on the rue Ordener has made Jules Bonnot and his friends famous—as has their green-and-black, twelve-horsepower, 1910 Delaunay-Belleville sedan. "Men of taste!" Francis explains to the young gendarme as he walks them out.

On the way back to Paris, both Francis and Marcel are delighted to have been mistaken for public enemies and dangerous anarchists, instantly forgetting the anxiety of their detainment, which they recount for Gabriële in such detail that she's soon sick of it. Francis immediately starts planning a Bonnot Gang party at the avenue Charles-Floquet apartment so that all of Paris will hear the story of how Marcel Duchamp was branded a "dangerous anarchist fellow-traveler." Marcel's older brothers are less than amused by the joke.

Raymond Duchamp-Villon has been remodeling his kitchen. For Christmas that year, he asks each of his friends and his brothers to contribute a small painting to liven up the room (Francis Picabia, we probably don't need to add, wasn't asked). Marcel produces a piece called *Coffee Mill*. Does he find his brother's request a bit . . . decorative? Is he reproaching Raymond for his enmity toward Francis? In any case, instead of painting a Cubist coffee mill for his brother's kitchen, Marcel paints the operation of the machine, a visual explanation of the mechanics of the mill. It's a humorous gift. And yet it's also a manifesto. Later, Marcel will become aware that this painting was, for him, a fundamental beginning. The next year, Francis Picabia will execute his own first mechanical piece.[2]

Something very important is happening as these two men

[2] The drawing *Mechanical expression seen through our own mechanical expression*, 1913.

turn away from Cubism. Of this period, Gabriële will recall, "What was really curious with Marcel and Francis was that they both immediately began to manipulate the *raison d'être* of machines, their utilitarian nature, and gave them other meanings." This reflection on mechanics and machinery is fueled by the emergence of the movement known as Futurism, founded in Italy by artists including Filippo Tommaso Marinetti. The Futurists hold their first Paris exhibition at the Galérie Bernheim-Jeune in February 1912. According to Gertrude Stein, the American collector, expatriate, and Pablo Picasso's great friend, "Everybody was excited."

On February 5, Gabriële attends the opening of the Futurist exhibit with Francis and Marcel. It's chaos. "So many people, it was hard to see the paintings," Duchamp will remember. The Futurist manifesto, written by Marinetti, begins as follows:

"We declare that the splendor of the world
has been enriched by a new beauty: the beauty of speed.

A racing automobile with its bonnet adorned with great tubes like serpents with explosive breath,

A roaring motor-car which seems to run on machine-gun fire,

is more beautiful than the *Victory of Samothrace*."

The Italian Futurists speak of starting over from scratch, of a blank slate, of the total elimination of the old way of painting. They urge the demolition of museums and libraries, which they compare to cemeteries. They're against moralism, determined to create a new generation of artists on the march for a revolution. They've given themselves ten years to change painting. And "when we are forty, let younger and stronger men than we throw us in the waste paper basket like useless manuscripts."

Francis and Marcel are deeply impressed by the zeal, fury, and above all radicality of the Futurists. Gabriële, though, is more circumspect. These Italians are a bit too eager to exalt the "new man" and the "slap and the blow with the fist" for her taste. They sing the praises of "the man at the wheel," but openly declare their contempt for women. At any rate, the Picabia-Duchamp trio's discussions quickly flare up like a bonfire the Futurists have stoked with new matches. Machine, movement, speed. Their attraction to mechanical innovation is the same; the Futurists speak of "the gliding flight of aeroplanes whose propeller sounds like the flapping of a flag." It's all there.

Later that same year, Marcel Duchamp visits the Exposition de la Locomotion Aérienne at the Grand Palais. Afterward, he goes straight to the Picabias' to tell them about it. "I happened to be there with the sculptor Brancusi, and also Fernand Léger. We were looking at an airplane propeller. And I said to Brancusi, 'Painting is finished. Who could ever create something better than this? I mean, can you do that?'"

"Good point," Picabia nods.

Marcel and Francis, each egging the other on, are in full creative flow, their artistic agenda radical, unrestrained, electrifying. Their respective works are now in dialogue with one another; for example, Duchamp's *Sad Young Man on a Train*, painted in late 1911, is echoed by Picabia's *Sad Figure*, produced in 1912.

For years, Francis has been on a quest to liberate painting from its imitative role and, under Gabriële's intellectual stewardship, to transform it into a symphonic composition. And now Marcel begins to use musical terms when he speaks of painting: a work of art must be made of "colors that are the different timbres of harmonic tone," he writes to his sister Suzanne. Francis undertakes various paintings, including *Port of Naples*, whose elements are "arranged . . . with the rhythm proper to musical composition." Duchamp, for his part, has just completed his *Nude Descending a Staircase, No. 2*—based on a small preparatory oil painting done in late 1911, hence the "No. 2." He rents a small boat to transport the piece down the Seine to the Grand Palais.

The painting is intended to represent (or imagine?) a moving figure (a descending nude form) in a fixed environment (a staircase). The palette is Cubist (brown, greenish, and brick-red shades) but the subject is Duchampian. The body is literally invisible, expressed only as a mechanical process, the idea of a moving body, an action so thoroughly broken down into its parts that it has nothing to do with naturalism, but rather a sequence so rapid and organic that the eye doesn't have the time to organize its perception for transmission to the brain except through the idea of a kind of overlapping jumble. It's a deconstruction of the construction of movement. However, the title is clearly written on the canvas itself, in capital letters at the bottom of the painting, and there can be no mistaking it: *NUDE DESCENDING A STAIRCASE.*

Marcel decides to exhibit his painting at the next Salon des Indépendants, in the room reserved for Cubists, with all the members of the Puteaux Group.

The morning before the Salon finds Gabriële drinking coffee on the terrace of La Rotonde, savoring a moment of calm on this exhibition eve. Opening nights always put Francis in a state of agitation, whether he's delirious with excitement and inviting all one hundred and fifty people at the vernissage home to dinner, or insulting every critic in sight and threatening to flee to a seaside hotel then and there. Gabriële knows the whole song and dance so well that she could write the Francis Picabia instruction manual. That would be quite fun, actually: *How to Operate a Spanish Painter.* He'd adore it, she thinks, smoking a cigarette.

She turns her attention to the newspaper. A copy of *Le Matin* dated today, Tuesday, March 19, that someone left on the counter. The terrace is still fairly empty, and Gaby takes advantage of the quiet to read an article devoted to the Bonnot Gang. Ever since the stranger-than-fiction arrest of her two companions, she's been closely following the twists and turns of the ongoing manhunt. One of the gang members has been insolent enough to write to the newspaper, deliberately provoking the police; he's even signed the letter with his fingerprint.

Absorbed in her reading, Gaby doesn't notice Marcel crossing the terrace to join her. He's nervous, awkward, bumping into chairs. She looks up, lowering the paper, and immediately sizes up his mood the way none but the closest of friends can do. Without consulting him, she beckons to a waiter and orders Marcel a Picon beer. Something is wrong.

Indeed, Marcel is furious. Livid. He starts to talk, but he can't even string a sentence together properly. It's frankly astonishing to see him so angry, almost out of control, this young man who's normally so unflappable.

"It's a *betrayal*, Gaby. My brothers showed up at my apartment. Dressed like morticians. To tell me that the Salon people want me to change the title of my painting."

"*Nude Descending a Staircase?*"

"Yes. I've been told to change it before the vernissage."

"Why, does the Bible say it's against the Cubist religion?" Gabriële asks wryly.

"No—their revolutionary little temple just can't understand how a nude can descend a staircase."

"What are you going to do?"

"Take down my painting."

"Fabulous. A phantom painting in the catalogue. Francis will love that."

The Salon des Indépendants was originally conceived as a place of freedom for painters. A place for the renewal of painting, a laboratory, totally free of juries and awards.

Yet it's this same self-styled "modern" salon that has just asked Marcel Duchamp to give his painting a completely different title—and not even twenty-four hours before the opening on March 20. A "gentle" way of breaking the news that his painting doesn't enjoy unanimous approval. More precisely, it's the "bouncers" of the Cubist room (the famous Room 41), namely Messieurs Gleizes and Metzinger, who don't like the painting—so they've ever-so-courageously asked Marcel's older brothers to persuade him to hide away the canvas they're determined to keep the public from seeing.

The incident makes Marcel Duchamp's blood boil. "To hell with them," he rages. Francis Picabia backs him all the way:

"Gleizes likes to think he's a revolutionary socialist, but he's never been anything but a petit-bourgeois from Courbevoie."

Marcel has no intention of bowing to popular opinion. For him, as for Francis, painting has already become, in this year of 1912, a bridge to somewhere else rather than an end in itself, much less a thing subject to etiquette. For the twenty-five-year-old Duchamp, still watched over by his brothers in the Puteaux Group, it's time to pull up stakes.

Marcel is devastated by the whole affair, humiliated, betrayed by his own family. The shocking cruelty of it—that a group of people he admires would force him to withdraw his painting from the exhibition—will have a lasting impact on him. He retreats to Neuilly to nurse his wounds. He stops going to Puteaux on Sundays, remains cold toward his brothers.

He doesn't even want to paint anymore, spending whole days reading. He finally develops a passion for Nietzsche, whose praises Picabia has been singing endlessly since they first met. Gabriële will remember: "Duchamp shut himself away in his studio in Neuilly, only staying in contact with a few friends, including us. Sometimes he'd "take a trip" into his room and disappear. A period of withdrawing into himself, during which the *Sad Young Man on a Train* was transmuted into the captivating, formidable embodiment of Lucifer."

Francis is worried about Marcel, determined to do something to help ease his friend's pain. He can identify with it. He understands it. So he turns to his network, makes the rounds of his friends and acquaintances, and manages to convince the well-known Catalan gallerist Josep Dalmau to exhibit the young man's painting. Shortly after the Salon des Indépendants insult, *Nude Descending a Staircase* is finally showcased in Barcelona, as part of the *Art Cubista* exhibition. It doesn't make much of a splash, but that hardly matters. What's important is that it's been accepted, displayed, and seen.

And in fact, the painting hasn't gone completely unnoticed. It's made an impression on one young man. A strong one. He's been struck by it. Mesmerized. That young man is the still-unknown Joan Miró, aged nineteen and a student at Francesc Galí's Escola d'Art. In 1937, Miró will produce the pencil and charcoal drawing *Naked Woman Climbing a Staircase* in obvious homage to Duchamp.

Days turn into weeks, then months. Marcel reconciles with his brothers. The Bonnot Gang is arrested in April 1912. The siege of the house where Jules Bonnot was hiding out is like a scene in a western, with the police dynamiting the building to finish Bonnot off. The manhunt eclipses almost every other news story, including the sinking of a luxury ocean liner off the coast of Nova Scotia—the *Titanic*. Gaby meets a survivor of the sinking during a "spontaneous getaway" to Amsterdam with Francis and his gallerist Hedelbert.

The Salon des Indépendants, at which Picabia has exhibited three paintings, closes on May 16. A sweltering heat wave blankets the capital. The mood is uneasy. After the April spring freeze, the mercury climbs relentlessly, with temperatures in Paris exceeding thirty degrees Celsius in the shade. Francis paints completely nude in an attempt to beat the heat, a sort of *Nude Painting a Picture* scenario that terrifies the children. Laure-Marie has just turned two, a quiet little girl but one who's always dragging little Gabriel/Pancho around by the hand; the one-year-old is only just starting to walk.

In the humidity of a Parisian evening, the trio goes to the Théâtre Antoine for the opening performance of Raymond Roussel's *Impressions of Africa*. They're eager to see the play. It's quickly become the talk of the town in recent days—but why?

The author is a young writer hardly older than Gabriële, known for wearing dandyish dark suits and extravagant bow ties. Gabriële has heard that he originally wanted to be a musician, even a composer, but abandoned that dream. People say he's had a luxury caravan built for himself, with gold taps and servants' quarters. He likes to play the starving artist, but his family is a wealthy one that made its money in finance.

Having started out as a novelist, Roussel then made the leap to theater. A few acerbic tongues mutter that the real reason for the change was to seek the acclaim and recognition his novels had failed to earn. The play *Impressions of Africa* is taken from his novel of the same name. The first time he staged it, it was a flop. "It was more than unsuccessful, it was catastrophic," Roussel will recall. "People said I was mad, they heckled the actors, they threw coins onstage and wrote outraged letters to the director." Far from being discouraged, the playwright is now trying a new staging. He has put up posters for the play all over Paris, comic strips showing the principal scenes. The piece features a dwarf called Philippo who has a head as big as his body, a zither-playing earthworm, a whalebone-corset statue that rolls on rails made of calves' lungs, a wall of dominoes that look like priests, a one-legged man who plays a flute made out of his own tibia (resourceful!), and (take a deep breath . . .) a rotting rubber tree with the corpse of the Black king Yaour IX lying on a stretcher beneath it, dressed in the traditional costume of Marguerite in *Faust*. The list is long and intriguing. Everyone starts to talk about it. The curiosity reaches a peak. Roussel is an eccentric and an all-or-nothing-ist, and one thing is certain: he knows how to put on an event.

Emerging from *Impressions of Africa*, the Buffet-Duchamp trio are in shock at what they've just seen. A keyed-up Francis exclaims, "It's the new *Ubu Roi!*"[3] He was particularly impressed by the beginning of the play, which "begins with a meticulous description of a series of representations, almost circus shows, in which ingenious and impossible artefacts act with perfect precision, like robots that cannot be controlled by man."

Gabriële is in a state of euphoria. She's just laughed for two hours straight. Marcel is dazed. Stunned. The play, he'll say later, transported him to another place. This great carnival, in the medieval sense of the term, where fools become kings, where reason ceases to exist, is seen by all three of them as a brilliant overturning, a reversal, and if everything is reversed, if the impossible becomes the new metric . . . then what? "It was incredible," says Duchamp, recalling that evening in May 1912, forty years later. "It's important for you to know how much I owe Raymond Roussel, who rescued me in 1912 from a whole 'physico-plastic' past I was already trying to escape."

What is the play about? A western ocean liner, the *Lyncée*, sinks off the coast of Africa. The local king, Talou VII, captures the survivors and forces them to perform a variety of amazing acts for a grand show called the Gala of the Incomparables, tormenting them all the while. They aren't freed until the day after the show.

Roussel's writing process was based on word association. His explanations of his own method give us an idea of the level of strangeness his play's audience was faced with. "I took the word *palmier* and decided to think about both meanings of it, the pastry and the tree. Then, in thinking about the pastry, I tried to match it, using the preposition *à*, with another word that could also be understood in two different ways. This gave me (and let me say again, this was a long and difficult process)

---

[3] An 1896 play by Alfred Jarry, considered by many to be the first modernist play

un palmier (pastry) *à restauration* (restaurant where pastries are served), which then also gave me *un palmier* (tree) *à restauration* (in the sense of restoring a royal dynasty to a throne). And in the end, I had the *palmier* from the Place des Trophées dedicated to the restoration of the Talou dynasty."

The play's language is undoubtedly extremely confusing for its audience on that hot Paris night; most of the people in the room probably find it totally incoherent. But for others, such as Duchamp, Gaby, and Francis, the night is full of unexpected poetic gifts. Language turned music, a clamor, a burst of sound euphonic and dysphonic by turns. The immense and the miniature, overarching narrative and minute detail evoked pell-mell in the same breath. Everything possessing meaning, or creating meaning, with no consideration for hierarchy or scale.

Then there is the Gala of the Incomparables, a series of spectacles within the spectacle that is the play, Roussel having lavished a wealth of resources and imagination on the creation of incredible machinery, including a machine that paints! We can imagine the jolt felt by Duchamp and Picabia, who are just beginning to develop their passionate mutual interest in mechanics, during that part of the act, feeding as it does into their own speculations and feelings.

The play, Marcel Duchamp will remember, "showed [him] the way to create something with no echo of the outside world." Roussel has opened up new horizons of expectation for the young man. "Even today," he will later write, "I consider Raymond Roussel all the more significant because he never gained widespread popularity."

But let's take this memory for what it also was at that moment in time, a moment we can never truly capture, the real truth of which evaporates almost as soon as it comes into being: simply a night at the theater, the surprise so great that they don't even listen to the dialogue, that the whole room is drunk without alcohol, calling out to the actors, luxuriating in the scandal of it all. It's a breath of absolute freedom.

And they laugh.

Marcel, Gabriële, and Francis laugh until their ribs ache.

Ribs bound by whalebone corsets, or maybe encircling calves' lungs.

We could speculate endlessly, contort ourselves into impossible knots trying to understand how Marcel became *Duchamp*, or how Francis became *Picabia*. But what Gabriële will remember is how happy they were that night. All three of them. And that is everything and nothing, all at once.

The month of May is searingly hot. Gabriële feels as if she's trapped in an airless jar. She wishes she could go away somewhere, far from Paris. Alone. Without Francis and the constant chaos he generates; without Marcel, with whom her bond is so intense that it sometimes frightens her. She can't completely disregard his physical presence, his body, his attention always on her. She often catches him gazing at her, so gravely, so openly, in cafés crammed with sweating, entangled people and brimming with the noise of their conversations. So many overexcited people. She finds Marcel irresistible, but in the way a too-clever child is irresistible. They've become so close. The two of them. The *three* of them. That's what it is, really—that it always has to be the three of them.

Some nights, at the apartment on avenue Charles-Floquet, she falls asleep between the two men in a bed that is now, figuratively at least, without a frame, without limits, listening to their mingled breathing, their two breaths harmonizing within her like a free and deconstructed melody.

She'd never understood those stories of physical lust, of some primal, animal hunger driving you wild with the desire to devour another person. Absurd. The hot jolt in the pit of your stomach at the mere sight of a person's face. Ridiculous. The idea of the hollows and creases and depressions of a strange body fascinating you so deeply that you'd sacrifice your whole identity without batting an eyelash to lie down in that foreign landscape. To lose yourself in him, in the other. To grasp, and take, and be vulnerable. To surrender everything.

When she sees Marcel, she wants him. In a new and insistent way.

A guillotine.

That's what it is.

I should go to England for a while, she thinks.

12

AMOROUS PARADE

May 1912. Gabriële is preparing to leave for Hythe with the children. The night before her departure, Marcel Duchamp calls her on the telephone. He asks her for the address of the villa where she'll be staying, the way one might extract information from a covert ally. Has he sensed her desire for him and been emboldened by it? Does he know she's running away to avoid succumbing to temptation? He's called her in an uncharacteristic fluster to tell her one thing, and one thing only.

That he loves her.

I love you, Gabriële.

He says it in the tone of a revolutionary.

With the kind of performative boldness that transforms the words into an event.

She stays calm.

Of course they love each other.

But did it have to be said out loud?

Should she tell him, just like that?

He demands her address. "I want to know where you are, I want to be able to find you, write to you." She gives it to him, the way she would have given herself.

The trio smolders. The triangle has become treacherous.

They've never hidden anything from one another before. None of them.

But everything is shattering. Gaby is going away. Marcel decides to leave Paris for Germany.

He, too, must flee, shake off the traces of Gabriële in his day-to-day life. As Kornelia Von Berswordt-Wallrabe will later write, "His decision to confess his love to Gabrielle Buffet-Picabia strikes at least her as sufficient to explain his abrupt departure from Paris and his trip to Munich." He doesn't have the strength to see Francis again before he catches his train. Francis, his big brother in painting, his sun in perpetual eclipse. He loves him. And he loves Francis's wife. He doesn't know, anymore, which of them he loves more. He doesn't know if he's committing an act of betrayal, or if the true, the real love they share consists of loving the same woman,

He must leave Paris. He's suffocating. He must go as soon as possible . . .

Marcel finishes his painting *King and Queen Surrounded by Swift Nudes*, the terminus of a series of pieces on movement: *Two Nudes: One Strong and One Swift*; *King and Queen Traversed by Swift Nudes at High Speed*; *King and Queen Surrounded by Swift Nudes*.

King and Queen.

King Picabia.

Queen Gabriële.

Before Gaby's departure, he leaves *Two Nudes: One Strong and One Swift* at her door.

Too meaningful a gift?

So yes, she gives him her address in England.

She gives it to this man who is so intense. This all-devouring angel.

She leaves for Hythe.

One strong and one swift. Francis and Marcel.

How to choose? She must not choose. Everything fits together. Everything holds together. *Together*. She'll never leave Picabia. It's impossible. They could destroy each other, tear each other apart, anything. And anyway, it hardly matters. Gabriële doesn't fear the reality of solitude at all. But nothing will separate her and Francis.

They *are*. One body. A subject. To be pondered. To be painted.

But if Marcel wants to write to her.
He's welcome.
Welcome with them.

Gabriële arrives in Hythe with Laure-Marie and Pancho. "Having chosen that distant seaside village to escape from the turmoil of Paris for a while, it seemed to me that crossing the Channel would be just the thing to give myself some distance," she'll write—with restraint, but her meaning is clear enough, for those who can read between the lines. What she can't escape, though—the unconscious effect of the journey—is the emotion she feels at Marcel's absence. She misses him. She's not as strong without him. Unexpectedly, their relationship grows even more intense. Which only strengthens her desire to be far away. She really does need to put a sea between herself and the two men in her life.

The gracious coastal resort of Hythe is in the southeastern English county of Kent. Cobbled streets, a few churches, the sea. A polyglot, Gabriële admires the English language, relishing its wonderful poetic efficiency. She's rented a villa belonging to an old lady, its décor as British as one could possibly imagine, full of dried flowers and seashells. The owner of the place has a passion for collages, which she creates from pictures cut out of newspapers and magazines, glues onto a backing, frames, and hangs on the walls. As Gabriële will trenchantly observe, "Other people escape the pressures of everyday life by writing those endless novels that are among the great charms of English literature. Instead, this lady spent her solitary leisure time crafting quite ingenuously indecent little scenes." It's easy to imagine the collages only narrowly escaping being used as kindling for the fireplace.

Gabriële settles in (somewhat) and, leaving Marie and Pancho to play with the nanny, sets about indulging in her private ritual, walking barefoot on the beach, eventually shucking off her dress, taking down her hair, and plunging into the watery *elsewhere*, far from the rest of the world.

One morning, she receives a letter with a German stamp. Marcel. Sensing that its content will shake her deeply, she doesn't open it right away.

Marcel Duchamp arrived in Munich on June 21. There to greet him was the painter Max Bergmann, whom he nicknames "the cow-painter." His friend has found lodgings for him, a small room at 65 Barerstrasse, near the Alte Pinakothek. Marcel will quickly develop the routine of going to the museum each day to admire the nudes of Cranach the Elder. Other than his letter to Gabriële, he won't communicate much with his loved ones, as if deliberately draping a veil of mystery over his Munich interlude.

Duchamp cloaks himself in solitude. He smokes short-tipped cigars called Virginias and shies away from meeting the members of the local artistic community in person—preferring to read them, as in the case of Kandinsky, whose *Concerning the Spiritual in Art* he buys on Gaby's recommendation. He trawls exhibitions, galleries, museums (including the replica of an alchemist's laboratory in the Deutsches Museum). He discovers Paul Klee and the *Blaue Reiter*, or Blue Rider, a group of avant-garde artists urging the spiritual renewal of civilization. But he keeps himself apart from it all.

Munich suits Marcel's melancholic lethargy to a tee. He's able to come to grips with his romantic disappointment—or romantic aporia, rather—in a city where he's anonymous, where no one and nothing is reflecting his own heartache back at him. "I went to Munich, where I spent two months shut up in a hotel room without seeing a single person," he'll remember fifty years later. He'll say, too, that during that same time, a kind of survival instinct will drive him to transform his frustrated passion into artistic inspiration, letting himself be imbued with the pain, enabling him to explore new possibilities, invent revolutionary new visual language.

Young Marcel is experiencing a pivotal transition, shedding any remaining outside influence and forging a completely new path: going beyond the visible and toward the "non-retinal." Following the example of many other Cubist artists, from 1911 onward Duchamp introduces into his work the idea of a fourth dimension, corresponding to the invisible, which it's the job of art to show. A 2014 retrospective of his work at the Centre Pompidou will describe it this way: "What is this 'invisible' Duchamp wants to show? That of ideas, of the soul and the body's movements, of erotic impulses, of time and space deforming." The work Marcel begins in Munich is a process that will last more than ten years. As he later writes, "I sketched out the overall plan for a large work that would end up taking me a long time because of the many new technical problems to be solved." It's in Munich that Duchamp drafts his first study for *The Bride Stripped Bare by the Bachelors*.

The "bride," of course, is an abstract concept, an idea. Just like the "virgin," the theme of two other pieces also completed in Germany (*Virgin no. 1* and *Virgin no. 2*). These two "ideas" are paired in another piece, *The Passage from Virgin to Bride*. Virgin or bride. The image is emerging of a woman who is forbidden, unfathomable, the focal point of Duchamp's obsessions during his stay in Munich. The bride is Gabriële.

In Germany, Marcel also produces a drawing showing two fencers in combat, their bodies robot-like. "Was he poking fun at his own situation, through the theme of two men fighting, perhaps for the love of a woman?" Judith Houssez, a future biographer, will wonder. These aren't the only examples of pieces that reflect Gabriële's place in Marcel's life. As Herbert Molderings will write, "Indeed, it offers sufficient evidence to suggest that Duchamp's vain attempt at wooing the wife of his friend served as his starting point for the sketch *Mechanism of Chastity* and, by the same token, the new large-size painting, *The Bride Stripped Bare by Her Bachelors, Even*." Likewise, Von Berswordt-Wallrabe will write of Duchamp's sketch *Two Characters and a Car (Study)* that it "applies caustic irony to create a touching image of the apparently intractable situation in which he finds himself with his love for Gabrielle Buffet-Picabia." Another, lesser-known piece, *To Have the Apprentice in the Sun*, is a drawing of a cyclist done on a sheet of paper ruled for music; Von Berswordt-Wallrabe writes, "the tiny loop may signify not only the 'sol' (Latin for *soleil*, or sun), but also as the key of 'sol,' or G. Surely we are not supposed to think of Gabrielle Buffet-Picabia . . . "

Mechanism of Chastity; The Bride Stripped Nude by Her Bachelors, Even; Two Characters and a Car (Study); King and Queen Traversed by Swift Nudes at High Speed . . . The number of works inspired by Gabriële Buffet is not insignificant in relation to Duchamp's total output.

In Hythe, Gaby receives Marcel Duchamp's letter. A letter declaring his love, but a love he knows is impossible.

What is he thinking? she wonders.

Their trio fit together so perfectly. Such a smooth triangle. Flawless. She hadn't expected . . . what, exactly? This outburst. And she, herself, so strong, so imperturbable. A rock. A mountain. Fissured—yes—fractured, by this turn of events.

In his letter, Marcel compares their situation to that of Jérôme and Alissa, the hero and heroine of André Gide's novel *Strait Is the Gate*. Published three years earlier, this is the tale of two sisters who love the same man. The heroine, Alissa, sacrifices herself so that her sister can marry the man they both love. What follows is a series of romantic twists and turns, with the death of feelings mingling with physical death. "The path you're showing us, Lord, is a narrow one—so narrow that we cannot walk it side by side," the heroine writes. On Earth, the love between the soulmates proves to be impossible.

Duchamp's allusion is surprising, to say the least. To symbolize his passion for Gabriële, Marcel has chosen a story of incestuous love: in Gide's novel, Jérôme and Alissa are cousins. Indeed, it's true that Marcel and Francis are like brothers.

Or lovers. In 1966, Duchamp will say that "Another characteristic of the century is that artists have tended to pair off: Picasso-Braque, Delaunay-Léger, Picabia-Duchamp. It was a curious marriage, a sort of artistic pederasty." Gabriële is his sister, and the wife of his brother/lover, with the two spouses themselves having a kind of ambiguous brother-sister relationship. It's enough to make one's head spin. Gabriële is six years older than Marcel Duchamp, and back then, that counted. He's very young, seen as a confirmed bachelor, a man without sentimental attachments, while she's a mature woman, a wife and mother. Hers is the body of a woman who has already given birth twice. Duchamp has chosen to love a multiple fantasy. A *femme totale*, an incarnation of all that is possible and all that is forbidden, an all-encompassing woman, superior, one that can be broken down into a multitude of evocative figures, like his *Nude Descending a Staircase.*

A goddess both earthly and intellectual.

He swore his love over the telephone, then left Paris. Sought refuge in distance immediately after opening a dangerous can of worms. Marcel creates disruption, then flees. He can moon over his fantasy-object from afar, suffer from lovesickness, wallow in despair. But what does he want? Or, more precisely, does he just want to play in a universe of absolutes, in the certainty that reality will never intrude to tarnish the spiritual (to borrow once again the central theme of *Strait Is the Gate*)? In Munich in 1912, Marcel has a nightmare, as Robert Lebel will later recount: "One night, after drinking too much beer at a brasserie, he fell asleep in the hotel room where he was completing work on *The Bride* and dreamed that she—the bride—had become an enormous beetle-type insect and was slashing him hideously with her elytra."[4] Beyond the Kafkaesque quality of the dream, we can see in it the overweening female figure, monstrous and

---

[4] Elytra: A beetle's hardened forewings, used for protection

devouring; the feminine mystery, the BRIDE already loved by another, possessed by another; but also the VIRGIN, that is, metaphysical, transcendental.

Just as Francis and Gabriële Picabia seem to blossom and flourish within the love triangle, so young Marcel draws his passion from the unconventional bonds present in the relationship, the start and source of a life defined as a work of art, whose artistic creations stem from the same wellspring as the choices he makes in his personal and everyday life. Everything is mixed; all is one. "So, if you like," he'll say, "my art is that of living, each second, each breath a piece that is written nowhere, that is neither visual nor cerebral. It's a kind of constant euphoria."

And so, breaking the completeness, the perfection of the triangle by fleeing as he has done is perhaps a significant act in itself. Marcel isn't seeking to possess Gabriële or to eliminate Picabia, whom he loves intensely. What he's doing is entering the fourth dimension.

He's creating a *tableau vivant*. A living painting.

One morning, through the kitchen window of her chocolate-box English cottage, Gabriële hears a noise she knows all too well, elephantine and mechanical. The roar of an engine. *Already?* she thinks. She knew her husband would show up without warning sooner or later.

The engine stops in front of her villa. Gabriële watches as Francis gets out of the car, followed by another man.

Gaby's heart starts to pound. Could Francis have gone looking for Marcel in Germany and brought him here to reform their trio? He's perfectly capable of it, she knows. But then she sees the immense male figure unfolding and extracting itself from the car, dusting itself off and smiling. He's a big man, quite overweight, who could just as easily be thirty as forty years old. Hard to put an age to this fellow in the rather old-fashioned suit. Well! It's certainly not Marcel Duchamp who has made the journey here at Picabia's side.

The two men arrive in a commotion of noise and dust. Dirty, because Francis likes to remove the windshields and mudguards of his cars to gain speed. They're in a riotously good mood, and famished. Gaby improvises a dinner of bread and butter, roast beef, steamed pudding, jam, omelets, pâté, and potatoes. Their stomachs are like bottomless pits. "They ate and drank almost without pausing for breath," she'll remember, "and I just kept on supplying them, all while they carried on a conversation full of inside jokes, references, and mysterious allusions that delighted them both."

The travelers may have robbed her of both her tranquility and the contents of her pantry, but Gabriële finds herself carried along on the wave of their happiness. She studies the new arrival. His name is Guillaume Apollinaire. The poet and resident of the famous Bateau-Lavoir building. The art critic. So *this* is Apollinaire. Everyone knows him by reputation, along with the rest of his crowd, the painters championed by Daniel-Henry Kahnweiler's gallery, Picasso foremost among them. But this is the first time she's ended up at his table. Or rather, that he's ended up at hers.

Francis and Apollinaire tell Gabriële the story of how they decided to come to Hythe on the spur of the moment. In this month of June 1912, with his wife in England and Marcel in Munich, Picabia had found himself alone in Paris, like a lone donkey in a field. Picabia knew Apollinaire, of course, but he'd never had a very good impression of him, as the man consistently failed to mention Francis in his exhibition write-ups, omissions that aggravated the painter greatly. But suddenly, there they were, speaking for the first time. Summers in deserted cities tend to foster encounters that might not otherwise happen. And, as always with Picabia, once the two met, they were inseparable. An "ostentatious rapprochement" intended, perhaps, as revenge on Picasso. As it happened, Marie Laurencin had just left Guillaume, who had no objections to drowning his romantic sorrows in good company—and what better companion in excess than Francis Picabia?

"We met almost every night to smoke opium with friends," Francis will recount. "It was very amusing to listen to dear Guillaume launch into interminable discussions with these little society ladies, particularly the ones in Montmartre and Montparnasse, about the charms of literature or love." They got drunk, roamed the streets, played tag on the Champ de Mars in the middle of the night, went for aimless drives, picked up prostitutes—their sisters in shadowy pleasure—ate and drank until dawn. Guillaume was a gourmand, and with him, life was a party. They talked for hours, whole nights together. About painting. Art. Poetry. Guillaume didn't agree with Picabia's artistic vision, but he was enraptured by the intensity that lay beneath the charming but superficial veneer of jokes, laughter, and hijinks. And Francis, who'd been wary at first of the overly sensitive, overly traditional poet, discovered a man of depth and seriousness, forceful and modern. *In fine*, the two of them spoke the same language—the language of madmen.

Soon enough, Francis had only one thing on his mind: to introduce Guillaume to Gabriële. He was certain Apollinaire would be bowled over by his wife's intelligence. And of course, he couldn't truly love another person if Gaby wasn't there to love them, too.

Eventually the two of them had ended up at the Café de la Paix with the poet Paul-Jean Toulet and Claude Debussy, whom Gabriële knew well. They'd just imbibed a number of cocktails when Picabia suggested to Apollinaire that they leave *immediately* for England; he wanted to introduce him to Gaby.

"All we have to do is drive to Boulogne, and we can take the ferry from there!" The only problem was that Apollinaire was scheduled to give a lecture that very night.

"I can't disappoint the public. It's in two hours. The whole thing is planned already."

"Oh, well that's perfect! I'll kidnap you! Even better—I'll *steal* you!"

And Francis, who never has to be told twice to start up a car's engine, whisked Guillaume away then and there, lecture be damned. The two travelers stopped at Étaples in the Pas-de-Calais, where Derain had spent time painting (two birds, one stone, and all that). Then they'd headed for Boulogne-sur-Mer and taken the boat. They hadn't let Gabriële know; it would be a surprise. For a fellow to be so bent on introducing his wife to a new friend as soon as possible, that wife must be something quite special, Guillaume had thought. He didn't know much about Gabriële, though he'd seen her before, of course.

And now Gabriële finds herself struck by Apollinaire's cheerfulness, the rough-hewn kindliness so at odds with his outsized intellect. He talks endlessly, commenting with equal enthusiasm on a book he read last week and the pâté he's in the midst of devouring, using the same superlatives for both of them. He's charmingly delighted with everything around him, not missing a detail. He fills the space. The journey was wonderful, the villa is wonderful, the curtains, the children— all wonderful. Everything pleases him. He explores the house, admiring every nook and cranny, every knick-knack. The little collages hung on the walls in droves by the villa's owner, like a doll-size exhibition, enrapture him. He pretends to swoon dramatically: *how extraordinary these are! That one is surely worth more than a Picasso!* He's exuberant, facetious. You never know whether to take what he's saying ironically, or seriously, or as the ravings of a lunatic.

She's wary of him initially, because he comes across as a liar.

On first arriving in Hythe, he claims to speak fluent English. Yet, as he's admiring the proprietor's infamous collages, it dawns on her that the poet can't read their titles. He must not actually speak a single bloody word of English! She's still fuming over this when they come to a small drawing with a strange title that she hasn't been able to decipher herself, assuming that it's some kind of Old English, so outdated as to be incomprehensible. But then, suddenly, Apollinaire reels off the title perfectly in French, declaring that it's *obviously* a very old Irish dialect—a translation later proven to be correct. "Needless to say, he was right," Gabriële will recall. "The story of the 'Irish dialect,' embellished and spread around as only Picabia could do it, made the rounds of Paris when we got back home." Guillaume makes Gabriële laugh, but still it takes some time for her fully to appreciate his eccentric, sometimes bombastic intellect.

For that is Apollinaire in a nutshell: all grandiloquence and charm. It's impossible to tell what's truth and what is invention, so endless is the stream of gab and improbable anecdotes, the detailed accounts, the pronouncements on art and life in general. It *is* true that Apollinaire is a tutor at the Bibliothèque Nationale, which explains his impressive and wide-ranging knowledge, Gaby thinks. He's curious, passionate, intense, and he soon comes to feel like part of the family. A family of men able to see reality differently. However, he remains vague about himself, his childhood, his past. His exuberant façade concealing but not dispelling the secret man beneath. He is a man wholly invested in the present, the now. The next discussion, the next project. All of it fills him up, and yet he confides in no one. He's impressed by Gabriële, and she by him. He immediately grasps her extraordinary intelligence, the anti-conformism and humor behind the serious face. A remarkable woman, he thinks. The sort one doesn't meet very often.

At the age of thirty-two, Guillaume Apollinaire is a well-established writer. In addition to the numerous articles and columns he pens, he's also published works of prose including *The Enchanter Rotting* and *The Heresiarch & Co.*, as well as his first collection of poems, *The Bestiary or Orpheus's Retinue* (not to mention his erotic novel *The Eleven Thousand Rods*, published semi-anonymously under his initials, G.A., and sold under the table). He's best known for his art reviews, which are more nuanced snapshots than objective or theoretical critiques. He haunts salons and nurtures close relationships with painters, Picasso foremost among them, but also Max Jacob, Henri "Le Douanier" Rousseau, and Georges Braque, among many others—including Marie Laurencin, with whom he had a stormy affair beginning in 1907. He is a man described by most as being of impressive stature, a keen-eyed, sentimental colossus.

Guillaume has occasionally mentioned Francis to Pablo Picasso, and each time he's sensed an immediate, groundless loathing. The two Spanish painters avoid each other's company, disliking one another on principle. One of them, poor as Job, has spent much of his adult life living hand-to-mouth, while the other was born with a silver spoon in his mouth. Two different worlds.

Picasso and Apollinaire were once the best of friends—until a nasty business became the source of a thousand rumors, the talk of sophisticated dinner tables and countless inches of newsprint. Gabriële and Francis have never been completely clear on the details of what happened, but tonight they'll hear the whole story of the "theft of the *Mona Lisa*"—and straight from the mouth of one of its main characters.

This is how it goes.

Apollinaire meets Picasso in 1905, and they're immediately inseparable. They're deeply fond of one another, supportive, almost like brothers. But on August 22, 1911, the wall of the Salon Carré, where the da Vinci masterpiece *La Joconde* had hung, is bare. Pandemonium erupts. The Louvre's staff, arriving in the morning before the museum opens, are aghast: the

Mona Lisa has been taken. An investigation is opened, and the already unbelievable story becomes even more bizarre when one trail followed by the police leads to the poet Guillaume Apollinaire. It turns out that, four years earlier, he was mixed up in a matter involving some Iberian statuettes stolen from the famous museum. His secretary at the time, one Guy Piéret, was the true culprit behind the shady acquisition. He'd then given the valuable objects to Apollinaire who, without giving much thought to their provenance, had sold them to Pablo Picasso. Those very statuettes had inspired Picasso to paint his *Brothel of Avignon*, which would become the luminous *Young Ladies of Avignon* (named after a street in Barcelona's red-light district, the "Carrer d'Avinyó," and nothing to do with the French city of popish fame). The result of all this was that Guillaume Apollinaire's name was registered with the French police, and comes up again in August 1911, during the investigation into the theft of the *Mona Lisa*.

Apollinaire, who has nothing to do with the robbery, is nonetheless alarmed by the prospect of the old statuette business being raked up again. In early September, he asks Pablo Picasso, then in Spain, to return to Paris immediately and get rid of those damned Iberian statues once and for all. The two friends initially plan to throw them into the Seine, but Apollinaire can't bring himself to do it, so, on the morning of September 5, 1911 (two weeks after the disappearance of the *Mona Lisa*), he has them dropped off anonymously at the *Paris-Journal* newspaper offices, so that they can be discreetly returned to the museum.

But the police have their eye on Apollinaire. On September 7, he's arrested and detained at La Santé Prison to be formally questioned. A "sensation of death" grips the prisoner, who feels as if he's being "destroyed." After several days, the investigating judge summons Picasso to be questioned along with Apollinaire. In the judge's chambers, the painter, interrogated about his links to the accused, looks away from Guillaume and declares firmly, "I've never seen this man before."

In the absence of proof, Apollinaire is freed. But he remains devastated by Picasso's attitude and by his time in La Santé, which will inspire a future poetry collection, *Alcohols*. Recounting the whole sorry tale to his then-lover in a 1915 letter, Apollinaire will call his former friend "a great artist but utterly without scruples."

The happy chance that brings friendships into being notwithstanding, it's worth noting that Francis and Guillaume become friends at around the same time the latter's relationship with Picasso is ending.

After they've listened to the stranger-than-fiction story of "the theft of *La Joconde*," during which Francis hasn't been at all displeased to hear his rival Picasso characterized as a coward and a backstabber, Gabriële suggests that they go out. She takes the two men to a sort of rural music hall being held in a circus tent. One by one, past-their-prime singers made up to look like American stars, performers both comical and visibly depressed, do their best to earn applause in the dust-laden beams of pinkish spotlights. The men find the whole thing uproariously funny—and all the more so because they don't understand a word of the artists' speeches. Gabriële, seated between Guillaume and Francis (as is only proper), acts as interpreter, translating a word or a phrase on the fly, first to her right and then her left, both men clamoring for explanations. They applaud each act wildly, as delighted as if they were at the premiere of a Raymond Roussel play.

"After the show, we came across the performers in a little bar on the pier," Gabriële will remember. "In their beach clothes and sandals, they looked quite poor, but they continued to laugh, dance, hug, and kiss one another just as they'd done onstage, though now it was only for each other, and it was clear that they meant it. The sight of such purity and good humor, so unexpected and so very un-French, had already charmed me the previous evening, and the obvious pleasure the new arrivals took in it, too, only made me happier still." As an old lady, Gabriële will recall that "that English evening completely devoid of art and literature, combined with a beautiful, warm summer night, has remained vivid in my memory, amid the fog of the distant past, like a rare and precious jewel."

The next morning, Guillaume and Francis, unable to stay still, decide that they must return to Paris immediately and convince Gabriële to come back with them. Their belongings and the children are duly packed up. Gabriële is one of those individuals able to live every day as a potential adventure, never knowing exactly who they'll dine with that night, or in what city they'll go to bed, or who they might marry on a drunken whim. It's certainly one way of living. She leaves Hythe with no regret, and much earlier than planned. Going away for a proper rest, when you're Francis Picabia's wife, is all but impossible.

The family takes the ferry across the Channel, Gabriële watching the English coastline recede into the distance—along with Marcel's letter, which she left in a dresser drawer at the villa in Hythe. It was a deliberate act. The words are inside her, along with the turmoil they've caused. For her only, in her only.

The new trio pauses to refresh themselves in a little café near the Boulogne-sur-Mer pier after the crossing. Years later, Gabriële will recount the men's exchange in detail, describing Apollinaire as anxious, resistant to Francis's artistic evolution:

"'It's inhuman, incomprehensible art, alien to feeling . . . ' he said. 'It risks being decorative and nothing else.'

"'Are red and blue incomprehensible?' Francis shot back. 'Isn't it possible to understand circles and triangles, volumes and colors just as easily as we understand this table or this cup?'

"'And is it not rational,' I added, 'to envision a use of color and pure form that are to the visual what music is to sound?'"

Back in Paris, the trio remains inseparable. Instead of Marcel, it's now Guillaume who shows up at the avenue

Charles-Floquet apartment each night, becoming "the usual companion in all sorts of outings both wholesome and otherwise, all the unplanned excursions for which he was always ready." Marcel, still in Germany, has journeyed to Berlin, where he posts letters to his brothers: "I'm writing to you in a so-called literary café . . . there are mostly a lot of women here with nothing literary about them."

In July, Apollinaire, Francis, and Gabriële attend the "Prince of Poets" ceremony together, a lovely tradition dating back to Clément Marot and Ronsard that consists, as its name indicates, of electing a "prince" of French poets for life. Leconte de Lisle and Paul Verlaine have worn the laurel wreath in the past, and the man who had held it since 1898, the Parnassian Léon Dierx, died on June 11. A vote was held to name Dierx's successor, and the Symbolist poet Paul Fort was elected. On July 12, the literary and artistic paper *Comœdia* marks the occasion by holding an enormous banquet in the gardens of the Bois de Boulogne, near the Luna Park fairground, and Guillaume Apollinaire invites the Picabias to celebrate the new prince.

After the banquet, at which the tables are afloat on a papier-mâché sea, the guests scatter into the fairground, which glitters with thrill-rides and animals in costume. Giddy from their Dionysian evening, the three friends pose in front of a photographer's hut made to look like the deck of a ship complete with railing and life-preserver. Gabriële stands between her husband and the bow-tied Apollinaire, wearing a hat and a vague smile.

A marvelous three-headed hydra. The new trio immortalized on film.

They haven't known each other for very long, but in this photo, this split-second frozen for eternity, they look as if they've been friends forever. "I never had a companion jollier, or wittier, or with as much zest for life as Apollinaire," Francis will say. Gabriële loves the way Guillaume laughs, covering his mouth with his hand as if in apology. She loves his compulsive inclination to create constant astonishment, to scorn the conventional, to seek out the bizarre. "His real genius lay in the choice he made to surround himself with words and things and people he would then imbue with his own precious values and reasons for being, all through a kind of sleight-of-hand," she will write.

The true strength of Francis and Guillaume's friendship lies in conflict; it's their disagreements that stimulate and enrich them. Unlike Francis and Duchamp, whose relationship is like that of two brothers bound by a mutual artistic vision, Apollinaire and Francis aren't brothers—they're enemies who love spending time together. "Being close to Picabia meant that Guillaume discovered an aspect of the evolution of art that made him very nervous, but the force and momentum of which he couldn't deny," Gabriële will recall. Together, they have a thousand ideas, a thousand arguments to champion, both of them thrilled by the artistic atmosphere that exists between them, where every thought is ripe for being taken apart and put back together again. They butt heads and question each other; they joke and get closer. A powerful energy binds the two men to each other, as well as to Gabriële, whose background and education have made her into a formidable rhetorician; as she will later put it, " . . . I was fully equipped for these debates, and I'd take my part in them by providing references and comparisons." One day, Gaby will remember, Guillaume Apollinaire announces that he's thought of a name for this new form of painting: "There is Cubism and there is Futurism, and you will now stand alongside them as representatives of Orphism." He's including several painters in the blanket term "you," including Robert Delaunay, Fernand Léger, Francis Picabia, and Marcel Duchamp. Gabriële knows she had a little something to do with this brainwave, but unlike most people, she chooses to rewrite history to minimize her role. In truth, multiple accounts suggest that the term "Orphism" was invented by Gabriële herself and then borrowed by Apollinaire. In his book *Le Flux et le Fixe*, Jean-Nöel von der Weid calls the term

"Orphism" "[a] neologism coined on the prompting, it's said, of a young avant-garde musician and former pupil of Busoni in Berlin, Gabriële Buffet, the first wife of Picabia." But what is the point, at the end of the day, of rendering unto Caesar what is Caesar's, if Caesar himself doesn't want it? What counts is that Apollinaire, in defining the new style of painting, places it firmly within Gabriële's territory: music. Because the mythological hero Orpheus, who descends into Hades in search of his wife, is a musician.

The trio's sometimes-humorous, sometimes-serious verbal jousting eventually gives rise to a plan that Picabia has already been pondering for several months: a grand dissident exhibition, to provide wider exposure for the Cubist aesthetic. An event that will help anchor and consolidate the movement's development and bring together a number of painters from "outside the Rue Vignon group," 28 rue Vignon being the address of the Galerie Kahnweiler, where Picasso, Braque, Gris, and Derain—who also published Apollinaire's 1909 novel *The Enchanter, Rotting*—display and sell their work. Picabia is determined that Cubism won't belong solely to Picasso, and intends to make that point by holding a Cubist exhibition without the creators of Cubism. His obsession with Picasso is growing, starting to gnaw away at his brain. It's damaging, but it also compels him to act, undertake, organize. And by contributing to the project, he's putting on a show of support for his new friends and further detaching himself from his old ones. Apollinaire is preparing to give a major talk, one intended to systematize this new artistic vision that exists intuitively and spontaneously in Picasso and Braque, and to create a theoretical framework for it. For their part, Metzinger and Gleizes are currently putting the finishing touches on their book, *On Cubism*, set to be published in late 1912.

Apollinaire and Francis decide that their exhibition will take place in October, boldly asserting itself as an alternative to the Salon d'Automne. Their announcement of the event triggers a sudden avalanche of activity, and Gabriële is at the heart of it. About this period, she will write, "Thus began a series of meetings to establish a firm plan for this project that had started out as something quite vague, merely one of a hundred more or less ridiculous propositions of the sort Picabia and Apollinaire were always flinging out when mired in their discussions of paradox. These meetings always took place at the avenue Charles-Floquet apartment where we were living at that time; decisions had to be made about painters, pieces, location . . . "

Gabriële, whose English holiday was cut so brutally short, decides to leave the avenue Charles-Floquet flat, a hive of activity, to its own agitation, retreating to the quiet restfulness of Étival. She'll leave the children to enjoy the Jura, far from the August heat of Paris, and travel back and forth between the capital and the mountains according to her whims—and Francis's ability to manage without her.

Gabriële needs to be alone so she can think about Marcel.

14
ADAM AND EVE

Since Marcel's unexpected declaration of love over the phone, the triangular game being played by Duchamp and the Picabias has changed—precisely because those words of love were not playful in the least, and have brought an unaccustomed element of seriousness to the whole situation. Marcel is waiting for a response to his letter. What should she tell him? She *is* attracted to him, to his youth and disarming beauty. He makes her feel alive. Gaby would like to have it all: the intensity of forbidden passion *and* the dreamy lightness of an unconventional relationship. But Francis Picabia, with all his flaws, and against all logic, is the only man to whom she can devote her entire life.

In his June letter, Marcel begged to see Gabriële alone. So far, she hasn't given in. She writes to him about the evenings spent with Apollinaire, about the exhibition taking shape for October (which they've decided to call the Salon de la Section d'Or, or Golden Section), about Étival with its scents of forest humus in the autumn and hay in the summer, the floral aromas of pollen in the spring and the smell of woodsmoke in the winter. She describes the trees whose songs she alone can hear, the cathedral-like pines and the absolute silence of the night, more intense than all the ringing and clanging of a Parisian evening. She encourages him to meet with Kandinsky. She imagines him in Munich, standing before Cranach's paintings, propping his elbows on brasserie counters and sharing steins of beer with the anonymous crowds. She knows Germany so well; through Marcel she experiences once again the freedom of Berlin, so vivid and so dear in her memory.

And all the same, she dares to write at the bottom of the page that she misses him, and at last she suggests that they meet in the Jura. She has to go back to Paris for a few days, she explains to Marcel, because Picabia is calling for her, he needs her—he *always* needs her. She'll leave the children with her mother. Her train journey, she writes, will include a stop at the station in Andelot, at the junction of the Paris and Étival lines, and she'll have a stopover of an hour. One hour when she'll be alone, because that's what he wants. Words that knock on the narrow door. But the rendezvous is impossible. Marcel won't be able to get there from Munich, and Gabriële knows it. She chooses the game. The meeting she's dangling in front of him, the way medieval ladies used to drop their handkerchiefs to see whether they'd be picked up, is merely a lure, an illusion.

Except that there, on the platform at the station in Andelot, is Marcel.

Gabriële steps off the train. She can't believe her eyes. You have to imagine, today, the difficulty of traveling from Munich to Andelot in 1912.

It's madness.

For a single stolen hour.

To know.

To *live*.

An *idée fixe*: to see Gabriële alone. Marcel didn't hesitate for a moment before undertaking the forty-eight-hour journey. As Thomas Girst, a future biographer, will recount, "Duchamp rode third class [on] an over 700-kilometer stretch that entailed countless station transfers, one that would shuttle [him] from Lake Constance to Austria into Switzerland, past Lake Geneva and through the mountains."

Gabriële will not speak of this moment until the very end of her life. When all the other protagonists are dead, and she is the last survivor of an unparalleled era.

Andelot Station is in the middle of nowhere, and it's deserted. It's a warm evening, but growing cooler as the sun goes down. Marcel and Gaby sit on a little wooden bench. A trunk abandoned, stoic, on the platform. There's no secluded corner, nowhere to go eat something or have a drink, to give any kind of structure or a semblance of context or purpose to this insane rendezvous. No stage directions. The stark setting is cold comfort for warm hearts.

After an hour, the train for Paris arrives. The situation grows larger than both of them, every word weighted with magnetic intensity, every move becoming symbolic of something else.

Gabriële hesitates. Lets the train leave without her.

The next train, too. And the next.

Until there are no more trains.

Night has fallen, and they're the only two people in the world.

Gaby teases Marcel at first. As she remembers years later, "It was a kind of madness, idiocy, to travel from Munich to the Jura to pass a few hours of the night with me."

But after a little while she stops poking fun, because she can't conceal the way her heart is pounding.

Maybe they spoke of nothing but the two of them.

Of the couple they could never be.

Of bodies in motion, but captive.

Of hearts confounded by not always beating in the same place.

Maybe Marcel kissed Gabriële.

Maybe Gabriële kissed Marcel.

They'd embraced before. Many times. But not like this. Not all kisses are the same.

This whole journey, this time together, stolen in the name of a spiritual love, a Gidean love without flesh and without saliva.

A pure rendezvous.

A living painting.

"It was utterly inhumane to sit next to a being whom you sense desires you so much and not even to have been touched," Gabriële will remember. "Above all, I thought, I must be very careful with everything I say to him because he understands things in quite an alarming way, in an absolute way."

Early morning.
The rumble of the dawn train.
Strands of hair escaping the chignon, strands that didn't resist the night, loose and wild.
Gaby takes the train.
Marcel stays beside her until the absolute last moment, helping her aboard through the small, narrow door of the train car.
A last press of their hands.
The feel of skin.
This is ours alone.
We seal the vow.

Marcel Duchamp, left alone, slowly breathes in the air of Andelot Station. Air turned combustible. Then he takes the first train in the opposite direction. And returns to Germany, a thousand kilometers away. *Sad Young Man on a Train.*

* * *

Station platforms
Are silent nowheres
Men slowing, easing
Dropping their masks
Women cool and open as basins
Their flames turned low
in the night, gentle farewells,
melodious boys

Station platforms

Are silent nowheres
Where men traveling empty-handed
Dare forbidden things
And persuade language
To fight on, in a green box,
The next train of chance
Carrying far and wide
Nought but the eyes

During the month of August 1912, Marcel Duchamp produces his famous oil painting *The Bride*. It depicts a body broken down into its organs, viscera, and veins, arranged into a kind of strange mechanical apparatus that takes up the whole canvas. The browns, flesh tones, and shades of apricot and purple are similar to those used in Cranach's nudes, the ones Marcel spent so much time studying at the Pinakotek. "I love those Cranachs," he'll say later. "I love them. Cranach the old man. The tall nudes. That nature and substance of his nudes inspired me for the flesh colour."

He leaves Munich almost as alone as he was when he arrived. He visits the Museum of Technology, with its more than seven thousand objects in wooden display cases tracing the history of machines. He also becomes acquainted with the work of Karl Valentin, an artist who performs in Munich bistros as a clown and musician, playing twenty instruments at once, all by himself, using a mechanism of his own invention. Valentin also recently put together a humorous exhibit featuring all kinds of ridiculous objects. At the entrance to this satirical museum, the visitor was warned: *People without a sense of humor not allowed.* Objects on mock-serious display included "An old broom"—directly next to "The *Mona Lisa*, the painting recently stolen from the Louvre in Paris."

Returning to France in early October 1912, Marcel makes a beeline for the Picabias, where his first act is to present Francis with *The Bride*. A gift to a beloved rival, intended to strike a balance: *I give, in exchange for what I have taken from you. Secretly.* A subtly carnal gift, as writer Thomas Girst will later observe: "In *Bride*, however, he applies the paint with tactile sensuality, sometimes spreading it with his bare fingers. On one occasion, he will call *Bride* the one painting he preferred among all he had produced."

The trio reforms instantly, with the same enthusiasm as before. The separation has changed nothing; together, they feel as if their bodies are floating above everyone else's. And yet, they aren't exactly the same people they used to be. Francis is grieving the death of his grandfather, Alphonse Davanne. Though he refrains from putting on a show of his pain, Gabriële and Marcel know that Francis has lost the guiding figure of his childhood, and he's devastated. Alphonse is mourned with great pomp and ceremony and honored, as the former president of the Société Française de Photographie, for his achievements as a researcher and inventor. Marcel and Gaby are there for Francis on the day of the burial, bracing him and supporting him, Andelot Station their own private secret—a secret deeply buried, but an act of silent rebellion nonetheless.

Duchamp, too, has changed. Made cynical by the art world's backroom dealings, its authoritarian collectivity, and humiliated by the Salon des Indépendants' rejection of his painting, he's in a state of total revolt. Like Arthur Rimbaud, who stopped writing overnight, Marcel decides he's done with painting. He wants to work, to get in touch with normal life. Reality. The harshness of labor. Biographer Bernard Marcadé will later call it "a kind of intellectual posturing against the manual servitude of the artist." Gabriële and Francis have their doubts. How is Marcel, whom they see as a bit of a social misfit, going to handle a nine-to-five office job? Who would hire him? He couldn't sell anything to anyone. The Picabias cast about for a solution, some easy position that would enable Marcel to earn money while still remaining in his bubble. Francis asks his maternal uncle Maurice Davanne, the one who's a curator at the Sainte-Geneviève Library, to find Marcel a job as a librarian.

"I was twenty-five years old," Marcel will recall in an

interview years later. "I'd been told a man should earn his own living, and I believed it."

The Sainte-Geneviève Library is located on the Place du Panthéon. Several times a week, Gaby walks up the rue Soufflot, in this quarter that reminds her of her studies at the Schola Cantorum, bringing lunch to Marcel. They sit on one of the stone benches outside the library, and the young librarian tells Gaby about the rare books he's able to consult. He's passionately interested in the ancient philosophers and in treatises on optics and perspective, including those of Jean du Treuil, Jean-François Niceron, and Abraham Bosse. Marcel and Gaby make a game out of deciphering the names etched into the façade of the library. It's some time before they figure out that the names' placement on the wall corresponds to the location, inside the library, of the shelves dedicated to those authors' work.

The Salon d'Automne opens on October 1 beneath the glass roof of the Grand Palais. The borrowing of these premises for the exhibition has stirred up controversy; one Pierre Lampué, a fifth-arrondissement city councilor for the district of Val-de-Grâce, called for the event to be prohibited, horrified by the negative influence of Cubism on respectable people. He didn't carry the day, but the Cubists have been relegated to an inconspicuous, dimly lit room—the latter in the hopes that the low lighting will help lessen the shock to people viewing the art inside. Two canvases by Francis Picabia are on display, including *Dances at the Spring*.

At the vernissage, Gabriële ends up in conversation with František Kupka, whose *Fugue in Two Colors* has been hung near Francis's paintings. Kupka is explaining to Gabriële that his work plays on line and color the way Bach's music plays on cadence and sound, when suddenly they hear a visitor standing in front of one of Francis's canvases cry out: "If I could get my hands on the painter who did this, I'd kill him!"

The next day, Gaby reads in *Le Petit Parisien*, "The record for unbridled imagination is held this year by [Monsieur] Picabia." And so the Salon d'Automne proceeds with its usual batch of polemics and more or less fanatical debates, conducted in the pages of newspapers and magazines. But the real event of the season, the one all of Paris is awaiting with bated breath and which promises to deliver the most violent skirmishes, is the Salon de la Section d'Or—its name coined by Marcel Duchamp's older brother, Jacques Villon, who read the term in both Leonardo da Vinci's *Treatise on Painting* and Luca Pacioli's *The Divine Proportion*. The *nombre d'or*, or golden ratio, corresponds to a geometric ideal, a cornerstone of aesthetic theory. The members of the Puteaux Group have chosen it as a way to avoid the "Cubist" label, to keep from aligning themselves with the crowd, to distance themselves from all the other "*—ism*" movements and groups. Their exhibition will deal in absolute beauty: the golden section.

The Salon de la Section d'Or opens at 9:00 P.M. on October 9, at Floury's gallery at 64 bis rue de la Boétie, one week after the Salon d'Automne vernissage. It's Picabia who has financed the project and chosen the site, delighted to be using the premises of a former furniture-seller and not a "traditional" gallery. The space is unusual, iconoclastic—and perfectly suited to the dimensions of the canvases on display.

One hundred and eighty-five paintings are exhibited, including several produced by Marcel in Munich. His *Nude Descending a Staircase* is finally shown in Paris. There are also thirteen of Francis Picabia's creations, including five new ones, painted that summer, as yet unseen by the public. The exhibition is a collective display of modern paintings, all chosen without a jury, without a selection committee. Thirty artists are exhibiting their work, including the Duchamp brothers, František Kupka, Fernand Léger, Juan Gris, and Robert Delaunay. Ten thousand invitations have been sent out, on the subject of which

Apollinaire has written a short article entitled *"Jeunes peintres, ne vous frappez pas!"*—"Young Painters, Never Fear!"

Guillaume also delivers his lecture, in which he explains Orphic Cubism to his audience, a mixture of young artists, art enthusiasts, critics, and journalists. It is "the second great trend in modern painting," he says. "It is the art of painting new wholes with elements taken not from visual reality, but wholly created by the artist and endowed by him with a powerful reality."

"I'm sure," Gabriële will remember, "it was on this same occasion that he quoted an aphorism that one of us had tossed out in an embryonic, questioning form during one of our usual discussions, which went something like this: the new style of painting is to representative painting what music is to poetry; the one can neither replace nor eliminate the raison d'être of the other."

One of us, says Gabriële, the ever self-effacing Gabriële . . .

It's the biggest Cubist exhibition ever held.

Gabriële participates in the work of planning the Section d'Or, of course, but as usual, she vanishes the moment the party begins. With her stage-director's soul, she's perfected the art of slipping backstage before the curtain goes up. Having worked to the point of exhaustion to produce the salon with Francis, she skips the vernissage and retreats to Étival the moment the calendar shows October. A strange woman. Gabriële's escapes reveal a deep truth about her. She's at the heart of everything, working physically and mentally, communicating and arranging, suggesting and supporting, reviving flagging spirits and untangling knots, refining ideas—but when at last the fruits of all her toil are brought to light, she's never there, leaving the men to bask in the glow. Leaving the men to have their egos stroked.

Yet Francis does beg her to stay. This is no order, nor a

demonstration of his masculine authority. No. He's afraid. He needs her by his side, he insists. This salon is very different from all the others; it's he who's bearing the responsibility for it. Without her, he'll never be able to face the crowds of journalists and curious spectators. Gabriële kisses him, reassures him, and promises to send all the energy he needs from her mountain hideaway. And then she boards her train, baggage and children in hand. In the Jura, she can breathe. She can rest her fingers at last on the keys of the grand piano in the dining room. Her soul, though refined in the sophisticated salons of Paris, remains that of a *montagnarde*. She needs rocky terrain, the sky blending with the earth, pine needles and sturdy boots laced up past the ankles, meals eaten in silence after the strenuous physical effort of the hike and the climb. Here, she cleanses herself of Paris.

On the evening of the Section d'Or vernissage, after the children have been put to bed, Gabriële sits by the fire with her mother. She smiles, thinking that at this very instant she should be wearing an evening gown, corseted and perfumed, explaining the concept of Orphism to a bunch of art critics. But she's four hundred kilometers away from Paris, the logs snapping in the fireplace, the room filled with the scent of pine, faces glowing in the firelight, and there's nowhere in the world she'd rather be than here, in her childhood home. Never has she reveled more deeply in silence, in tranquility, in the warmth of the fire, than in knowing she's avoided an obligation she didn't think she had a prayer of escaping. It's a malady Francis and Gabriële share—the impulse to flee situations imposed by circumstance. It's how they both test and luxuriate in their freedom, even at the risk of angering their friends.

In the middle of the night, as Gabriële lies asleep in a big bed with sheets warmed by hot stones taken from the fireplace, a car horn blares.

Gabriële, who's never totally surprised now by the sound of

an automobile arriving from somewhere far off, is astonished. Francis should be shepherding everyone to a late supper at the Closerie des Lilas right now, to celebrate the end of the vernissage. It *can't* be his car rattling up the road toward the house; that would mean he's missed his own opening night.

Gripped by anxiety, her heart thumping, Gabriële gets out of bed to watch the car noisily approaching the house. A light goes on; her mother's been woken up, too, and is stepping out into the cold, her husband's shotgun at the ready—nothing unusual in that, for a woman living alone in the middle of nowhere.

Three figures emerge from the car, hollering like sailors passing the Straits of Gibraltar, covered in dust, oil, and grease. Gabriële and her mother recognize Francis's voice, of course; he's shouting about his empty stomach. He's followed by Marcel Duchamp and Guillaume Apollinaire. From the open front door, Madame Buffet, pragmatic as ever, tells them to get inside before they let all the heat out of the house, while Gabriële, speechless, gathers back to her (vital, irreplaceable) feminine bosom her three men, her three boys. They're cheerful but exhausted, and as hungry as when they arrived in Hythe. Gaby goes to the kitchen to whip up a cheese omelet, watching the first rays of dawn streak the sky beyond the window, laughing to herself. *My husband is completely off his rocker*, she muses. It's at moments like these, her soul stirred irresistibly to life, that she's reminded of how madly she loves this man.

Bellies full, warmed by the fire, the three men stagger upstairs to collapse in the house's various bedrooms. Guillaume isn't even aware of falling asleep next to a little brown-haired boy—Pancho, Gaby's son, the child utterly nonplussed by the appearance of this ogre in the night. It's not until the next morning, when the boys have recovered from their nocturnal odyssey, that—over cups of strong coffee artfully brewed by Madame Buffet *mère*—they tell the tale of their desertion.

The night before the Section d'Or vernissage, Francis had felt his anxiety mounting until, as was usual with him, it exploded into one of his spur-of-the-moment impulses. The truth was, he wanted to be with Gabriële. Without her, his heart beat too fast, until it felt as if it might burst out of his chest. Without her, he thought he might die then and there.

So, right in the middle of the vernissage cocktail reception, he seized Marcel and Guillaume by the arms, plucking their glasses of champagne out of their hands and setting them down on a table, and all but frogmarched them out of the crowded room. In front of the gallery, with groups of guests still arriving, Picabia asked his two friends to wait for him there; his new Peugeot 141 was parked on the rue La Boétie. Marcel and Guillaume waited obediently, of course, knowing there was no point in asking questions. Francis pulled up a few moments later and bundled them into the car like so much luggage.

"Where are we going?" Apollinaire asked.

"To see the Jura," his kidnapper replied.

Marcel was relieved. He hated vernissages, cocktail parties, and all those superficial events requiring him to make a good impression, to sell himself. And of course, he'd always been delighted by the unexpected. That famous "constant euphoria." He was the first to get into Francis's car, grabbing one of the grayish driving blankets as he did so. Thinking, privately, that this wouldn't actually be his first time discovering the Jura—for that matter, not even his first time traveling there impulsively. Cherishing the thought that neither of his companions had any idea about that. Eager to see Gaby again. To surprise her. And pleased, too, that it would be in the company of these two friends, his adopted big brothers—men who, unlike his real brothers, actually respected and admired him.

Guillaume, of course, was always ready to crisscross France at night in a screaming metal death-trap. Nothing better. "One can be a poet in every domain," he'd said. "You just have to be bold and seek out new adventures." For him, the words weren't just a figure of speech.

The route was an extremely dangerous one, and they'd

driven all night in a lashing rainstorm. Exhilarated by the danger, "Apollinaire and Picabia challenged each other, egged each other on, shouted bizarre, often ungrammatical encouragements, punctuated at the appropriate moments by Duchamp, with his clear, precise voice." The roads were steep, sometimes almost impassable, muddy and pocked with unseen holes. They'd narrowly avoided crashing more than once.

Yet they were sure of themselves, filled with joy.

Invincible.

Guillaume had sung a little song of his own composition again and again, as if to ward off bad luck:

Tanguy du Gana
N'as-tu pas vu mon gas
Qui jouait de la trombone
Qui jouait de la flute à mes gas
Qui jouait de la flute!

Nearing their destination, Picabia had explained to his companions that the region where Gabriële lives is called "the Zone," a designation going back to the eighteenth century. After a good word had been put in by the philosopher Voltaire, who'd settled in Ferney, the king of France had, in 1776, granted the region of Gex—in which Étival is located—the status of "free zone." A free zone benefited from more relaxed trade regulations, particularly with bordering countries. Apollinaire would allude to a memory of this particularity in a calligram: "And I smoke Zone tobacco"—in other words, cheap tobacco.

It may be the Zone, but in this year of 1912, electricity has already reached Étival. They were surprised, as they drove through the village, to see carbon-filament bulbs glowing in the windows of the houses—an unexpected touch of modernity for such a remote corner of the mountains—an early arrival explained by the recent construction of small hydroelectric power stations in this part of the Jura, Apollinaire had told them, knowledgeable as always.

Now, Guillaume is especially delighted to have made the acquaintance of Laurence Buffet, née Jussieu. The matriarch. Gabriële's *alma mater*.

"With that supreme adaptability that came so naturally to him, Guillaume matched his tone to my mother's, drawing her out and keeping her chatting," Gabriële will recall. "She was delighted to trot out all the old reminiscences we didn't usually show much interest in. She and Guillaume seemed to be charmed by one another, which pleased me greatly, but the thing that *really* surprised me was hearing Apollinaire tell anecdotes about the finest minds of my mother's time as if he'd been there, too."

Gabriële can't believe it; Guillaume's even familiar with the work of her grandfather Jussieu, who wrote short volumes exalting civic virtues. Up to now, she thought his erudition was largely a figment of his incredible imagination. She's often told Francis that she adores Apo's ability to make his friends believe that the crazy things he makes up are true. And she's always found it endearing how upset he becomes when anyone questions the veracity of his observations, because really, at the end of the day, who cares if they're true or false; in the moment, they're poetry. But in talking with Madame Buffet, Guillaume has proven to Gabriële how wrong she was to take his scholarliness so lightly. She will write, "I never again dared assume he was putting on an act when he gave us the exact recipe for the soy sauce used in China to prepare the newborn girls they ate like grain-fed chickens."

The little colony quickly settles into a routine.

During the day, everyone works or takes long walks. Whenever it stops raining, they set out on exploratory expeditions toward the "free" boundary, which is also the border with Switzerland, bundling up in the heavy sheepskin coats hanging in the entryway and sweaters dating from the last century. Returning soaked from these mountain tramps, they settle down by the fire to play with the children at *jonchet*, a game of skill similar to the Mikado, involving little sticks made of wood, bone, or ivory. Then they troop into the kitchen to cook, directed by Apollinaire, who dons a servant's apron and rolls up his sleeves, while Marcel, delighted to be useful, peels vegetables with intense concentration. These activities keep their hands busy and free up their minds; they talk of poetry, painting, revolution. Perhaps the sweetest hours are the ones spent in shared silence, Apo and Gabriële reading quietly while Marcel and Francis sketch. They rediscover something of childhood here in Étival; they're like four brothers and sisters, or four cousins, lazing in the pleasant boredom of a family holiday. Marcel captures Guillaume's profile on one page of a school notebook, pipe in mouth, his gaze turned inward.

As evening approaches, Laurence Buffet sets the table with a feast of regional foods: "morels, wild game, the most delicious cream, wine from the plains—the Low Countries, as they say in the mountains." Every day is a banquet. Apo all but swoons with ecstasy at the sight of the bags filled with delicacies brought back from the market. On long walks during which they try to pry fossils out of the hillsides with a small hammer, Guillaume and Francis lay out a plan for *Aesthetic Meditations*, a book on Cubism that Apollinaire dreams of publishing. Francis offers to finance it, and the deal is done in the rain, sitting in the middle of a field full of cows, the bouquet of gentian flowers they've plucked starting to wilt beside them. Shaking hands on the agreement during a brief pause in the downpour, they hear the village's church bell striking the Angelus.

They could happily live this way for a hundred years.

Marcel and Gabriële brush against one another in the hallways, heavy and light with their secret. People tend to become braver when they're not in the normal world, and Étival isn't the normal world. It's an island. Whenever they find themselves alone together for a brief moment, time ceases to exist; the memory of Andelot, so chaste, burns them, and one evening

Gaby clasps it all to her. The whole of Marcel Duchamp. Flesh and bone.

Laurence, the elderly matriarch, watches over these young souls in turmoil, not at all angry that a bunch of rowdy Parisians have come to disrupt her Jurassian solitude. She turns a blind eye to their mischievous behavior, which sometimes veers over the line into rudeness; for example, the three young men make fun, openly and nastily, of the paintings done by her son Jean Challié, Gabriële's brother, which Madame Buffet has on display throughout the house. Though he wasn't present during their visit, his influence hung over the group, for Jean has recently, and publicly, declared his opposition to Cubism. As a result, his canvases become the target of pointed insults—and salad dressing. Which is still kinder than the fate that was reserved for old Aunt Alphonsine's work. Francis and Gabriële exulted in the sight and smell of burning oil. An exorcism. Like merciless demons, they liquidated their heritage.

After dinner, they decamp to the lounge, staying there late into the night. It's "a large, charming room, unpretentious and rustic—but with an *authentic* rusticity, with rough, exposed ceiling beams and a hooded fireplace burning enormous pine logs, the overall impression being perfectly "'romantic.'" Guillaume enjoys declaiming for his companions the verses he's written that day, standing in the middle of the room and speaking sometimes softly, sometimes passionately, playing with the melody of the rhymes. There, in that candlelit mountain room, they attend the iconoclastic mass of Apollinaire's words.

As Gaby will recall in her memoir, "He recited several poems from the collection *Alcohols*, which hadn't yet been published at the time, and one of them, which told the story of his life, his childhood and misfortunes, made a deep impression on my mother:

There it is the young street and you still but a small child
Your mother always dresses you in blue and white
You are very pious and with Rene Dalize your oldest crony
Nothing delights you more than church ceremony
Now you walk in Paris alone among the crowd
Herds of bellowing buses hemming you about
Anguish of love parching you within
As though you were never to be loved again

"My mother asked him the title of the poem. 'It isn't finished,' he replied, "and it doesn't have a name yet." Then, suddenly and very sweetly, he turned to her and said, 'I shall call it "Zone."'"

The opening poem in the collection *Alcohols*, which will be published the following year in 1913, finds its name in the heart of the Jura:

In the end you are weary of this ancient world
This morning the bridges are bleating Eiffel Tower oh herd
Weary of living in Roman antiquity and Greek

Each day the four friends say to each other, *We'll go back tomorrow*. Paris is waiting for them; they have to arrange for the Section d'Or paintings to be taken down, compile press clippings, take stock of the exhibition. It's Apollinaire who has the most pressing engagements; he's scheduled to give a series of lectures on the subject of Cubism. But every day, it's Apo who comes up with a reason not to leave the Jura. Instead of spending two days in Étival, they spend two weeks, as attested to by the various postcards they send to friends. A snippet in the *Paris-Journal* announces on October 19 that "Guillaume Apollinaire, who is ill, will be unable to give his lecture at the Université Populaire this evening, and will be replaced by Olivier Hourcade." And in the newspaper *Gil Blas*, the art critic Louis Vauxcelles, after having noted sardonically that Apollinaire begged off due to a cold, hints that he knows perfectly well why he's shirking his responsibilities: "The rat was last seen riding away in the automobile of a certain gilded Cubist . . . "

It isn't the first time Apollinaire has played hooky. That very evening at dinner, Francis and Apo regale Madame Buffet—who's torn between laughter and dismay—with stories of all the missed lectures. Sweeping the poet away from his obligations is one of Francis Picabia's favorite games. They tell the tale like a comedy duo:

"Another time—we were having dinner together then, too—Apollinaire says to me that he's in a hurry," Francis says.

"I had to give an important lecture that evening," Guillaume explains to Madame Buffet.

"But *I* needed some fresh air . . . "

"So Francis tells me off: 'Stop being an idiot, forget your lecture!'" Apo says, in a perfect imitation of Francis.

"I just wanted to take a little drive!" Picabia protests with feigned naivety.

"I tell Francis it's impossible, Delaunay will be furious, I'd promised to talk about him . . . "

"And his wife!"

"Yes. Sonia. I was supposed to talk about the 'simultaneous' curtains she'd embroidered for my study . . . "

"Fortunately, five hours later we were already in Chartres!" Francis concludes, thumping Guillaume on the shoulder.

And Madame Buffet bursts out laughing, simply happy to see the young generation, scruffy and childish though it might act sometimes, enjoying itself under her roof. The next day, Apollinaire, having been reminded of Delaunay, sends a postcard to his friend. It's dated October 19, 1912.

"*Hello. Weather superb. Best, Guillaume Apollinaire. From the house of Madame Buffet, Étival near Clairvaux (Jura).*"

This gives Francis an idea.

Picabia, who is (and will remain to his dying day) obsessed with Pablo Picasso, suggests that Apo send him a card, as well. He's desperate, though he'd never admit it, for Picasso to know that Apollinaire has now become *his* best friend. He wants to make him jealous, to annoy him, like a child. Except that Guillaume is now stuck between a rock and a hard place. If he refuses to send the poisoned-pen missive, he risks angering Francis, who is after all a much better, more loyal friend than Pablo Picasso. But if he sends the post-card, he knows Picasso will take it very badly, and he doesn't want that. Yes, it's true that Picasso broke his heart when he claimed at the police station that "he'd never seen this man"—Apollinaire—"in his life." The wound is still raw, still deeply painful. Yet Guillaume still shudders at the thought of being rude to him.

And so he finds himself caught between two Spaniards. A delicate situation. After a few days of consideration, Apollinaire hits on a solution that should spare him any embarrassment: he buys a postcard for Pablo and then, in his beautiful handwriting, as Francis watches with satisfaction, he writes:

> *"October 23, 1912*
> *Hello!*
> *From the house of Madame Buffet, Étival near Clairvaux."*

Francis was expecting more enthusiasm and verbosity than a single *Hello!*, but it will do.

Then, with Francis still watching, Apollinaire affixes a stamp to the postcard and drops it into the letterbox. But what Francis doesn't know is that Apo has "accidentally" made an error in Picasso's address. Instead of sending the postcard to 242 boulevard Raspail, he's sent it to 142. And so the card never reaches its destination. It will be returned to the Buffet home a few weeks later, bearing the handwritten notes "Pablo Picasso: unknown" and "Return to sender." Guillaume will blame the mistake on the incompetence of the post office, neatly avoiding ill will on both sides.

On the same day as they mail the postcard, October 23, 1912, the four friends bid Madame Buffet farewell and depart Étival together in Picabia's Peugeot—Gabriële having left the children behind and joined the men on the drive back to the boiling bathtub that is Paris. As they're exchanging goodbye hugs and kisses, Gaby surprises herself by getting a bit emotional, realizing how much she's enjoyed sharing the company of such brilliant men with Madame Buffet. It's been an unexpected small joy for this lady, a holdover from another era, another world, to have had this glimpse into her daughter's life. These will be Gabriële's most treasured moments with her mother.

The four people now making their way back toward Paris aren't quite the same as they were when they arrived in Étival. Gaby will recall that the time spent in the mountains was "like a sort of womb, where the alchemy of their combined minds allowed each of them to unlock their own creative energies, in the spirit of what might be called proto-Dada." They stop to rest in Avallon, where Apollinaire sends one last postcard to the painter formerly known as Ludwik Kazimierz Wladyslaw Markus—it's Guillaume who advised this Polish friend with the unpronounceable moniker to Frenchify his name (as Apollinaire himself did), and suggested the name of a village near Paris, and so Ludwik became Louis Marcoussis.

On the way home, Francis's mind is occupied by *Aesthetic Meditations*, which he's promised to finance. Guillaume, for his part, is currently consumed body and soul by the poems that will eventually make up his collection *Alcohols*: free verses, wholly mad verses that glow in the night, verses born of the roads and landscapes flashing past at inhuman speed.

Marcel, too, has been changed by the road trip, and by everything that passed during their mountain stay. It's during these two weeks that he's begun to develop his idea for *The Large Glass*. On arriving home, he'll write a note entitled "The Jura–Paris Road," describing an approach tending "towards the pure geometrical line without thickness." The note evokes an ideal fusion of man and machine, symbolized by a "headlight child" that "could, graphically, be a comet, which would have its tail in front, this tail being an appendage of the headlight child appendage which absorbs by crushing (gold dust, graphically) this Jura–Paris road."

During the drive, the noise of the car is so deafening that any conversations have to be shouted. Leaving the men to rib each other, Gaby closes her eyes, turns her face into the wind, and allows images from the last two weeks to replay in her mind. She etches into her memory for the decades to come the sight of Guillaume and Francis walking together in the forest, hatching plans, completely blind to the trees surrounding them but delighted to have their feet in the mud. And Marcel, so handsome, so mysterious in the aphrodisiac glow of the firelight.

With mixed elation and apprehension, she concludes that these October weeks spent together in Étival may well be the most beautiful time the four of them ever spend together.

In his note inspired by the trip, Marcel will speak of the "machine with 5 hearts"—with the fifth heart being that of the car.

To all appearances, at least.

Because Gabriële knows, as they leave Étival, that she has conceived a fifth heart there, one already beating inside her.

The child born of this magical interlude.

* * *

I went to spend a few days in Étival. The big lounge, with its ageless furniture comfortably arranged around an imposing stone fireplace, is the nerve center of the house. A door in this room opens onto a magnificent garden, puncturing the warm cocoon with a view of the horizon. An escape route. You can see Mont Paradis out the window, a tall hill beloved by anyone who's ever lived around there. It's behind Mont Paradis that the sun rises, flooding it with magenta light, and it's Mont Paradis that overlooks Étival's lakes, which, family lore has it, used to belong to the Buffets.

The lounge is an impressive room. Hanging on the wall is a veritable gallery of ancestors. The portrait of Gabriële's grandmother, Laure de Jussieu, immediately draws the eye. Our great-great-great-grandmother, the writer, painted at age thirty. She watches over Étival, unsettlingly beautiful.

Nothing has changed in this room since that 1912 visit.

Just as you suspend an organic object in formaldehyde to preserve it, this room was closed up and left exactly as it was from 1953 to 2006. It was called "the museum." Frozen in time. Stepping inside it for the first time, I found myself deeply moved, imagining Apollinaire standing next to the fireplace, reciting his poems that didn't yet have titles. *Anguish of love parching you within.* I was pregnant, and, as it happened, I was only violently ill once in my whole pregnancy—at Étival. Dizziness, cramps, endless nausea. I couldn't even get up. Brooking no refusal, they parked me in the lounge-museum with blankets, soft music, and cups of herbal tea, and I stayed there, flat on my back, for three days. I dozed on and off, not even really able to tell the difference between my dreams and reality, my senses dulled by illness. Appalled by this body that now refused to obey me, that was revolting, transforming. We were only just starting to collaborate on this book. I wondered how on earth my sister and I were going to tell the story of Gabriële's life. Where to start?

In my pre-partum torpor, I studied my ancestors and watched them come to life, emerging from their frames. They were all there in the paintings on the walls. All but Gabriële. I pointed this out and was told that Gaby's portrait was hanging by itself in another room, the dining room. Why? No one seemed to know; that was just how it was, as if someone had wanted to isolate the dreaded and mysterious Gabriële.

To put her away.

B ack from Étival and galvanized by the energy of Paris, the foursome is eager to get started on the projects they devised while away.

Guillaume's latest idea is to bring together, centering on a journal entitled *Poème et Drame*, a new artistic circle. A kind of "Mont-Passy"—there are "Mont-Parnasse" and "Mont-Martre" circles, after all—with dinners held at the home of Honoré de Balzac, in the Passy district. He asks Gabriële to help him.

Apollinaire's energetic nature and his capacity for new undertakings, driven by his own desires, match well with Gaby's character. Guillaume is one of those people who *do*—a new journal, a collective, articles, a new exhibition—where others only talk or daydream, where Francis veers between manic phases and periods of lethargy, where Marcel needs impossible amounts of time to make even the smallest decision, often withdrawing into solitude.

Guillaume is a man who gets things done. He's put together a group to organize his dinners that includes Sébastien Voirol and Henri-Martin Barzun, an experimental poet and founder of an experimental utopian community called the Abbaye Group (inspired by Rabelais's Abbaye de Thélème) which is determined to escape "the commercialization of the mind and of artistic creation."

The idea Henri-Martin and Apollinaire have come up with involves a new kind of gathering, one based on dinners organized by artists. Gabriële loves it. She rolls up her sleeves and dives in. There are menus to be planned, invitations to be sent, tables to be decorated, chefs to be hired. It was Guillaume's decision to hold the dinners in Balzac's residence on the rue Raynouard, a house with two entrances (handy for dodging bill-collectors!), to which admittance could only be gained, in the author's lifetime, by giving the maid the correct password.

They have tremendous fun organizing the dinner in Passy. Gabriële runs all over Paris making arrangements for the food and décor. Monsieur de Royaumont, the caretaker who looks after the house like a museum curator, gives them permission to use the renowned writer's own dishes, including his famous coffeepot marked with the initials *HB*. Leaving the house, the side of which faces the rue Berton, and looking up from the lane at the bottom of the hill, they can see "Dr. Blanche's old clinic," where, Guillaume explains to Gaby, the physician used to treat "all kinds of celebrities from artistic and literary circles, including Nerval and Maupassant." The clinic strikes Gaby as a bad omen. Her husband has been deeply morose for some time now.

Marcel and Francis have no interest in Guillaume and Gabriële's Balzacian flurry. They've agreed to attend the dinner, of course, to avoid causing annoyance, but that doesn't keep either of them from poking a bit of fun at the new project.

Neither Francis nor Marcel is fond of groups. Nor do they like it that Gabriële is being taken away from them, putting all that energy of hers to use for someone else, even if he is their close friend. At the last minute they threaten not to come, pre-ferring to shut themselves up in Francis's studio to talk—and to be conspicuous by their absence. But Gabriële gets angry. They *promised*. It's not fair for them to be so fickle, or so flippant. And in the end Francis and Marcel are there "chez Guillaume de Balzac," as they teasingly call Apo, gleefully mocking the bourgeois taste in home décor of the *Human Comedy*'s author. Also seated at the dinner table are Jean Crotti, future husband of Suzanne Duchamp; the painter Georges Ribemont-Dessaignes, who has become one of Francis's close friends; the poet Paul

Fort; the Duchamp brothers; Albert Gleizes; and the architect brothers Auguste, Gustave, and Claude Perret. Gabriële is the only woman. She's used to it.

Skeptical at first, by the end of dinner Marcel and Francis don't want to leave. They're having the time of their lives, smoking and drinking into the wee hours in Balzac's garden, which, in 1912, must still have overlooked open countryside. The atmosphere is relaxed, Francis deep in conversation with Barzun, whose modernist vision of the beauty of "fluids and forces" he finds extremely interesting. The guests, who spent the first part of dinner in awkward silence, are now—thanks to copious amounts of wine—giving each other great comradely thumps on the back and vowing eternal friendship. And Gabriële? Exhausted from planning the dinner, she's curled up in Honoré de Balzac's bed and gone to sleep. No one notices her absence. When men's mutual-adoration hour rolls around, female voices tend to disappear amid the alcohol vapors.

A few days later, Gabriële and Francis are visited by the young American painter Walter Pach, a sturdily built, good-looking 29-year-old sporting an impressive mustache. They've met before, Walter having attended some of the Puteaux Sundays. He's one of those American artists who have come to "learn the ropes" in Paris, floating between Montmartre and Montparnasse learning the European style of painting they admire so fervently. As Gabriële will attest, "Certainly in the United States, a whole generation of young painters was watching the goings-on in Europe with great interest"—though she will add, with her usual wry humor, that the opposite was not the case. The French artists, supremely self-absorbed, cruelly mocked everything happening on the other side of the Atlantic.

Walter Pach tells them about an event he's organizing in the United States, a monumental exhibition that he's eager for Picabia to contribute some paintings to—ideally new ones. The event is the brainchild of a handful of New York artists who dream of holding "the world's greatest modern art exhibition." The New Yorkers are planning to assemble more than a thousand works from all over the world in one gigantic hall able to accommodate hundreds of thousands of visitors.

"How very American," Gaby comments, smiling around her cigarette.

As Walter Pach is crisscrossing Europe, sending entire crates of modern paintings back across the Atlantic, the organizers in New York are busy raising funds and scouting out the perfect place to hold their exhibition. Gertrude Stein receives a letter from one female member of the planning committee that reads: "There is going to be a tumult . . . [This is] the most important event since the Declaration of Independence."

Francis Picabia agrees to take part. As do Claude Monet, Henri Matisse, Auguste Rodin, Edvard Munch, Auguste Renoir, Constantin Brancusi, Odilon Redon, Georges Braque, Pablo Picasso, Robert Delaunay, Maurice Denis, all three Duchamp brothers, Raoul Dufy, Pierre Bonnard, Fernand Léger, Marie Laurencin, Vassily Kandinsky, Jules Pascin, Felix Vallotton, Maurice de Vlaminck, Édouard Vuillard, Alexander Archipenko, and many others. The exhibition is set to take place in New York in early 1913. But none of the European artists are planning to attend in person. Go to America? To do what? America comes to France so often. And it's an expensive journey. Risky, too.

As Christmas 1912 approaches, Francis's mood remains black. The holiday season has been depressing for him ever since he was a motherless little boy. And people are saying, he's heard, that the last few exhibits haven't gone so well for him. He's underrepresented, he thinks. Underexposed. Misunderstood. Not to mention the death of his grandfather. And then there are his financial woes. He sinks into a state of deep melancholy. Marcel Duchamp and Guillaume Apollinaire are the only people he can tolerate—along with his indomitable Gaby, of course. But everyone else is an imbecile. He shuts himself up in his studio, refusing to see anyone.

On his doctor's advice, Francis has stopped using opium. Instead, he's been prescribed cocaine, recommended by physicians of the period as a remedy "for the treatment of melancholy, hypochondria and dyspepsia." Freud also believed it an excellent remedy for altitude sickness and a means of increasing sexual potency.

Gabriële, a woman who never dwells on her own problems, is anxious to snap Francis out of his depression. She can see that the atmosphere of Paris is weighing heavily on him; he's completely without energy or enthusiasm—except when he's on *coco* (his nickname for the new medicine, which he loves). He's begun joking about his sudden new fondness for "winter sports," skiing down "slopes powdered with *coco*," as he'll write in *Caravansérail*. Gaby can't help noting the fact that, ironically, it was one of her very own Jussieu ancestors who introduced cocaine to France, bringing coca plants back from Bolivia in 1750.

Much of Francis's suffering, Gaby knows, is due to lack of acclaim. His efforts since giving up the comfortable status of Impressionist *wunderkind* haven't really paid off. It's Georges Braque and—especially—Pablo Picasso that everyone's talking about when they discuss Cubism, not Francis Picabia, who remains overshadowed by these rivals. His past fame is proving hard to shake, making his newer work, as revolutionary as it is, harder for people to accept. It's not easy for him to be "downgraded" as an artist. He's still full of swagger in public, of course, loudly proclaiming his satisfaction at having left facile painting behind and ventured into modern art. But behind the façade, Gabriële can see his terror of not succeeding, the humiliation of not being recognized the way he deserves, the shame of his reduced earnings. "Francis had been extremely successful in his Impressionist period, and his name was internationally recognized. But once he became an avant-garde leader in painting, he had nothing but detractors left in France. Everyone washed their hands of him: the Arts et Lettres officials, his admirers, his art dealers, the entire press!"

Something has got to change, Gabriële thinks.

Why not start with a change of scenery?

She proposes to Francis that they travel to America for the vernissage of Walter Pach's exhibition.

No one's going. So why not them?

Gabriële, who has traveled a great deal in her life, knows that geographic changes cause internal changes, too, beneficial ones. She also remembers that in 1905 her teacher Vincent d'Indy left the Schola Cantorum for several weeks and went to America, where he received a rapturous welcome, far beyond what he was used to in France. They even organized a lecture at Harvard in his honor! D'Indy returned home galvanized by the trip, by the honors heaped on him. *That's* what Francis needs, to lighten his black mood.

But the trip is expensive.

Now that he's stopped selling Impressionist paintings, and they have four mouths to feed, and since he's been spending most of what income he does bring in on his "medicine," not to mention his umpteenth car, Francis's finances aren't in the best of health.

Gabriële asks her father-in-law for help. But the latter categorically refuses; it's out of the question for him to support such a folly. And furthermore, Monsieur Picabia says, he doesn't approve of Francis and Gabriële's behavior, the way they spend money as if they had it to burn. Good thing Gaby hasn't told him she's pregnant again. Actually, she hasn't told anyone. Not even her husband.

When Gabriële tells Francis that his father is giving them neither his blessing nor the money for the trip, Picabia becomes even more dead set on going. As she will put it in a later interview, "Despite our family's gloomy advice against going, it was all the more tempting!"

And so Francis dispatches Gabriële to buy two tickets for the French Line, which offers crossings between Le Havre and New York. Money is no object; Francis has rediscovered his zest for life since announcing to everyone that the Picabias are sailing for America on an ocean liner. In December 1911, Gabriële visits the offices of the Compagnie Générale Transatlantique, or Transat, at 6 rue Auber in the Opéra district. The sales office is gleamingly modern, its displays state-of-the-art, with posters showing the skyscrapers of Manhattan and leaflets vaunting the splendor of its steamships. This is exactly what Francis needs: luxury, travel, and speed.

But the bloom is quickly off the rose. The first- and second-class ticket prices are quite simply prohibitive. The six-day crossing costs as much as a year's rent! They just can't do it. And as for third class—well, that's for migrants . . .

Gabriële is about to leave when the clerk shows her a brochure for the "third-class cabin" option, a sort of intermediary class between second and third. Gabriële hesitates; they could just about afford two tickets at this price. But what are the conditions like? Then, however, it occurs to her that, if they can't bask in the ship's luxury accommodations, Francis can always find inspiration in the beauty of propellers and machinery.

She buys two tickets for the steamship *Lorraine*.

Next stop: America.

The evening before their departure, Francis invites all their friends to Prunier, a restaurant with a lovely turquoise-blue façade located at 16 avenue Victor Hugo, where they dine on oysters and shellfish. Everyone is there . . . except Guillaume. Why? Francis is hurt by his absence. In a postcard dated January 29, just after their arrival in New York, he asks his friend: "Why didn't you come to dinner at Prunier the night before we left? We were counting on you." A rhetorical question, for Francis knows the answer. The only one capable of stealing Apollinaire from him is, still and always, Picasso. Despite their previous differences, despite Pablo's shameless betrayal of his friend, when Picasso whistles, Guillaume comes running. And Francis can't bear it.

Marcel, though, *was* there at Prunier. "Why are you running away from me?" his insistent looks at Gabriële seem to say. He feels abandoned by his friends/lovers. What about their trio? What about their secret? What Marcel can't understand, is too young to understand, is that only Picabia has staying power in Gabriële's heart. It's brutal, but her husband is so fragile, and she's willing to make a clean sweep of everything else to prevent his collapse.

The morning after the dinner at Prunier, the Picabias travel to Le Havre. The city has changed so much since Claude Monet painted it fifty years ago, the port hardly recognizable now that Transat has moved in. It resembles nothing so much as an ant colony now, each worker going busily about the task assigned to them.

Francis and Gabriële watch the upper-class ladies in their fur coats and stylish hats, the nurses in their uniforms and the children dressed like adults, the top-hatted men and soldiers on leave, the penniless students dreaming of adventure, the young couples on honeymoon, the businessmen on a mission. There are politicians on holiday, tourists eager to discover the New World, migrant families from the East fleeing for their lives, and aristocratic families that detest America but enjoy the luxury of a first-class crossing. And there are the crew members. So many of them, one for every two passengers. Sailors, captains, mechanics, carpenters, woodworkers, cooks, bakers, pastry chefs, stewards, butchers, poissonniers, sommeliers, baggage-handlers, barmen, headwaiters, grooms, chambermaids, doctors, hairdressers, nurses, store clerks, secretaries, printers, receptionists, switchboard operators, firemen, security officers, breakfast cooks, buffet attendants, cellarmen, paymasters, bridge and salon attendants, shoeshine boys, musicians, and even a dentist.

And in addition to all these there are the crowds of onlookers who aren't boarding the ship, but have just come to watch the spectacle of the massive vessel being loaded with cargo, as well as with the many live animals required to feed almost three thousand people for six days. The *Lorraine* is equipped with refrigerators, but it's still necessary to carry on board the equivalent of a large farm: cows, pigs, chickens, geese, and ducks, in order to guarantee fresh meat for the passengers.

The ocean liner is a colossus. Gabriële and Francis are stunned speechless. The noise of Transat employees loading trunks and suitcases aboard with the help of a crane is so overpowering that Francis is already abandoning himself happily to the ambient madness. Gabriële can see the light returning to her husband's eyes, his spirits visibly boosted by all this energy. Reassured, she congratulates herself on making the right choice: adventure.

The Picabias start up the gangway, following the flow of stylishly dressed passengers, but when they reach the top, they're informed that they're in the wrong place. Their third-class cabin tickets mean that they board at the other end of the ship. The message is clear: they will be officially prohibited from entering the first- and second-class areas of the *Lorraine*. Banned from lounges and smoking rooms, Francis is humiliated—especially when a young crewman elbows him aside peremptorily to clear the way for a young woman everyone is staring at. A kind of ripple precedes her, the crowd parting for the star—a dancer who also makes movies. People whisper as she passes. *C'est La Napierkowska*, they murmur. A young lady of unique beauty. At the sight of this glittering star, Francis bows his head, his expression closed, white-faced with shame.

Silently, the Picabias make their way to their cabin, which they're sharing with two other couples, in vertical bunks. It's luxurious compared to the dormitories in third class (no cabin), where migrant families sleep (between 1830 and 1920, more than three million of them will make the crossing from Le

Havre). Gabriële watches as Francis puts his suitcase, a luxury brand, down on their narrow bunk. She still has the receipt for the suitcase and will keep it all her life. It's dated January 26, 1909, just a few days after their wedding. Francis strapped that very case to their car when they went off on honeymoon. It's a beautiful piece that has been well used.

For the very first time since they met, Gabriële senses that Francis is angry at her. She's sorry she ever bought the tickets and afraid this trip to America will harm their relationship, that one day they'll wake up and the electricity between them will be gone.

The ocean liner's massive engines rumble to life. Sirens blare, announcing their departure, triggering an acrid-sweaty rush of adrenaline. Francis refuses even to be spoken to; he merely stretches out on his bed, fully clothed. Gabriële knows what he's thinking; he's imagining all those talentless fools above their heads at this very moment, settling into their chic cabins and luxuriously appointed suites, laughing in their spacious bathrooms, changing into evening dress to sip cocktails while an orchestra plays. It should be him up there, not them. He would have been in top form at the captain's table; in a matter of a few hours, he would have been the object of everyone's attention, the topic of every conversation over coffee on the boat deck and in the wing chairs of the smoking room. Everyone would have been vying for his company, because Picabia is a prince wherever he goes.

The air in their miserable cabin is thick with silence, the porthole over their heads gleaming like a perfect, false metal moon. It's eleven o'clock at night. The third-class dining room has emptied out. The first-class passengers have returned to their suites, the last notes of music dissipating in the ocean breeze.

Gabriële is praying, but not to God.

She's reciting a magical prayer, for the energy around them to change.

A gust of wind causes the ship to rock slightly.

Then another.

And again, and again. Someone, something, is blowing across the sea angrily. The ocean heaves and roars, growing angry in its turn, the waves rising and swelling. Lightning rips the sky, the porthole flickering white as if caught in a camera's flash. *A miracle*, Gabriële thinks. Also known as a storm—and an opportunity to reroll the dice of chance.

The *Lorraine* was a Compagnie Générale Transatlantique steamship that first sailed the Le Havre–New York service on August 11, 1900. It was the largest French ocean liner in service at the time and the most luxurious, equipped with every modern amenity despite its comfortably old-fashioned Second Empire décor. The ship's architecture was designed to offer passengers every conceivable form of entertainment; there were sports and exercise rooms, shopping arcades, a theater, concert venues, bridge parlors, music rooms, smoking rooms. Passengers were meant to completely forget that they were no longer on *terra firma*, but at sea. Not in any danger, but in the most opulent Parisian pleasure-palace.

Except, of course, in the event of a storm.

In this month of January 1913, the unprecedented storm in which the Picabias' ocean liner is caught is lashing the coast, threatening a large part of the seaboard and washing away dams and dikes. As Gabriële will recall, "Our *Lorraine* found itself in the clutches of a storm even the sailors found terrifyingly violent. The ship would be carried up to the top of waves 10 or 20 meters high, its propellors wailing helplessly, then swallowed up by moving mountains. It seemed impossible that it could survive such an onslaught."

No one can help but remember the famous sinkings of the previous century; the papers had wallowed in them, publishing apocalyptic accounts by survivors, of men unhesitatingly drowning women and children with their own hands to gain a place in the lifeboat. The *Lorraine*'s passengers are seized with panic. All of them, but one.

The storm has reinvigorated Francis Picabia. Disasters always get his blood pumping. Flirting with danger, as he does when he drives at top speed, makes him feel alive. Eros and Thanatos. The passengers, ill and terrified, hardly dare leave their cabins. There is one thing to be said for seasickness: it brings everyone down to the same level. The pitch and roll of the sea are hellish, the waves leaving no stomach unturned. With most of the crew vomiting in their bunks, Francis takes the opportunity to go on a self-guided tour of the ship. No one shows up to check his ticket and so, like a high-wire artist, he wanders the corridors freely, gazing dreamily down passages that seem to reflect infinitely in the mirrors lining them. Eagerly he climbs the spectacular staircase leading to the first-class dining room, whose straight and austere lines give the space an imposing air rather like an embassy. The ship continues to heave and tilt in the storm, and he bumps into the Empire-style furniture more than once, gouging himself painfully on table corners, but none of it stops him; he continues his solo exploration of the monumental lounges and salons decorated with images of laurel leaves, stars, palm leaves, and bees that seem to flit around in his honor. Then, suddenly, in the reading room, among the elegant chairs with their striped upholstery, he sees her. The woman he was subconsciously looking for.

The dancer.

Stacia Napierkowska.

This goddess is giving a performance for a courageous few, their eyes bulging with fear and desire. It's quite the spectacle, to say the least, as Stacia dances almost nude and with sublime grace, as if there were no storm, as if the world has stopped just for her. Francis is overcome by the sight of her creamy skin, barely covered by a scanty Eastern costume that emphasizes the curves of a body sculpted expressly to make the senses go haywire. Francis wants to feel that expanse of white skin against his own. To lose himself in it.

Stacia Napierkowska is twenty-two years old. She began her career as a chorus girl with the Folies-Bergère. Then, she was "noticed" by the director of the Opéra-Comique, who hired her to perform in the Fêtes Romaines at the ancient Théâtre d'Orange. From there she moved into acting, playing in silent films opposite the famous Max Linder, and quickly became a star. This voyage to the United States is intended to launch her international career; she's signed a contract with Transat to put on shows aboard the ocean liner to pay for her crossing.

For the next six days, as the storm continues to rage, Francis goes every night to the near-empty salon where Stacia is dancing for a handful of lovestruck men. As Gabriële will recall, the small audience includes a man of the cloth, a Dominican priest. She imagines the holy man regaining the sanctuary of his cabin, trembling with desire, trying to calm the fever in his body by praying over his Bible, his missal, his crucifix. Gabriële is no fool; she knows exactly why her husband is dressing to the nines every evening and braving the storm to sneak into the first-class salons. She's aware that Stacia is particularly known for a number called the Fire and Bee Dance. And she senses, too, that the dancer is not impervious to her husband's charms.

But Gabriële is unruffled. Her sense of her own superiority to other women, no matter how sensual, acts as a kind of armor. Such is the strength of her relationship, its untouchability, that she doesn't feel threatened by her husband's desire for other bodies. She knows that Picabia draws his creative energy from seduction, from sex. "There are really no limits to imagination and emotion except those imposed by habit or convention," he will tell an American journalist. He has to have models who make him want to paint; he has to have conquests that make him want to transcend himself. Gabriële knows that if, out of jealousy, she prevented him from having these extracurricular experiences, his painting would pay the price. And Gaby's in love with a man who paints. Not a faithful husband.

Gabriële Buffet will write, "A woman whose husband has a lot of mistresses isn't necessarily a wronged wife. No, he wasn't unfaithful. To conclude otherwise is stupid, but also very subtle." Reading these last few sentences gives us a glimpse into the circuitous—and unique—workings of Gabriële's mind. For her, Francis wasn't unfaithful; he respected their union's indestructibility. In this passage, she uses the word "subtle" in an ancient, almost vanished sense of the word, meaning "that which insinuates itself with great ease." For her, anyone who considered her a wronged wife had commonplace judgment. An easy, mundane way of thinking. And in 1911, La Napierkowska doesn't worry her one bit.

The Atlantic crossing is nearing its end. The storm has passed. The painter returns to his third-class cabin *heureux qui, comme Ulysse.*[5] He lies down on the bed next to Gabriële, his unsinkable wife who functions like a modern machine, full steam ahead. The passenger decks reopen at last, and the travelers glimpse the skyscrapers of Manhattan in the distance, like the promise of a party in full swing. There's a kind of tense excitement in the air. Francis and Gabriële board one of the little pilot boats ferrying passengers from the ship to the port. Suddenly, they hear an American voice:

"Hey! Mister Peek-a-bia!"

They turn. It's a reporter, come to pepper the artist with questions. But Francis is silent. So the reporter tries his luck with Gabriële.

"Madam Peek-a-bia, what do you think of American women?"

---

[5] *Heureux qui, comme Ulysse*: From the 1558 sonnet by Joachim du Bellay, which begins "Happy as he who, like Ulysses, has returned triumphant from his travels . . . "

"I don't know them yet. Wait until I meet them and then I will tell you," she replies, laughing, in fluent English.

Francis stares at Gaby, dumbstruck. He didn't even know his wife spoke English. There's no question; she is his ace in the hole. How would he survive without her? She'll get him through this. Among the crowds awaiting the *Lorraine*'s arrival is a group of journalists who have come to greet the "Peek-a-bias" as if they were a presidential couple. On the dock, several men in shirtsleeves, hats jammed low on their heads and cigarettes in their mouths, fire questions at them. Gaby, a bit taken aback, tries to answer them one by one. Francis, who doesn't understand a word of English, is blinded by popping flashbulbs. And the dancer Stacia recedes into the distance with the rest of their fellow travelers, unnoticed. "We never saw her again," Gabriële will write.

This trip will mark the beginning of a very important phase in Picabia's work. Over the next few months he'll paint a number of canvases inspired by the dancer that are among the most revolutionary of his entire output. "I want to make this point very clear," Gabriële will say, "because that dancer was the inspiration for some of his most beautiful paintings. That crossing marked an extraordinary period in his life."

A crossing that was Gaby's idea. A stroke of genius.

No jealousy. No bitterness. And art as the only thing that truly matters.

MUSIC IS LIKE PAINTING

I t was a rather strange entry to America," Gabriële will say, remembering that January 20, 1913, and their extraordinary arrival at the Hotel Lafayette, in the heart of Greenwich Village. Hardly have they set foot in their room when the telephone starts to ring and doesn't stop. Requests for interviews, meetings, photo shoots. Gabriële has to manage everything all at once, since she's the only one who can speak to the callers in English. The situation is as exciting as it is overwhelming. The next day, the front pages of both the *New York Herald* and the *New York City American* feature photos of Francis in front of the ocean liner, captioned ARRIVAL OF LEADING CUBIST. The vernissage of the modern art exhibition is touted everywhere as "a riot and a revolution." The *New York Sunday* makes the mistake of informing readers that the Picabias are staying at the Hotel Lafayette, and then they have no choice but to move, as the mob of reporters clamoring to meet them becomes too much to handle.

Of the many invitations they receive (it's impossible to accommodate them all), Francis and Gabriële accept one from Mabel Dodge, a society lady who's an active supporter of the exhibition. Mabel is a wealthy heiress, the daughter of Charles Ganson, a prosperous Buffalo banker. Married at 21 and widowed with relief at 23, she embarked on an affair with the most well-known gynecologist in Buffalo before her husband was even cold. Her parents dispatched her to France to remove her from that scandal, but she only went from the proverbial frying pan into the fire, discovering the bohemian lifestyle of Paris and the joys of bisexuality—and marrying a rich architect along the way. Back in the United States, she settled in New York (there could be no question of burying herself alive at her parents' home near Niagara Falls) and decided to establish a salon modeled after the one hosted by Gertrude Stein. A salon decorated entirely in white, which is unheard of anywhere else at the time.

Unlike Gertrude Stein, who is known to be highly selective about her guests, Mabel Dodge opens her doors to anyone "from the moment the person becomes interesting." Passionately fond of politics, she soon becomes known as "the queen of the radical set in downtown New York." Her salon becomes the most highly regarded of its kind in the city. She receives every Wednesday.

Mabel has had her heart set on hosting the Picabias since their arrival. "We went, mostly out of curiosity," Gaby will remember. "Mabel greeted us reclining on a divan, a nurse fluttering busily around her. She was quite attractive and spoke a bit of French. She began telling Picabia all about how she couldn't bear New York anymore and was planning to emigrate to the New Mexican desert to free her mind and escape the dissoluteness and unpredictability of the city. Picabia responded with a couple of jokes that—fortunately—she didn't understand."

Mabel urges them to move to the Brevoort Hotel, which is across the street from her house. The Picabias find the idea both agreeable and opportune, as it will get them away from the throngs of journalists. Once they're neighbors, Mabel and the Picabias see each other daily, and at her salon the couple makes the acquaintance of numerous political activists. Gabriële hits it off with Margaret Sanger, a former midwife turned sexual-education advocate regularly arrested for her articles on birth control. She's also dazzled by the Russian anarchist Emma Goldman, founder of the magazine *Mother Earth*, arrested more than once herself for her fight on behalf of women. In this month of January 1913, hundreds of women demonstrate beneath the Washington Square Arch, demanding that their rights be respected. Gabriële watches them marching proudly arm-in-arm, finding them beautiful in their anger.

Mabel Dodge's salon might be highly feminist in its way, but the presence of men there is equally important. The lady of the house is currently embroiled in a passionate affair with the journalist and militant communist Jack Reed. Gabriële and Francis make the acquaintance at her salon of Max Forrester Eastman, editor of the socialist magazine *The Masses*. They also meet a man nicknamed "Big Bill Haywood," one of the most important figures in the American workers' movement.

Another of the invitations Francis and Gabriële accept soon after their arrival will prove decisive for the events that follow—and for the history of art. This encounter is with Alfred Stieglitz, an extremely influential New York gallerist. They meet him through Paul Haviland, a handsome man born in France to American parents, who also acts as kind of interpreter for Francis and Stieglitz. Paul's father is immensely rich, having made his fortune selling Limoges porcelain under the name "Haviland" all over America, while his mother is the daughter of an art critic who was friends with numerous artists; little Paul posed for Renoir at age four.

Paul Haviland knows painting, but what he loves above all is photography. This is what led to his friendship with Alfred Stieglitz, who operates the highly influential gallery called 291, named after its location at 291 Fifth Avenue. Sieglitz is also the founder of the photography magazine *Camera Work*, a benchmark publication.

The problem is that this new art form doesn't bring in much money, and when Haviland meets Stieglitz, the gallerist is struggling to make ends meet. To save 291, Paul pays three years of rent in advance—and becomes Stieglitz's closest collaborator. From time to time, they put on art shows between photography exhibits. But this isn't just any artwork; they display only non-academic work. Man Ray, who is at the time still a painter and not yet the great photographer he will become, will recall of 291, "It was there that I saw my first Brancusi sculptures, my first Picasso collages. For me, it was a revelation." Later, Man Ray will understand why Alfred Stieglitz took such an interest in these unusual artists before any other American did: because they were non-figurative and, as such, posed no threat to the photographers he exhibited.

Stieglitz and Picabia are virtually guaranteed to get along. Once again, it's Gabriële who facilitates things, for Alfred lived in Berlin as a student, and so the conversation can shift from one language to another. Their talk focuses, naturally, on the conflict between painting and photography. Francis Picabia, thanks to his photographer grandfather Alphonse Davanne, has a deep knowledge of the subject. Stieglitz is impressed; it's rare to meet anyone with that kind of expertise. The two men agree that painting cannot continue to reproduce reality as such, and that emerging painters must "decline to go on doing merely what the camera does better" and do something *new* instead. Stieglitz has long discussions with Gabriële, too, about the renewal and rejuvenation of painting. Discussions that will result in an article entitled "The First Great 'Clinic to Revitalize Art,'" published in the *New York American*.

The vernissage for the International Exhibition of Modern Art is held on February 17, 1913. The event is nicknamed the "Armory Show," since it's held at the 69th Regiment Armory building at 305 Lexington Avenue, on the corner of 25th Street, bordering Greenwich Village and Madison Avenue. An enormous artillery depot rented by the organizers for the sum of four thousand dollars.

It's already dark when the heavy medieval-style doors open to admit the buzzing crowd. Students hawk programs and badges inscribed with the words "The New Spirit," which the women pin to their evening gowns. The spirit is new and the atmosphere frenzied. One thousand two hundred canvases have been hung, and three times that number of visitors attend the vernissage. It's monumental. As Gabriële will write, the opening night takes place "in an unprecedented atmosphere simultaneously reminiscent of a religious ceremony and a carnival. The evening of the vernissage, until late into the night, a veritable mob gathered in front of the paintings." The works have been hung with didactic intent. In the European section, the visit begins with paintings by Goya, and then the classics— Ingres, Delacroix, Courbet—followed by the Impressionists, the Nabis, and the Fauves, ending with the famous Cubists everyone's talking about: Picasso, Braque, Gleizes, Léger, Archipenko, Jacques Villon, Duchamp-Villon, Manolo. Marcel Duchamp and Francis Picabia are hung next to each other, in a part of the display set slightly back from the rest—which draws the eye to them all the more effectively.

The Armory Show's organizers have given Gabriële a special assignment: to act as a kind of private guide for a wealthy attorney, Arthur J. Eddy, who has supported the exhibition financially. Eddy is a lover of European figurative art, already the owner of pieces by Whistler and Rodin. Now it's Gaby's job to make him understand the language of the modernists—and encourage him to buy some Cubist paintings. Taking Eddy by the arm, she steers him over to "even the most difficult to understand, the most off-putting canvases."

"The bizarre paintings you see here are linked to technical progress," she explains. "Because photography, and now cinema, have taken away painting's most important role. Painting used to be intended to freeze a moment of human life in time. But now all that has changed."

"All of a sudden," she will later write, "I realized that a sizable group of listeners had gathered behind me and were straining to understand my arguments, and my bad English." The reality is that a crowd eager for an interpretation of the paintings on display is hanging on every word uttered by the charismatic Gabriële Buffet. Some members of this audience are reporters, who hand Gaby their cards in the hope of interviews or meetings with her in the days to come.

Thanks to the illuminating explanations of his unrehearsed guide, Arthur J. Eddy buys three paintings: Francis Picabia's *Dances at the Spring [I]* (purchased for four hundred dollars) and *Portrait of Chess Players* and *The King and Queen Surrounded by Swift Nudes*, both by Marcel Duchamp. At the time, Gaby has the impression that Eddy is taking out an option on the future, "the way some people buy land on the Moon just in case it becomes valuable," she'll say later. Indeed, these paintings will be considered masterpieces of twentieth-century art. And Arthur J. Eddy will establish himself as one of the most forward-thinking art collectors of his time.

Thank you, Gaby.

"It wasn't a success; it was a scandal!" The words are Man Ray's. The Armory Show stirs up an unprecedented mixture of dismay, fascination, and outrage within American society. The exhibition becomes a veritable phenomenon, and Francis Picabia is its hero. There isn't a newspaper or magazine or review that doesn't paint a portrait of "the rebel who has come to defend the new movement." Every paper from the *New York Times* to the *Tribune* publishes interviews packed with declarations calculated to further stir up their readers. Former president Theodore Roosevelt mocks the Cubists in an article in *Outlook Magazine*, asking why they shouldn't call themselves "Octagonists" or "Knights of the Isoceles Triangle." Even the mayor of Chicago joins the fray, denouncing Picabia's *Dances at the Spring* as proof of Cubist painters' immorality. And Marcel Duchamp's *Nude Descending a Staircase*, which even his own brothers rejected? It becomes the most famous painting in the entire United States. Visitors stand in line for more than forty minutes to see it. "People camped out in front of the room," the artist Juliette Roche will remember. "There was one old gentleman who came every day, with a bag of sandwiches and a folding stool. He'd sit down in front of *Nude Descending a Staircase* and eat his sandwiches until closing time. Then he'd come back the next day!" Everyone has an opinion, even Theodore Roosevelt, who says Duchamp's painting reminds him of the "really good Navajo rug" in his bathroom.

Even with the Atlantic Ocean separating them, Duchamp and Picabia remain inextricably linked. United in an extraordinary success they'll never experience in their own country. And Gabriële's role in all of this is decisive. In a matter of days, Marcel Duchamp becomes the subject of crazed media attention, and it's Gaby who's pulling the strings. It's she who, from the shadows, unleashes the phenomenon that is *Nude Descending a Staircase*—the fame of which will extend all the way to its being put on an American postage stamp!

It's Gabriële Buffet who "filters" the Cubist movement in such a way as to make it accessible to the American public. The proof: when we read Francis Picabia's statements to the New York press, it's clear that they were dictated, word for word, by Gaby, and for good reason; Francis still doesn't speak a word of English. Moreover, everything "he" says about painting harks back to music, so much so that art critics and historians will speak of a "musicalist" period in his work.

For example, in a *World Magazine* interview dated February 9, 1913, Picabia says, "I simply equilibrize in color or shadow tones the sensations which those things give me. They are like the motives in symphonic music."

In the *Globe and Commercial Advertiser* on February 20, 1913: "Art resembles music, [Picabia] says, in some important respects. To a musician the words are obstacles to musical expression, just as objects are obstacles to pure art expression."

In the same interview: "The attempt of art is to make us dream, as music does. It expresses a spiritual state, it makes that state real by projecting on to the canvas the finally analyzed means of producing that state in the observer."

In the *New York Tribune* on March 9, 1913: "Modern music has won its way; this modern painting, too, will find appreciation and understanding in the days to come."

And in *New York American* magazine on March 30, 1913: "I improvise my pictures as a musician improvises music."

Knowing that Francis knew nothing about music before he met his wife, how can we not see and hear Gabriële behind every statement? The Americans of the period aren't deceived. They treat Madame Picabia as an eminent intellectual. Journalists are impressed by the couple's complementarity, and by Gabriële's conceptual solidarity with her husband. In the *New York American*: "Incidentally, one should not speak of Mr. Picabia, without mentioning his Madame Picabia, who has come to New York with him and who talks as fluently and as charmingly of her husband's work as he does himself. And to her other charms Madame Picabia adds a remarkable knowledge of the English language." And in the *New York Tribune*: "Madame has, moreover, the advantage of being able to discourse of post-impressionism in exceptionally fluent English and German."

Years later, when interviewing her about her memories, a journalist will emphasize her perfect mastery of English even when discussing concepts that were abstract, to say the least. Eyes dancing, Gaby retorts:

"A mastery I didn't possess when it came to buying myself a pair of stockings!"

Gabriële is invited to give lectures, pressed for interviews. When asked about the condition of women in America, she replies, "They are considered, and legally treated, as equal to men; every situation is open to them, whereas in every other country women are treated if not as slaves, at least as permanent minors." The Americans love to hear her talk about the differences between the United States and France; she has the ability to analyze, in quite a structuralist way, the similarities and contrasts between the two systems:

"Your legends have to do with speed, space, functional efficiency, machinery. Whereas ours have their roots in mythology and imagination."

A Roland Barthes ahead of her time. The journalists adore Gabriële. But as always, she doesn't take herself seriously. She isn't here to forge her own myth, but that of her husband.

One day in March 1913, Francis and Gabriële receive an intriguing invitation: the editor-in-chief of the *Cincinnati Enquirer* has "a surprise" to show them. He refuses to say any more. The Picabias have to come and see it for themselves.

Arriving at the newspaper's New York office, they're led down to the basement archive. There, the editor-in-chief proudly hands them a sheaf of photos. They're snapshots of Francis and Gabriële, taken in Cassis in October 1909, a few days after they first met. The Picabias are dumbfounded. Not only did they not know they'd been photographed, but what kind of journey could these stolen photos have taken, to reappear years later in an American basement? The paper publishes the photographs a few days later, captioned WONDERFUL NEW ART CLAIMED BY FRENCHMAN.

Remembering this particular newspaper item, Gabriële will characterize the American press as a "fearful thousand-tentacled hydra, willing to employ any investigative means whatsoever to satisfy its appetite."

What she doesn't reveal is the storm of emotion kindled within her at the sight of that other Gaby, the one from before Picabia. The Gaby who could still have gone back to Berlin, never gotten married, never had children. Who could have been a creator in her own right and not just an inspirational muse for someone else. A muse who keeps to the shadows, out of the light. The thoughts make her head whirl. She chose Picabia, and she will make a show of standing by that choice. It's her own act of creation.

The Picabias had originally planned to spend two weeks in America, but they end up staying for three months. Alfred Stieglitz offers to put on a show of Francis's work at 291. Francis immediately fills their hotel room with painting supplies and gets to work; the walls of the Brevoort are soon covered with canvases. "Watercolors," Gaby will recall, "each of them more extraordinary than the next, and still avant-garde even today." Picabia produces thirty or forty paintings in a few days and nights, most of them on cardboard, with incredible speed—and exhilaration. The more uninhabitable their room becomes, the more immersed Francis becomes, body and soul, in his work. "Picabia adores the very smell of paint," Gabriële knows. It was Marcel who coined the expression.

Naturally, Alfred Stieglitz asks Gabriële to write the preface to the exhibition catalogue: "This collection of works completed at the Brevoort Hotel is remarkable: it is utterly new, even compared to what is being done today. Here are lines, strokes, the most complete abstraction." The show at 291 is a success. It takes place two days after the Armory Show closes. The sixteen paintings exhibited were all inspired by the ocean liner crossing and the city of New York. Stieglitz's magazine *Camera Work* devotes an entire special issue to Picabia's work. It includes an article written by Gaby, titled "Modern Art and the Public": "The number of people who really understand the interest and beauty of the Primitives and of El Greco and Rembrandt is as limited as the number of those who genuinely appreciate modern painting. This misunderstanding arises because the public looks upon art merely as a pastime, a form of entertainment that is due to it."

All the watercolors sell, or nearly. After the vernissage, Francis and Gabriële walk back to the Brevoort, where they've been staying almost since their arrival. They've come to feel at home in this immense building entered by climbing a majestic staircase, an ancient oak tree arching overhead. The hotel's owner, a Frenchman named Raymond Orteig, even has a Parisian-style café on the ground floor. This evening, he offers the Picabias a glass of champagne to toast the success of the exhibition. Gaby and Francis, who by now speak to Orteig as if he were an old friend, ask him why some parts of the hotel remain outdated, even run-down. Why doesn't he modernize his establishment a bit, for the comfort of his guests?

His reply? *"Mais quelle horreur!* People would say it's no longer French!"

Francis and Gaby laugh. This is the reputation of the French: bon vivants and gourmands, but dirty. France. They don't miss it at all. They're happier than they've ever been, living like exiles, their lives devoted wholly to art, far from family pressures and the worries of everyday life. Unfortunately, though, they'll have to go back eventually.

The day before their departure, on April 9, 1913, Gaby gives a talk on modern art at the request of the Civitas Club, an anarchist organization. "That anarchist club quickly disabused me of my European ideas about what a meeting of that type would be like. Instead of the militant fanatics I was expecting, I found myself in the presence of an impressive number of women who, despite the early hour—it was nine A.M.—were heavily decked out in jewels and enormous ostrich feathers. I'd never seen so much elegance in one place, so many beautiful cars (O surprise of the New World)!"

The next day, the Picabias sail—regretfully—for France. Alfred Stieglitz writes in a letter dated April 11, 1913, "Picabia left yesterday. Everybody at 291 will miss him. He and his wife have been undoubtedly the cleanest propositions I have ever met in my whole career. They were a hundred per cent purity. This, together with their marvelous intelligence, made them both a constant source of delight." His description of the couple as "pure" is ironic, to say the least. During the voyage home, Francis sends Guillaume Apollinaire a telegram, technically referred to as an "Ocean-Letter." Apo, charmed by the term, will turn it into a poem—the first of his calligrams.

As their ocean liner steams back toward Le Havre, Gabriële reflects on the happiness of the past few weeks, the exhilaration and intensity of life with Francis, who hasn't had a single attack of nerves during the whole time they've been away. She watches him dressing, this madman of hers, in a white dinner jacket he had custom-tailored in New York—the captain has invited them to dine at his table tonight. And after dinner, blissfully tipsy, they go to bed in their first-class cabin.

* * *

I was talking about Gabriële with some friends yesterday, trying to explain why we want to rescue her from obscurity, erase her erasure. Someone said that the "feminist" sheen we're putting on her life is debatable. I was shocked by that at first, because the list of women whose talent has been stifled by men is so very long. I got quite irritated, even offended. And as I was trying to think of a comeback to that remark, a vague idea occurred to me. I thought that maybe it was true, that Gabriële's case actually *was* different. Because what's so troubling about her is that no one prevented her from being famous or successful. *She* was the one who wanted to be forgotten. And unlike the other women we were talking about, Gabriële wasn't an artist in the strict sense of the word. Her perspective was something new. *Other*. She was like a kind of medium. A messiah, but one who never proselytized.

Back in Paris, Francis withdraws into his studio, afraid to let his New York energy dissipate in the Parisian air. Refusing to see anyone, he orders a number of enormous canvases, two by three meters, which he fills feverishly, rapidly, painting day and night. He doesn't speak, doesn't go out, doesn't eat.

Meanwhile, Gabriële settles in Saint-Cloud with the children. It's a bit dull compared to her American life, but she takes the opportunity to wake her fingers up by playing the piano. It's deeply pleasurable to renew her acquaintance with music, as if—after having lived in someone else's house for a long time—she's back in her own home, surrounded by its familiar scents. Music will forever be her student room, her intrinsic identity.

Since Francis is painting nonstop, Gaby takes herself to a few concerts, going out alone in the evening, leaving the Saint-Cloud house as excited as a teenage girl in the provinces sneaking off to see Paris. On May 29, 1913, she goes to the newly opened Théâtre des Champs-Élysees to see *The Rite of Spring*, composed by Igor Stravinsky and choreographed by Vaslav Nijinsky for Sergei Diaghilev's Ballets Russes. Half of the audience doesn't understand a bit of it. The other half doesn't, either, but abandons itself to the extraordinary modernity of the piece. The ballet doesn't tell a story, per se. *The Rite of Spring* stages a series of "tableaus" that show the pagan myths and rituals of ancient Russia. The dancers execute choreographed "hymns to the Earth," during which they enter ecstatic trances, before an adolescent girl is sacrificed to a nature god named Iarilo. Their traditional costumes make it look as if shamanic witches and wizards have invaded the stage. These strange beings move with forceful, disconcertingly jerky movements that might seem grotesque or ridiculous to many, even unpleasant to watch. To top it all off, the music is "antisymphonic"—that is, non-melodious to the ear.

Stravinsky's score will remain a seminal work in modern music. Some audience members are so shocked that they scream. Gabriel Astruc, the theater manager, begs these irate customers to wait for the ballet to finish before hissing in disapproval, so the rest of the room can at least hear the music! Nijinsky and Diaghilev call for the curtain to be dropped in order to protect the artists. But the dancers and musicians fight on to the end. The commotion reaches its peak during the bows, when shouted insults mingle with cries of approval—and even blows—in every part of the theater. The society ladies demand to have their subscriptions reimbursed, while the Stravinsky admirers in the room ridicule them as *grues du faubourg.*, unimaginative biddies.

Gabriële, of course, has "gotten" Stravinsky as few others in the room would then have been in a position to do.

Recalling the performance, she'll remember being "one of the people who defended him." On the way home late that night, she's staggered by what she's just experienced. Stravinsky, she thinks, is a revolutionary, a genius, and "the difference between talent and genius is a new and unfamiliar contribution, something that takes hold and makes itself essential even if you don't understand it. It's very mysterious, something beyond mankind." Later, much later, Gabriële will have an affair with Igor Stravinsky. But tonight, alone in the car gliding through the night toward the calm suburbs of Paris, she's filled with a kind of violent euphoria, which makes her think of Marcel. She really must arrange to see him again; she abandoned him for so long. They didn't even write to one another while Gabriële was in America. What will their reunion be like?

From Marcel's nervousness, from the way he looks at her, Gabriële can tell he's still in love with her. Time and distance have only heightened his desire. It's extraordinary to her. Singular. Unfamiliar. So yes—Francis may be like her own body, her own blood, but it's Marcel who kindles that body, who strips it bare. Physical love has many outlets.

Gabriële tells Marcel about the phenomenal success of his paintings in the United States, showing him a stack of press clippings she's saved, translating them for him enthusiastically. Marcel can hardly believe it. He looks at the articles suspiciously, as if they might be fakes. He does the same with the banknotes she's brought back, the money received for the sale of his canvases. So much! A fortune! He takes the bills tentatively, unable to resist asking if it was Francis who arranged this to play a prank on him, or maybe as a way of giving him money surreptitiously. No, Gabriële swears. The cash is from his paintings, which are garnering rapturous acclaim on the other side of the Atlantic.

Still skeptical, Marcel puts both the money and the press clippings away in a drawer. None of it means much to him anyway, deep down. What he wants is to be left alone, to read, work, and play chess in peace. And to think. It's not the success of his work in America he's interested in, but life in New York. He wants Gaby to describe everything in detail. He loves her clear and precise way of expressing herself, her razor-sharp eye transforming the stories of her travels into a visceral experience, as if one were actually there. She lingers on one incident in particular—something she saw in the display window of a New York department store. It was an automobile tire, set upright, alone and isolated behind the glass. The tire was thrown into sharp relief by the intense illumination of several spotlights, and behind it in the distance was the scene of an opulent living room complete with a grand piano, a transparent vase of white orchids sitting atop it, standing out against a backdrop of black velvet curtains. "The mismatch of those decorative elements, intended to hype up a brand of tires, was something we delighted in and talked about for a long time afterward," Gabriële Buffet will say later.

A tire, you say. Alone and isolated.

Marcel is so interested by this that he almost forgets the very important thing he wants to show Gabriële. He was thinking of her while he worked during her absence; he "composed." Yes—he's written two pieces of music with improbable titles: "Erratum Musical, for Three Voices" and *"The Bride Stripped Bare by Her Bachelors, Even*/Erratum Musical for Keyboard or Other New Instruments."

This is "conceptual" music, which seeks to eliminate the sensitive or expressive qualities of musical notes. Marcel spreads out for Gaby all his notes, scraps of paper, cards. It's an extraordinary clutter. She looks at it, smiling graciously, amused, waiting for him to explain.

"'Erratum Musical' is repeated three times by three people, each creating their own music composed of notes drawn from a hat," he says.

Gabriële has her own ideas about why Marcel seems to be obsessed with the number three, but this isn't the time to comment on that, as the young man is fiercely intent on this new creation. Getting down on his knees, Marcel divides up the cards on the floor. He asks Gabriële to write musical notes on the dozens of scraps of paper he's also dumped in front of her, then puts these into a hat. Gaby must then draw notes at random and rewrite these onto a piece of sheet music. Then the whole process is repeated—twenty-five times! Gabriële's head is spinning, but she patiently follows orders, chuckling, realizing how much she's missed Marcel's joy, his childlike enthusiasm—not to mention his crazy desire for her. He's an intense young man. Sometimes she wonders if they didn't make a mistake, she and Francis, by bringing him into the noisy chaos of their romantic life.

She doesn't mention the captivating Igor Stravinsky to Marcel. She doesn't want to make him jealous.

This new endeavor of Marcel's, this gift of love, is touching, but one might also wonder if he isn't trying—subconsciously—to encroach on Gabriële's territory. One thing is certain—both of the men in her life, Francis *and* Marcel, could have pushed her to compose. Built up her confidence. Treated her as a creative peer.

But no. The only man pushing Gabriële to express herself during this period is Guillaume Apollinaire. When it really comes down to it, he's the only one who truly *saw* her.

Gabriële finds Guillaume in the middle of moving house. As a housewarming gift, she gives him a miniature set of kitchen utensils made of coins. Apo is delighted and immediately hangs the set on the wall. Then, amid the pots and pans and the boxes waiting to be unpacked, she tells him about the trip to New York. Guillaume can tell how much she enjoyed writing articles and giving lectures in America, and so he commissions her to write an article about music for the magazine *Les Soirées de Paris*, of which he's the new editor and owner. Gabriële, touched, can't tell him how honored she is by the proposition. She accepts.

That evening Guillaume and Gabriële have dinner with Francis, who has momentarily poked his head out of his studio. They've agreed to meet at Paris's only Chinese restaurant, on the rue Royer-Collard near the Pantheon in the fifth arrondissement, where the clientele is composed almost exclusively of Asians because Chinese cuisine is still virtually unknown to Parisians. There's a veritable giant seated at the table next to theirs, a Chinese wrestler wolfing down his dinner before a match. Francis and Guillaume are fascinated by what Gaby later describes as "his grimacing mask, like some cruel idol, squinting at [them] with his strange slitted eyes." They follow him out of the restaurant when he leaves and attend the match. A few days later, Francis draws on this memory to produce one of his most famous paintings, which he calls *Catch As Catch Can*.

Guillaume has finally published *The Cubist Painters, Aesthetic Meditations*, financed in large part by Francis Picabia. In it, Apollinaire discusses his various theories on Cubism and introduces the ten most important painters in the movement. The release of a book is always tricky, and Gabriële is there to assist Guillaume in dealing with the challenges of the moment, having proactively made the rounds of New York's bookstores (including Brentano's in Union Square) to encourage them to order copies. In Paris, her support is mostly psychological. The book is greeted with derision by those members of the press who don't understand Cubism. The polite reviewers say things like, "If I didn't know who Guillaume Apollinaire was, I would explain away his 'case' as an effort to call attention to himself, or perhaps to impress his contemporaries. But I can't consider him either a snob or a charming phony, so I prefer to admit that the book made no sense to me." But most of them are nasty.

Guillaume is used to being mocked by critics, but Picasso's rejection of his book comes as a shock—all the more so because he's written of the Spanish artist as the greatest of Cubists, lavishing praise on his work. Yet Picasso makes it known all over Paris that he dislikes the book. Guillaume is furious and inconsolable, the old wound of the stolen *Mona Lisa* business opening up all over again.

Gabriële tries to soothe her friend, But Apollinaire, cut to the quick, sends Picasso a letter: "I hear that you've deemed what I say about painting uninteresting, which seems to me quite extraordinary on your part. As a writer, I've championed painters whom you only admired after I did. And do you really think it wise to tear down someone who, at the end of the day, is the only one capable of laying the foundation for future artistic understanding?"

On June 18, 1913, still painting like a man possessed, Francis gets a telephone call begging him to return immediately to Saint-Cloud. He hangs up the receiver, so absorbed in his work that he didn't even listen to the reasons why his wife is in such urgent need of him.

In Saint-Cloud, he finds Gabriële in bed. Worried, he wonders if she's had some kind of accident.

"Why are you in bed?" he demands.

"Not just in bed," she retorts, laughing. "In *child*bed!"

Gabriële has just delivered her third child. A little girl. Gabriële-Cécile, but always called Jeanine.

This baby's birth goes almost unnoticed.

Even so, she will be Francis's favorite.

Let's look back at the countdown to Jeanine's birth.

Gabriële became pregnant during the stay in Étival. It was perhaps because she was expecting another child that she decided to sail to America, either to put some distance between herself and the mesmerizing Marcel, or to distract Francis from the fact that she was putting on pregnancy weight. According to the math, Gabriële endured the storm on the *Lorraine* when she was already three or four months pregnant. Then there was the whole American adventure: the exhibitions, the meetings, all the travel around the city. All of that without ever even mentioning that she was pregnant. Shocking, when you think about it. Today we'd call that "denial."

With the approach of summer, Francis's mood does an about-face. As usual, he goes from one extreme to the other. After all those weeks shut away by himself, now he wants to socialize every night, go out for long drives, spend hours in conversation with Marcel and Guillaume, hold court at Maxim's. He calls the roll of his friends; he wants everyone around him. Max Jacob, nursing a hand injury, writes to refuse one of his invitations: "With you, one always paints the town red, and I can't paint the town red at the moment, much as I enjoy your company." All the others, though, accept with pleasure, because partying with Picabia is always a memorable experience, elevated to an art form.

Gaby would like to go with them; it isn't lack of desire that stops her, but her body's failure to cooperate. She's just had her third baby, and it takes time to recover. After four months of extreme closeness with Francis, he's pulling his disappearing act again. How unfair it is to be a woman in a world where everything enjoyable is organized by men, for men.

True to form, though, Gabriële isn't spiteful. She takes advantage of her solitude to make contact with Gertrude Stein. So far, the high priestess of modern art (and close friend of Picasso) hasn't deigned to take an interest in Picabia. But Gaby uses the success of the Armory Show, plus Mabel Dodge's recommendation, as an excuse to introduce her husband. And while Gertrude will show a preference for Gaby, whom she deems truly *smart*, once she meets Francis, she—like everyone else—quickly falls under his charismatic spell. Gertrude and her brother Leo Stein are charmed by his humor and his carefree manner, his gift for witty repartee.

Later, emboldened by her success with Francis, Gabriële will ask Gertrude if she can introduce her to young Marcel Duchamp . . .

Alice B. Toklas, Gertrude Stein's companion and a famous cook, even allows Francis into her kitchen, to show her his recipe for scrambled eggs, which she dubs "Oeufs Francis Picabia."

OEUFS FRANCIS PICABIA

Break 8 eggs into a bowl and mix them well with a fork, add salt but no pepper. Pour them into a saucepan—yes, a saucepan, no, not a frying pan. Put the saucepan over a very, very low flame, keep turning them with a fork while very slowly adding in very small quantities 1/2 lb. butter—not a speck less, rather more if you can bring yourself to it. It should take 1/2 hour to prepare this dish. The eggs of course are not scrambled but with the butter, no substitute admitted, produce a suave consistency that perhaps only *gourmets* will appreciate.

Once his euphoria has passed, however, the return to Paris plunges Francis into despair. He feels ill, claustrophobic, as if the city is a museum and its inhabitants wax statues. He yearns to be near the Mediterranean again, to paint bare-chested in the southern sun. And so he takes the whole family back to Cassis. In June 1913, Francis sends a postcard to Guillaume with the words: "I hope you've recovered and healed from your ordeal. Here it's bouillabaisse, sun, fresh air, etc. Shame you aren't with us."

In mid-July, Francis drives to Amiens and back to attend the Grand Prix automobile race in Picardie, organized by the Automobile Club of France. He comes back alive and in one piece, which is a miracle in itself. And then he produces a group of paintings with strange titles. Outsized, sublime paintings inspired by his memories of the dancer Stacia Napierkowska.

Meanwhile, Gabriële takes advantage of the break to launch an endeavor she's been dreaming of since New York: opening a gallery in Paris. She conceives it along the lines of Stieglitz's gallery, 291, and discusses it frequently with the gallerist himself in her letters. Alfred Stieglitz encourages her and assures her of his support, and so she decides to take the leap and starts buying paintings, acquiring Picassos and Braques with confidence and a keen eye. She envisions the new gallery as a fresh and modern place in which her gifts as an artistic facilitator can be given free reign. Reinvigorated by New York's energy, she wants to recreate in Paris what she saw in the American city: a tiny, self-contained artistic and avant-gardist community. Most importantly, her concept is devoid of any hint of commercialism. She has no intention of being an art dealer. Quite the contrary, she will be an exhibitor. An illuminator. An astute and sophisticated assembler and gatherer.

Picabia, obsessed with his own work, only half-listens to Gabriële's plans, which he approves of in principle but declines to be a part of. He just doesn't have the time, he says. Gabriële, who has actively supported his every move since the moment they met, absorbs the rejection without blinking. She isn't surprised, or even hurt. She knows her husband only too well. And so she turns to the painter Georges Ribemont-Dessaignes, a habitué of the Puteaux Group and longtime friend of both the Picabias and the Duchamps, who agrees to the partnership with alacrity. Gabriële buys a small space (her finances are limited) at 29 rue d'Astorg in the eighth arrondissement and christens her newborn gallery *L'Ours*. The Bear.

A surprising choice of name. Why L'Ours?

Gabriële has just returned from America, and it was there that her idea for a gallery was born. And so it seems fitting to choose a word with an English homonym: "ours," meant to symbolize the notion of New York ideas finding a home in France. And perhaps—why not?—Gabriële thinks of herself, too, as a kind of bear-tamer, an *art*-tamer, showing people the very wild thing they fear.

That summer of 1913 is the most creative time, buzzing with ideas, that the Picabias have known since they met. While Gabriële builds castles in the air, Francis paints a number of important works, including two canvases entitled *Udnie* and *Edtaonisl*. In a letter to Stieglitz in New York, Francis writes that these paintings, "no longer having titles, will each be given a name embodying its relationship to pictorial expression, a name created solely for it." *Udnie* is an anagram of "indue," a reference to the Hindu-style Indian dances of La Napierkowska, and also to Jean d'Udine, author of the 1910 book *L'Art et le Geste*, a theoretical study on the origins of art in which he posits a correspondence between sounds, colors, and rhythm. As for *Edtaonisl*, it's an anagram of "dans etoil"—"danseuse étoile": star dancer.

To Gabriële, these are the most beautiful paintings Francis has yet produced, despite their obvious homage to the dancer Stacia Napierkowska. She was watching, rapt, as he painted them.

Gabriële never tires of watching Francis paint. She's

witnessed the evolution of his style since their marriage. It's not only the subjects of his canvases that have changed, but also—above all—his physical method of painting them. He's freed himself from the static, focused stance he used to adopt, standing outdoors at his easel. Now, he literally dances as he paints, executing a series of movements of which he seems totally in control, his brushstrokes the result of a sequence of energetic actions. Abruptly he crouches down, as if to be dominated, devoured, bowled over by the canvas. This uncomfortable position causes him to undulate like an eel, gesticulating, miming with his body the movement he wants the image he's painting to contain. Then he rises, turning his back on his creation like a man disappointed, despairing. He walks toward the door with an air of finality—but at the last moment he returns to his easel and, like an actor or a child might do, tries to look at his painting through another's eyes, as if seeing it for the first time. Then he dashes toward it, seizing his tubes of paint and applying the color as it comes, without mixing, without shade. He smears paint even on the floor, the parquet becoming his palette. He wipes his brushes on it furiously, grinding in the color with fierce, powerful strokes. The tubes yield their contents ecstatically. He rarely mixes colors, preferring crudity, the spurting of the paint from the tube, inexhaustible. At his mercy. He whips, slaps, strikes, "almost never retouch[ing] his brushwork." He always seems totally sure of himself, like a man running with eyes shut to capture a phantom image. His technical control of the painting is so complete that he can easily take it apart again, manipulating it to suit his vision. What precedes each assault on a blank canvas is a fascinating mystery to Gabriële, who will later say, "It was as if he was projecting onto the paper fleeting impressions taken from dreams or distortions." Picabia sees something in his head and engages in a kind of all-out battle to convey it, to the point of total exhaustion. And Gaby shares in his blood, sweat, and tears.

Gabriële writes about *Udnie* and *Edtaonisl,* the two paintings whose births she's witnessed, in a letter to Alfred Stieglitz, describing the power that emanates from them, their strength and beauty. They are, she explains, a fierce and intense encapsulation of her husband's feelings while in New York.

But the Salon d'Automne selection committee doesn't share her opinion. The jury scowls at the sight of the photos Francis submits. They dislike *Udnie* and *Edtaonisl,* but they can't easily refuse them. After much deliberation, the committee hits on a diplomatic solution: Picabia's paintings will be displayed in the stairwell. At a blind angle, to be less visible.

This decision devastates Francis. He'd really thought his "new evolution," as he calls it, would be understood and appreciated by the French. And now the reverse turns out to be true. Once again, his efforts go unrewarded. Gaby pours out her anger in another letter to Stieglitz, floored by her contemporaries' inability to understand her husband's work. She's afraid Francis will become "neurasthenic" again. How is it possible for him to be so disparaged in his own country? Apollinaire has his own opinions on the subject, which he explains to Gaby: Francis has the bad taste not only to be rich, but to show it. Other artists might be heirs like him or be earning large amounts from the sale of their art, but they have the sense not to advertise their wealth. In squandering his fortune the way he does, buying himself cars and inviting his pals to lavish meals at Prunier, Francis is making people jealous. Just as infuriating as his conspicuous displays of wealth is his refusal to be "categorized" alongside any of his fellow artists, his disdaining of any association with either his traditional or modernist colleagues. For him, "a free spirit takes liberties even with respect to freedom."

And he'll be made to pay dearly for that.

Combing the newspapers, Gabriële realizes with bitterness that most Parisian critics aren't even mentioning the Picabia paintings on display at the Salon d'Automne. Hidden away beneath the stairs, they're invisible. The only exceptions are the *Chronique Française* of November 30, 1913, containing the terse note, "Run from Picabia, run," and the December 3 issue of *La Démocratie*, in which the reporter advises his readers to avoid the vicinity of the staircase because of Kupka ("frightening") and Picabia ("who has made a concerted effort to create something hellish").

During this same period, on October 9, 1913, Kupka tells a *New York Times* critic: "I am still feeling my way in the dark, but I believe I'm on the threshold of discovering something halfway between sight and hearing."

A reporter from *Le Matin*, one of the few inquiring minds to take an interest in the enigmatic art of the stairwell, seeks the painter out at home to ask him some questions, where both Picabias do their best to unpack the titles of *Udnie* and *Edtaonisl* for the unfortunate man. They "don't mean anything," they explain, because there's "nothing to understand." They spend hours with him, expounding in great detail on the theories behind abstract art. It's quite enjoyable giving an interview together again, actually; it makes them feel like they're back in America. Gabriële provides the reporter with examples, using a famous Mendelssohn song called "Bees' Wedding" to illustrate their theories:

"You agree that this piece of music, while excellent, in no way makes you think of a wasp or a hornet, right?"

The journalist nods.

"And yet you accept its title without question?"

He nods again.

"Well then, why can't a painting be the same thing? A piece that doesn't evoke a conventional title?"

The journalist keeps nodding. He seems convinced. He takes his leave of the couple and goes off to write his article, which his paper runs two days later.

On December 1, 1913, Gabriële hurries to a newsstand to buy that day's *Le Matin*. She flips feverishly through the pages until she finds the following headline, captioning an image of *Udnie*:
DON'T LAUGH, IT'S ART!
It's the final blow.

Already upset by his disdainful treatment at the Salon d'Automne and everything that followed, Francis sinks back into depression. A few days later, Guillaume Apollinaire receives this letter: "Dear friend, I'm in Gstaad with my wife for a few weeks, being in dire need of peace and complete rest." Gabriële remains at Francis's bedside, supporting and sustaining him, this man whose melancholia weighs on him so very heavily. As always, she simply copes, without ever asking questions or setting conditions. Francis comes before anything else. He comes before the children, before any easy happiness. He is her husband. Her project. Her lifeblood.

Francis is "neurasthenic and exhausted," Gabriële tells Alfred Stieglitz in a letter. Louis Aragon, will later use Picabia as the basis for a character in his novel *Aurélien*, writing, "He'd never quite come to terms with the fact that he was rather a marginal figure. He knew he was more intelligent than other painters, and had come to the conclusion, once and for all, that talent is a matter of intelligence."

Once Picabia has regained his strength, Gabriële turns her attention to planning the grand opening of her gallery, L'Ours. It's set for January 1, 1914—a good way to start the new year, and a nice distraction for Francis. The newspaper *Gil Blas* runs a piece on December 31 announcing the opening of the new gallery which, it says, promises to display original artwork—including paintings by Picabia. The strange final line of the article is addressed to the reader: "Will your bears be taken? That is the question."

But the gallery opening ends up being delayed, because the Picabias decide to travel to Saint-Tropez—or rather, Francis, depressed again, suddenly feels the need to get away from Paris and its social obligations. His mood swings are becoming both more abrupt and more frequent. Gabriële tries to take advantage of the trip to write the article Apollinaire has commissioned from her; he keeps asking for it, anxious to publish it in his magazine *Les Soirées de Paris*. Eager for her to share her views, her opinions, her brilliance. But she struggles to finish the piece, for she's hopelessly entangled in Francis's net, captive to his demands for attention. His support is only ever, at best, tepid for her personal endeavors. For anything that takes her away from *him*.

> *St-Tropez, January 11, 1914*
> *My dear Apollinaire,*
> *We've been in Saint-Tropez for 4 days and to [illegible]. Don't worry about the color proofs; one of our friends will go to keep an eye on the printing.*
> *My wife hasn't finished her article on music, so it will have to be for the February issue, if possible. I couldn't give my friend the printer's address. Please send it to me. I'm going to exhibit 2 pieces at the Indépendants,* Negro Song *and* Physical Culture. *I'm planning to work and hoping for peace and quiet to do it.*
> *Write to us, dear friend, and love from us both.*
> *Your F. Picabia*
> *Hôtel Sube*
> *Inc.!*

> *St-Tropez*
> *Tuesday, February 24, 1914*
> *My dear friend, I'm not very good at keeping my promises, am I?? Finally, a few months late, here it is, just the beginning of an article, but still worth something, and you can use it however you see fit if you think it's interesting enough for your magazine. It's been incredibly stormy here for the past four days, and St-Tropez isn't very pleasant.*

Francis is working a great deal and asks me to send his
fondest wishes, which I add to my own.
Send me the final proofs.

Gabriële Picabia

A few weeks later, on March 15, 1914, Apollinaire publishes reproductions of six Picabia paintings (including two in full color, as trumpeted on the cover) and the article "Music Today," by Gabrielle Buffet (with two l's). Thus, the two Picabias are brought together, side by side, in issue 22 of the magazine *Les Soirées de Paris*.

In her article, Gabriële describes her artistic vision in theoretical terms. "With the perfection of mechanized sound-producers, an objective recreation of our sound-life would become possible. We would be able to experience the forms of sound outside conventional music, something quite similar to witnessing the abandonment by painting of objective representation in favor of pure speculation." The piece harks back to her discussions with Edgard Varèse during their time in Berlin. She thinks about the handsome Edgard sometimes, and it's like imagining a strange parallel world, one that might have, *could* have existed, if she hadn't crossed paths with a certain Spanish painter.

The Salon des Indépendants opens in March, but Francis, uncharacteristically, decides not to participate. The Picabias seem to be doing their best to freeze time instead.

Like the painter Paul Signac, who came to Saint-Tropez to escape the "intellectual shit" of Paris and never left, a prisoner to the delights of the old port and its heady salt air, Gabriële and Francis grow languid in the shadow of the town's famous citadel, showing no inclination to return to the capital. Signac occasionally asks them round for a glass of excellent cassis and a little sail on his boat. He always mounts an energetic defense of pointillism, which makes Francis laugh, but all in all he's an easygoing fellow who's never really looking for a fight and likes spending time with other painters who bring him spicy tidbits of city gossip—though he also bemoans the "invasion" of the town he calls the eighth marvel of the world, and talks about leaving soon, if Parisian sophisticates continue to insist on colonizing his little slice of heaven.

Gabriële, as fond of her solitary walks as ever, particularly likes to visit the chapel of Saint Anne, tucked away amid the pines, always pausing in front of the century-old votive offerings left by sailors in gratitude for their patron saint's protection. Here, amid the silence of the cracked and ancient stones, far from the odors of oil and turpentine, she can think about music, gaining a few moments' respite from the "forms of sound" in this otherworldly place.

She's not unhappy, she finds, to be missing the Salon des Indépendants this time around.

Neither of the two paintings Francis has submitted attract much notice. Even the compliments paid to them by Guillaume Apollinaire are lukewarm, at best: "In contrast, the slightly dry, but precise and elegant refinement of the two Picabia canvases, *Negro Song* and *Physical Culture*, shall not go unnoticed, and the influence already enjoyed by this embattled painter stands as proof of his importance."

The real talking point of the salon is a farcical duel between Apollinaire and one Arthur Cravan. No one really knows much about this strange man, whom Gabriële will describe later as a colossus who "stood more than two meters high. His admirably proportioned, athletic body supported an Olympian head with strikingly regular features, but his eyes often had an odd, vague expression." His real name isn't Cravan, but Fabien Lloyd. When asked his occupation, he replies "poet and boxer." Before each of his matches, he insists that the referee tell the audience—who has come to watch a boxing match—that he's related to Oscar Wilde on his mother's side. A unique character to say the least, he is, first and foremost, an agitator.

On the occasion of this year's Salon des Indépendants, Arthur Cravan decides to set about ridiculing Apollinaire's art reviews. He founds his own magazine, called *Maintenant*, or "Now," wheeling piles of copies around in a barrow and handing them out to salon visitors like religious tracts. The articles in the magazine are written for the express purpose of crucifying all those painters whose artwork has been hung in favorable positions, the critics' darlings: "Chagall, or *chacal*,[6] will treat you to the sight of a man pouring gasoline into a cow's asshole." "I'd rather spend two minutes underwater than in front of that painting; I'd feel less like I were suffocating." "Suzanne Valadon is well acquainted with small ideas, but simplifying isn't the same thing as making simple, you old bitch!" "Metzinger, a failed artist riding the coattails of Cubism. His colors have a German accent." "It might seem like I have something against Cubism. Quite the contrary; I prefer the eccentricities of even a banal mind to the dull art of a bourgeois imbecile."

The Delaunays are at the receiving end of an especially vicious attack: "Monsieur Delaunay, who has the face of a flaming pig, or perhaps some wealthy family's coachman, would have done better, with that mug of his, to try his hand at a more brutish kind of art. [. . .] Madame Delaunay, who is oh-so-cerebra-a-a-a-al, though she knows even less than I do, which is really saying something, has stuffed his head with ideas that aren't groundbreaking, just bizarre." Guillaume Apollinaire is particularly singled out, as is his onetime love Marie Laurencin: "Now here's one who needs someone to lift her skirts and stick a big . . . somewhere, to teach her that art is more than just a cute little pose in front of a mirror. Oh! You sissy! (shut the fuck up!) Painting is walking, running, drinking, eating, sleeping, and shitting. You may say I'm disgusting, but it's all of that."

[6] Chacal: Jackal

The artists targeted by Cravan's articles are not amused. Sonia Delaunay presses charges. And Apollinaire, never one for restraint, sends his seconds to challenge Cravan to a duel, to avenge Marie Laurencin's honor. Gabriële anxiously tries to dissuade him, but it's no easy matter from all the way in Saint-Tropez. The poet-boxer, who wanted only to amuse and provoke, sends Guillaume a highly facetious letter of "apology" in which he insists that his words have been misunderstood: "As far as Mademoiselle Laurencin is concerned, the full sentence should have gone: 'Now here's one who needs someone to lift her skirts and stick her with a big volume of paleontology at the Théâtre des Variétés."

The duel does not take place.

But the press continues to dwell on the affair for another month, doing its best to rekindle the argument. Cravan is sentenced to eight days in prison for committing libel against Sonia Delaunay.

At last, the Picabias decide to stop haunting Saint-Tropez like a pair of sentimental ghosts and return to Paris. Francis applies himself to the watercolors he's planning to send to Amsterdam, where there will be an exhibition in the spring. He amuses himself by picking Latin phrases from the pink pages of his Larousse and translating them on the fly to use as titles for his paintings, resulting in *Comic Force* and *French Impetuosity*. He's also working on two large canvases for the next Salon d'Automne, *Comic Wedlock* and *I See Again in Memory My Dear Udnie*, both immense abstract compositions. It's likely that *I See Again in Memory My Dear Udnie* is a response, or perhaps an echo, of Duchamp's *The Bride*, which he painted in Munich and gave to Francis as a gift. As William Camfield will write in his essay "Picabia's Life and Work," "There is a general similarity between their quasi-visceral/quasi-mechanical shapes as well as a more specific one between a form in the upper left of *Bride* that resembles (reversed) a hanging form in the upper right of Picabia's painting."

In May, Gabriële plays host to Marius de Zayas, who has made the Atlantic crossing to Paris to borrow some paintings for an exhibition in New York. Gabriële gives him access to her small collection, originally intended for L'Ours, her still-born gallery project. Put on the back burner when the Picabias departed for Saint-Tropez, Gaby's dream ended as quickly as it had begun—and yet it wasn't all for nothing, for in a June 1914 letter to Alfred Stieglitz, Marius de Zayas writes that he's in negotiations with Madame Picabia to purchase from her the "eighteen Picassos" she acquired for her late gallery. Zayas also writes of being impressed by *I See Again in Memory My Dear Udnie,* telling Stieglitz that he'd like to hold a Picabia exhibition and bring the painting to New York for the occasion.

Gabriële also introduces Marius de Zayas to Guillaume Apollinaire. The two men hit it off right away and immediately start discussing ideas for a collaboration between their two magazines, with de Zayas, Picabia, Apollinaire, and Duchamp planning a collaborative pantomime called *What Time Does a Train Leave for Paris?*, based on a poem of Guillaume's.

It's the summer of 1914, and our whole group of artists is brimming with creative energy. Plans are being made, friendships are flourishing. Guillaume is busy writing for the 291 gallery; de Zayas is thrilled by the many possibilities opening up through his Parisian travels; Picabia is immersed in pure and abstract painting; and Duchamp is creating his first proto-readymades (the term "readymade" won't actually be coined until later). He buys a bottle-drying rack at the department store BHV, turning the simple purchase into an act he will later describe as "a reaction of visual indifference, simultaneously combined with the total absence of good or bad taste." At the same time, he's starting work on a piece consisting of a supply box filled with drawings, notes, and scraps of paper, later titled

The Box of 1914. And in addition to all this, Marcel is executing studies on the walls of his apartment for what will become *The Large Glass.*

Ideas are coming thick and fast, and it seems that nothing can stop this bounty of artistic vision and zeal.

But on August 3, 1914, war is declared.

"After that," Gabriële Buffet will write, "the war scattered plans and families and friends, dissolving for a while the dazzling mirages of that extraordinary period of intellectual profligacy."

* * *

Gabriële owned a significant art collection, given to her by the artists she inspired and aided. She also bought many pieces from friends.

Yet when she died in 1985 at the age of 104, her apartment was virtually empty.

The paintings by Picabia and Picasso had vanished. Gone were the drawings by Marcel Duchamp. Her letters from Guillaume Apollinaire were no longer in her desk drawers. Nothing remained but a bed, a few pieces of well-used furniture, and a dusty refrigerator emptied by the neighborhood vagrants. Gabriële had stopped closing her front door long before she died. Whenever she heard a noise, she would call out to the invisible intruder, in her quavering centenarian's voice: "There should still be a few yogurts in the icebox. Help yourself." The tramps took the yogurts. Others took her keepsakes.

Where did Gabriële's treasures go? The answer is simple: we have no idea. This supreme archive of Dadaism was scattered to the wind. Everything is gone. It was all taken, from her Calder jewelry to her most insignificant administrative document. Gabriële Buffet died stripped of everything she possessed.

She didn't react to much anymore. She'd already left the world, mostly. She spent most of her time lying down, often on the floor, her soul floating above that decrepit body. A silent struggle between half-life and half-death. She could stay like that for days at a time. And then one morning she'd get up, pour herself a glass of whiskey as if to get her engine running again, shake off the specter of the beyond, pull herself together, and realize that she was still here. Any visitor who showed up at one of these times would be shocked by the vibrancy of the old lady who could engage in a fluid and razor-sharp conversation on any subject.

Until she broke free of her body completely.

Gabriële Buffet passed away one day, setting sail for the last time. A frail corpse, freed of itself, a shadow dispersed into the air like a bar of soap left for too long in water. Stripped of her belongings, certainly, but peaceful, unbothered, all her richness retained within. Her spirit, and her memories.

The history of art is made of passions, betrayals, broken friendships, men and women disappointed in love. The history of art is made of vital seed, as in the painting given by Marcel Duchamp in 1946 to the woman he was in love with, a painting called *Faulty Landscape*, actually a jet of his own semen on black satin. In the magazine *XXe Siècle*, Gabriële writes: "We speak and write a great deal on the arts. Eminent critics dissect works of art, explain them, criticize or praise them. It seems to me that they rarely speak from the perspective that interests art itself." What is this perspective? Life. The lives of those who create. The lives of those who look. The routine, pragmatic, but also occasionally sublime and dangerous lives of bodies and spirits. The fact that Braque glued a piece of newspaper to a canvas one day because he didn't have enough money to buy a tube of gray paint in no way diminishes the reality that that day marked the birth of the collage, and it was revolutionary. Our great-aunt Anne Picabia (the wife of Gabriel/Pancho), with whom Yves Klein was madly in love, used to say, drunk and laughing on the terrace of La Mascotte on the rue des Abbesses, "International Klein Blue? He bought it at the corner haberdashery!" That unique, mystical blue, the subject of a thousand theories about the mysterious way it was produced. But the fact of Yves Klein Blue's being bought at a haberdashery takes nothing away from its sacredness, if you want a shade of blue to be metaphysical.

So yes, of course, sometimes, after the fact, we slightly rewrite the lives of these people who became towering figures to make them fit the legend. We leave out some things and emphasize others, we make anecdotes symbolic, all to shape the myth. What makes the case of Gabriële Buffet so unique is that, unlike most people, she rewrote her own legend to take herself out of the story, to erase herself, to minimize her role among the artists of her day. In general, people tend to do the exact opposite. They puff themselves up; they give themselves importance. The challenge we set for ourselves, a daunting one, was to shine the spotlight on someone who preferred to remain in shadow.

19
MACHINE WITH NO NAME

The general mobilization begins on August 1, 1914, the day after pacifist Jean Jaurès is assassinated with a bullet to the head right in the middle of Paris. "General mobilization" is the national call-up of all men eligible for military service—the draft—and this is the first time it's ever been initiated in France (only professional soldiers were called up for the 1870 war).

When a war breaks out, people invariably separate into two camps: those who fight, and those who refuse. And so, in 1914, the artistic sphere finds itself completely, vehemently divided. Aesthetic debates are replaced by political ones. It's no longer a question of who's Cubist and who isn't, but one of who will flee and who will die.

Marcel and Francis have never tried to hide their anti-militarist stance. They jeer openly at the sight of anyone in uniform and are, as a matter of principle, firmly opposed to any service in the armed forces.

Guillaume Apollinaire, on the other hand, dreams of fighting for France. On August 5, he applies to join the army voluntarily, writing on the form that he is "Russian (Polish)," "an educated man" who can swim, speak German and Italian, ride "a bit," and shoot "a bit." All his friends make fun of him. Picabia is stunned by his poet friend's enlistment; like everyone else, he finds Apo's patriotism ridiculously bourgeois and old-fashioned. Only Gabriële sees things differently. "When Guillaume told us about Nîmes, after a long silence, his enlistment and joining of an artillery regiment, that noble act worthy of the most heroic French petit-bourgeois that astonished all his friends, seemed to me to be born of something else entirely, of everything he had repressed, of the traditional and the instinctive mingling, just as they did in his life and his literary style."

Despite their opposing feelings and viewpoints, Francis and Guillaume continue to write to each other and to love each other. For the first time, Francis uses the informal *tu* in his letters to Apollinaire. Troubled times tend to do away with posturing. We go back to basics.

Marcel Duchamp, declared unfit for service due to a heart murmur, escapes the draft. "I've been condemned to remain a civilian for the duration of the war. They've deemed me too ill to be a soldier. As you well know, I'm not too upset by this decision," he writes to Walter Pach.

His brother Gaston leaves for the front.

His brother Raymond is made a medical officer, working with his wife Yvonne at the military hospital in Saint-Germain-en-Laye. Yvonne disapproves of Marcel's behavior, which she views as a shirking of his duty. "The call to arms," Gabriële will remember, "affected everyone around us. This return to the old cookie-cutter values caused a great deal of anguish for our little group. Our world of abstraction and speculation, our castle in the air, dissipated into nothingness."

For the Picabias, it's panic. Francis castigates himself for not having become a Spanish or Cuban citizen at age twenty-one. He's called up, which plunges him into a state of near-catatonia. Fortunately, Gabriële—her father's daughter—has connections in the army. She takes the matter in hand and manages to pull a few strings so that Francis is given a post as driver for a general who happens to be a friend of the Buffet family and lives at the La Tour-Maubourg garrison, not far from the Picabias themselves. Not only is Francis safe from dying in combat, but he can even sleep in his own bed every night. Gaby the mother-goddess has protected her husband, her everything, once again.

In the meantime, Gabriële herself joins the Red Cross. Like many women, she feels the need to be of use from the very start of the conflict, and this means joining one of the three subsidiary organizations of the French Red Cross: The French Society for the Aid of Wounded Soldiers (SSBM), the Association of French Ladies (ADF), and the Union of French Women (UFF).

Dressed in a white blouse, her hair covered with a coif, Gabriële performs whatever duties are needed: putting together parcels for soldiers, working in canteens set up for the public, sorting clothes, assisting with the setup of auxiliary hospitals. She's left the children with her mother to keep her hands free—all the more necessary because Francis doesn't seem to comprehend the seriousness of the situation, taking delight in terrifying the general by driving him at excessive speeds. And not only does he drive like a madman; he also can't resist giving his opinions on the military and the war. At first, General Boissons politely pretends not to hear his driver's subversive rantings, but after a while the seditious remarks, combined with Francis's ever-more reckless driving (more dangerous than life at the front), become too much to take. Out of friendship, he warns Gabriële to curb her husband's behavior, reminding her of what it means to be "the second-class Picabia." Her duties and obligations. Gabriële, afraid Francis will be sent into combat, begs him to act more reasonably.

The Battle of the Marne is fought that September. The French government is forced to withdraw to Bordeaux.

And Francis with it.

Where Gaby soon joins him.

Marius de Zayas writes to Alfred Stieglitz in October, describing the axe-blow that has fallen on their French friends: "Since the beginning of the war," he says, "all the intellectuals seem to have disappeared." "I think that this war," he prophesies gloomily, "is going to kill a lot of modern artists, and, undoubtedly, modern art."

De Zayas returns to New York with three important paintings by Francis Picabia (originally intended for a Salon d'Automne that will no longer be held): *I See Again in Memory My Dear Udnie*, *Comic Wedlock*, and *This Has to Do with Me*. In a letter to Walter Pach, Duchamp writes of the grim bleakness of war: "Life in Paris is as stupid as ever. Since yesterday, we've had to keep from giving off any light that might make Paris visible to the zeppelins: shops half-closed after six o'clock, no more lighted signs, streets only dimly lit, and, at the first hint of danger, total darkness!"

In late October, Guillaume, stationed in Nîmes, writes to Francis, who is still in Bordeaux. In the letter, he asks Francis to use his military connections to help him obtain permission to enter the war zone on behalf of "a very pleasant and charming lady." This is the Comtesse de Cologny-Châtillon, whom he calls "Lou," and with whom he's embroiled in a stormy relationship. Apollinaire also asks Francis to help him financially, if possible. The lovers need money in order to meet. Guillaume assures Francis of his happiness at having been declared fit for military service, and describes his daily routine. It's "cold as a witch's tit," he says, and deadly dull in the barracks when you don't have any money to go out, and they've made him grow a mustache. "But for some nonsensical reason, we don't seem to be having anything at all to do with the war." Francis and Gaby resolve to do everything they can to help the young lovers.

Francis returns to the capital in November, terrified at the prospect of being called to the front. The situation is ominous, men departing en masse. Francis's father, Pancho Martinez Picabia, who holds a position at the Cuban embassy in Paris, manages to secure an unlikely "mission" for his son: to negotiate with the Cuban government to purchase sugar and molasses for France.

The opportunity is more than they could have hoped for.

Francis is instructed to complete the Cuban mission before summer. Already he's trying to think of a way to fit in a side trip to New York to see his friends. This isn't a holiday, Gabriële reminds him; she urges him to carry out the mission first. It's important to stay on the government's good side. But Francis argues that this is a perfect opportunity to kill two birds with one stone. He has another mission, too: Mission Duchamp. Encouraged by Walter Pach, who's a great admirer of his work, Marcel has decided to travel to the United States. Francis is helping to pay for his journey and wants to meet up with him in New York, before going to Cuba, to introduce him to his friends there. Gabriële is unconvinced. She knows Marcel can handle himself perfectly well on his own and that Francis is just looking for an excuse to have a good time and drag out the sugar-and-molasses negotiations. Before summer, she reminds him again and again. You have to complete the mission before summer.

Picabia sets sail on May 27, 1915. Followed a few days later by Marcel Duchamp, who has kept his preparations for the trip secret from his brothers. "I haven't told anyone of my plans," he writes to Walter Pach. "So please reply to me on the subject on a separate sheet from your letter so that my brothers don't find out."

As her husband's ship steams away, Gabriële feels as if he's not simply leaving, but *escaping*. "Picabia's not leaving France just to get away from the war; it's the stresses, too: marriage, fatherhood, family." Their eldest daughter Laure-Marie is five years old now, Pancho four, and Jeanine twenty-three months, and, it must be said, Francis isn't wholly enchanted by the noisy little beings that are his offspring. But even being abandoned this way is preferable, for Gabriële, to watching her husband march off to fight. She can endure everything, bear anything, except that.

And so, in the early summer of 1915, Gabriële finds herself alone, the head of her family. It's complete carnage at the front, a horrifying waste of human flesh and blood. Apollinaire writes to her, telling her his news the way most soldiers reassure their families with comforting words. He has the grace, the elegance, to talk to her about herself. As usual, he encourages her to write, suggesting subjects for articles he's sure she would execute beautifully. Guillaume is one of those longtime friends who worries that he's annoying people with his own problems, a Cyrano de Bergerac concealing his head wound as he reads to the convent-bound Roxane in the dark. So kind, so considerate that he does all he can to spare Gaby the slightest worry, while she, for her part, continues to send him money and does small favors for Lou, his latest love, whenever she can. He never fails to thank her, calling her "my very dear friend"—and always asks about the children, too: "Pancho and his happy ways, Laure-Marie with her queenly bearing." He describes for her, in detail, his soldierly routine: the guns, the advances on horseback, his hopes for promotion. He is the only one she talks to about Francis, her worries about his moods and behavior. Guillaume always ends his letters to Gaby by sending her a "brotherly" kiss.

She decides to go to Étival with the children. The mountain air will do them good, the bountiful terrain offering both food and protection. The region where the village lies is nowhere near the front and has been spared any combat or destruction. Still, the war is omnipresent. Gabriële frequently sees squadrons of French and Allied troops passing through the villages, and the area's hospitals are overflowing—so much so that schools are transformed into auxiliary hospitals managed by the Red Cross. Gaby busies herself tending to these young men, their bodies broken and torn, trying not to flinch at their agony. She falls into bed exhausted at night, utterly drained, but something is worrying her more and more all the time: she still hasn't heard anything from Marcel and Francis.

The summer of 1915 passes in a strange blur of mountain walks with the children and days spent at the hospital. Gabriële's anxiety continues to mount. Then, at the end of August, a letter arrives from her husband. At last. It's about time.

She rips open the envelope, her heart thumping. Reads the letter at a glance, stops to breathe, and, suddenly, bursts out laughing. It's laughter born of relief—Francis is alive, blessedly alive—and anger—Francis is the most arrogant man she's ever met—and bitter irony; how could she have thought, even for a moment, that her husband would ever put himself in danger?

Francis isn't dying. He hasn't been assassinated by Cubans or thrown into a French military prison. No, he's in the process of opening an art gallery in New York—The Modern Gallery, it's called—on the corner of Fifth Avenue and 42nd Street. The grand opening is set for October, with a show of his paintings, obviously, and so he needs some pieces of his from the studio in Paris. That's where Gabriële comes in; Francis wants her to bring the canvases to New York as a matter of urgency. As soon as she can. And make sure nothing happens to them during the crossing, he concludes. End of letter. Gaby is thunderstruck. Disbelieving. The man is quite simply out of his mind.

She hasn't laughed in so long. Since Francis left, in fact. This is why she loves that incorrigible husband of hers so much. With him, mundanity and routine simply don't exist.

She puts the letter down, thinking of Francis. Without even realizing it, during these long weeks of his absence, she'd forbidden herself to think of him. As a kind of self-protection. But now, here he is again, suddenly, bursting into her mind, flooding it to overflowing. How she's missed him, this too-noisy, too-talented, too-vibrant husband of hers who never thinks of anything but painting, because painting is the only thing that gives him the courage to involve himself in life and to look at people, this husband who will do anything to avoid dwelling on the small oval portrait of his dead mother, this husband who always knows the right thing to say to make you laugh, to charm you, who has the gift of improvising, of poking fun at the world and everyone around him. This husband so bored by the changeless countryside that he eats leaves off the trees to amuse his wife.

Gabriële remembers their last few days together before his departure. One evening, he'd invited all the people he'd encountered that day to dinner at their house: a famous jockey, a chess player, a ravishingly beautiful young woman with her two female cousins and their mothers, a banker who'd known "a fellow" he once met on a boat, and a young author who hadn't yet written any books but who Francis was certain was a literary genius. There was also an art dealer who'd come to visit the studio, who had asked him, a bit acidly:

"Doesn't it bother you when people watch you paint?"

"Not at all," Francis had replied calmly.

"But great painters always seem to detest being watched," the man had persisted.

Francis had sensed the barb aimed at him from behind the false naivety of the remark, of course. But, in the same tone of voice, as if nothing were wrong, he'd simply answered, smiling:

"Indeed! What fantastic lovers they must make!"

The whole room had dissolved into laughter. That was the last time Gabriële laughed. And it's taken this letter to make her laugh again.

But it's more than that.

This letter is a call, the call of the open sea.

The call of adventure. Excitement.

A return to New York.

Gabriële snaps into action. She has to find somewhere safe to put the children (which turns out to be a boarding school in Gstaad), get back to Paris, pick up Francis's paintings (which are enormous and very heavy), and sail for America . . .

"I was like a man," she will say years later. "I didn't want to put any limits on my life. I've always lived like an adventurer, allowing myself to do things others wouldn't allow themselves. I would have liked to travel a great deal more. I was frustrated, sometimes, at not being able to have all the adventures I wanted, and so I had those adventures within the relationships I had with people."

20

The City of New York Perceived through the Body

G aby arrives in the United States in October 1915. The New York reunion, though, doesn't go the way she'd hoped it would. Francis is tired and on edge, focused on his gallery opening. When she thinks of how she was forced to abandon her *own* gallery—her Ours—Gabriële's heart clenches in her chest. He can't even be bothered to ask for news of the children, or the war; he just pounces on the paintings Gabriële has brought and looks at them for a long time— then throws himself on the bed of their room at the Brevoort in despair. They're not as good as he remembered them. He's devastated.

Gaby glances around. The room looks virtually uninhabited. It's very likely that Francis only just checked in. Where was he staying before this? *Don't ask too many questions*, she warns herself. *Start with the most important.*

"How did Cuba go?"

" ... what? Cuba?" Francis repeats, looking totally confused.

"Yes. Your mission. How was it?"

"Oh ... I haven't gone."

Gabriële is appalled. It isn't a question of ethics; she's fully aware that painting in New York is more interesting to him than carrying out a "sugar mission" in Havana. But the sugar mission is a hell of a lot better than being in a trench on the front. Francis is putting himself at risk of being court-mar-tialed, and if they find out he's opening an art gallery on Fifth Avenue instead of doing his bit for the war effort—well, it's unthinkable. Francis buries his face in the pillow and moans as if Gabriële were responsible for the situation. *He's such a child*, she thinks, sighing. She'll buy tickets for Cuba first thing tomorrow, and they'll leave as soon as Francis's art show is underway.

The Modern Gallery opens on October 24, 1915. Address: 500 Fifth Avenue. The *New York Tribune* publishes an article devoted to the French artists who have settled in New York since the start of the war in Europe. Francis has insisted on the reporter's mentioning in print that he's on a "secret mission" and not in exile. The paintings on display at the gallery, Gabriële thinks, mark the beginning of an artistic quest that is utterly new, with nothing of glossy pre-war lyricism. The paintings are serious, hard, inspired by highly simplified machine diagrams and accompanied by phrases.

This time, however, Francis Picabia doesn't ask his wife to interpret for him when he speaks to the press, or to relay his concepts for the works. His English has improved, and now he speaks for himself, about himself, visibly pleased by his emancipation.

Once the vernissage is over, Gabriële manages to convince Francis to sail for Havana. They spend much of the voyage arguing. Gaby's known ever since her arrival in New York that her husband was diverting himself in the arms of other women during their time apart. But that isn't the problem, and it's nothing new, anyway. What she can't bear is that he tried to hide it from her, and that he lied. That's what hurts. Francis confesses to a long affair with Isadora Duncan—another dancer. He was living with her until Gaby arrived.

Gabriële is humiliated. Not by having been cheated on, but because her husband lied to her by making her believe he was living at the Brevoort, and claiming he didn't know the woman they glimpsed on the evening of the vernissage. It's an insult to Gaby's intelligence. It diminishes her in the eyes of others, who saw her having the wool pulled over her eyes by her own husband. How dare he behave as if they were some petit-bourgeois couple straight out of a Feydeau bedroom farce? Francis can't come up with an adequate reply.

The trip to Cuba doesn't go well. The couple lands in Havana, then travels to the seaport of Colón in Panama. The mission turns out to be lengthier and more complicated than they expected, and they run up against copious amounts of bureaucratic red tape. By sheer chance, the French consul happens to be a Jussieu, related to Gabriële. Taking mercy on the Picabias, he procures all the documentation necessary for Francis to complete his "mission."

On November 21, Gabriële celebrates her thirty-fourth birthday in Peru. A strange sort of birthday. The atmosphere is heavy, like the body that's been put through the torture of three pregnancies, and which she wears like a too-thickly padded coat. Francis makes an effort for the evening, but she can tell that her husband's mind is elsewhere, in New York. He sends a postcard to Alfred Stieglitz from Miraflores: "I think I'll arrive at the same time as this card, dear friend." He doesn't think so, Gaby tells herself, he *hopes* so.

In Jamaica, they write to Apollinaire: "A thousand faraway and affectionate remembrances." The card, sent from Kingston, has a picture of a fountain in the Castleton Botanical Garden. It reaches Guillaume in the heat of battle. Hoping for promotion, he's requested a transfer to the infantry, whose ranks have been decimated. And so he's now an officer, under his real name, Kostrowitzky (his fellow soldiers have nicknamed him "Cointreau-Whiskey"—easier to pronounce). Guillaume is always delighted to receive any news from his friends. There's no jealousy when he hears that they're traveling, thousands of miles away from the war. He's exactly where he wants to be, on the field of battle. And he hopes, quietly, that Gabriële and Francis are rediscovering the divine madness that has always bound them.

Sadly, this isn't the case. Back in New York, Francis sets his bags down at the hotel and immediately announces that he's going out. He's expected at the home of Alfred Stieglitz, where he'll hand-paint the series of mechanical drawings he's done for *291* magazine. Every copy must be colored by hand, one by one, a task that will take up most of the evening. By the time Gaby thinks of going with him, he's already gone, leaving behind a scrap of paper on which he's scribbled the address of where he'll be when he's finished at Stieglitz's: "33 W 67th Street/Mr. and Mrs. Arensberg." Is this an invitation? Gaby isn't sure. Sighing, she pours herself a whiskey—with a drop of Cointreau—and thinks of Guillaume. For the first time, she feels the reality of war. Realizes that this enormous, ridiculous disaster could actually cause his death.

At nightfall, after some dithering, she decides to go to the address Francis left for her. It's at least better than staying at the hotel and drowning her disappointment in her peaty drink. Walking alone through the streets of New York, she recovers a semblance of energy and excitement, but no more than that. On the way up Bowery Street, she realizes that she has to face the obvious: her coming to the United States hasn't reestablished the marital bond like she'd hoped it would. Francis remains distant, preoccupied. In the past, he would have insisted on her coming along to advise him on the *291* drawings. Would have been proud to introduce her to everyone. But it's nothing like that now. He's left her at the hotel like a cumbersome piece of luggage. Worse—like a *wife*. He might as well have suggested that she go shopping or get her hair done while waiting for his return. Gaby finds the whole thing quite upsetting, and very mysterious. What's going on? Is Francis in love with that Isadora Duncan? No, he's sworn to her that he isn't, that it was only a fling—dancers are unbearable to live with, but he couldn't resist her, and besides, Isadora is already engaged to another man. As for Marcel, Gaby hasn't even seen him since her arrival in New York. Both men seem to have been drawn away into something. But what? Gabriële has a feeling the answer lies with Mr. and Mrs. Arensberg, and it's with curiosity that she heads for their home.

The Arensbergs live near Central Park, on a street given a rather Gothic look by its red-brick structures topped with eagles and oak leaves like in some dark fairy tale. The entrance to their building looks like the door of a medieval castle, complete with pointed arches and carved animal heads. In the lobby, golden mosaics gleam in the light of electric bulbs. Gabriële understands now why Francis didn't indicate which floor the Arensbergs live on; all she has to do is follow the noise.

She enters an apartment filled with people, the atmosphere buzzing with energy. Taking off her coat, she steps into a vast, rather low-ceilinged, rectangular living room whose walls, she notices, are covered with Armory Show art: lithographs by Paul Cézanne and Paul Gauguin, a small painting by Jacques Villon . . . and a drawing she instantly recognizes as having been done by Francis. It's strange, seeing a piece of his that she isn't familiar with. It's like a message that she isn't part of his life here. A small knife-wound to the heart.

Louise Arensberg, the lady of the house, is an extremely charming woman of thirty-six, married to a friend of her brother's from Harvard, Walter Arensberg. Louise and Walter are a good match: the same age, both from wealthy families, both interested in the arts. Music for her, poetry for him. In 1913, during a stay in New York, they visited the Armory Show and, struck as if by a revelation, decided to start a collection. They set themselves up as patrons of the arts, moved to the city, and opened wide the doors of their apartment to anyone claiming membership in New York's original and avant-garde artistic community: photographers, painters, poets, writers, dancers, musicians. They arrive to eat and drink as soon as the sun sets, impassioned and insatiable, modern-day vampires.

Tonight, the evening has only just begun. Gabriële observes the discussions, the chess-players in one corner, the sandwich-eaters in another, the cigarette-smokers and scotch-drinkers. She drifts, smiles at a familiar face or two, makes the acquaintance of Walter Arensberg, speaks at length with Man Ray and spots the painter Jules Pascin across the room. Francis finally makes his appearance around an hour later, accompanied by the whole *291* magazine crew, walking into the Arensbergs' flat as if he owns the place. Everyone knows him, everyone has been waiting for him, everyone has something they want to tell him—the American ladies especially, all of them, have something to slip in his ear, a pink tongue or a bon mot. Francis isn't altogether pleased to see Gabriële there. He introduces her distractedly to his friends, the way you might present a country cousin.

At the stroke of midnight sharp, a dazzling woman makes her grand entrance into the salon. From the uneasy glances aimed her way, Gabriële gathers that this must be the dancer. Isadora Duncan. The one for whom her husband was willing to lie. She turns her head to look at the woman's face and recognizes her. She and Francis saw her dance at the Gaîté-Lyrique in 1909, back when no one in Paris could talk about anything but *La Duncan*. After the performance, Isadora had had a signed card delivered to Picabia, inviting him to dinner. *Now this is a woman who knows how to follow through on her ideas,* Gabriële thinks. Francis hadn't seemed overly impressed by her in 1909. He'd even taken mercenary advantage of her interest in him to convince her to buy one of Marcel's paintings, which she hadn't even really liked and had quickly gotten rid of, giving it to a friend as a birthday gift. The painting had then vanished into thin air. Perhaps it's for sale even now, sitting between a used pepper mill and an embroidered tablecloth at some weekend flea market. Who knows?

Gabriële has no desire for any direct contact with Isadora Duncan, so she takes refuge in the kitchen, where an extroverted American woman loudly begins telling her about a recent disappointment in love. Gabriële doesn't give a rat's arse, but this is a good hiding place; there's wine within easy reach and a cigarette case someone has mislaid. So she smokes her heaven-sent cigarettes and listens to the American, who's besotted with a certain "Victor" who unfortunately doesn't love her back. The woman ends by asking Gaby's advice on the best way to seduce Frenchmen; sleeping with them is easy, she says—they're born bed-hoppers, all of them—but making them fall in love is a different story. Gaby doesn't really know how to respond, so she asks questions about Victor instead, just to pass the time. He's a real womanizer, she's informed, a collector of women and a seducer of rare skill. He's also drop-dead handsome, the heartthrob of the Arensbergs' salon. He rarely talks when he first shows up, just remains silent and mysterious, even seeming a bit shy. But after a few drinks, he relaxes, turns rakish, his eyes lighting up, and suddenly he's as forward as anything, seizing women and kissing them, groping their breasts and buttocks in the semidarkness of the hallways. Eventually he chooses one and takes her to his studio—he lives right here in the Arensbergs' building, in rooms they've lent him on the courtyard side. He'll make love to any woman, but he never gives his heart to any of them.

Gabriële, vaguely curious, is wondering just who this "Victor" might be when, abruptly, people start singing "La Marseillaise" in the next room. Everyone hurries into the salon: Isadora Duncan has decided to treat the company to a dance "in homage to a France at war." Her dances usually end with her stripping naked, so, unsurprisingly, there's quite a rush to catch the act.

The American woman takes advantage of the opportunity to grasp Gabriële's arm and point out the famous Victor, who's just arrived. Gaby stands on tiptoe trying to catch a glimpse of this ladykiller, this Frenchman who's seduced half of New York. And then—ah, yes, of course. Everything becomes clear. Victor is Marcel.

Marcel Duchamp no longer bears any resemblance to the

reserved, aloof young man Gaby knew in Paris. Far away from his brothers, his family, he's taken on a completely new personality. Alcohol has liberated him from his shyness—alcohol which he now consumes daily, and in staggering quantities, to shake off his inhibitions around women. It's the exhilaration of life in exile that Marcel is tasting for the first time; that sudden, dizzying ability to reinvent oneself, to slip on another identity like a new suit. He arrived in New York preceded by unaccustomed fame, with everyone, men and women, eager to meet him. Since the Armory Show, he has become, "along with Napoleon and Sarah Bernhardt, the best-known Frenchman" in America. In New York, he's become a supreme playboy, ready for anything. And it's working a charm.

Later, Gabriële will say that she found in Marcel a man who had seamlessly adapted to the mad rhythm of life in New York: "In intellectual circles, he was a hero to artists and girls alike. He went from quasi-monastic solitude to throwing himself into every kind of drunken debauchery, every American excess." A discreet way of putting it. But in the privacy of her letters, Gaby nicknames him her "archangel with cloven hooves." To her, young Marcel has turned into a demon.

To earn a living, Marcel is giving French lessons for two dollars an hour. "Lessons in love to American women," Francis says, laughing. Naturally, all his "students" throw themselves at him. "He'd started drinking heavily, but without ever losing control of himself. He was very different, very seductive," Gabriële Buffet will later confide to her friend Malitte Marta.

Marcel has been rechristened "Victor" by Henri-Pierre Roché, who has become his best friend. A sometime writer and journalist, Henri-Pierre Roché works as a translator and intermediary for foreign press correspondents on behalf of his native France, but mostly he's a habitué at nightclubs and parties. Where, in Francis, Marcel found an older brother who would never disappoint him, in Roché, he finds a twin. The two men look a great deal alike, though Roché is older. "Marcel," Roché will write, "was a creator of legends, like a young prophet who wrote almost nothing down but whose words were nevertheless on everyone's lips. Anecdotes from his daily life came to seem like miracles. He loved life and was light-heartedness incarnate." Marcel and Henri-Pierre met at the Arensbergs' one evening when both tried to seduce the same woman. At around three in the morning, Marcel won the battle. Henri-Pierre wanted to congratulate him, but he was so drunk he'd forgotten his first name—so he called him "Victor," for Marcel's *victory* in their romantic duel. And with that, Henri-Pierre Roché fell immediately, literally in love with Marcel. "Spending time with him was a privilege and a gift—and he was totally unaware of it." They played the same game again and again during the nights that followed: the game of picking out a woman and competing to seduce her. Sometimes Marcel won, and sometimes Henri-Pierre won, and sometimes their conquest would get them mixed up, forgetting which one of them was which, and that always amused them. There was no jealousy between them; the ultimate goal was for the young lady to agree to spend the night with *both* of them.

For example, on April 18, 1917, Henri-Pierre writes in his diary: "First time with Louise Norton, Duchamp, and me. Delightful night for all three of us; I gave her cunnilingus once and fucked her twice. I had to help Duchamp, who managed to make love to her once. Then, tired, I went home and spent an hour with Beatrice Wood." This is actually a translation, as Roché wrote his private diary in code so that no one would be able to read his recollections of his exploits. The original reads: "First time. With Luiz. Tor and I sp. Delightful night for three. Kpf. 2sp. I help Tor. He 1 sp. Tired. Home, 1:00. Beah." (This scandalous diary, which Roché will keep all his life, will provide invaluable source material for his novel about a pre-war relationship, entitled *Jules and Jim*.)

Gabriële decides to leave the Arensberg soirée and walk back to the Brevoort. Without saying goodbye to anyone, she gathers her coat and her courage and steps out onto 67th Street, intending to head for Greenwich Village. But she's hardly set foot outside the building when there's a shout out the window: "Oh, Gaby!" Francis and Marcel, both drunk as lords, barrel down the stairs and out into the street. They each seize one of her arms and lift her off her feet, and Gabriële is borne away into the New York night.

"We'll walk you back! Heads or tails!"

Later, Robert Desnos will explain this game: "Picabia and Duchamp spent their time in America playing one long game of 'heads or tails.' Heads or tails to take this street or that street; heads or tails to get up or lie down, to stay awake or go to sleep, etc." It takes them hours to get back to the Brevoort.

Despite the familiar laughter, Gaby knows everything has changed. She'd had a feeling already, and tonight at the Arensbergs', it became clear to her why life in America won't be the same as it was in Paris. She's no longer the subject of a sophisticated erotic fantasy. The diamond-bright flaring of secret desire, the passionate caresses and stolen brushings of skin against skin—all of it ended with the war, with their vanished youth. It might as well be a hundred years ago. Marcel is twenty-eight years old now, Francis thirty-six. By day they work tirelessly, but at night, their real interest is in what goes on between women's legs. That's it, the great mystery. That's why they go to the Arensbergs' every evening. Times have changed, and it's all about sex now. As Gaby will recall, "At parties, and after dancing, people kissed and petted like mad. 'It doesn't mean anything here,' Henri-Pierre Roché had warned me. It wasn't so much about companionship, just a very sexual game. In my opinion, one that pushed the very limits of the words 'game' and 'sexuality.'" The Arensbergs' salon, and Mabel Dodge's too, are laboratories for artistic and political experimentation, but also experimentation with sex and drugs. "Just before the war, Mabel had organized a peyote party for all her friends," Gabriële will recall. She's no prude, but, quite simply, all of that just isn't her *thing*. When she "trips," it's on ideas, plans, words, discussions that last for hours. And so there's only one conclusion left to be drawn: their love triangle no longer exists. She's always known that desires are changeable, that emotional balances are unstable and fleeting. And she knows, too, that the brain, no matter how powerful, is no match for the sexual urge.

Gabriële has no desire to stifle her husband's freedom; it would go against her whole way of living and thinking. She could pack her bags and return to Paris. But she chafes at the thought of playing the part society wants to assign her, that of the responsible wife and mother who does her duty and looks after her children in a country at war. She's never been cut out for the role of *Mother Courage*. No, she doesn't owe anyone anything. She's going to stay in America. If the men want to act like adolescent boys, fine. Let them. She'll just have to get back in touch with her own girlish self.

And as if on cue, as so often in Gabriële's life, fate steps in, suddenly and bounteously, and throws into her path a ghost from the past, a beautiful memory from her youth, a tall, wild-haired musician. On December 19, 1916, the Brevoort Hotel steward informs her that an old friend has been waiting for her for more than three hours in the bar of the Café Français. It's been seven years since she last saw him: that stormy and brooding prince, Edgard Varèse. Gaby recognizes him instantly, and with delight, embracing him warmly, this youth potion in human form. He has changed—he's even more handsome. "A head like a Greek statue and a manner that charmed everyone he met," Gabriële will recall. The flame of a romantic friendship never quite dies when it's never been consummated. A chemical frisson passes between them. All at once, Gaby feels light-hearted. Desirable. Stripped bare by Edgard's eyes.

He arrived in New York yesterday aboard the *Rochambeau*, with a grand total of thirty-two dollars in his pocket, fleeing the war and a France unable to comprehend his creative aspirations. He'd heard talk in Paris that Gabriële Buffet had left for

New York with her husband. And so he'd taken a chance. He'd wondered how he would find her in this enormous foreign city, but in the end it hadn't even taken twenty-four hours because Picabia was so well-known in New York. And so Edgard came straight to the Brevoort, to wait for Gaby. And voilà.

It's taken a war to bring two friends who met in Berlin together in New York. It's funny, they agree: when they lived in Paris, their mutual home city, they never saw each other. Now it's time to make up for the lost years. Edgard and his wife Suzanne had a little girl, Claude, now aged five, but divorced shortly after her birth; two artists in a couple is always one artist too many. Suzanne has since joined the Théâtre du Vieux-Colombier, and Edgard has devoted himself to music. Gabriële tells him about her marriage to Francis, her three children. Edgard congratulates her, awkwardly, on having married such a famous painter. Gabriële can hear in his voice that he's jealous of the other man, with his own work still misunderstood and maligned, his career still a struggle. In Berlin, they were both students, with the same hopes, the same ambition. Peers. But today, things are different. Despite his aspirations, Varèse has yet to break through, to make his music heard, while Gabriële—in Edgard's eyes—is part of the artistic elite. She's "arrived." And yet, she's jealous too. She envies him his freedom to live and to create, jealous of his having stayed in the music world. This mutual jealousy will draw them to one another like magnets.

Gaby and Edgard wander the streets of New York just like they used to do in Berlin, pausing from time to time to look around them at the hustle and bustle, like two actors blending into the scenery. "The look of the city, from the neon advertising signs unknown back home to the often-grand architecture, struck us as truly new, genuinely astonishing," Gaby will remember.

She asks him for news of the musical world, the world she left behind. Vincent d'Indy, their old teacher at the Schola, is more fanatically patriotic than ever; he even tried to enlist, writing to

the War Ministry that: "Despite my 62 years, I still have a good
eye, a strong stomach, and sturdy legs." Rather than being sent
to the front, though, he's been forced to content himself with
composing fanfares for the Chasseurs Alpins, the French army's
elite mountain infantry. He's also established, in collaboration
with Camille Saint-Saëns, a National League for the Defense of
French Music, aimed at making it illegal to play German music.
Debussy, too, is in the grip of a violent nationalist fervor. Ill with
cancer and so unable to contribute physically, he's begun signing his compositions as "Claude Debussy, French musician."
Maurice Ravel has likewise begged to join the French army, but
was rejected due to his skinniness and short stature: "I'm two
kilos short of being permitted to join this glorious fight." And
Eugène Ysaÿe, too old for combat, goes out to the trenches,
alone, to play his violin for the soldiers: "I want to play something beautiful for you, because I respect you and love you."

Hearing these names from her youth, Gabriële feels a kind
of acid burning in her heart. She thinks of the card Vincent
d'Indy sent her after the birth of Laure-Marie, her first daughter. "Congratulations. Please forgive the brevity of this note;
I will write at more length soon." The promised letter never
arrived. Gabriële understands, now, her teacher's disappointment. From then on, he'd considered her lost from their cause.

Edgard tells Gabriële about how he finally managed to stage
his symphonic poem *Bourgogne*, the piece they spent a whole
night working on together in Berlin. The performance ended up
being a failure, if not an outright scandal, Edgard lamenting the
"aesthetic prudishness of his homeland." As they talk, Edgard
and Gabriële realize that the two of them attended the very same
May 1913 performance of *The Rite of Spring* at the Théâtre des
Champs-Élysees. They discuss the show, and the theoretical issues Stravinsky has raised. Edgard tells Gaby about the new
instruments he wants to invent, new machines. He has all sorts
of plans: a new orchestra, new compositions. Gaby smiles. Her

dear Varèse hasn't changed; he always has a whole galaxy of ideas and flashes of brilliance swirling around in his head, but, as if weighed down by his own intelligence, he can never quite figure out what to do with it all.

The days pass in this same state of profound joy at rediscovering their old connection—and their shared obsession, music. Gabriële introduces her old friend to New York's nightlife, the city even more exciting at night than during the day, plunging him into a whirl of light and sound, of illuminated signs blinking hypnotically and spectacular stage revues "that make the Casino de Paris look shabby in comparison." They lose themselves together in seedy dockside bars and in jazz clubs, marveling at the rhythm and dexterity of the tap dancers, captivated by the beauty of their bodies and their ease in the dance. They go to music halls and laugh together at the nonsensical and sometimes shocking numbers with their typically American comic effects. Varèse is utterly enthralled. "The roar and rumble of New York became his inspiration," Gabriële will later write.

She also introduces him to jazz, a kind of music still unknown in France, which she compares to a drug that takes possession of the body, the gut, and the spirit. They spend hours listening together, lost in the rhythms and the disconcerting sounds of the music, sharing with each other their thoughts on the "tenderness" of the saxophone's "melodic line" and the "wild meter, interspersed with hitches and yet magnificently precise, the musical genius that inspires improvisations on saxophone that the accompanying instruments are able to follow and support all the way to the final meeting point."

Duchamp and Picabia are thunderstruck: Gaby, dropping out of sight with this fellow who showed up out of nowhere! She's stolen away from them. Or rather, *been* stolen. They spot her and Varèse together occasionally, deep in discussion at the Café des Beaux-Arts or Polly's. Everyone's intrigued by Gabriële's new friend; he's handsome, funny, and keenly interested in everyone. Beatrice Wood will say that he has "penetrating blue eyes that see everything" and that, when "he smiles, Heaven opens up." One evening, Gaby shows up at the Arensbergs' with Edgard.

"So, you're a musician?" Francis asks him.

"No, he arranges sounds," Gaby corrects him, smiling enigmatically.

"How?" Marcel asks.

"I'm going to invent instruments able to bypass the limits of certain sounds through the 'physical resonance of bodies,'" Edgard explains.

"His music will leave the realm of imagination behind and rediscover the objectivity of the world's 'noises,'" Gabriële translates.

Gaby and Edgard are the evening's star attraction. They're asked a thousand questions, giving answers that are precise but confusing as they explain the thought processes driving them. For Francis and Marcel, it's as if they're seeing Gaby again for the first time. With Edgard on her arm, she's intriguing, fascinating.

"Who is this man?" people ask Francis and Marcel.

"An old friend of Gaby's," they reply, jealous.

Hoisted by their own petard. Gaby has regained the upper hand, created envy, surprise, desire. Once again, it's she who's leading the dance, she who has established herself as a central figure among the artistic intelligentsia. In his 1916 poem about the Arensberg salon, the writer Allen Norton portrays her as one of the most important personages in attendance:

Where I first saw Time in the Nude
Where I met Mme Picabia
Where Christ would have had to sit down
And Moses might have been born with propriety

Francis had forgotten how much he admires her, this iconoclastic wife of his. Another man's desire has reignited his own.

This woman who doesn't pretend, in whom liberation isn't just a fashionable pose. As he will write in *Caravansérail*, "I found her so much more genuine, more beautiful, than all those women who use their pretty faces to entice men."

One evening, returning to their hotel room, Gabriële finds a gift on her pillow. A painting, wrapped in newspaper. Tearing open the wrapping, she finds a gouache, entitled *Gabrielle Buffet, She Corrects Manners While Laughing*. It's signed *le fidèle Picabia*. Francis likes to write *Gabrielle* with two "L"s, thus hiding in the name a pair of *ailes*—bird's wings.

Years later, Gabriële will point to that painting as an illustration of the unbreakable bond that existed between her and Francis at the time. He's portrayed her as an open windshield, showing that she's his protector, his bulwark, and a window to the world, all at once. The title comes from a Latin phrase in Larousse, *castigat ridendo mores*, which is the definition of "comedy," that theatrical genre that "corrects customs by laughing at them." And that, indeed, is Gabriële's great strength. She doesn't moralize, doesn't sulk, doesn't punish, simply reaches within herself to find a kind of life-force, then rallies, overcomes, reinvents herself. *This* is why Francis is *fidèle* to her; *this* is the reason he can't do without her. And neither can Marcel, who invites her to his studio one evening, where she discovers, to her amusement, his latest whim: "how attentively he watched his carefully depilated body for the slightest regrowth of hair, which he removed immediately."

Eventually, Gaby reintroduces Edgard Varèse to Francis Picabia. She's been in no hurry to do it, wanting to keep him to herself for a while, because she has a feeling they'll hit it off right away. They share an obsession: machines. Francis has drawn them for *291* magazine and in the pieces he's exhibiting at the Modern Gallery, industrial objects having become an endless source of inspiration for him. In an interview with an American reporter, he says, "The machine has become more than a mere adjunct of life. It is really a part of human life . . . perhaps the very soul . . . I have enlisted the machinery of the modern world, and introduced it into my studio." The machine as the soul of human life. For his part, Varèse, without knowing it yet, is already in the process of inventing electronic music. In an early 1916 letter to Sophie Kauffman, he writes, "I am trying to have the new electrical instruments I invented built. It will be wonderful."

But this fascination with machinery isn't the only thing Francis and Edgard have in common. More prosaically, "they both loved to go out and drink, and they didn't hold back," Gabriële will say. Francis is delighted by Varèse's sense of humor, especially when he exclaims, at the drop of a hat: *"C'est de la merde de Poincaré!"*—this is some Poincaré shit! The phrase is meaningless. It's just words. It's wonderful. Picabia loves it.

"Life with the two of them was never boring," Gaby will remember. "Once they came home in the wee hours, still full of energy. They'd invented a stupid game, where each one tested his strength by gripping the other's arm. That's it. Well, Picabia had apparently bent poor Varèse's arm and broken his wrist. They were laughing about it, though . . . "

But this immediate and intense friendship worries Gabriële, as is so often the case where Francis is concerned. First of all, Varèse is, by his own admission, a "maniac"—and two maniacs together are a recipe for trouble. Edgard ends up in the hospital one evening, having somehow gotten his foot run over and crushed by a taxi on Fifth Avenue (Gabriële will never be clear on how, exactly). Both men are drunk and howling with laughter. It's actually a stroke of luck, Francis insists to Gabriële, because the taxi driver's insurance will have to pay Varèse a lot of money. But Francis is burning through life too hard and too fast. Gaby becomes aware, gradually, that her husband's mood swings are worsening. And then the thread snaps. "Too much excess," she'll recall, "too much work, and too much nightlife inevitably led to Picabia's suffering a severe nervous depression, which manifested in attacks of paroxysmal tachycardia that left him weak and in terror of a recurrence." Everything starts to go wrong. And not even Gaby's laughter can put things right.

21

Spanish Night

Gabriële needs a break from Francis, whose changes of mood and personality are invisibly, insidiously poisoning their marriage. She makes a quick trip to Europe and back between March and April 1916 to see the children in Switzerland and pay their school fees.

The flying trip reunites her with her three children, Laure-Marie, Pancho, and Jeanine, who are all blooming and, she's happy to see, bursting with youthful gaiety and good health—but who are all but strangers to her. It's awkward. Gabriële's visit with them is brief.

The steamship that takes her back to America is called the *Chicago*. It's one of Transat's new "one-class" ocean liners. Restrictions have become quite stringent in wartime, and there are no more social distinctions, no more cabin-class. Every passenger is accommodated in the same style.

During the crossing, Gabriële spots a petite woman in the crowd of passengers, with whom she strikes up a conversation. Why this particular stranger, rather than any other of the hundreds on board? Perhaps because this young woman (she's twenty-six) has a unique look and an air of being lost. Perhaps it's Gabriële's special gift at work again, that ability to attract people who are extraordinary, even if they're not aware of it.

This young woman, whose first name is Elsa, has a lot in common with Gaby. Both of them can boast aristocratic lineage—Elsa, born in 1890 at the Palazzo Corsini, is a descendant of the Medicis—and both were raised in an intellectual atmosphere. Both of them pursued higher education, and both fled the familial cocoon in search of emancipation. And, finally, both of them married their husbands immediately after meeting them.

But unlike Gaby, Elsa hasn't been married for long. Her husband is an English lord, Count Wilhelm Wendt de Kerlor. He's extremely handsome, admittedly, but Gabriële doesn't trust him at all. Elsa, whose relationship with her new spouse is already rocky, regularly slips away from him to meet Gabriële for a good stiff whiskey in the ship's restaurant. Wilhelm, she tells Gaby, is a slippery one. A man of dubious substance but endless charm. You never know whether his stories about his life and past are true or not. He's a vegetarian, and a psychic. A few years ago, he advised his best friend against boarding a ship, due to a nightmare he'd had in which he saw the man struggling to survive amid a mass of people in the middle of the ocean, and drowning. The next year, his friend perished on the *Titanic*. De Kerlor went on to become an expert in theosophy and everything touching the paranormal, but he was soon accused of being a huckster and charges were filed against him, resulting in a nasty trial and conviction. "One year, almost to the day, after having married the man of my dreams, I find myself sharing his humiliating fate," Elsa tells Gaby, with clear-headed insight.

To avoid prison, the lord was obliged to pay a symbolic fine of five pounds and leave the country. He and Elsa packed their bags and went to live in France for a few months, then decided to leave for New York. And that's how Gabriële Buffet comes to make the shipboard acquaintance of Elsa Schiaparelli, who in just a few years' time will transform herself into a provocative, avant-garde fashion designer.

Elsa, a small woman with thick eyebrows sitting a bit too close to her eyeline, a slightly protruding chin, and a prominent forehead, is no paragon of prettiness. She was, she insists to Gabriële, an ugly little girl: "I had enormous eyes and looked half starved. And it was impossible for me to have any illusions about myself, because my mother was always comparing me to my older sisters, who were—of course—so cute they made everyone swoon!" To make up for the shame of being plain, she began taking extra care with her clothes and hair, always adding an original detail, a stylish little flourish that drew gazes and compliments.

Gaby feels extremely close to Elsa. Their hearts speak to one another. She shares her own childhood memories with the young woman: her loneliness, her perpetual sense of being a strange little girl.

It's the first female friendship Gaby has ever had.

The two women remain inseparable after their arrival in New York. Gaby convinces Elsa to move into the Brevoort Hotel with her husband and offers to act as their guide during their first few days in the city. She and Elsa made *plans* during the crossing. Gaby has brought back a quantity of French lingerie, which doesn't exist in America, and she's proposed to Elsa that they find a department store interested in buying the lingerie and then split any profits.

Gabriële introduces Elsa to Francis, who's even worse than he was before she left for Switzerland, experiencing intense depressive episodes. Physically, he looks a fright. He's acting like a bratty child, blaming his wife both for having left him and for coming back. What does he want? Is she supposed to feel sorry for him for having exhausted himself with his many excesses? Jealous of the women he continues to collect? Is she supposed to stop the war all by herself? Does he want her to stay or go?

Inside, Gaby is faltering. She's left three unrecognizable children in one country and returned to a husband in mid-breakdown in another. She doesn't know where she lives anymore. And so she takes refuge in Elsa's friendship, taking her to jazz clubs and city parks. Everywhere she goes, Gaby always seeks out trees. The two women take real comfort from one another. Elsa's emotional situation isn't much better than Gabriële's. Her husband is living off her dowry, which is dwindling alarmingly fast. Elsa isn't eating anything but oysters and ice cream—not out of snobbishness, but because those are the least expensive items on the Brevoort's menu! The women, both suffering the torment of a chaotic marriage, try to advise each other on ways to improve their predicament.

Francis isn't painting. He just sleeps, and he sleeps badly, hardly ever getting out of bed. He swallows pills by the handful but has virtually stopped drinking alcohol. His body is leaden, cumbersome, in need of detoxification. Gabriële, who's put up with so much from him over the years, has finally had enough. She's sick, suddenly, of being his watch dog, his failsafe. The atmosphere whenever they're in the same room is tense, close to explosion. She turns her husband over to the care of one Dr. Collins. Francis, for his part, has struck up a friendship with a wealthy French banker, Jacques Bordelongue, who, made aware of his condition, invites him to take a cure at the Gramathon Hotel, a luxurious complex near the city complete with golf, tennis, and cabarets. Picabia settles there with Bordelongue, who proves perfectly able to deal with the painter's mercurial moods. Meanwhile, Gaby relaxes with Elsa, introducing her to all her New York friends.

Some time later, Bordelongue finds himself obliged to travel to San Sebastian, and invites the Picabias to accompany him. Francis, nostalgic for Spain, urges Gabriële to come on the trip with him. She's hesitant, unsure whether going on a journey with her husband will bring them closer together or split them up for good. But Elsa encourages Gaby to go, and that makes up her mind. The two women promise to meet again, on this continent or another. And indeed, later, in Paris, Gabriële will introduce Elsa Schiaparelli to the couturier Paul Poiret, thus launching the career of one of the greatest stylists of the twentieth century.

From late 1915 until the Picabias' departure for Spain in June 1916, Francis Picabia appears to have virtually stopped painting. Only a single piece is thought to date from the period after Gaby's arrival in New York. Francis calls it *Music*

Is like Painting. According to the catalogue description, "Picabia draws inspiration here from a diagram illustrating the effects of a magnetic field on alpha, beta, and gamma particles." *We* saw it as a painting of the effects of the fusion of Gabriële and Francis. Who is the magnetic field acting on the other?

The Picabias sail for Algésiras on the British ocean liner *Canopic.* From there, they'll take the train to San Sebastian. But Francis's true destination is Barcelona. His homeland, as he calls it. The place where, as newlyweds, they sealed the pact between them, Gabriële thinks. A Faustian bargain.

Spain, as a neutral country in the war, has found itself playing host to numerous artists fleeing the conflict. Arriving in Barcelona, the Picabias find themselves *in medias res*— right in the midst of things—and this, of course, is familiar ground. Arthur Cravan, the provocateur from the Salon des Indépendants, has been here for several months, along with his brother Otto Lloyd and Otto's wife Olga Sacharoff, both painters. Arthur Cravan isn't writing in Barcelona; he's boxing. Two months ago, he made the ring shake in a match against world champion Jack Johnson—or rather, made the *room* shake, with shock and disbelief. He'd been knocked out almost at the first punch, provoking a storm of boos. Malingering, vanity, or drunkenness? In any case, the editor of *Maintenant* who so angered Guillaume Apollinaire has a knack for being at the center of strange situations. His suicidal intensity appeals greatly to Francis, who becomes absolutely desperate to meet Cravan, whose motto, "Every great artist has the sense of provocation," could've been uttered by Picabia himself. Likewise, Cravan's frequent public threats to kill himself can only enchant the painter.

Arthur Cravan, so harsh with most people—women, in particular—instinctively forms an unshakeable friendship with Gabriële, treating her with boundless generosity. He'll be characterized in a future biography as "close friends with the first wife of Francis Picabia, who step[ped] up to support him more than once."

The Picabias are happy to be reunited in Barcelona with Marie Laurencin (whom Cravan insulted so viciously in his magazine), and she's equally pleased. Marie, Guillaume Apollinaire's former lover, has been friends with Francis since they were both twenty years old, the two having participated in countless drunken nocturnal escapades together. Marie retains about her a whiff of Paris, so far away now, the Paris of before the war. But she has also sunk into the melancholy so common to the uprooted; she's been brooding, unable to paint, since coming to Spain. She was forced to flee France because of her marriage to a German, Otto von Wätjen, whom she'd only wedded a few months before the declaration of war. After the conflict began, Marie was stripped of her rights as a French citizen and tried for desertion, on the grounds of being "A French woman having deserted her country by marrying a German." After the trial, the couple had simply applied for permission to leave France. Marie recounts the trial for Gaby:

"How could you turn your back on your country like that, with a German husband?" the judge asked.

"But I'm not sleeping with him, I swear!" Marie protested.

Unfortunately for her, and to her own distress, this was the truth. Her husband, who had some odd beliefs, had said to her, "One doesn't sleep with members of his own family. And since we're married now, you're part of my family, so I can't sleep with you."

Gabriële, who's shocked by nothing, is silent for a long moment before commenting, laconically, "Strange things do happen."

The painter Albert Gleizes and his wife and fellow artist

Juliette Roche are in Barcelona, too, as is the poet Max Goth (real name Maximilien Gautier) and the Lyonnaise aristocrat Valentine de Saint-Point, a distant relative of Gaby's, both being great-grandnieces of the poet Alphonse de Lamartine. An iconoclastic *pasionaria*,[7] she published her *Manifesto of the Futurist Woman* in 1912, which began with the words: "Humanity is mediocre. The majority of women are neither superior nor inferior to the majority of men. Both are equal. Both deserve the same scorn."

So, it's a true artists' colony in exile that forms with the Picabias' arrival in July 1916. The merry band decamps to spend the rest of the summer at the seaside resort of Tossa de Mar, a small port town fifty kilometers from Barcelona. There they posed for a photo, all of them dressed in bathing suits, playful and smiling. The image is striking. They look like a bunch of tourists without a care in the world.

Picabia, in the far left of the photo, puffs out his chest and flexes his muscles in ironic imitation of Arthur Cravan. Gaby can be seen second from the right in a white hat, between Marie Laurencin and Olga Sacharoff.

Their bodies are relaxed, their expressions amused, in the middle of a war. Are they aware of the dissonance?

They seem almost a bit too cheerful, perhaps, as if forcing a summer happiness they don't truly feel. But yes—the intellectual games resume, they talk painting and poetry and dance the flamenco, they go to bullfights and dress up in costumes. Picabia quickly becomes the leader of the group, slipping easily back into the role of troublemaker-in-chief, organizer of games both sublime and ridiculous. He acquires a sailboat, a passion of his almost as intense as automobiles. Gleizes paints him several times, all with the same title: *Picabia's Boat*.

---

[7] *Pasionaria*: A female political activist, usually in a left-wing organization

Francis appears to be almost fully recovered from his neurasthenia.

Gabriële, on the other hand, can't stop thinking about the others, the ones who are fighting. She thinks about them far more than she does about the children. She thinks of Braque, Derain, Léger, the Duchamp brothers—and, especially, Apollinaire. They learned shortly after arriving in Spain that Guillaume had sustained a shrapnel wound to the head. He's alive, probably in convalescence, but they haven't heard any more details. Francis, like the rest of the group in Spain, is antimilitarist. There's no debating the question; for them, the war is pure nonsense. But the world is suffering, and people are getting hurt, and for Gabriële the water tastes especially salty, sometimes, there on the beach in Tossa de Mar.

In September, Francis writes to Guillaume, telling him that he and Gaby have been in Spain for two months now. He urges Apo to write and tell them how he is. "Write to me what you're doing, if you're happy." A strange question. Then: "Tell me about life as a soldier." The two men are clearly not on the same wavelength.

Everyone reads the newspapers every day, anxiously following every update, reading every letter from France to each other aloud, sharing every new piece of information. The United States is expected to enter the war soon, and hopes for an end to the conflict are faint. Not only that, but Barcelona is in the grip of its own violent struggle. The political situation has been unstable since 1914, when Catalonia created the *Mancomunitat de Catalunya*, or Commonwealth of Catalonia, an assembly made up of councilors from the region's four provinces. In other words, an autonomous government. Barcelona has been under siege from Madrid ever since, with frequent skirmishes between Catalanists, nationalists, and anarchists, and even the occasional bombing.

Francis isn't painting. He sketches views of Tossa de Mar

and portraits of his wife, but he—normally so prolific, so tire-less—does not paint.

What he *is* doing is writing. He hasn't stopped writing since the crossing on the *Canopic*. Poetry. Wrenching, trenchant, ironic, beautiful, and filthy. Poetry in response to a world at war, to brothers and comrades being blown apart and disfig-ured for the sake of nothing. A defecation of words, shrieking and egotistical, strange and formless.

Dada, already.

Painted poems.

The Spanish interlude temporarily soothes the friction be-tween the Picabias. But Francis needs a mother, a lover, a muse, a whore, an intellectual companion. Francis has so many needs, and Gaby can't be *everything* all at once. She's beginning to feel stifled by the "resort" atmosphere. Back from the "vacation" in Tossa de Mar, she feels an urgent need for silence and solitude. Her best excuse for getting away from the group is the chil-dren. She hasn't heard from them in weeks, she explains to the others, and she's decided to go and fetch them. Unsurprisingly, Francis doesn't offer to go with her.

Left alone, Francis blossoms like a dandelion in the sun. He begins an intense sexual relationship with Marie Laurencin, without a moment's moral qualm; it may even be that possess-ing the former lover of an old friend represents a transgression that, for him, only adds an extra bit of spice. He'll just have to hope Apollinaire never finds out.

And so Francis goes back to his old ways, the embracing of nightlife and excess. But Picabia is a creator above all. Sex and sunbathing are necessary, but secondary. The only thing that truly interests him is work. He and Marie Laurencin decide to found a magazine modeled on Stieglitz's New York publica-tion, *291*. An avant-gardist magazine that will allow intellects in exile to express themselves. To write, to reflect, to draw. Art must not cease, even in wartime. They give their magazine the obvious name: *391*.

When Gabriële returns, Francis rents a spacious apartment at 28 avenida República Argentina, big enough to accommodate their cumbersome progeny. A photograph shows the reunited family in Barcelona. All the children are carefully groomed, the girls with bows in their hair and Pancho in an immaculate little schoolboy's outfit. Gabriële isn't looking at the camera, but rests a hand gently on her son's neck, her body angled toward her children. She's perched on the arm of an elegant chair, a throne on which sits Francis Picabia, who is looking directly into the lens, his expression closed, arms hanging loosely in his lap, bow tie slightly askew. Seeming to ask the photographer, "Where the hell is the exit?"

Commenting on this photo decades later, Gabriële will remark dryly, with a hint of bitterness, "The royal family." And laugh.

Another photograph attests to Gabriële's presence in Spain during the month of December 1916. She's posing with Marie Laurencin, who nestles fondly against her. Gaby, who dominates the scene slightly, is looking straight at the camera this time, wearing a faint, knowing smile and a resolute expression. She's well aware that Francis and Marie began a *pasión* while she was away—quite simply because Picabia no longer hides anything from her, and also because everything he does, he does with passion. Remembering the story of the desertion trial Marie was forced to endure, and her amusing defense ("But I'm not sleeping with my husband!"), Gaby thinks to herself wryly that the woman has certainly found a husband willing to sleep with her now, even if he's married to someone else. Gallows humor. You can always count on Francis. Years later she'll say, about a portrait of Marie Laurencin drawn by Francis in Spain, which depicts her as a fan, "My husband always did need fresh air."

Gaby finds her own pleasure in spending time with Arthur Cravan. They meet every day in the cafés on Las Ramblas. One morning, the boxer doesn't show up. He's simply vanished, without saying goodbye. That's his style. Gaby feels a small ache in her heart, then stores it away with all the others.

The first issue of *391* magazine is published in January 1917. The cover features a wheel-and-cable machine called "NOVIA," which in Spanish can mean both *fiancée* and *bride*—a wink to Marcel Duchamp. The magazine is addressed to "primary occupant" and signed *le saint des saints Picabia.*

Francis, having rediscovered his old tireless energy, is the primary driving force behind the magazine. He publishes some of his writings in its pages, including an unsettling poem entitled "Mie." *La mie*, the soft inner part of a loaf of bread. The better part. Gaby.

Misunderstanding beyond reason,
Creation of vice at a higher degree
In sum I am not taken into account
She thinks that I am a monster
I chose her without being distracted
A single day had ignited within me
This wondrous and immortal bond.

Gabriële, completely without spite as always, is an active contributor to the magazine created by her husband and Marie Laurencin. She writes, organizes, and acts as author, copy editor, and production manager all at once.

One day, she is given the proofs for an issue containing a serious error. Max Jacob has sent a poem that mentions little birds, *petits oiseaux* in French. But the Catalan typographer, who doesn't speak French, has unknowingly printed the words as "polis soiteaux." Gabriële shows the proofs to Francis, laughing.

"We're going to leave it, aren't we?"

"You're right—it's much better like that."

During this same period, the Dada movement is being born in Switzerland. And *391*, without knowing it, is Dada already. Gabriële recalls in *Aires Abstraites* that "*391* was supposed to be a joke. And then it rapidly became a medium for people's grievances, for everything they wanted to say against society, the war, etc. Of course, all of that had to be hidden beneath a sort of black humor, which became more and more aggressive as *391* got bigger."

She'll also remember that it wasn't actually very astute of her, perhaps, to associate the two groups. For her, the French exiles weren't really contesting the established order, and didn't constitute a cohesive school of thought about art, unlike the group in Zurich. For her, only Picabia, through his writings, already embodied the Dada spirit.

Francis wants to return to the United States. As he writes to Apollinaire, "8 months in Spain is a long time." Guillaume, for his part, would have loved a trip to Barcelona. He's contributed to *391* from a distance, sending an exquisite calligram, "The Clock of Tomorrow." Picabia slipped an invitation to him into issue 3 of the magazine: "Only just recovered from his literary and martial triumphs, will we see Guillaume Apollinaire here? Many desire it. But will the God of Armies abandon his lieutenant? Saint Max Jacob, pray for us."

In March 1917, after Gaby has made another (lone) trip to Switzerland to drop off the children, the Picabias sail for America once again. It's possible that Francis had a run-in or two with the Spanish police, who may have intercepted one of his mechanical drawings and believed it to be a military diagram. The thought of Francis Picabia's being a suspected spy is amusing, to put it mildly. At any rate, the couple takes along a number of paintings by Marie Laurencin, to exhibit them in New York. Gabriële dithered a bit over this umpteenth voyage. She's lost her taste for America and would really prefer to return to Paris. Has she lost her taste for Francis, too? In the end, at her husband's insistence, she goes with him. Maybe she feels that another physical separation would be the final death-knell for their relationship. "We went back to New York because Picabia couldn't stay in one place for long," she'll say.

But it's also true that on April 10, 1917, the first exhibition of the new Society of Independent Artists, whose founders include Duchamp, Arensberg, and Man Ray, opens at the Grand Central Gallery. A vernissage that Francis and Gabriële wouldn't miss for the world.

22

ROTATING PANTIES

On the ocean liner from Barcelona to New York, time stops. Journeys by ship have the peculiar ability to suspend time during the crossing; you're not physically in any country, but at sea, in a no-man's land. You while away the days with light entertainment, easily forgetting the life you left behind on *terra firma*. This sense of unreality makes the Picabias' arrival in America even more of a shock.

On April 6, 1917, President Wilson declares war on Germany. The conflict is no longer solely a European one. Gabriële will remember their entry into the port of New York on the very day war was declared: "We were caught in enormous headlights coming from every direction. The atmosphere was shocking, unprecedented." It's world war. The first.

Canvas booths have been hastily set up on every street corner, doing duty as voluntary enlistment offices. Sexy girls are being used to motivate the troops, manning makeshift counters next to officers in uniform, calling out to passing young men and promising "a kiss and glory" to anyone who enlists. It strikes Gaby that this falsely puritanical America is appealing to its basest instincts in its efforts to recruit cannon fodder.

Francis is less mindful than Gabriële of the United States's entry into the war. Buoyed by his time in Barcelona and the success of *391* magazine, he's eager to be reunited with their New York friends so he can continue his artistic pursuits. All his attention is taken up by the opening of the first Society of Independent Artists show, where he's exhibiting two canvases, including *Painting Is Like Music*.

The new Society of Independent Artists is intended to be

a sister organization to the French body of the same name, currently holding its own exhibition in Paris—the same Salon des Indépendants that demanded that Marcel Duchamp rename or withdraw his *Nude Descending a Staircase* in 1911. This American version includes many of the same members who participated in the development of the Armory Show, but there are also newcomers including Marcel Duchamp, Walter Arensberg, and Man Ray.

Their founding principle is that every piece of artwork is eligible for exhibition, with no need for approval by a selection committee. All an artist has to do for their work to be hung is to pay a six-dollar fee and fill out a simple form. The pieces are then displayed democratically, in alphabetical order, rather than according to any "aesthetic judgment."

But there is one piece that proves problematic. It's been submitted by one Richard Mutt, an artist living in Philadelphia. The piece is a white porcelain basin of the type commonly found in public bathrooms. In other words, a urinal. The most banal and industrial object imaginable, straight out of a train station. The artist didn't even make it himself, but bought it in a store, then simply painted a title on it in black: *Fountain*. In short, a joke submission.

But this provocative schoolboy prank is the cause of vehement disagreement among the salon's organizing members. Directors William J. Glackens and Charles E. Prendergast are infuriated by the submission, which they deem absurd. But Walter Arensberg, Marcel Duchamp, and Man Ray insist that the piece should be kept, R. Mutt having paid his six dollars. The rules stipulate that all submissions must be accepted without being subject to any aesthetic criteria. And the rules are the rules.

The directors, unable to believe what they're hearing, impose their veto.

The artist Beatrice Wood, who's present at the meeting, later describes the scene for the newly returned Picabias:

"'We can't exhibit that!' exclaimed William J. Glackens.

"'Yes, we can, this man has paid his six dollars,' Walter Arensberg retorted calmly.

"'Impossible. It's disgusting!' Charles Prendergast cried.

"'No. It's white. And the lines are quite harmonious,' Marcel Duchamp remarked.

"'Are you telling me that if someone were to pay six dollars to submit a canvas painted with horseshit, we'd be obliged to hang it?'

"To which Arensberg replied, mock-regretfully, 'I fear we would, yes.'"

But the urinal's defenders are overruled. The directors refuse to withdraw their veto, and R. Mutt's contribution is not accepted. Marcel Duchamp, who takes the rejection personally, seeing in it an echo of what he once suffered, is furious. He agreed to participate in this society of artists for the sole purpose of creating an art show that would judge neither taste nor value. He resigns immediately from the society he helped to found.

The Picabias don't return to the Brevoort Hotel, for lack of funds. They're out of money. Completely broke. A friend of theirs, Louise Norton—who's in the midst of divorcing the poet Allen Norton—offers to put them up in her house on 88th Street. A lover of France and the arts, Louise can be relied on to host any exiled, penniless French national. Albert Gleizes and his wife Juliette (the same Gleizes who once sent Marcel's brothers to talk to him about renaming *Nude Descending a Staircase*) live on the second floor. Francis and Gabriële settle on the ground floor, and even Arthur Cravan sleeps on Louise's sofa from time to time. He's reappeared as suddenly as he vanished. The Barcelona group is reunited. In the same building.

Francis quickly comes to feel at home in Louise's house, having afterparties there almost every night. "The Picabias' ground floor was an incredible place," Juliette Gleizes will remember. "There was always a group of people around Francis, a rather motley bunch. Cravan was there, too. They'd troop in at two or three o'clock in the morning and make merry into the wee hours." In the morning, Picabia pours out to Juliette all the anguish brought on by his hangover, tromping upstairs with a pile of newspapers filled with war bulletins and giving her the latest update. "Then," she'll say, "he'd go back downstairs and say to his wife, 'I've depressed Juliette, I feel much better!'"

Living in the same house as the Picabias is less than relaxing for the Gleizes. One night, Marcel and Francis devour the entire leg of lamb Albert is keeping in the refrigerator of their shared kitchen, leaving a check beneath the denuded bone after their feast. Gleizes appreciates neither the joke nor Francis's mindset. On the other hand, the house's owner has ample reason to be delighted by the Picabias' boisterous presence in her home—it's thanks to them that Louise meets the man who will become her second husband: Edgard Varèse.

Marcel and Francis quickly resume their bachelor lifestyle, Francis taking up with the dancer Isadora Duncan once again. One day, Isadora urgently summons Marcel Duchamp to her home. She can't tell him the reason over the phone, she says, but begs him to hurry. When Marcel arrives, Isadora takes his hand and leads him mysteriously into her bedroom. There, she indicates the closed door of a large closet. "I have a work of art to show you," she says. Duchamp opens the door. And there, completely nude, is Francis, drinking a cup of hot chocolate.

Marcel himself has a habit of getting entangled in messy romantic situations, carrying on chaotic dalliances with the Stettheimer sisters (pupils of his); with Beatrice Wood, the mistress of Henri-Pierre Roché; with the playwright Sophie Treadwell; and with the modernist poet Mina Loy, for whose attentions he competes with Arthur Cravan—and loses. None of this prevents his heart from leaping the first time he sees Gaby in New York again after her eight-month sojourn in Spain.

"*Bonjour*, Monsieur R. Mutt," she says. Marcel can only smile in amazement. She figured it out. Of course.

Gaby is one of the few people who knows. Marcel keeps up the hoax for as long as possible. He dedicates the May issue of his magazine *The Blind Man* to the rejection of *Fountain*, calling it "The Richard Mutt Case." Gaby also contributes an article. Duchamp's article addresses the scandal: "Whether Mr. Mutt with his own hands made the fountain or not has no importance. He CHOSE it. He took an ordinary article of life, placed it so that its useful significance disappeared under the new title and point of view—created a new thought for that object."

Gaby is blown away by Marcel's daring, which has turned established convention on its head and will surely have a transformative effect on ways of thinking, artistic creation, and production methods. He's the maddest of them all, she knows, and the strongest. He seems to belong, himself, to a whole different dimension. She sees an image in her memory of his gray eyes, the mesmerizing focal point in the awkward body of that young country boy newly arrived in Paris, back when they first met in front of Hedelbert's gallery. Those eyes, the hue of wild anthracite, are still there, but now they belong to the man who has become Marcel Duchamp the *star*, as the Americans say.

A star. It's fitting. He is otherworldly indeed.

Alongside *The Blind Man*, Marcel has co-founded another magazine, this one in collaboration with Henri-Pierre Roché, called *Rongwrong* (it was originally supposed to be titled *Wrongwrong*, but an amusing typographical error determined the final name). Francis starts to become jealous of the friendship between "his" Marcel and Roché, and so he throws down a gauntlet. It's disguised as a game, but in truth it's a battle, one intended to redefine intellectual territories and the balance of power.

Francis challenges Henri-Pierre Roché to a chess match, to

be played in the Arensbergs' lounge. The loser, Picabia says, must give up his magazine. If he loses, he'll stop publishing *391*. If Henri-Pierre loses, he must nip *Rongwrong* in the bud. The whole Arensberg salon gathers to watch the adversaries face off over the black and white tiles. Francis wins without breaking a sweat. *391* is saved, and *Rongwrong* is no more.

Chess is no joke.

Since their return to New York, Gaby's life has become one long party, with no distinction made between day and night. Francis can't tolerate solitude or silence; he invites everyone he meets to come wherever he's going and never makes a move without an entourage of odd characters around him. He has a deep need to be surrounded, paid court to, entertained, by a bizarre and permanent circus. Marcel, for his part, is compulsively pushing his own limits. During a fundraising reception for *The Blind Man*, he narrowly avoids killing himself by climbing a flagpole while staggering drunk. On another evening he climbs to the top of the Washington Square Arch and declares "the independence of Greenwich Village" at the top of his lungs. One night at Joel's Bohemia (an all-night restaurant near Times Square, well known as an artists' hangout) he gets into an altercation with some Americans ("far drunker than we were," he notes) and takes a few punches. "I'm still bleeding and swollen. Nothing serious."

Gabriële feels as if she's witnessing some sort of apocalyptic bacchanal. Francis is clearly in a state of intense restlessness and agitation, the phase that invariably precedes a neurasthenic crash. The more frenzied the merrymaking, the more uneasy she becomes. The parties are spinning out of control; everything, even disaster and darkness, is a source of entertainment. Every day is like Carnaval. For Juliette Gleizes, these evenings gradually take on a hallucinatory quality. "There was something end-of-the-world about them."

Gaby finds some comfort in her friend Elsa Schiaparelli.

She's introduced Elsa to everyone but prefers, these days, to see her one-on-one. They prop each other up and give each other strength, exchanging information that can be helpful when going out in a country that isn't their own, or having husbands who've lost their taste for marriage. Gabriële also enjoys spending time with Arthur Cravan. She's worried about him. He's penniless, roaming the city and spending his nights at the homes of various friends. When the weather is mild, he sometimes sleeps in the entrance to a subway station he's dubbed his "villa," and even, occasionally, under the stars in Central Park. Gabriële gives him money to help him get by and suggests that he come and live with them, but he replies with disarming graciousness that he prefers the green space of Central Park: "The squirrels have become my friends; they sleep in my pockets."

In April 1917, the Picabias' friend Heidi Roosevelt, newly returned to New York, proposes that Marcel and Francis give an "educational" talk on the evolution of art. They would need to simplify their new artistic experimentations for an exclusive, snobbish, and sophisticated audience. Duchamp and Picabia accept, and the invitations are sent out. The men's quick acceptance of Heidi's proposition worries Gabriële; they normally hate these types of events, sneering at them and doing everything they can to avoid them.

"Don't worry, Gaby, we aren't going to talk to them about painting," Marcel reassures her.

"We're just going to explain to them that they're all complete shits," Francis adds.

"'All complete shits,'" Gabriële will repeat later, recounting the prank. Their goal is to recreate a scandal, like the one Arthur Cravan stirred up with *Maintenant*, which had almost earned him a duel with Guillaume Apollinaire.

The day before the event, they inform Heidi Roosevelt that Arthur Cravan will be giving the lecture instead of them. Heidi is rather crestfallen because her guests are coming for the express purpose of meeting "Duchamp and Picabia," the two stars. Not to worry, Marcel and Francis assure her, they'll still be present in the audience, and they promise to answer all her guests' questions after the talk is finished.

On the appointed day, they invite Arthur Cravan to lunch at the Brevoort. Gabriële, who's there too, gradually figures out their plan. Marcel and Francis have set out to get Arthur drunk. One drink, then another, and another. Once he's well soused, they "warm him up" like before a boxing match: all these people are arseholes, they don't even deserve to be spoken to, etc. All three men emerge from the restaurant well and truly tanked, and head directly for the venue.

Once there, Arthur Cravan staggers to the dais. Wobbling and overheated, he strips off his jacket, then his shirt and suspenders, as the audience watches, dumbfounded. Reaching the podium, he drops his trousers. And then he turns around and moons the shocked society ladies before unleashing a tirade of insults at the crowd. Completely out of control.

Duchamp smiles happily at Gaby. "What a lovely lecture!" And it actually was, Gaby will later remember. "A true Dada exhibition before its time." But at what cost? For the police are called, and Arthur Cravan is escorted out in handcuffs, surrounded by cops. Walter Arensberg is obliged to pay a hefty bond to keep him out of prison. Gabriële isn't exactly enamored of the fact that Marcel and Francis got Arthur drunk and then fed him to the wolves—it reminds her unpleasantly of what the army does when recruiting soldiers. "Poor Cravan was very unhappy later," she'll remember. "He said they'd played a hell of a dirty trick on him."

Gabriële is starting to find the men around her tiresome. She's feeling a deep sense of disappointment. Ego clashes are gaining the upper hand over artistic creation. Everything is crumbling. 291 has closed, and the Modern Gallery is stuck in low gear. The relationship between Stieglitz and de Zayas has cooled considerably, and the same is true for Duchamp and the Arensbergs.

The parties are more like orgies. Discussions of art are lost in childish jokes and impulsive outbursts. Marcel, Henri-Pierre, Francis, and Arthur, she can see, are caught up in a sort of unconscious competition that no longer has anything to do with art; instead, it's about who can get the most women, the most attention, the most adoring public. The United States, too, is at war, but this little group seems to be disregarding that fact entirely. They're indifferent to what's happening in the world, indifferent to the reality that people are being butchered, a detachment resulting not from ignorance, but from their having decided that these things simply don't concern them.

Gaby feels as if she's suffocating. In August, she escapes for a few days to the Catskill Mountains in upstate New York. Mountains always have the effect of softening her view of the world. But on her return, she finds that her disgust at the unending circus, where nothing is taken seriously and everyone is obsessed with outperforming each other, where Picabia has become totally unmanageable, has only grown. She wants to leave America, but Francis's papers aren't in order for a return to France. Can she leave him there alone?

The summer, during which Picabia has caroused enough for ten lifetimes, draws to a close. His anxiety attacks have returned, violent and frightening. He talks of going back to Barcelona, as that city seems to calm his nightmares, and besides, he's been corresponding with a gallerist there, Josep Dalmau, about publishing a collection of poetry. He asks Gabriële to arrange the trip as soon as possible. And he wants her to go with him, of course.

But, for the first time, Gaby informs her husband that she won't be accompanying him. He can deal with his papers, his tickets, his nervous breakdowns, and his publishing contracts by himself. She, in the meantime, is leaving for Switzerland. She needs some time alone.

* * *

As we mentioned earlier, we've been struck, while writing this book, by how little we know about the Picabias. The silence surrounding them feels to us like a giant question mark. During our childhood, our mother never talked to us about Francis or Gabriële. We knew there was a painter in our family, and we'd heard our mother mention his name, and so we'd guessed that this "Francis Picabia" had some relationship to her. But what, exactly? It was all very vague.

We never knew our maternal grandfather, Vicente, Francis Picabia and Gabriële Buffet's fourth child (who hasn't been born yet at this point in the story). We never knew him because he died long before we were born, of an overdose, aged 27. Our mother was four years old. So she was raised without a father, and, later, she never spoke to us about him. Consequently, there was a hole in our family tree. No grandfather—and so no great-grandparents, obviously. The whole business was like some forbidden room in the house that no one ever went into, without the door's actually being deliberately locked. We just didn't talk about it. That was simply the way it was.

On the other hand, we had a maternal grandmother who was extremely visible: Myriam Rabinovitch. She had married Vicente, our phantom grandfather, during the war. He was 23 years old; she was 20. So *present* was she that, when we were little girls, our mother's family was "the Rabinovitch family" and not the Picabias at all.

We heard about the Rabinovitches almost every day. They'd all died in the camps, but their vanished lives permeated our childhood like a smothering identity. They took up every bit of the "ancestor" role in our household. Our Rabinovitch forebears had fled the pogroms of Russia and fallen eventually into the deathtrap that was France. Miraculously, our grandmother and our mother had escaped that fate. The Rabinovitches were so dominant in our lives that there was no room for any more ghosts.

It might also be true that we weren't interested in Francis and Gabriële because, quite simply, they weren't interested in us. When Gabriële died in 1985, we were three and six years old, and our older sister was twelve. We were her great-granddaughters. You'd think that those things count in a woman's life—her descendants. But no. She hadn't cared very much about our mother, either, even though she was her granddaughter. Why? Maybe because Gabriële felt responsible for the suicide of her son Vicente. Maybe she wanted to push all of that as far away as she could.

Push away the memory of the night when the police finally managed to reach her, to tell her that they'd found her son barely alive. Only just hanging on. He'd died on the way to the hospital. "There was nothing we could do." The problem was that, in all his twenty-seven years of life, nothing had ever been done for him. It was necessary for Gabriële to remain in denial about that. And that meant denying our mother, Lélia.

It was clear that she never wanted to hear anything about Francis Picabia or Gabriële Buffet, who had never wanted anything to do with her, never put their arms around the living child of their dead child. And yet, it's impossible not to be unsettled when we look at photos of Francis. Our mother looks so much like him. There's something monstrous in the realization. Like an echo of the reason for this book: there is no logic to family ties.

And so, the question we've been wrestling with while working on *Gabriële* has been: how can we write this story without betraying our mother?

It's painful for her that we've chosen to write about them. About these people. About this subject.

Maybe, if it hadn't been for each other, we wouldn't have done it.

Maybe it took two of us to shoulder the betrayal.

23
Paroxysm of Pain

Preparing to leave a place often gives rise to a morbid, fleeting thought: *Will I ever come back here again?* A quick chill that runs down the spine, gone almost as soon as you notice it. And then you think, a bit uneasily: *Odd . . . I was afraid . . .*

This is what Gaby feels in September 1917, on her last evening in New York. Her friends keep saying: "For your last night, we're taking you out to dinner!" And she wonders, *last* in terms of what? The war? The end of my relationship? The last in this beautiful, mesmerizing city that has bled me dry?

Francis insists on going for a drive, and then they go to dinner at the Mouquin Restaurant and Wine Company on Sixth Avenue. The place has its own house orchestra, and they order champagne, of course, and lobster for Gaby. They're still laughing; no one mentions the farewells to come. After the champagne, Gaby wants an ice-cold mint julep; in America, you drink cocktails. She looks at the men around her. There are lines bracketing their eyes now, shadowy commas betraying their excesses.

Marcel remains sublime, transcendent as always. This country has made him iconic. But she can still see, beneath the cavalier façade, a trace of the shy, intense young man from the time when Paris wasn't at war and Marcel wasn't Duchamp. She knows that she's the only one who can still see it, because it's become invisible. But she can see it all. The whole story.

Falling asleep in an American bed for the last time that night, she thinks of the journey to come tomorrow. Francis will accompany her to the ship. She's sure he won't even mention the children, not out of unkindness, but simple oversight. He'll kiss his wife, one of those tight embraces that happen when they're about to be separated for an indefinite period, as if their bodies need a running start.

On the ship bound for France, she'll be alone. Finally. And every day at sea will bring her that much closer to Switzerland, to the trees. Already she's dreaming of reconnecting with nature, with her self, on those long walks that leave her in a state of lifegiving exhaustion. Already she's yearning for that music only she can hear.

The children have grown so much she hardly recognizes them. Jeanine is bolder, feistier than Laure-Marie, the younger sister often taking the older one's hand and leading her off to play. Pancho is a cheerful boy, charming like his father. Less fragile.

Gabriële travels back and forth between Gstaad and Paris. Her time in France is spent trying to untangle the snarl of bureaucratic red tape that is Picabia's government file so she can get him a valid passport. In Switzerland, she spends her time in the mountains, cleansing her lungs with cold sweat, allowing herself to feel at one with the rocky landscape.

Francis writes to her from Barcelona. Many letters. Poems. Funny, she thinks; when he had her right there next to him in New York, he had nothing to say to her, but now that she's gone, he's an inexhaustible source of words. He tells her absolutely everything in the smallest detail; his letters are crammed with pointless information, the way a child would write to his mother. He lists what he eats and everything he does each day (he's seen Picasso at a bullfight) and asks for her advice on the order of the poems in his first collection, which is soon to be released. The poems are clearly foremost in his mind, and he wants to know his wife's opinion on each one of them. Gaby remains his eyes and ears even when they're not in the same country.

Stepping inside the marital home on avenue Charles-Floquet, Gaby is reminded of Pompeii and Herculaneum, those ancient cities frozen for eternity in the mundanity of everyday life. Everything is exactly as it was at the start of the war, here in this large apartment with its white plasterwork and Louis XVI moldings. All the Picabias' mess and clutter sits dully beneath the layer of dust coating the paintings leaning against every wall, the books piled on the floor in precarious stacks, the papers and magazines, and the cards and letters shoved into the gaps between them, the oil lamps and model ships and hats with little veils, the African statues atop the long grand piano. Francis's racing bicycle suspended from the ceiling where a chandelier should be, gleaming in the light filtering through the embroidered pink crêpe de Chine curtains. In the studio, the floor is still strewn with papers, abandoned drawings, and cigarette butts. Cups still ringed with tea-stains sit on the kitchen counters, toys in the children's bedrooms, and, on a small slate flung to the floor, its owner's first name written in a round, childish hand.

Gabriële sleeps there, but doesn't touch anything or make any attempt to tidy up. It's as if this place shouldn't come back to life until Francis and the children are there, someday. Like they were before the war. She finds herself hoping for it, recreating in her mind scenes of familial happiness that may never have existed. Regarding all these domestic objects as if their presence here together stands as a kind of promise that things will start over again one day. One evening, she paints in large black letters on the foyer wall: BONJOUR PICABIA!

Gaby has also been reunited with Guillaume. Her trepanned poet. Nearly killed. A piece of shrapnel to the head. She meets him at the offices of *Paris-Midi*, where he's working, and they go to lunch together.

The first time she sees him, it's as if her heart bursts into glittering rainbow shards. He's alive. And he isn't even much changed. She realizes, suddenly, how big of a void his absence had created in her life. How deeply worried she'd been for his safety. Her dear friend, gone off to play soldier. Ecstatic at being reunited with his Gabriële, Guillaume wraps her in a bear hug and lifts her off her feet. They have so much to tell each other about the different wars they've each been fighting. "He'd gotten even bigger," Gabriële will recall, "and still had his goatee, and on his head, to protect his scar, he wore a kind of protective helmet that accentuated his Roman look. He was in his infantry lieutenant's uniform and spoke happily about his heroic adventures; he said the noise of the cannons was the only thing he found unbearable and told me how he was wounded. He almost hadn't noticed it at the time; he was reading *Le Mercure de France*, leaning against a tree, and the sudden spreading pool of blood on the pages made him realize he'd been seriously wounded; he'd thought it was nothing more than a tree branch falling on his head."

How very typical of Guillaume, to confuse a bullet with a falling branch. He loves talking about the war, and about his wound. He tells Gaby about a young man, assigned to the hospital in Nantes as a medic, who's been sending him letters and poems. The boy's only twenty years old, but he's clever and not lacking in life experience, Guillaume explains to Gabriële. His name is André Breton, and he and Francis Picabia would get on splendidly.

When Apollinaire asks her about Francis, Gaby admits to him that their relationship is in trouble, which upsets Guillaume almost more than it does her. They *can't* separate, he repeats again and again, deliberately using the word "can't" rather than "shouldn't," as if he genuinely believes that neither Gabriële nor Francis can exist without the other. Full stop. The idea of a separation seems more shocking to him than any of the dramatic war stories being told all over Paris. Apollinaire as marital counselor: what a joke. These stolen moments with her tenderhearted poet brighten the grim months of autumn 1917. Gaby only feels good when she's with him. She's never met any other man as naturally kind and thoughtful as Guillaume, or as genuinely selfless. A heart precious as Carrara marble.

One evening when they've planned to meet at the Âne Rouge restaurant, Guillaume shows up with Max Jacob. The dinner starts out well, with both men in top form, competing to see who can make Gabriële laugh the most with their witty wordplay. But things break down abruptly. Max, whose face has turned red with fury in the span of a few seconds, rips into Guillaume: "You steal all my ideas; you'd be nothing without me!"

Gabriële tries to defuse the tension, to steer the two men back toward a mood of humor and lightness, but Guillaume sits stony-faced, refusing to look at his friend, who continues to lash out. All of a sudden, she can't bear the intensity of their anger. She excuses herself and leaves, pleading fatigue.

On the way back home, Gaby trips on a cobblestone and almost falls. The near miss jerks her out of her reverie, and she realizes that she's lost. How is it possible to get lost on such a familiar route, one she's walked so many times? She feels slightly dizzy. Then, at once, she realizes why she's so distracted. Francis will be able to return to France soon, but she's uneasy, afraid of what their reunion will bring. Filled with a sense of foreboding. The next day, she buys a ticket to visit the children.

Picabia arrives in Paris in November 1917, after more than two and a half years away. Gaby has already been in Gstaad for several days by then, and so Francis comes home to an empty apartment with its message of welcome, BONJOUR PICABIA! The black paint has dripped down the wall as it dried, leaving long inky trails all the way to the floor. Francis smiles and doesn't turn on the light.

Gabriële had told him that she wouldn't be there to greet him. Now Francis, who hates to be alone, stretches out on the leather sofa in the living room without taking off his shoes, feeling his heart pound. He lies there for a long time, motionless, feeling as if he's going mad, listening to the shuddering beat of his heart.

Gabriële returns to Paris a month later, in late December. She lets herself into the Charles-Floquet apartment—and jumps. Picabia is standing there in the foyer, solemn-faced, as tense as a little boy who's done something wrong and is trying not to let on. Gaby doesn't speak, just sets down her bags and takes off her coat and hat, her movements slow and graceful. Then she stands, facing her husband, and waits.

The two Picabias look at each other for a long time, as if examining a strange yet familiar image in a tarnished mirror. But nothing happens. Nothing. Until Francis turns and leaves the foyer. Now out of sight, he says to her: "I need to tell you about a woman. Germaine."

Ah, Gaby thinks. *So here we are.*

Francis and Gabriële spent the whole night talking. In the wee hours, they curled up together in bed to get some sleep. The nearness of their bodies turned into an embrace, and they made love, melding for a few moments into a single being. Now they're deeply asleep, two knocked-out boxers, bruised and weary, drained by the dark flow of hours of conversation.

Gaby understood the situation immediately. For the first time since they met, her husband has fallen in love with another woman. It was bound to happen one day. He fell in love and fell ill at the same time. He's tormented, for he genuinely can't live without Gabriële. This man who lost his mother can't bear the idea of a separation. But he misses Germaine so much that it's physically painful. In his agony, he pleads with Gaby to find a "solution." Otherwise, he says, he might go mad.

At around noon, Gabriële detaches herself from her husband's body and goes into the kitchen to make herself a very strong coffee, hoping it'll help her think straight. She knows that steps need to be taken, and quickly. Francis's threats aren't to be taken lightly, for the madness that lives inside him, bursting out from time to time like an evil genie, is no put-on. "The devil follows me day and night because he's afraid of being alone," he sometimes says, and Gabriële knows it isn't a joke.

The first item on the agenda is to meet the other woman, Germaine Everling, to assess the situation. Gaby picks up the phone and dials the number Francis has given her.

"Madame Germaine Everling? This is Madame Picabia."

There's a stunned silence on the other end of the line. Germaine has been waiting anxiously for a call from her lover. Not from his wife. She'll remember the astonishing phone call in her memoirs, entitled *L'Anneau de Saturne*, or *Saturn's Ring*. Hearing Gabriële for the first time, Germaine will say she found her voice to have "a rare musicality, sweet and sharp at the same time, like certain fruits that are sweet when bitten into but leave a sour taste on the lips."

"I returned from Switzerland last night," Gaby continues. "When I came home, I felt at first as if my house had been burned down while I was gone. Then we talked about you, all night, my husband and I, and now I feel a great desire to know you. Come and have dinner with us tonight."

Germaine accepts immediately, unthinkingly, so shaken by this unexpected invitation that she doesn't know what else to say. Gabriële, for her part, is relieved; her husband's mistress doesn't seem to be the hysterical sort, or a troublemaker. Maybe they'll be able to reach an understanding.

Francis, meanwhile, has sunk into a depressive trance. A delirium tremens linked to the revelation of his secret; to anxiety about the future; a cold, greasy, feverish sweat. Yet again he wants everything and nothing. To be alone, to have Gabriële and Germaine at once. He wants one of the two women to vanish forever, sometimes Gaby, sometimes Germaine; he wants it to be understood that he isn't a "beautiful monster," as he describes himself occasionally, but a victim: of women, of physical love, of marital obligations. It's consuming him, so much so that he bites at his bed linens with rage.

If she were listening to her own mind alone, Gabriële would turn her back on this mess immediately. Leave it all behind and disappear. The problem is that Francis can't live without her. He is her child. If she abandons him, she'll be putting him in real danger.

The doorbell rings in the apartment on avenue Charles-Floquet at six P.M. sharp. Gabriële tries to conceal her anxiety, to appear calm, detached, smiling. She opens the door to reveal Germaine, a pretty little thing with a frank, open face. Gaby suggests that they take tea in the living room. Germaine agrees, dazed and mesmerized.

The two women now sipping tea together are absolutely terrified of one another. They eye each other, scrutinizing and assessing, all while remaining impeccably polite and gracious. The blood is pounding in their temples, and their hearts are hammering as if they might explode, but they'd both rather die than show it. Gaby's personality quickly makes a strong impression on Germaine: "Picabia had bragged to me so much about his partner's intelligence, the clarity of her mind, her absolute understanding of all things, that I was quite fearful of facing such a superior being." Gabriële, for her part, finds Germaine very beautiful, just as she'd imagined her. "Francis loved being surrounded by lovely, elegant women." But she didn't expect to see such a keen spark of intellect in the other woman's eye. This gives her confidence for the negotiations to come—it's always best to have a level playing field—but unnerves her slightly, as well. Germaine Everling isn't going to be manipulated so easily.

To conceal the new fear coursing through her, Gabriële picks up a nail file and goes to work on her nails, apologetically. This not only gives her something to do with her trembling hands, but it allows her to establish a kind of informality between them, as well—not to mention reminding Germaine that Gabriële is in her own home, on her territory. Germaine, struck, sees the gesture as an assertion of power on her rival's part. As she'll recall in her memoirs: "And with that, she ran a buffer repeatedly over her fingernails, just the way a businessman would light a cigarette at the start of a pivotal conversation."

Gabriële makes her opening gambit by asking a few questions. It rapidly becomes clear to her that Germaine Everling, happily, is no naïve little goose. She's already experienced the failure of a first marriage; she has a son named Michel and is currently going through a painful divorce. She's a *woman*, not a young girl, someone with whom Gaby will be able to talk "man-to-man," as it were. More than anything, Gaby's reassured that this is no gold-digger, but a beautiful bourgeoise Parisienne, a modern Madame Bovary trying to follow the dictates of her heart and her passions, but without being mercenary or thoughtless. "She was a woman of the world," Gaby will write later, "and she was in love."

As they keep talking, Gabriële realizes that Francis has lied shamefully to his new mistress. He's led her to believe that he'd been living alone and hopeless since his wife abandoned him even though he was very sick, on the brink of death. When she hears this, Gabriële doesn't know whether to laugh or cry. Mostly, she just feels a monumental sense of exhaustion. She concentrates on buffing her nails, trying to keep her face impassive.

Abruptly, Germaine Everling breaks off, unsettled. She's just spotted a photograph of Gaby and Francis on a bookcase, taken during their honeymoon in Martigues. In it, Germaine recognizes the façade of the hotel where Francis took her for their first intimate night together. She remembers, now, how the hotel manager had mistaken her for "Madame Picabia" before correcting himself, embarrassed by his blunder. How she'd felt a brief, nauseating surge of unease. The next day, on the beach, Francis had spoken to her for the first time of the "other" woman, his wife Gabriële, while tossing pebbles into the sea.

The two women have no idea that they experienced a near-identical scene ten years apart, one that could be entitled "Stoic Woman on a Beach with a Picabia," with the male protagonist dramatically announcing the existence of another woman while angrily throwing stones into the waves.

An hour of conversation later, Germaine has answered all of Gabriële's questions. Now it's her turn to steer the boat, though she finds it difficult, seeing Gabriële Buffet as "a being far above average—indisputably a true *personality*." Summoning all her courage, she tells Madame Picabia that Francis wants to move out of the family apartment and into the one she shares with her son. She launches into an interminable explanation of the well-being Francis feels when he's in her home, that he loves the morning light for writing his poems, that he appreciates the arrangement and decoration of the rooms, finding them conducive to his creative process, etc. Gabriële listens in silence, wanting neither to hurt Germaine nor to interrupt her charming monologue about Picabia's ideal working conditions. How can she break it to the younger woman, without being cruel, that Francis has changed his mind, that he no longer wants to move in with her but isn't brave enough to tell her? He's spent the whole day begging Gabriële to find him an excuse. He wants to stay in the avenue Charles-Floquet apartment, in his longtime home, with his own furnishings, but doesn't know how to give his mistress the news.

And so Gaby takes on the dirty job herself.

"You know that I make no claim whatsoever to owning my husband," she begins. "If he'd rather live with you, I wouldn't think of standing in his way. It's just that he's ill. I've had the doctor in, and he's ordered complete rest and quiet."

"I don't understand . . . he seemed absolutely fine when he left me yesterday . . . "

"My dear," Gaby says, cutting Germaine off, "you'll find that Francis's attacks are severe and always unexpected. We'll talk about this more later—I have a lot to tell you about it. But let me finish first. I don't want to separate you. I've never particularly wanted to be a nurse, myself, and I also have a lot to do. Francis's affairs were neglected while I was away. So, here's my suggestion: you should come here every day and keep him company. He's restricted to his room for now; his heart wouldn't be able to stand any kind of move in his current condition. In the meantime, please feel free to stay for dinner whenever you like; it would make me very happy. I believe that both you and I are quite beyond being bound by bourgeois convention."

Gabriële makes these outrageous, even indecent suggestions in a calm, matter-of-fact tone. She knows it's mad to be proposing such things—unacceptable—but this is what Francis wants: to live with his mistress in his wife's home. And so Gaby goes for broke, out of love for him, and pity, too. Far from breaking down in this crisis situation, she's doing what she always does: organizing the chaos.

Against all expectations, Germaine agrees to the arrangement. An intelligent opponent indeed. And yet she'll describe herself as captivated, bowled over by Gaby's conduct. "What loftiness of spirit, I thought, and what unconditional fondness she must have for her husband, to accept a situation that so many other women would find humiliating."

Their negotiations concluded, Gaby and Germaine go into Francis's room together. Germaine will recall, "He was sitting up in bed, wearing a black silk shirt and eating a bowl of *potage au lait*!" He reaches out to take Germaine's hand and kiss it, looking questioningly at Gaby.

"We're quite in agreement. Germaine—may I call you Germaine?—Germaine will keep you company while I'm away, which will be often."

And so, there they are, the three of them, in the semi-darkness of the Picabias' marital bedroom at dusk. The alliance between the spouses is unbounded, the role of each remarkable, extraordinary. It's Gabriële who's playing hostess to the mistress while Francis stays in bed, eating his soup, like an overgrown little boy with the flu. It's Gaby who shoulders the burden of leadership, assigning the roles and managing the agendas of each.

Gaby the orchestra conductor. Francis's face lights up with an unsettling yellowish illumination as he smokes one cigarette after another—"cigarettes brought back from Switzerland, a thoughtful wifely gesture," as Germaine will recall in her memoirs.

25
COWARDICE OF SUBTLE BARBARISM

From the next day onward, Germaine shows up each day at the avenue Charles-Floquet apartment, regular as a Swiss cuckoo clock, to keep Francis company. When friends are present, Gaby is audacious enough to introduce the new arrival as "my husband's nurse," always with an ambiguous smile.

Germaine tolerates it all, reassured by the love poems Francis slips her, words meant for her alone:

You are the sweetest imaginable,
The marvel of the Spanish serenaders,
Mine like a precious relic.
My little girl is devoted to me,
And I'm feeling much better.

A little girl. A relic. She has a sweetness all her own. She's almost a fetish object, a child-woman who yields, who indulges, who caresses. Submissive. The total opposite of Gabriële. Gaby sometimes reads the poems addressed to Germaine, for Francis leaves them shamelessly all over the apartment. Their mawkishness makes her roll her eyes.

As crazy as it might seem, Gaby wants to protect Germaine Everling from the entourage of ne'er-do-wells she herself helped to put in place. She worries about Germaine, who seems thinner, tired, often sad. She encourages the younger woman to take her mind off things, to go to the movies or out with friends, to immerse herself in a healthier environment. But Germaine, like those women who lie about their unhappy situations at home for fear of being thought a victim, has stopped speaking to her old friends at all. Her only refuge is her passionate love. Francis is a drug.

But Gaby is afraid Germaine will sink. A respectable woman like her is ill-equipped to fight in this war. She imagines Germaine returning to her apartment on the rue Émile-Augier in the evenings, falling asleep wracked with anxiety: *Who is this couple I've gotten myself mixed up with, really? Are they mad?*

To reassure herself, Gaby projects onto Germaine the questions she's really asking herself. Why go along with all of this? She knows her own answer, at least. In a final act of loyalty to Francis Picabia, she is orchestrating the passing of the torch.

So that she will, finally, be able to rest.

Francis writes at length to his mistress, complaining of his deep melancholy. He's feeling worse and worse. It's simply too much. Gabriële is scrambling, questioning everyone she knows in her efforts to find the best doctor in Europe. Someone recommends a highly regarded neurologist in Lausanne, Dr. Brunschwiller. Gabriële makes an appointment and arranges the trip, then calls Germaine to explain the situation. Germaine is frankly stunned by the thought of Francis going somewhere five hundred kilometers away with his wife.

But: "Who's talking about separating you? I wouldn't dream of it. Let me take my husband to Switzerland, and you can join us just as soon as we've settled in."

Germaine, not entirely reassured, slips Francis a gushing love letter just before he departs.

In response, she receives a brief, almost terse note: "We're first and foremost the best of friends, and we count on each other. Francis, February 16, 1918."

Nothing makes sense to Germaine Everling anymore.

Gabriële, who saw Francis's note, is equally confused.

One might think that this journey to Switzerland is a

subterfuge designed by Gaby to get Francis away from Germaine without any fuss, but no. She's truly concerned about the state of her husband's health. Deep down, Germaine's presence has allowed her to share the burden that Francis poses when he's in the grip of a serious depressive episode. The younger woman is like a partner in crime. And in the last weeks of 1917, Picabia sank deeper and deeper into an alarming darkness, even if he did put on a show of high spirits at times. Now, as always, Gabriële frequently comes to his rescue, handling problems for him. She is his structural element, his spinal column. She's taking him to Switzerland so that he can be cared for by the best doctors, breathe cleaner air than there is to be found in the capital, reunite with their children—and be far away from the temptations of Paris, particularly alcohol and drugs. And Germaine, as his devoted nurse, is an important part of the plan.

The Picabias settle at the Winter Palace Hotel in Gstaad. Gabriële blossoms like a flower in the whiteness of her mountains, the restorative bite of the frozen air that cuts to her bones on her solitary walks. Francis remains bedridden in the hotel room, hardly speaking, withdrawn into himself. He hates Switzerland.

Germaine, meanwhile, is eagerly preparing to join them. She arranges to meet Francis at the Hotel Mirabeau in Lausanne, but Europe is still at war, and, unlike the Picabias, who have friends in high places to facilitate their travels, she gets stuck in the border town of Bellegarde for eight days.

When she finally reaches her destination, she finds only a note Francis has left for her at the Hotel Mirabeau's reception desk, informing her that he's been delayed, as his son Pancho is very ill.

Picabia does show up in the end, restless and evasive. The young woman in love who was expecting a rapturous reunion after her difficult journey is disappointed. Francis is distracted, returning again and again to his son's worrying condition. Germaine demands an explanation, and the reply is a firm one for Francis:

"It's awful. I don't think I'll ever be brave enough to leave my wife and children." He excuses himself; he needs rest, he's leaving for Gstaad with Gabriële. He promises to come back to her very soon, but in the meantime, could she go and visit poor Pancho, who's still at the Montbrion clinic in Lausanne?

It's unacceptable. Germaine knows this. But as she'll say later, she's blinded by love, like anyone in the throes of uncontrollable passion. And, yet again, she has no idea of the truth: that it's *Gaby* who instructed Francis to bring Germaine to Switzerland because he was, as ever, too mercurial and irresolute to make the decision. One day Germaine is the love of his life; the next, he's mooning over a young Belgian beauty seen in the hotel lobby. It's Gabriële who works to soothe the torments of his heart, to find concrete solutions, as if she were his best friend and not his wife.

Gabriële and Francis, astonishing as it might seem, are more tightly bonded than ever. Picabia conceals absolutely nothing from his wife. He relies on her. She is his double, his family, his partner. Even if they decided not to live together anymore, it would change nothing. They're connected, like twin flames, for life.

She still goes for long walks every day; it's her salvation. This woman, so cerebral, turns sensual upon contact with pines and lakes and snowy peaks, as if the hard beauty of the landscape enables her to be wholly herself, to let herself go.

When Germaine Everling visits the Picabias' young son as requested, she receives a bit of a shock. Pancho is doing wonderfully well, playing contentedly in his room. At the sight of her astonished expression, the nurse reassures her about the boy's condition: yes, he's still convalescent, but he's been on the mend for at least a week and a half, and his mother comes to see him regularly. Nothing to worry about.

Germaine returns to her hotel, troubled by Francis's lies and prevarications. A few days later, he tells her on the phone that Gaby is going off to the mountains by herself for a bit, and asks if she'll join him in Gstaad.

Of course. Germaine duly arrives, but Gaby returns from her trip earlier than planned. Germaine can't believe it. Gabriële is omnipresent—omniscient, even. An unnerving goddess. Nothing escapes her. It has to be said that she is and will always remain Francis's main confidante. That's just the way it is. Little by little, Germaine comes to understand this.

Their menage à trois resumes. One can only imagine the hotel gossip. It buzzes around them when they sit down to dinner, or a drink in the bar. The Picabias, that scandalous pair. The whole little group makes frequent trips between Lausanne and Gstaad, depending on their moods and on the various doctors to be consulted.

Gaby's calm self-confidence begins to crack.

She remains the soul of the brilliant Picabia, the confidante of the great Francis, but, she wonders, is the cost to herself too great? She writes to her friend, her brother, Lieutenant Guillaume Apollinaire. How wonderful it would be if he joined her in Switzerland. His presence would give her new strength. Her message is pressing but betrays none of her unhappiness:

> *March 1, 1918*
> *If you could come here for a bit of relaxation it would make me very happy. So do come if you can. I think it would be so splendid to form a little community here—is that impossible?*
> *Warmly yours,*
>
> *Gabriële Picabia*

But Guillaume can't make the trip. Neither of the Picabias seems to be truly aware that Europe is at war, and that this isn't the time to travel for pleasure. But in the end, it doesn't matter, for a few weeks later Gabriële returns to Paris. She says it's to "take care of some things," but really it's to see Guillaume. He's told her about an "event" at which he'd like her to be present, leaving the whole thing tantalizingly mysterious.

Hardly has she set foot in the avenue Charles-Floquet apartment when Gabriële receives a note from Apollinaire: "Would you like to be a witness at my wedding?" Gaby smiles, delighted. At least one of them is lucky in love. Her friendship with the poet is unique, based entirely on mutual generosity. During the war, it was Gaby who sent money and little care packages to Apollinaire wherever he was stationed, and Guillaume who urged Gabriële to keep writing, to use her magnificent mind. There's never been the slightest hint of competitiveness between them, never the smallest disagreement. They recognized each other, from the beginning and forever, as sibling souls.

Gabriële is already acquainted with the woman who's won Guillaume's heart. Apo met this "pretty redheaded" painter, who sometimes goes by Jacqueline, sometimes Ruby (though her real name is Amélia Kolb), in the summer of 1917. Engaged at the time to Madeleine Pagès, Guillaume had simply noted that Jacqueline had "hair like the sun." But he'd broken the engagement to Madeleine soon afterward and taken up with Amélia, dedicating a poem to her in his collection *Calligrams*, published in April 1918:

> *She comes and attracts me like a magnet draws iron*
> *Her complexion the charming one*
> *Of a beautiful redhead.*

Gabriële chooses her gown for the wedding with unusual care, wanting to do justice to the importance of the occasion. It's a frock by her friend, the couturier Paul Poiret, known as "Poiret le magnifique." She's set to meet Guillaume and his fiancée at ten o'clock in the morning at the courthouse of Paris's seventh arrondissement. It's May 2, 1918. Apollinaire has invited only a select few people to the ceremony, which he describes as "so sacred and so intimate." No family, no friends. Only the witnesses chosen by the couple. Guillaume's witnesses are Pablo Picasso and Gabriële Buffet. An odd pair. If Picabia knew, he'd be furious.

After the civil wedding, the merry little group follows the couple to their religious ceremony at the church of Saint Thomas Aquinas, then decamps to Poccardi, on the boulevard des Italiens, for lunch. "The ceremony was followed by a feast so exquisitely chosen, and accompanied by such lovely wines, that I'll admit my memories of the rest of the day's events are a bit hazy," Gabriële will write. On the menu: hors d'oeuvres, ravioli *al pollo*, filet of turbot, entrecôte of beef, asparagus, and wild strawberries, washed down with Chianti and Asti Spumante (!).

Gabriële also takes advantage of this Parisian interlude, these few days alone in the capital without children or husband—or husband's mistress—to recover her own spirits. It's going to take strength for her to go back to Gstaad.

She departs for Switzerland a few days later, reinvigorated. And as it turns out, a happy surprise is awaiting her. Picabia has regained some color, she sees immediately—and in every sense of the term, because he's painting again. She studies his latest composition: a fairly complex machine, composed of multiple turbines, interwoven and overlapping one another. It's very interesting. But before she can give any opinion at all:

"I'm calling it *Brilliant Vagina*."

Yes. Francis is definitely feeling better.

So much better, in fact, that he's embarked on an affair with a married woman, another hotel guest. This woman is a French painter of keen intelligence, charismatic and beautiful. Her first name is Charlotte, but she goes by Carlos. Her husband, Costica Gregori, is a tall blond Romanian, pale and retiring, diagnosed with a "nervous ailment."

Several weeks before, the Gregoris took a shine to Germaine Everling, so much so that they came to serve as her confidants on those evenings when the young woman stole off into the hotel corridors to cry. They've followed the bizarre daily saga of the Picabia trio ever since, their curiosity particularly piqued because they know Francis, at least by name and reputation. Then they're introduced to the Picabias themselves, and eventually the inevitable happens: Charlotte, otherwise known as Carlos, falls in love with Francis, and the moment Germaine leaves on a brief trip to Paris to look after her son, she tumbles into bed with him.

Gabriële sits alone in the hotel's plush lounge one evening, nursing a glass of whiskey, enjoying a bit of solitude before dinner. Germaine is in France, Francis taking a bath. As for the Gregoris, it's been several days since they last dined with them. Costica has noticed the loving looks his wife's been aiming in Picabia's direction and, pathologically jealous, has locked her in their room.

How peaceful this is, Gabriële thinks, savoring the sharp bite of her favorite tipple with its soothing coppery-amber glow. But suddenly she hears the sound of gunshots coming from the hotel lobby. Startled, she looks around at the other people in the room, who wear similarly anxious expressions. Everyone turns. The bartender crouches reflexively behind his bar. Children start screaming.

And then Gabriële sees her husband. He's running down the hall, pursued by a disheveled Costica Gregori, his normally pale face crimson with rage. The betrayed husband is quite simply trying to kill Picabia.

A bullet grazes Francis, and then the wronged husband is seized by hotel staff. Gaby regretfully sets down her glass.

Wouldn't it have been easier if he'd killed him? she thinks, for a flashing instant.

"Who's going to explain all this to Germaine?" she asks a few moments later as she bandages Picabia's wound, which is barely more than a scratch. Three more days, and the mistress will be back from Paris. "Not me," Gaby adds quickly, before Francis can open his mouth. She's had enough of his *surréaliste* banter—to use the wonderful term coined by Apollinaire as a subtitle for his play *The Breasts of Tiresias*, when the revised version was staged in June 1917.

On the day of Germaine's return, on Gaby's orders, Francis goes to meet her at the station. He's very sick, he warns her, as she steps off the train. He's sorry, but he can't even help her carry her baggage (!). The two walk side-by-side, Germaine silent, disappointed by the chilly welcome. Then, abruptly, as if he can't hold the announcement in any longer, Francis blurts:

"Costica shot at me twice in the lobby of the Hôtel Beau Séjour."

"*What?* Why?"

"Jealousy. I slept with his wife."

Germaine, thunderstruck, doesn't say anything. After a pause, Francis adds, without looking at her:

"What can I say? I'm Francis Picabia. It's my weakness."

26
FUNNY GUY

The Spanish flu is ravaging Europe. The newspapers are censoring information about it, but rumors are rife. There are murmurs of another plague, of many thousands of deaths; they say people are turning black and dying in the space of a single night and being hurriedly buried. The news is alarming, to say the least. In Lausanne, with the situation worsening, Picabia decides to leave for Bex with both women and all the children: "Best not to be separated, in these anxious times!" he says. The blended family moves into the Hôtel des Salines, reserving three rooms—with Francis claiming the one in the middle.

The tenderhearted Germaine is extremely fond of the three Picabia children, especially Jeanine, the youngest, whom she hoists onto her shoulders for fast-paced "horseback" rides "astride my cob." Gabriële, for her part, quite likes Germaine's son Michel, a strapping teenager enamored by the mountains, taking him on daily walks and introducing him to mountaineering. Solitary by nature, she comes to appreciate the quiet yet enthusiastic company of this young man.

August 4, 1918
My dear Guillaume,
I'd very much like to hear from you; what are you doing with yourself? Where are you? I've been working a great deal recently but am also very tired and on complete rest at Bex—I've finished my little book, which was published in Lausanne:
Poems and Drawings of the Girl Born Without a Mother. *I'd have loved to send you a copy but I don't think it's possible to*

post anything to France at the moment. The war news is very good; we have to hope we're at the end, don't you think? My best wishes to your wife, and I clasp your hands affectionately in my own.

Francis Picabia
Do write!

As he often does, Picabia decorates this letter with sketches—his previous correspondence with Apo has included things like a boat on an ocean, or the rugged face of a bullfighter. On this particular missive, mailed from Bex-les-Bains on August 4, he draws himself in profile gazing at two small dogs next to him, writing in parentheses above the drawing: "I have two dogs."

No comment.

At around this same time, the Picabias get a letter from Duchamp, complaining about how bored he is in the United States: "Everything's changed, and there's far less to do. I've been working a little. Nothing finished. How I'd love a game of chess with the two of you."

Marcel is about to leave New York on an open-ended trip to Buenos Aires, disgusted by everything and determined to "cut ties completely with that part of the world." He plans to be away for at least two years, if not "several years, most likely," looking forward to hiding himself away in a country where no one knows who he is—and no one will talk to him about painting. He asks his friends and family to respect his desire for exile and silence. But the day before his departure for Argentina, he writes this letter to Francis and Gaby, like a final flinching before the leap into the void: "Meet me there, both of you, and if we don't like it, we'll find ourselves an island. The advantage is that it's far away."

Gaby surprises herself by dreaming of Marcel, of being reunited with him, *far away*, on an exotic journey. For the first time, she wants to be alone together, just the two of them.

Or just the three of them.

She could leave on a whim, of course, *à la Picabia*. Join Duchamp in Argentina, appearing out of nowhere like a mirage, the way Marcel once did on the platform at Andelot Station.

But there's something new keeping Gabriële at her husband's side. Something powerful, intoxicating, wild. It's Francis's poetry. Picabia has begun writing like a madman, and reading his poems aloud to Gabriële. She's always known him as a painter, but now she finds herself more and more attracted by his explorations of language. A poet of an altogether new kind. Gaby is enraptured by his poetry, possessed by the urgent need to share it with the world, just as she's done with his painting since the day they met, and indeed one is an extension of the other, the words Francis's latest artistic medium. The name of his collection, *Girl Born Without a Mother*, is for Gaby a definition of the machine, a pictorial matter Picabia and Duchamp have been trying to resolve for years. This penetration of the object field as artistic subject, she believes, is truly revolutionary. She assists with the editing and publication of the slim volume, provides explanations to the public, and writes articles to accompany this strange assembly of poems and drawings with their themes, jumbled together pell-mell, of sex, anger, drugs, Switzerland, art, and machines.

"Picabia's written works," Gabriële opines, "are missing none of the revolutionary qualities of his paintings. They are produced by the same alchemy, and have the same power to shock and enthrall."

Gabriële doesn't merely serve as copy editor for the poems. Francis asks her to insert her own words into his verse. On the whiteness of the page, the Picabias become a couple once more. "At his request, I frequently added a few words of my own to his texts."

In Zurich, a copy of *Girl Born Without a Mother* ends up in the hands of a young Romanian poet named Tristan Tzara and the members of Dada, the artistic movement he's helped to found. These fellow members include Jean Arp, Richard Huelsenbeck, Hugo Ball, Marcel Janco, Emmy Hennings, and Sophie Taeuber. Gabriële will write of them: "Their work was similar in many ways to that of the 391 group, but its attitude was less egotistical, more mystical and naïve, the yearning for recourse to primal forces."

On August 21, Francis receives a letter from Tzara, who identifies himself as the publisher of a modern art magazine and says he'd be honored to collaborate with him. Francis replies immediately, thus beginning a compulsive epistolary exchange with each man sending the other his magazines: *Dada* for Tzara, and *391* for Picabia. Both are delighted to find that they speak the same language.

Francis cheerfully ignores the advice of Dr. Harb, who admonishes him to rest, and throws himself headfirst into his plans with the passionate Tzara. Gabriële, greatly interested by Dada herself, also begins corresponding with the young Romanian.

It's all very new and very exciting.

But Gaby is summoned urgently back to Paris to see Guillaume. Those close to him have informed her that he's ill, even though he doesn't want to worry her, and she wants to see for herself that he's all right.

Gaby does find Apollinaire somewhat changed; he's short of breath and paler than usual. But she's reassured by the fact that, as soon as he starts talking, he's the same old enthusiastic Guillaume he's always been. He demands the latest news and, hearing the stories from Switzerland, repeats like a priest chanting an incantation that she must not leave Francis. Changing the subject, Gaby peppers him with questions of her own, about his latest collection of poems and his future plans; what is he working on at the moment? But Guillaume only wants to talk about her. He cuts her off, asking that simple yet profound question exclusively reserved for true friendship:

"How are you *really*, Gabriële?"

The question hits her like a knife in the gut. She falters, suddenly aware that no one ever asks her that anymore. The mighty, untouchable Gabriële. And then, all at once, the mask drops. She opens her soul to her poet. Feelings bubble to the surface, feelings she's been unwilling to acknowledge, that she's quashed in her determination to keep a tight grip on her own psyche. The superhuman dam that has been holding back the anger, the frustration, the humiliation fleetingly felt and then repressed, breaks.

Guillaume comforts her, supports her as she accepts the truth. She is deeply sad.

Apollinaire is her subconscious. Her guardian angel.

Gabriële has to return to Lausanne, so Guillaume proposes that they meet for dinner at the Gare de Lyon before her train. His wife Jacqueline is the first to arrive. She confides in Gaby that she's worried about Guillaume's health. Gaby is puzzled; he didn't seem very ill to her. The opposite, in fact. But just then he joins them, and the trio takes a table at Le Train Bleu. They talk of the imminent end of the war, of what they'll do afterward when all their friends are together again, of life resuming as before in Montmartre and Montparnasse. Then it's time for Gaby's train, and the Kostrowitzkys accompany her to the carriage door. Hugs and kisses are exchanged, and the locomotive rumbles to life. As the train pulls away, Gaby sees Guillaume's bearlike arms, waving as high as he can manage, prolonging the farewell, staying with her as far as he can.

At Bellegarde, the border is completely closed. Panic. There's talk of an armistice, but the bulletins remain hazy, and there are no newspapers or mail available. Travelers who had intended to cross into Switzerland are instead bundled into cheap hotels to wait for the situation to become clearer. For the moment, nothing is happening, and no one moves. Gaby shares a room with a few other unfortunates on standby.

At five o'clock in the morning on November 11, 1918, the announcement comes that a train is about to depart for Switzerland. Gaby hurries to the station, because there won't be enough seats for everyone, and manages to board. In Geneva there are shouts of "Armistice," everyone riotously happy. The train goes on to Lausanne.

Disembarking, Gaby looks for a French newspaper, eager for news from her own country.

The atmosphere of jubilation is growing and growing, people draping flags in their windows. At last she finds a French paper, scans the headlines, flips through the pages. And stumbles across a brief obituary:

"The poet and critic Guillaume Apollinaire died in Paris on November 9."

All the joy goes dark.

Dots of light, distorted sounds.

Guillaume is dead.

Gabriële weeps.

For the first time in her life.

"I still don't know anything about Guillaume Apollinaire's death, have only just read about it in the papers," Francis writes to Tristan Tzara. "The flu struck and killed him in the space of only a few days. It must have been very fast, because my wife had dinner with him and Madame Apollinaire at the Gare de Lyon, on the evening of her return to Switzerland from France, only a week before, and he sent me his best regards. Apparently, he seemed his usual active self, in perfect health, engaged in numerous projects. There was even talk of spending a few weeks in the mountains together.

"His death still seems impossible to me. Guillaume Apollinaire is one of those rare individuals who witnessed the entire evolution of modern art and understood it completely; he championed it valiantly and honestly because he loved it, just as he loved life, and every kind of new venture. His mind was rich, sumptuous even, supple and sensitive, proud and childlike. His work is full of variety, spirit, and invention.

Francis Picabia."

Reunited, Francis and Gabriële hold each other tightly in mutual, unfathomable grief. Wordless.

With the end of the war, they'll be able to move back to Paris. But how will they live without Apo?

Paris is a tomb. Going back would mean burying their friend too soon. Their grief is simply too raw.

To escape it, they accept Tristan Tzara's invitation to join him in Zurich.

Tzara and the painter Jean Arp have arranged to meet the Picabias at the Hôtel Élite. When they arrive, they find Francis and Gabriële bent with childlike concentration over something on a table. Assisted by Gaby, Francis is in the process of dismantling the alarm clock from their room, dipping each tiny piece of machinery in ink and pressing it to a sheet of paper.

Everyone finds the result inspirational.

They all embrace as warmly as if they were old friends, their exchanges of letters and ideas having already created a familiarity between them despite this January 1919 encounter being their first meeting in person.

The atmosphere is celebratory. Jean Arp is immediately enchanted by Gabriële Buffet, whom he finds visionary and exciting. And Tzara is delighted by Picabia, his double, his brother.

Francis adores the name "dada," repeating it over and over like a magical incantation. The term was first used in 1916 by the poet Richard Huelsenbeck and the writer Hugo Ball: trying to come up with a name for a number at the Cabaret Voltaire nightclub, they'd riffled through the pages of a dictionary, stopping on a word at random: Dada.

Dada. It's perfect. Universal. Primitive. The word, repeated—dada, dada—restores a kind of lightness, a lifesaving energy, to the Picabias' dynamic. The long, lethargic, inactive months, the sense of being frozen in time by Francis's neurasthenia, all seem very far away. The little group becomes inseparable. It's clear that they're all on the same page, breathing the same air. *391* and Dada merge, like two rivers finally flowing into the sea. Barcelona, Zurich, New York: everything intertwines, overlaps, and fits together. As the historian Philippe Dagen will later write, "The destruction of the old artistic language became complete just as the Old World destroyed itself with the war."

Gaby becomes a full-fledged member of the community, which welcomes her with open arms. She finds all the men talented, funny, and full of wit, and the feeling is mutual, even more than it was with the *391* circle, the Dadaists being less misogynistic. Man, woman, child, or animal, everyone is equal before the great Dada! The excitement of this new atmosphere in Zurich makes the Picabias forget about the friction in their marriage for the time being. There's so much intellectual work to be done that there isn't a moment to waste.

Their new friends have an ongoing collaboration with an anarchist printer, with whom Gabriële gets on particularly well; she loves talking politics with nihilists. They meet every day in a lakeside café to discuss their future projects, which continue to multiply like the bread and wine of a Christ filled with mighty, righteous rage.

Issue eight of *391* magazine is published in Zurich in January 1919. The pink cover features a grid, with some squares bearing names. Gabriële Buffet's name sits in the middle square of the top row, like the queen on a chessboard drawn in chalk. The only woman present. (To the Dadaists, Gabriële truly is a queen—and even a king. Jean Arp will write this magnificent description of her: "Gabriële is a King, Gabriële is a Queen. She adores bewitchment. Even caught in a spider web, she remains bright as day.")

The rightmost column of the grid contains the names of Arensberg, Stieglitz, de Zayas, Varèse, and Guillaume Apollinaire. The leftmost, Tzara and Pharamousse (a pseudonym of Francis's). Near the bottom are Marcel Duchamp, Crotti, and Ribemont-Dessaignes. Featured, too, are the names of various magazines created during the war. At the center of the grid is a drawing of a machine with wheels and a ladder. The whole image is entitled CONSTRUCTION/MOLECULAR.

The New York and Zurich branches of the family, together at last.

A surprising article by Gabriële opens the issue: a "Little Manifesto." Surprising because it isn't a theorist's text, but rather a *cri Dada* that begins: "These explanations will be like a ringing in the ear. But you've asked me for them, and now I'll give them to you until your whole head is buzzing."

Gaby's pen is iconoclastic, determined, scathing.

She attacks, she challenges, she deconstructs.

Ultimately, it's her voice, in all its power, that leads the charge. She creates the phenomenon of self-questioning in a text of ultramodern poeticism: "But don't fear: the thing that's terrifying you now is the shadow of your navel—it can hold only a single drop of water—that frightening noise is the beating of your heart."

After that come writings and drawings by Picabia, Arp, and Tzara. One of the texts co-signed by Picabia and Tzara is the first known example of automatic writing; that is, written and guided by the unconscious and published as is, without editing. Issue 4-5 of *Dada* magazine is released almost immediately afterward, its cover image the famous autopsied and ink-dipped alarm clock.

Francis is doing well, Gaby observes. Like a sudden break in the clouds in a lowering, gray sky.

Jean Arp becomes a true friend; occasionally she realizes with a slight jolt that he reminds her, in his brotherly kindness and sensitivity, of Guillaume Apollinaire, who feels more alive within her than ever. The current flurry of creative productivity would have made him so happy. Gabriële surprises herself by talking to him sometimes, silently. Years later, she'll describe the time in Zurich as "an extraordinary period of mental activity, vibrant and healthy exchanges, and extravagant theories, in which even the most firmly entrenched appearances were done away with, the most disconcerting suggestions going hand-in-hand with the joint creation of automatic masterpieces."

Their planned departure date approaches. Back to Lausanne first, then Paris. But Gaby pushes it back, dreading the ghosts. Avenue Charles-Floquet. Germaine Everling. Guillaume's grave.

In Lausanne, Francis and Gabriële play game after game of chess. She wins sometimes. One day, as they're hunched over the black and white tiles in a concentrated silence, she says: "I'm pregnant."

Francis doesn't seem upset, or surprised, or happy.

Just annoyed. He doesn't like to be distracted when he's playing.

* * *

The Picabias' relationship with their children is a mystery.

There's no physical abuse, no intentional mistreatment. Just calm indifference. The children are there. A mere statement of fact. They're cared for year after year by an army of successive nannies with their hair in identical tight buns. They're sweet little burdens, cumbersome baggage, an inconvenience for parents that like to travel light—baggage usually carried by an employee or two in return for a few banknotes.

The Picabias never mention them. They simply aren't a topic of conversation. In all their voluminous correspondence that has come down to us, there's hardly a line concerning their four children.

It's no accident that the children are a phantom presence in this book. Small intruders, arbitrary hostages of a pair of monsters—monstrous geniuses, monsters in the original, ancient, sense of the term: outliers. Those who are strange, unusual. Those who don't fit the norm.

All four of the Picabias' children changed their names from the ones they were given at birth. Laure-Marie became Marie Catilina; Gabriel, Pancho; Gabrielle-Cécile, Jeanine; and Lorenzo, Vicente. It's as labyrinthine and confusing as a Russian novel. Gabriële gave her first name to two of her children, a boy and a girl. The advantage of having a gender-ambiguous name. Pancho is a Spanish diminutive of Francisco—*Francis*. The parents may have given up even before they tried, but they gave their children their names, and their last name. If nothing else.

In this family, as in any other, first names are Freudian slips, identity constructs that your parents compel you to bear. Weighty first birthday gifts for your developing brains. But the Picabia children, *all* of them, decide to rechristen themselves.

We never knew any of them. Not our grandfather Vicente, or his brothers and sisters, or their children, or their children's children, our distant cousins.

Writing this book meant reaching out to our Picabia relatives, meeting them for the first time. This is how we came to know Gillian-Joy, whose father was the son of Jeanine, Francis and Gabriële's third child.

Gillian-Joy's dark eyes are deep and merry, and in this they doubtless resemble the eyes of Gabriële, our mutual great-grandmother.

We're all happy that this book has brought us together, and that the family conflicts involving previous generations have dissipated over time. After so many decades, only curiosity and the desire to know one another remain. We spend hours asking Gillian-Joy questions about Gabriële, for she and her mother Armelle have very clear memories of her.

Every anecdote they recount for us is more incredible than

the next. Gillian-Joy refers to Gabriële as "Mémé." *Mémé*. The word is hard for us to hear. Startling, too. A little child's word, a sweet word, a word of everyday closeness. It's a strange feeling to find out, as an adult, that we could have had a "mémé"— who had no interest in meeting us.

"Mémé was living in Étival full-time," our cousin tells us. "At one point they had the most beautiful house; it was like a castle. A stunning place where Gabriële spent a lot of time in her childhood. She even spent a summer there with the sculptor Brancusi. There was a long lane lined with trees in front of the chateau, and she had the trees cut down and the wood sold to make some money. But after that, she thought the chateau had become extremely ugly, and so she sold it to a local farmer for absolute peanuts. That was Mémé. She just didn't care."

That she didn't care about *anything* is crystal-clear. As evidenced by the fact that she didn't give a tinker's damn about us.

Gillian-Joy continues telling us about "Mémé," who really seems to have enjoyed cutting things down. "Once, Mémé, who had just gotten a new pair of garden shears, called for her daughter. She wanted to make sure the shears would cut well. Without saying a word, she cut Jeanine's braids right off."

Apparently, Gabriële would even tell her children, looking at them with those penetrating eyes of hers, "My darlings, I'll outlive you all!"

A mother who broke the ultimate taboos.

* * *

Another taboo.

When Francis Picabia died in 1953, Vicente, his youngest son with Gabriële, had already been buried in the family vault for six years. This meant that there was no room to deposit the body of the man who had been her husband. Without a qualm, Gabriële had her son's body exhumed and Francis's installed in the crypt in its place. Why? Because, even thirty-five years after their divorce, Gabriële Buffet preferred Francis to any other man on earth. Even her own son.

The body of her son Vicente. That poor body, eternally young, mishandled, displaced. Denied.

Our grandfather.

* * *

We've learned about things Gabriële said and did to her children that we find difficult to believe. Abusive, cruel, strange words. Things that speak of an *abnormality*. Another piece of the puzzle that was this extraordinary woman's psyche.

A strange old lady, a strange mother. It's equally important not to underestimate the deliberatively provocative nature of her bizarre statements about motherhood. The truth is always murky. A gray area.

In an unpublished text, Gabriële writes: "I didn't understand the role of mother at the time I had my children. Only later, much later, did I really give it any thought. My love for that man [Francis] was so intense that it left no room for anything else. I've regretted not feeling maternal, not experiencing the bond between mother and child. My husband's love was, for me, like music, like a perpetual, soothing lullaby."

* * *

We're in the last stages of writing this book. Our mother, who's never talked to us about her grandparents, suddenly tells us that she attended Gabriële's funeral in 1985. We're stunned. She's never told us that, not even in all the time we've been working on this manuscript. We ask her what the funeral was like.

"It's strange; I remember being in my car on the way there, but I have no memory of anything after that," Lélia answers.

"But why did you go in the first place?"

"I don't know."

Paris, July 1919.

Gaby receives by courier a small parcel prettily wrapped in chestnut-brown paper, her name written on it with two "L"s like bird's wings. She unwraps it and finds a brand-new copy of Francis's latest collection of poems, *Thoughts Without Language*. The dedication on the first page reads: "Dear friends Gabrielle Buffet, Ribemont-Dessaignes, Marcel Duchamp, Tristan Tzara, I dedicate this poem to you in light of our elective affinity." *Our elective affinity*. Very Goethe. She wouldn't have put it that way herself, Gabriële thinks. She flips through the volume. It consists of a single, long poem. Certain words jump out at her.

"she is pregnant
isolated in the dormitory of humiliating situations

the household is breaking up
and the woman in love
is seeking the lost diamond
one definitely must not
drag along heavy things
anatomical regrets"

The dedication "dear friends" says it all, really. Gabriële is no longer Francis's wife, but his friend. This is the great truth, and it will permeate the whole rest of their lives. The problem is that the baby growing in Gaby's womb doesn't need a pair of friends. He or she would benefit far more from having parents right now.

Francis has gone to live with Germaine Everling. Who is pregnant, as well. Gaby remains in the avenue Charles-Floquet apartment. Alone. With the first three children, the detritus of her married life, and the fourth child, who's a bit late to the party. BONJOUR PICABIA! still greets them, wincingly, every time they enter the apartment. Some days, Gaby's able to convince herself that none of this is that bad compared to the devastation of Guillaume's death. Other days, she's consumed by rage, wishing none of it had ever happened: "I'd written a sonata, and unfortunately I tore it up, because with Picabia, it was finished." Gabriële, so filled up by her life-creating womb, is completely drained.

She's 38 years old.

She reads the poem "Zone" again, and it's like having her guts ripped out. She can't get over the loss of her dearest, kindest Apollinaire. She can just see him standing in the living room in Étival, snapping out the words, and it's as if he's speaking to her, scolding her, ordering her to come through this whole damned sorry mess alive and with her head held high. She is *not* going to do what he did, dying two days before an armistice. What an exit. So she reads the poem again, and again.

Grievous and joyous voyages you made
Before you knew what falsehood was and age
At twenty you suffered from love and at thirty again
My life was folly and my days in vain

Marcel, once again, comes to her rescue. It's been more than four years since he left France. He, too, has suffered the pain of loss: his brother Raymond has succumbed to typhoid fever. On learning the news in August, Marcel immediately made arrangements to find a ship and sail from Buenos Aires. "I knew he was ill," he will say later in an interview, "but you can never really know how ill a person is." Marcel hadn't seen his brother since the war began, back when he'd schemed to prevent his family from finding out that he was leaving for America. It seems so long ago now. Not so much because of the actual time that has passed, but because he was such a different man then. Personal metamorphoses cause temporal distortions.

Marcel returns to a Paris sweltering in a heat wave. He moves in with Gaby, naturally, at the avenue Charles-Floquet apartment. But he visits Francis on rue Émile-Augier every day. He loves them both, and nothing will change that. Gabriële's archangel is still as handsome as ever. He contracted lice in Buenos Aires and had to shave his head, but she finds that it suits him. She strokes his head, and he strokes her rounded belly. They're happy to be together again.

Marcel asks her to help him: he wants a star shape shaven into the stubble on his head, with a tail pointing toward his forehead to make a shooting star. A tribute to the 1912 Jura–Paris road trip and the note that resulted: " . . . a comet, which would have its tail in front, this tail being an appendage of the headlight child." He likes for Gabriële to run her hand over his starry head, closing his eyes and smiling. Man Ray, then in Paris, photographs Marcel's celestial tonsure. The image shows him from the back, smoking a pipe.

One morning, a few minutes after leaving the apartment on avenue Charles-Floquet, Marcel goes into a pharmacy on the rue Blomet and asks for some vials of saline solution. Glass vials. The pharmacist nods and is about to fetch them when Marcel specifies: "I actually only want one vial, and would it be possible to empty out the contents and then seal it again?" The pharmacist looks dubious. "I want to capture some of the room's air inside," Marcel explains.

Returning to Gabriële's apartment with his precious purchase, Marcel attaches a label to the vial on which he writes: *Paris Air*.

"Look, Gaby. It's a gift for Arensberg. A gift money can't buy."

Gabriële peers at the object, contemplating it with a faraway look in her eye, then asks, "Could we seal Picabia's soul in a glass vial, do you think?"

"*You're* Picabia's soul," Marcel Duchamp replies.

On September 15, 1919, at three o'clock in the morning, Gabriële tells Marcel that her water has broken. No panic; a baby is a kind of *readymade*, isn't it? On that Monday, Gabriële Buffet-Picabia brings her fourth child into the world. At age thirty-eight, she isn't a young girl anymore; she knows the whole business by heart and is prepared to deal with the pain. She gives instructions calmly and firmly.

Lying in bed, Gaby watches as Marcel Duchamp brings her a basin of very hot water, a stack of clean cloths, a pair of sterilized scissors, a cigarette and a glass of whiskey to aid in relaxation . . . all the usual birth paraphernalia. Marcel, who's been living with Gabriële for two months, has one quality in particular that makes him perfectly suited to assist with a premature delivery: he's handy. He can make anything imaginable out of whatever's available to him. A tinkerer *par excellence*.

The contractions grow closer together. Gaby is sweating. No choice but to finish this now and see what it ends up being, this baby who's making its mother cry out in pain. Daughter or son? Marcel thinks it'll be a girl, one he can teach to play chess. But the head that emerges belongs to a tiny boy. Olive-skinned, with raven hair and eyes black as pitch. This screaming little machine is his father's son, no doubt about that.

Marcel takes the baby and places him gently in a small, open suitcase on the floor in which he's arranged a nest of soft blankets—no one has thought to buy a cradle. Then he picks up the phone and calls Francis to tell him that his son has just been born. The child's birth will have to be registered at the town hall, which is done early the next morning. Francis, accompanied by Germaine Everling—herself pregnant—duly registers the birth of his son, Lorenzo Picabia.

That baby was our grandfather. According to his sister Jeanine, he was a great tinkerer.

Three months later, Germaine Everling gives birth in her turn, also to a little boy. His name? Lorenzo. Wait, him too? The same name as the first baby? No! *Yes.* It's glorious! It's Dada! Champagne! *More* champagne! And *vive* the two Lorenzos! Twin brothers with different mothers! He's got nerve, that Picabia.

Lorenzo Number One will choose to go by his middle name, to differentiate himself. We don't blame him. He'll be Vicente Picabia.

Our grandfather has just been born.

And so have we, finally, after . . . how many pages?

Epilogue

We're ending the book here, on a kitchen table covered in blood and sweat. A delivery that marks both a beginning and an end.

An end because, after 1919, Gabriële will never live with Picabia again, though this singular couple will never truly separate. They'll continue to see each other and to write regularly, several letters a week. Francis will keep sending love poems to Gabriële, mad, magnificent poems. Reading them, it's easy to imagine the elderly Francis sneaking away from a new young wife who is forever jealous of Queen Gaby. The dialogue between the two will remain unbreakable until one of them dies.

Picabia will go first. He dies on November 30, 1953, in the same apartment on the rue des Petit-Champs where he was born. On learning of his death, Marcel Duchamp sends him this telegram from New York: "See you soon, dear Francis."

It feels strange to leave Gabriële here, to say goodbye. In 1919, she hasn't even lived half her life yet, and the years to come will be no less adventurous, no less extraordinary for this remarkable woman.

She'll return to New York, where she will, at last, have a monogamous romantic relationship with Marcel Duchamp.

She'll help Elsa Schiaparelli to become a fashion designer in Paris.

She'll form close friendships with Calder, Arp, Brancusi.

She'll live with the composer Igor Stravinsky, years after he first dazzled her in 1913.

In 1939, she'll work alongside the writer Samuel Beckett as part of the Gloria SMH resistance network.

It's Gabriële, too, who will help the wife of her son Vicente, Myriam Rabinovitch, our grandmother, to hide and escape deportation.

Francis and Gabriële will never parent their youngest child Vicente. An unwanted child. Unloved by parents who loved each other too much. Our grandfather will die by suicide, aged 27, after taking an overdose. He'll leave no note, but he will leave behind a four-year-old girl, Lélia.

A very unusual Hebrew name meaning *night*.

That's all he will leave to Lélia. That, and the name Picabia. A legacy of darkness.

Our mother never knew any of her Picabia family.

She never talked to us about her phantom father. And then, one day, out of nowhere, she wrote to us:

"The most striking absence is that of my father, Vicente. He existed, because I do, but I don't know what his laugh sounded like, what his anger felt like, how deep his voice was. I have no memory of his loving looks, the movements of his hands, the warmth of his arms. I don't know the scent of his skin or the feel of his hair tickling my nose, his favorite expressions or the foods he liked best, the stories that interested him or the painful things that made him cry. All I've ever known is the photo of a young man who very quickly became younger than me. How can a person be the daughter of a man younger than her? The brain struggles to resolve the question, then gives up. My father is a photo."

This book ends, then, with a birth.
The birth of Lorenzo, who will go by Vicente.
A handsome boy with dark eyes and a tormented soul.

For our mother Lélia,
we've tried to illuminate the night.

Gabriële is a true novel about our great-grandparents. To write it, we spent three years delving into archives—including a great deal of unpublished material—and conducted interviews with many historians. We undertook a thorough investigation to shed light on the life of Gabriële Buffet, a figure who had remained forever behind the scenes in the history of art. Armed with our research, we then allowed our work as novelists to take over, bringing this woman's life to life. Art historians, or discerning admirers of Francis Picabia's work, who may want to know the precise sources of the scenes and details we recount, might turn to the French edition, which includes many footnotes. Instead, here, for the English edition, we include a full bibliography of those same sources.

Anne and Claire Berest

BIBLIOGRAPHY

Anglim, Paule. "A conversation with Gabrielle Buffet-Picabia (1976)." In *The New Brick Reader*, edited by Tara Quinn. House of Anansi Press, 2013.

Apollinaire, Guillaume. *Alcohols*. Translated by Samuel Beckett. Dolmen Press, 1972.

Apollinaire, Guillaume. *Chroniques d'art, 1902–1918*. Gallimard, 1960.

Apollinaire, Guillaume. *Correspondance avec les artistes, 1903–1918*. Edited by Laurence Campa and Peter Read. Gallimard, 2009.

Apollinaire, Guillaume. *L'Esprit nouveau et les poètes: Conférence donnée au Vieux Colombier le 26 novembre 1917*. Altamira, 1997.

Apollinaire, Guillaume. *Le Flâneur des deux rives*. Éditions de la Sirène, 1918.

Aragon, Louis. *Aurélien*. Gallimard, 1986. First published 1944 by Gallimard.

Bernheim, Cathy. *Picabia*. Éditions du Félin, 1995.

Borràs, Maria Lluïsa. *Picabia*. Translated by Kenneth Lyons. Rizzoli, 1985.

Boulbès, Carole. *Picabia, le saint masqué*. Jean-Michel Place, 1998.

Buffet, Gabriële. "Edgard Varèse." Unpublished text.

Buffet, Gabriële. "Igor Stravinsky." Unpublished text.

Buffet, Gabriële. "Modern Art and the Public." *Camera Work*, special no. (June 1913): 10–14. https://doi.org/10.11588/diglit.31330.5.

Buffet, Gabriële. "Picabia." Unpublished text.

Buffet, Gabriële. "Picabia et Gabriële Buffet." Unpublished text.

Buffet, Gabriële. Video interview. In *Les heures chaudes de Montparnasse*. Chapter 4, *1914–1918*. INA archives.

Buffet, Gabriële, and Malitte Matta. 1974 interview. In *Paris–New York 1908–1968*. Éditions du Centre Pompidou, 1991. First published in 1977, following the exhibition *Paris–New York 1908–1968* at the Centre Pompidou, Paris, France.

Buffet, Gabrielle. "La Section d'Or." *Art d'aujourd'hui* 4, no. 3–4 (May/June 1953): 74–76.

Buffet-Picabia, Gabriële. *Aires abstraites*. Pierre Cailler, 1957.

Buffet-Picabia, Gabriële. Video interview. In "Dada: Part 1," *RETROSPECTIVE archives du XXe siècle*, 1971.

Buffet-Picabia, Gabrielle. *Rencontres*. Belfond, 1977.

Camfield, William. *Francis Picabia: His Art, Life and Times*. Princeton University Press, 1979.

Campa, Laurence. *Guillaume Apollinaire*. Gallimard, 2013.

Caradec, François. *Raymond Roussel*. Fayard, 1997.

Caumont, Jacques, and Françoise Le Penven. *Système D*. Pauvert, 2010.

Centre Pompidou. "Marcel Duchamp: La peinture, même." http://mediation.centrepompidou.fr/education/ressources/ENS-Duchamp_peinture.

Chavasse, Paul. "Mémoire du siècle. Gabriële Buffet." *La nuit rêvée de . . . Hervé Poulain*, Les Nuits de France Culture, February 17, 2013. Podcast, 28 min. https://www.radiofrance.fr/franceculture/podcasts/les-nuits-de-france-culture/la-nuit-revee-de-herve-poulain-9977860.

Clemenceau, Georges. *Correspondance (1858–1929)*. Edited by Sylvie Brodziac and Jean-Noël Jeanneney. Robert Laffont/BNF, 2008.

Dagen, Philippe. *Le Silence des peintres: Les artistes face à la Grande Guerre*. Fayard, 1996.

Debussy, Claude. *Monsieur Croche et autres écrits (1901–1914)*. Gallimard, 1987.

De Challié, Laure (née Jussieu). *Essai sur la liberté, l'égalité et la fraternité*. Gaume Frères, 1849.

De Fraguer, Marguerite-Marie. *Vincent d'Indy: souvenirs d'une élève*. Jean Naert, 1934.

De la Fuente, Véronique. *Dada à Barcelone 1914–1918*. Éditions des Albères, 2001.

De La Hire, Marie. *Modèle nu*. Bibliothèque indépendante d'édition, 1908.

De Moncan, Patrice. *Paris inondé: La Grande Crue de 1910*. Les Éditions du Mécène, 2009.

Des Cars, Laurence, ed. *Apollinaire: Le regard du poète*. Gallimard, 2016.

Desnos, Robert. *Nouvelles Hébrides et autres textes, 1922–1930*. Gallimard, 1978.

D'Indy, Vincent. *Ma Vie*. Séguier, 2001.

Duchamp, Marcel. *Affectionately, Marcel: The Selected Correspondence of Marcel Duchamp*. Edited by Francis N. Naumann and Hector Obalk. Thames & Hudson, 2000.

Duchamp, Marcel. *Duchamp du signe: Écrits*. Edited by Michel Sanouillet. Flammarion, 1976.

Duchamp, Marcel. *Entretiens avec Marcel Duchamp (1960)*. Edited by Georges Charbonnier. André Dimanche, 1994.

Duchamp, Marcel. "Preface." In *Francis Picabia*, edited by William Camfield. Losfeld, 1972.

Duchamp, Marcel. *The Writings of Marcel Duchamp*. Edited by Michel Sanouillet and Elmer Peterson. Da Capo, 1973.

Duchamp, Marcel, and Pierre Cabanne. *Entretiens avec Pierre Cabanne*. Allia, 2014.

Estèbe, Françoise. "Raymond Roussel (1877–1933)." *Une vie, une œuvre*. France Culture, April 27, 2013. Podcast, 59 min. https://www.radiofrance.fr/franceculture/podcasts/une-vie-une-oeuvre/raymond-roussel-1877-1933-4528152.

Everling, Germaine. *L'Anneau de Saturne*. Fayard, 1970.

Fouquier, Marcel. "L'Exposition Picabia." *Le Journal*, February 10, 1905.

Friedel, Helmut, ed. *Marcel Duchamp in Munich, 1912.* Schirmer/Mosel, 2012.

Gauguin, Paul. "Diverses choses." Unpublished notes made between 1896 and 1897, Paris, Louvre, inventory of Department of Graphic Arts.

Gauguin, Paul, and André Fontainas. *Lettres à André Fontainas.* Échoppe, 1994.

Gide, André. *La Porte étroite.* Mercure de France, 1909.

Gough-Cooper, Jennifer, and Jacques Caumont. *Marcel Duchamp: Work and Life.* Edited by Pontus Hulten. MIT Press, 1993.

Guitard, Louis, and Louis Aubert. "Entretien avec Louis Aubert." *La Table ronde*, no. 165 (October 1961).

Hapgood, Hutchins. "A Paris Painter." *Globe and Commercial Advertiser*, February 20, 1913.

Hegel, G. W. F. *Hegel's Aesthetics: Lectures on Fine Art.* Vol. 1. Translated by T. M. Knox. Oxford University Press, 1998.

Hélias, Pierre-Jakez. *Le Cheval d'orgueil.* Plon, 1975.

Housez, Judith. *Marcel Duchamp.* Grasset, 2006.

Huard, Charles. *Berlin comme je l'ai vu.* Eugène Rey, 1907.

Jayle, Didier. "Freud, Mariani et la publicité, ou comment la cocaïne a conquis l'Europe," *Swaps*, no. 58 (2010), pp. 5–8.

Jebb, Katerina. *Musée Réattu.* Skira, 1916.

Lacarelle, Bertrand. *Arthur Cravan précipité.* Grasset, 2010.

Launay, Florence. *Les compositrices en France au XIXe siècle.* Fayard, 2006.

Lebel, Robert. *Sur Marcel Duchamp.* Éditions du Centre Pompidou, 1996.

Le Bon, Laurent. *Dada.* Éditions du Centre Pompidou, 2001.

Le Bot, Marc. *Francis Picabia et la crise des valeurs figuratives: 1900–1925.* Klincksieck, 1968.

Leggio, James. *Music and Modern Art.* Routledge, 2001.

Lemoine, Serge, ed. *Aux origines de l'abstraction, 1800–1914.* Réunion des musées nationaux, 2003. Published following the exhibition *Aux origines de l'abstraction, 1800–1914* at the Musée d'Orsay, Paris, France.

Live, Yu-Sion. "Les Chinois de Paris depuis le début du siècle. Présence urbaine et activités économiques." *Revue européenne des migrations internationales* 8, no. 3 (1992): 155–173.

Lunday, Elizabeth. *The Modern Art Invasion*. Lyons Press, 2013.

Macmonnies, Frederick. "French Artists Spur on American Art," *New York Tribune*, October 24, 1915.

Marcadé, Bernard. *Marcel Duchamp*. Flammarion, 2007.

Marinetti, F.T. "The Futurist Manifesto." Translated by James Joll. Originally written in 1909. http://bactra.org/T4PM/futurist-manifesto.html.

Marnat, Marcel. *Maurice Ravel*. Fayard, 1986.

Monod-Fontaine, Isabelle, Claude Laugier, and Sylvie Warnier. *Daniel-Henry Kahnweiler, marchand, éditeur, écrivain*. Éditions du Centre Pompidou, 1984.

Montjaret, Anne. *La Sainte-Catherine: Culture festive dans l'entreprise*. Éditions du CTHS, 1997.

Morel, Guillaume. *Paquebots–Le Triomphe de l'art déco–L'art du voyage à la française*. Éditions Place des Victoires, 2015.

Munson-Williams-Proctor Arts Institute. *1913 Armory Show 50th Anniversary Exhibition 1963*. Henry Street Settlement, 1963. Published following the exhibition *1913 Armory Show 50th Anniversary Exhibition 1963* at the Munson-Williams-Proctor Arts Institute, Utica, NY.

Musée des Beaux-Arts de Nîmes. *Catalogue de l'exposition Francis Picabia musée des Beaux-Arts Nîmes*. 1986. Published following the exhibition *Francis Picabia* at the Musée des Beaux-Arts, Nîmes, France.

Naumann, Francis M. *New York Dada 1915–1923*. Harry N. Abrams, 1994.

Nectoux, Jean-Michel. *Gabriel Fauré*. Fayard, 2008.

Ouellette, Fernand. *Edgard Varèse*. Edited by C. Bourgois. Seghers, 1989.

Ouellette, Fernand, ed. *Visages d'Edgard Varèse*. Éditions de l'Hexagone, 1959.

Pauly, Emmanuel. *Le Jura et les Jurassiens dans la Première Guerre Mondiale.* Service Éducatif des Archives Départementales du Jura, 2015.

Picabia, Francis. "Albums Picabia." Thirteen of the painter's personal notebooks, digitized, Fonds Doucet archives.

Picabia, Francis. *Caravansérail.* Belfond, 2013. Unpublished manuscript originally from 1924.

Picabia, Francis. *Catalogue raisonné.* Vol. 1, *1898–1914.* English translation by Imogen Forster. Mercatorfonds, 2014.

Picabia, Francis. *Catalogue raisonné.* Vol. 2, *1915–1927.* English translation by Annette David. Mercatorfonds, 2016.

Picabia, Francis. *Écrits.* Vol. 2. Belfond, 1978.

Picabia, Francis. *Écrits critiques.* Edited by Carole Boulbès. Mémoire du livre, 2005.

Picabia, Francis. "Guillaume Apollinaire." *L'Esprit nouveau,* no. 26 (October 1924).

Picabia, Francis. "How New York Looks to Me," *New York American,* March 30, 1913.

Picabia, Francis. *Lettres à Christine 1945–1951.* Edited by Jean Sireuil and Marc Dachy. Gérard Lebovici, 1988.

Picabia, Francis. *Lettres à Léonce Rosenberg, 1929–1940.* Éditions du Centre Pompidou, 2000.

Picabia, Francis. "Ne riez pas, c'est de la peinture et ça représente une jeune américaine." *Le Matin,* December 1, 1913.

Pierre, Arnauld. *La Peinture sans aura.* Gallimard, 2002.

Picasso, Pablo, and Guillaume Apollinaire. *Correspondance.* Edited by Hélène Seckel and Pierre Caizergues. Gallimard, 1992.

Polizzotti, Mark. *André Breton.* Gallimard, 1999.

"A Post-Cubist's Impressions of New York," *New York Tribune,* March 9, 1913.

Proust, Marcel. *Correspondance de Marcel Proust.* Vol. 1. Edited, dated, and annotated by Philip Kolb. Plon, 1970.

Ray, Man. Video interview. In "Dada: Part 1," *RETROSPECTIVE archives du XXe siècle,* 1971.

Reliquet, Scarlett, and Philippe. *Henri-Pierre Roché: L'Enchanteur collectionneur*. Ramsay, 1999.

Roche, Juliette. Video interview. In "Dada: Part 1," *RETROSPECTIVE archives du XXe siècle*, 1971.

Roussel, Raymond. *Comment j'ai écrit certains des mes livres*. Pauvert, 1963.

La Route Jura–Paris: 1912–2012 Centenaire. Association Ressort International, 2012. Published following the event La Route Jura–Paris in Étival, France, October 2012.

Ruhrberg, Karl. *L'Art au XXe siècle*. Vol. 1, *Peinture*. Edited by Ingo F. Walther. Taschen, 2002.

Sanouillet, Michel. *Dada à Paris*. CNRS Éditions, 2005.

Sarazin-Levassor, Lydie. *Un échec matrimonial*. Les Presses du Réel, 2004.

Schiaparelli, Elsa. *Shocking Life, an Autobiography*. E. Dutton, 1954.

Schwartz, Manuela, ed. *Vincent d'Indy et son temps*. Mardaga, 2006.

Secrest, Meryle. *Elsa Schiaparelli, A Biography*. Knopf, 2014.

Steegmuller, Francis. "Duchamp: Fifty Years Later," *Show*, February 1963. Scrapbook, Archives Marcel Duchamp, Association Marcel Duchamp, Paris. https://www.duchamparchives.org/amd/archive/component/SBK2_1961-63_26/.

Stauffer, Serge, ed. *Marcel Duchamp: Interviews und Statements*. Cantz, 1992.

Stieglitz, Alfred. "The First Great 'Clinic to Revitalize Art." *New York American*, January 26, 1913.

Stein, Gertrude. *The Autobiography of Alice B. Toklas*. Penguin, 2020. First published 1933 by Harcourt, Brace, & Co.

Stévance, Sophie. "Les operations musicales mentales de Duchamp. De la 'musique en creux.'" *Images re-vues*, no. 7 (2009). https://doi.org/10.4000/imagesrevues.375.

Suquet, Jean. *Miroir de la mariée*. Flammarion, 1974.

Toklas, Alice B. *The Alice B. Toklas Cook Book*. Harper Perennial, 2021.

Tomkins, Calvin. *Duchamp: A Biography*. Henry Holt and Company, 1996.

Tyrrell, Henry. "Oh You High Art! Advance Guard of the Post-Impressionists Has Reached New York. One of Their Leaders, M. Picabia, Explains How He Puts His Soul on Canvas." *The World Magazine*, February 9, 1913.

Vallier, Dora. *L'Intérieur de l'art: Entretiens avec Braque, Léger, Villon, Miró, Brancusi, 1954–1960*. Éditions du Seuil, 1982.

Warszawski, Jean-Marc. "Le clavecin pour les yeux du père Castel." In *La couleur réfléchie,* edited by Jacques Le Rider, Michel Costantini, and François Soulages. Harmattan, 2001/2002. First given as a 1999 lecture at the conference La couleur réfléchie, Université Paris 8. https://www.musicologie.org/publirem/castel.html.

Ysaÿe, Antoine. *Eugène Ysaÿe: sa vie, son oeuvre, son influence*. L'Écran du Monde, 1947.

ACKNOWLEDGMENTS

The authors are grateful to their families and friends, to Pierre Belfond and the many people who have helped bring this book to fruition.

And, especially, Grégoire Chertok and Albéric de Gayardon.